AN INARTICULATE SEA

TAMSEN SCHULTZ

*everafter*ROMANCE

EverAfter Romance
A Division of Diversion Publishing Corp.
443 Park Avenue South, Suite 1008
New York, New York 10016
www.EverAfterRomance.com

Cover Design by Sian Foulkes
Edited by Julie Molinari

This is a work of fiction. Names, characters, places and incidents either are the
product of the author's imagination or are used fictitiously. Any resemblance to
actual persons, living or dead, events or locales is entirely coincidental.

For more information, email info@everafterromance.com

First EverAfter Romance edition March 2017.
Print ISBN: 978-1-63576-039-2

I've decided not to dedicate this book to any one person, but rather to life itself, and all the ups and downs—or potential plots, as we writers like to call them—it brings me.

CHAPTER ONE

"IT SHOULD BE YOU," CARLY Drummond said to her partner, Marcus Brown, as they climbed out of their newly issued police SUV.

"Actually, it should be Ian," Marcus countered calmly. He was right, of course. But his logic did nothing to assuage her agitation, as unfounded as it might be.

Roughly, she zipped her jacket against the chill of the fall morning and started toward the door of her friend's home.

It had been just over a year since Marcus had been seriously injured in a near-fatal incident. And twelve months since Carly had been appointed to his former position of deputy chief of police. Three months ago, after being deemed fit for duty, Marcus had come back to work. Two months ago, she had requested that Vic Ballard, Windsor's chief of police, reinstate Marcus as deputy chief of police, but he'd refused and, much to her irritation, left her in charge. Two days ago, she'd had to miss most of a big fall leaf-peeping party she'd been looking forward to for months—a fundraiser thrown by two of her friends, Kit Forrester and Garret Cantona, to help raise money for one of the orphanages they supported—because, once again, duty had called. And to top it all off, just twenty minutes ago, Carly had received a call from Ian McAllister, the county sheriff and her good friend and mentor, telling her that some of Kit's lingering houseguests had found a dead body.

Yes, a dead body.

The last year had not been easy for her—and this day wasn't shaping up to be much better.

As Carly reached Kit and Garret's front door, Marcus came up alongside her and she paused to scan the area. Technically, the house was in county territory, so Marcus was right in that Ian, as sheriff, should be the one leading the investigation. But he'd been tied up with a multi-car accident in the southern-most part of the county, so he'd called in a favor—a favor she couldn't have turned down even if she'd wanted to.

"It will be fine," Marcus said.

"Says the man who has significantly more experience than I have," she retorted as she rang the bell.

She wasn't actually too concerned about whatever would come next; she was good at her job, had a solid—if small—team, and decent relationships with the assisting agencies. But she was tired—not physically, but mentally—from the last year.

"I've been out of the game for over a year. If anyone is rusty, it's me," Marcus countered.

Just when she was about to point out that, since he had been an MP before becoming a police officer, he still had her beat when it came to the number of investigations he'd been a part of, the door swung open to reveal a striking blonde woman whom Carly recognized from the fundraiser. But because she hadn't been able to stay very long, she hadn't been introduced to any of the guests, including this one.

"I'm Carly Drummond, Deputy Chief of Police," she said, holding out her hand.

The woman smiled then opened the door wider. "Dani Fuller, please call me Dani," she replied, then added, "I think you knew already that Kit and Garret left for Rwanda yesterday." She tried extending her hand somewhat out to the side to accommodate her exceptionally large, rounded belly. Something resembling shock must have shown in Carly's expression because Dani laughed. "I'm having twins, I'm actually only six months along, so you don't have to worry about me going into labor any minute, despite appearances to the contrary."

Only moments into the investigation and already she'd lost her "cop face." Taking a deep breath, Carly pulled on her metaphorical "big girl panties" and straightened her shoulders.

"Congratulations," she said. "This is Officer Marcus Brown. Dispatch reported a call about a possible body?"

"There's no 'possible' about it," came a voice from behind Dani. A voice Carly remembered more easily than she ought to. *This Monday morning just keeps getting better*, she thought.

Drew Carmichael's tall, lean frame appeared behind Dani's shoulders. He was tugging on leather gloves while his knee-length black jacket hung open, revealing a button-down shirt that was just about the same blue as his eyes and a pair of dark gray wool slacks. She'd met him a handful of times before: four or five times while investigating an attack on Kit that had happened outside Carly's old apartment, and then again, several months later in New York City, when she and Kit had gone out for a girls' night and run into him out on a date.

Hailing from a wealthy family that ran several businesses out of a New York City headquarters, Drew was a man who wore his wealth and power as comfortably as an old pair of jeans—although he didn't seem like the type who would actually *wear* an old pair of jeans.

But despite his sophistication, he had an odd sort of edge Carly hadn't quite figured out. Back when Kit had been assaulted, he'd inserted himself into the investigation like he'd had every right to be there. That alone wasn't a surprise, given his personality, but what *had* surprised her was that he'd seemed to know what he was talking about. And she had yet to puzzle out why a businessman from New York would have understood the intricacies of a criminal investigation.

"Deputy Chief Drummond." As he spoke, he gave a curt nod in her direction; then his eyes darted to Marcus.

"Mr. Carmichael." Carly responded with her own nod. "This

is Officer Marcus Brown. I assume you're the one who called it in?"
A fact that didn't bode well. Before knowing Drew was involved,
she'd held some hope that the "body" would turn out to be nothing
more than an animal decomposed beyond easy recognition. Now,
that thin thread of hope vanished, because if there was one thing
she'd learned from her interactions with Drew, it was that if he
bothered to make an assertion, it was only because it was true.

"Call me Drew," he all but ordered. He'd issued the same
command several times before, but so far, she hadn't quite brought
herself to follow it. "And no, it wasn't me. It was Ty, Dani's husband, who called. He and I were out for a morning walk when
we saw her. He stayed with the body; I came back to show you
the way."

Her eyes bounced to Dani, who seemed concerned about the
situation, but surprisingly calm at the fact that her husband was
out somewhere sitting with a dead body. Carly had a moment's
reflection on the fact that Kit had some interesting friends.

Dani smiled. "My husband was a Navy SEAL and also a detective with Portland Vice for several years. While finding a body on
a hike, especially here in Windsor, isn't exactly what he would have
expected from his morning, he's not going to fall apart—and he
also won't contaminate your scene." She added the last part with a
small emphasis.

Carly felt a flush of embarrassment because contamination of
her crime scene was exactly what she'd been worried about, and
it hadn't been very charitable of her to be thinking that way. As
a human being, she should have been at least a little concerned
about Ty Fuller and his state of mind. Internally, she sighed.

"Thank you," she said to Dani before turning her gaze back
to Drew, who was watching her with a look of patience that, to
her mind, bordered on condescension. "Can you give us a rough
idea of where the body is? The medical examiner will be coming
along soon, as will the state police, and we'll need to give them
a location."

"We followed that path there," he said, still standing behind

Dani in the open doorway as he pointed to a trail that led east, away from Kit's driveway. "I didn't have my GPS, so I can't give you a specific location, but we found her not far from a dirt road about twenty to twenty-five minutes up that trail."

Carly turned to Marcus. "Churchkill Road, do you think?"

Marcus's eyes went to the path and, after a moment, he nodded. "Probably. Lancaster Road is the main road that goes back into those hills, but Churchkill forks off and follows the ridge when Lancaster turns east. I'm pretty sure the fork happens before that trail comes out," he said.

"Were there any distinguishing landmarks on the road that you can remember?" Carly asked Drew.

He seemed to give the question some consideration before answering. "There weren't any houses nearby, but when I made my way to the road there was a bend not far to the north of the trail, and from there I could see a farm down in the valley. It had a large yellowish house and two big brown barns."

"The Kirby place," she confirmed. The Kirby family had been providing local beef to the Hudson Valley for generations; their farm was well known.

"Churchkill Road it is," Marcus said.

"Why don't you take the SUV and wait down where County 17 meets Lancaster Road?" she asked Marcus. "When the State Patrol and Vivi get there, you can lead them up Lancaster to Churchkill. By then, I should have reached the site and will be able to give an exact location."

Marcus agreed and she handed him the keys.

"Is it just this trail here I should take, Mr. Carmichael, or did you turn off at any point?" Carly gestured to the path that clearly started between two trees but was quickly engulfed in forest and greenery.

"Call me Drew. And I'll show you the way. As for you," he said, stepping through the doorway and turning to Dani. "You need to lie down and put your feet up. Ty will have my head if he finds out you've been running around while he's been gone."

"I wouldn't mind seeing that," Dani retorted with a grin.

Drew let out a long-suffering sigh. "Dani."

Dani let out her own sigh. "Fine, *Dad*," she said with obvious sarcasm. Then she turned to Carly and Marcus. "It was nice to meet you, Deputy Chief Drummond, Officer Brown. I wish it had been under better circumstances."

Carly smiled, somewhat intrigued by the interchange between these two guests of Kit's. Their age difference didn't appear to be more than a few years, but she hadn't missed the paternal tone of concern in Drew's voice when he'd issued his order to Dani. The obvious and easy affection between the two surprised her since she'd only ever seen him as cool and efficient.

Brushing the thought away, Carly stepped back to let him pass by, then she and Marcus followed him onto the driveway as Dani shut the door behind them. Her partner veered off to the SUV, as she and Drew continued toward the woods. She paused while Marcus backed out, then lifted a hand to him as he pulled out of the driveway. He answered with a small wave of his own before turning around the side of the house and out of sight, leaving her alone with the enigmatic Drew in the silence of the fall morning.

She exhaled into the clean, crisp morning air. The fall, with its cool nights and mornings, had settled in like a familiar blanket over the Hudson Valley. And with the drop in temperatures, the trees had turned the colors of fire; the hills were lit with reds, yellows, and brilliant oranges that contrasted sharply against a pale blue sky.

It was a beautiful day to find a body.

"Shall we?" he gestured toward the trail.

Carly nodded and preceded him into the woods without a word. They walked for several minutes in a silence punctuated by the sound of their feet landing on the dry ground and the occasional call of a bird or rustle of an autumn breeze through the dying leaves. As they walked, Carly turned her thoughts to what might lay ahead.

She *hoped* what Drew had come upon was simply the result

of a tragic accident. Crime in Windsor, with a few exceptions, was primarily made up of thefts or an occasional assault. Even so, she harbored no illusions about the Hudson Valley. Crime happened everywhere, even amongst the rolling hills and hay fields of her county. Still, she wanted to believe that the people she served and protected wouldn't violate their own community by committing murder. At least she hoped they wouldn't.

With this thought in mind, she took a deep breath, inhaling the comforting scents of fall as they began to climb the slight slope toward the ridge of the hill. It did not escape her notice that, even in hoping for the best, "the best" would still be a dead body.

"Churchkill?" Drew asked from behind her.

Coming seemingly out of nowhere, his word interrupted her thoughts and she wondered if she'd missed something he'd said earlier. When she paused and turned toward him to ask, she caught him by surprise. He nearly walked into her, but pulled up abruptly and stopped just short; then he stepped back a few inches to put some space between them.

"Churchkill," he repeated, presumably at her questioning look. "It's an unusual name, but I've noticed a lot of towns and roads in this area have the word 'kill' in them. I know there were a lot of revolutionaries around here back in the 1700s, but they couldn't have been *that* bloodthirsty."

That actually made Carly smile: his certainty in the morals of their founding fathers. She shook her head as she turned around and started walking up the trail again.

"No, they weren't. Or not any more so than they needed to be, I would imagine. Before the revolution, in the early 1700s, the area was settled heavily by the Dutch." As she spoke, the trail started a brief but steep ascent. Vain as she was, she tipped her hat to Murphy and his laws and accepted that she was going to be huffing and puffing as she talked. She'd either sound like a phone-sex operator or an out-of-shape cop, and after a fleeting moment's consideration, she thought it would be significantly more embarrassing to be thought of as the latter.

"And?" he prompted.

"The word 'kill' is the equivalent of 'creek' in Dutch, or in the Dutch language of the time." She unzipped her jacket then tucked an errant curl behind her ear as they continued. Thankfully, she could see the end of the rise ahead and she knew it would level out after that. "Churchkill Road ends at the Kirby farm now, but back in the day, it continued on and into one of the local hamlets. There's a church there, and at the edge of the church's property is a creek. It's a popular swimming and picnicking area today—and it was back then too."

"And because the road was the road that took people to the church creek, it became Churchkill Road," he concluded.

"Most likely, yes," she agreed.

"And you said the church is still there?" he asked as they started down the now-level path.

"It is. The whole hamlet is still there, but you can't reach it from this side anymore. There's a county road, a paved one, that will take you to it now."

They walked another minute in silence before he surprised her with another question.

"You love this area, don't you?"

Again, Carly came to a halt—this time at the personal nature of the question—and turned around. From where they stood, she could see the gentle roll of the hills, green fields cut out of the woods, and trees rioting with color.

She must have paused long enough because, beside her, Drew turned too.

"What's not to love?" she asked, not bothering to hide the wistfulness in her voice. Dotted with old farms and new gardens, the county stretched out before them, peaceful and inviting. She could see the old clock tower in town peeking through the trees miles away. In a few hours, she knew she'd hear the siren at the volunteer fire department echoing through the valley as it did every day at noon. The Kirby farm produced fresh local beef, the Zucchini Patch the most sought after fruits and vegetables, and, this time of year, The Apple Barn had apple cider donuts that were, well, not quite worth killing for, but definitely worth the thirty-minute drive. It was a place so achingly beautiful in so many ways—a place that felt very nearly enchanted at times—that she still had a difficult time absorbing the fact that she lived there. That she was a part of it.

And, as if to give voice to that difficulty, a familiar, uncomfortable feeling began to creep into her mind as she stood there taking it all in. Her chest began to tighten and her heartbeat thudded in her ears as the old recognizable panic set in, reminding her that no matter how much she felt like she belonged there, it could all be taken from her in an instant.

Abruptly, she turned and started back up the trail.

"It is lovely," Drew said, as he followed her.

Carly let out a little breath. "Yes, it is," she agreed, because that was what he would expect her to say.

She turned her attention back to their more immediate surroundings and several more minutes passed as they continued their walk. At one point, she stumbled over a tree root, and as she felt the pull of her uniform across her body, she also became uncomfortably aware of just how poorly police uniforms fit. Of course, a flattering fit wasn't the point and she knew she shouldn't even be thinking about it. But having someone so immaculately put together breezing along behind her wasn't putting her in the most charitable, or reasonable, of moods.

"Is it much farther?" she asked.

"Just around the bend," Drew answered with a gesture to their right.

Knowing how close they were to the scene sharpened her focus, making her more alert and aware of everything around her. Despite her doubts about her personal life and wardrobe, Carly *was* confident about her job. It was the one area of her life in which she felt completely and utterly competent. The certainty she felt concerning her professional life was like a security web that held the rest of her life together.

"Drew?" a male voice called from their right.

"Yes, it's us," Drew answered as they rounded the bend.

Carly stopped to take in the scene before acknowledging the other man.

The trail continued on to her right, but her eyes were drawn to the hill that rose sharply in front of her. She knew if she forged ahead, Churchkill Road lay less than two-hundred yards up the rise. But between where she stood and where the road ran, the land was uneven and littered with the leaves of past seasons. It was also dotted with enough trees to cast the area into a shadowed darkness, with sunlight managing to filter through the few spaces made by branches that had already shed their leaves.

Covered in leaves and debris and lying about three quarters of the way between the road and where Carly stood was the body of a woman. A body that looked as if it had rolled down the hill and come to an awkward and final stop.

She lay mostly on her stomach, but with the pitch of the hill, she'd rolled slightly onto her side, giving Carly a view of her back. The woman was wearing a dark rose-colored lightweight knit sweater that was covered in bits of leaves and small twigs, both of which were also tangled in her long, dark brown hair, which fell across her back and the ground behind her.

Though Carly could not see her face, there was no question in her mind that she was looking at the form of a woman. With the discernable dip of her waist and curve of her hip, the woman's body lay much like Carly's own did when she reclined on her side. Also, one of the woman's arms was thrown over her head, leaving a delicate, feminine hand in view. Those details, along with her hair and her petite feet—feet that were bare—left Carly with no doubt that Drew had been right when he'd first referred to the body as "her."

Moving her focus from the body back to the area around it, Carly scanned the hillside. It wasn't a bad spot for a body dump, and though she would need to wait for Vivi, the medical examiner, to make the official call and then for all the evidence to come in, it was pretty obvious to her that that was exactly what this spot was—a body dump. Whoever the woman was, Carly knew she hadn't died there, not given what she was—and wasn't—wearing. Which led her to believe that she probably hadn't died naturally, either. There was something reckless in the way the woman had been left, something that spoke of a careless disregard for human life.

"Carly?"

Turning to look at Drew, she caught a look of concern on his face.

"Yes?" she responded, wary of what he might be concerned about. There was, of course, the body to be apprehensive about, but it was also possible that he was wondering why she was just standing there—apparently doing nothing. Maybe he was even considering whether or not she had the ability to do the job at hand. It was a lot to read into a single word, but between being a woman in a male-dominated profession, and a younger woman at that, she almost couldn't blame him. Almost.

"You let out a big sigh, everything okay?"

She frowned. She hadn't remembered sighing. Then again, she'd been caught up in cataloging the scene.

"Other than her," Carly said with a small gesture of her head toward the woman, "everything is fine. I was just thinking that this scene isn't going to be the easiest to process."

"No, I doubt it is," came a response, this time from the man at Drew's side—presumably Dani Fuller's husband, Ty.

Carly switched her gaze from Drew to Ty. Both men had moved off to the side, well away from the body and the scene she and her team would need to comb through. Unlike Drew, with his lanky, sophisticated appearance, Ty Fuller came across as down-to-earth and *real* to her, or maybe just more like the men she was used to seeing where she lived. He was tall, almost as tall as Drew, and built more solidly—exactly what she would expect from a former SEAL—and definitely differently than Drew, whose physique looked like a swimmer's. Ty had dark hair and dark eyes, and in his jeans, boots, and leather jacket, he could have been any town's working man.

"You must be Ty Fuller," she said, walking forward to shake his hand.

"Call me Ty, please," he said before casting Drew a quick look.

"Ty, this is Deputy Chief Carly Drummond." Drew performed the introductions.

"Nice to meet you," Ty said. "I saw you briefly at the fundraiser, which would have been a more pleasant place to meet, but . . ." He stopped talking and shrugged in a gesture of "what can you do?"

"I was there but on duty and got called away about ten minutes after I arrived. I know Kit was happy you were all able to come. Now, I don't mean to be rude, but I need to radio my partner where we are, then I'd like to ask you a few questions. Both of you," she added.

The two men smiled politely as she stepped a short distance away to make her call to Marcus. She'd noted her GPS position when they'd arrived and relayed the information to him. She also gave him a quick debrief on the scene and asked him to warn the support vehicles to stay to the center of the road. Churchkill Road was a dead end—whoever had brought that body there would have had to turn around somewhere. They'd look for tire impressions at the two spots where the dirt road widened enough to turn a vehicle around between where the body had been dumped and the Kirby farm. But she didn't want to rule out getting any additional impression matches from the road coming in. It wasn't likely they'd find much, but she'd rather play it safe and preserve as much of the road as possible.

When she turned back, Drew and Ty were both leaning against the trunk of a large fallen tree. Ty had his hands tucked into his jacket pockets and Drew's arms were crossed. Both were silent and seemed lost in thought.

"I know this isn't all together new to you," she said to Ty with another gesture toward the woman behind them. "But it must have come as a surprise this morning. Can you tell me everything that happened, including whether or not you touched anything?"

Carly almost smiled when Ty answered the last part first, as adept as his wife in knowing what was foremost on her mind. "We came around the bend and saw her. Drew stayed back, but I approached from there," he said, pointing out the path he'd taken from the trail to the body, "and felt for a pulse. I didn't move the body in the process as I was able to reach her artery by reaching into the gap created by the arm that's raised over her head and her neck. When it was clear she wasn't alive, and she was cold to the touch, I backed out the way I came and have pretty much been standing here ever since."

She glanced at the body then turned back to the men. "Thank you," she said, acknowledging their caution. "I'll let the evidence teams know. And now, can you tell me what happened?"

"At the risk of sounding cliché," Drew spoke before Ty had a chance, "there isn't much to tell. We were on a morning walk, the same walk we've been doing since we got here three days ago, and we came around the bend and saw her. Ty then checked to see if there were any signs of life, and when there weren't, he placed the call to the police and I went back to meet you."

Again, it struck Carly as curious that Drew seemed so matter-of-fact about coming across a dead body. There was no horror, no panic, nothing to indicate that finding the body of a woman was anything other than a minor blip in his day. Maybe corporate America was more cutthroat than she thought.

"Did you see anything else or maybe hear anything? A car or vehicle on the road?" she pressed.

Both men shook their heads. Which wasn't a surprise. There were only three other properties this far up Churchkill Road before it dead-ended at the Kirby farm. Two of those were weekend homes and the third was empty and for sale; it was not a high-traffic kind of road.

"And about what time did you find her?" As the question came out of her mouth, she realized that perhaps she should be more circumspect. It was the right question to ask, of course, but was it possible they hadn't just "found" her but put her there, too? Her gut said no, but her intellect knew she'd also have to pursue that line of questioning.

"About eight thirty or so, right before we called," Ty answered.

"And if you're wondering," Drew spoke, "we were all at Kit's house last night, all five of us, all night. She has an alarm system that tracks when doors or windows are opened. Feel free to check it."

"Five of you?" she asked.

"Ty, Dani, my brother, Jason, and his wife, Sam, who also happens to be Dani's sister, and myself, of course," he answered. Succinct and efficient as always.

Carly didn't miss the assessing look Ty gave his friend.

"It's interesting that you would offer that information," Carly commented.

"It was going to be your next question, wasn't it?" Drew countered.

She cocked her head. "It was. But in my experience, most people are surprised when asked to provide their whereabouts or an alibi. Have you been through something like this before?"

A ghost of a smile touched his lips at her not-so-subtle inquiry into his past. "Not this specifically, but I've been involved in more than my fair share of investigations."

She held his gaze as she let his enigmatic statement sift through her brain. She briefly considered asking several of the follow-up questions that popped into her mind, but just as quickly, she dismissed the strategy. The truth was, she no more thought he was involved than she was; and somehow, instinctively, she knew that if she pressed him, she'd get nothing other than more oblique answers until she was frustrated and, potentially, flustered. And she had no intention of letting either of these men put her on the defensive. She gave a curt nod and let it go for the time being.

"Thank you, both. Now, if you'll excuse me, I hear some vehicles on the road and suspect the support team is arriving. I'm going to go up and meet them. You're both welcome to head back to Kit's; if we need anything more, we know where to find you."

She didn't wait for a response from the two men, though she didn't anticipate either of them leaving for a good long while. Making her way up the hill, she stepped onto the road just as Marcus came into sight in the police SUV. Standing off to the side, she watched as he pulled up, followed by Vivi in the medical examiner van, Ian in his sheriff's truck, and two state trooper vans carrying the evidence response team.

When everyone had gathered around her, she gave them the details of the situation. She looked to Ian to put a plan into place—partly because he was the senior officer, but mostly because he loved his plans. But Ian simply stared back at her, making it clear that he expected her, the responding officer and deputy chief, to make the decisions. She knew it was Ian's way of mentoring her, of encouraging her to grow professionally—something he'd been doing since they'd first met—and that she should be grateful for the opportunity, but as it was, she felt more resigned than anything else as she issued orders and delegated tasks.

Having sent Marcus down the road to check the two areas where a car was most likely to have turned around, Carly watched Vivi and her assistant, Daniel Westerbrook, make their way down to the body, careful of where they tread.

"Everything okay?" Ian asked, coming up beside her.

She lifted a shoulder. "Yes, fine. I mean other than that poor woman, of course."

"Of course," Ian murmured in agreement. Carly was aware of the evidence collection team starting their work. They were always a buzz of activity—a systematic buzz, but a buzz nonetheless. However, even as they moved around the scene—taking pictures, placing markers, and making notes—she and Ian watched Vivi and Daniel.

"It's hard to believe he's the governor's son, isn't it?" Ian asked, speaking of Daniel.

She let out a little laugh, "I would say yes, but after seeing how hard he worked on that first case we worked together, it's hard to see him as anything other than a dedicated forensic anthropologist." Carly didn't need to go into detail about just which case she was referring to—it was one neither she nor Ian would ever forget. A serial killer had landed in Windsor and set his sights on Vivi. It was also the case that had brought Vivi and Ian, now married with a one-year-old son, together over two years ago.

"This should be your case, you know," she said after a short silence.

"And I'll be the officer of record, but there's no reason you can't lead the charge. After all, that's what good managers do, right? Manage down," he asked with a grin.

Carly all but rolled her eyes at him. He wasn't doing this to manage down, he was doing this because he thought it would be a good opportunity for her. And even though she wasn't entirely happy about embracing the opportunity, she knew he was right. Glancing at her former boss, she found herself wishing, not for the first time, that Ian hadn't left the Windsor Police department after his short stint as their deputy chief of police, the position she now held. Of course, she knew why he'd made the move and become the county sheriff, and she honestly believed it was the best move for him, but still, she missed having his daily guidance and support.

"Fine," she said with a small laugh. "Why don't you go manage the evidence team then? I'm going to join your wife at the body. Whoever she is, I hope we can figure out what happened to her, and quickly." She paused for a moment, letting the sounds of the scene filter through her mind. "No one deserves to be treated that way," she added quietly.

"It does speak of carelessness and maybe even some depravity," Ian replied.

And that was the part that really got to her: the thought of such depravity in Windsor. She knew that with 7,000 people, they would have their fair share of good and bad. But for the most part, crimes committed by *residents* of Windsor were pretty minor. And there was some measure of comfort in that knowledge.

But even as she approached the body and caught a few of Vivi's words as they were faithfully documented by Daniel, she knew that comfort was an illusion. Crime, even murder, could happen anywhere people lived. And today, it just happened to have landed on her doorstep.

"Rough time of death appears to be somewhere between eight and ten p.m. last night," Vivi reported without preamble as soon as Carly came to a stop a few feet from the body. "Female, obviously," she continued. "No ID in the pockets I can reach. Hard to say age without a closer examination, but judging by her hands and what I can see of her face, I'd say well into her forties. I won't know cause of the death until we get her back to the lab for an autopsy, but I can tell you now, it wasn't a natural death."

After working with Vivi for more than two years, Carly knew she shouldn't be surprised by what the medical examiner could determine so quickly with so little information, but she was. Of course, she'd suspected it wasn't a natural death, but to hear Vivi pronounce it was entirely different.

"How do you know?" Carly asked.

Vivi glanced up, ignoring the crime scene tech who was busy snapping pictures of the body, the flash going off at regular intervals in the tree-shaded area.

"See here and here?" Vivi asked, pointing to an area on the woman's jeans and another on her sweater. At first Carly saw nothing, but as she looked closer, she saw small spots of dark discoloration.

"I see the spots, but what are they?"

"Blood," Vivi pronounced as she sat back on her heels. "There are several areas like that on her clothing, areas where blood has seeped through, staining the fabric."

Carly was silent for a long moment, as was Vivi. No doubt, they were both wondering just what Vivi would find when she removed the victim's clothing back at the lab.

"How many areas?' Carly asked.

"Seven, so far," Daniel answered. "And we haven't turned the body yet."

"Any idea what caused them?"

Vivi shook her head. "And I don't want to lift her sweater to look while we're out here in the woods, I'd rather do that back at the lab."

"Of course," Carly murmured. "Are you almost ready to turn the body?" she asked, wanting to get a look at the face of the woman they were all focused on.

"I need a few more minutes and then we'll be ready," Vivi answered.

Carly watched Vivi and Daniel turn their attention back to the woman, then took a few steps up toward the road and caught sight of Ian talking with one of the evidence techs. With a wave, she got his attention, then gestured for him to join her with Vivi and Daniel.

Once he had made his way to her side, she spoke. "Vivi is going to turn her in a minute, and I want you here to see if you recognize her. There hasn't been any obvious identification found yet."

His head bobbed once in response.

Even though, in recent years, she'd been living in Windsor longer than Ian—she'd moved to the area five years earlier, and he'd only returned from the Army about two years after that—Ian had grown up in the small town and knew quite a few more people than she did, or at least he could recognize more than she could.

When Vivi and Daniel indicated that they were ready, Carly watched them brace the body. Taking care not to disturb anything more than necessary, the pair rotated the woman until she lay prone on her back.

Unexpectedly, Carly experienced a moment of hesitation. She didn't want to see the woman's face, she didn't want to know if it was someone from the community who had been tortured and killed—at least not yet, not until she'd had a moment to really brace herself for that option. And so her eyes went first to the woman's feet then slowly traveled up her legs. Now that she knew what to look for, she could see more signs of bleeding through the light blue denim of the jeans. Tracing her gaze upward, the rose-colored sweater had been hiked up enough to reveal a thin strip of flesh at the woman's waist, but it also looked like parts of the knit top were stuck to the victim's skin—perhaps from dried blood—leaving the general shape of the garment skewed.

It was when her eyes caught on a thin gold chain around the victim's neck that Carly's hesitation turned swiftly into a sense of foreboding that settled surely on her shoulders. For reasons she didn't understand, her instincts warred with her intellect for a moment and all she wanted was to be away. Far away.

"Carly?" Ian asked at her side.

Using him as a reprieve, she looked away from the scene and at her former boss. "Yes?"

"Do you recognize her? I don't. Vivi?" he added.

Carly turned her attention to Vivi, who was shaking her head.

"No ID that we can find, either," Daniel said having concluded his preliminary search of the jeans pockets.

Knowing she had to swallow the irrational fear that had gripped her, Carly took a deep breath. And looked down.

Years ago, when an infection had developed after she'd had her wisdom teeth extracted, a dentist had prescribed a painkiller and she would never forget the moment when it had kicked in. She'd been beyond grateful for the pain relief, but as the medication had washed through her body, she'd felt a disconcerting numbness spread from the top of her head down to her toes. She knew there were people who liked that feeling, but to Carly it had felt like the life, *her* life, was being drained from her own body, leaving nothing behind but a confused, emotionless empty shell. And that wasn't something she'd ever wanted to experience again.

But now, looking down at the face of the woman who had mostly likely been killed, then dumped, not ten miles from where Carly lived and worked, she had that exact same feeling.

Seconds passed, or maybe it had been minutes, when she

became dimly aware of Vivi's voice saying her name—once, then a second time. Then she felt Ian's hand on her shoulder. That touch, that solid, real touch, a touch that was meant for comfort, was just the reminder she needed. A reminder that there were special protocols she had to follow now—protocols that had nothing to do with processing the crime scene. No, the rules and procedures that came flooding back to her were ones that no one around her could know about.

She took a deep breath and pushed the fear crowding her brain back into the shadows.

"Yeah?" she answered, stepping away and looking at him.

"Do you know her?"

Carly glanced at the face again, then frowned. "No, she doesn't look familiar to me," she forced herself to answer. She didn't spare a glance for Vivi, knowing the trained forensic psychologist would pick up more than anyone else.

She let her gaze linger on the woman long enough to appear as if she was giving what she saw before her some consideration. "Can you tell us anything else, Vivi?" she asked. And only when she was sure Vivi had turned her attention back to the body did Carly look at her friend.

"No—no more than what we already know, but I can add that her face seems to confirm my original impression that she is well into her forties."

As Vivi spoke, movement to Carly's left caught her attention and she looked up to find Drew and Ty still leaning against the fallen trunk. Ty's eyes were on the body and she had little doubt that, as an ex-vice cop, he was probably asking himself all the questions cops ask—who, what, why, when, etc.

But not Drew. Drew wasn't looking at the body. No, he was watching her—as if the dead body at her feet were of no consequence and his only interest was in her. She held his gaze, wondering if he'd seen her reaction to the woman's face. Wondering if he thought that the sight of a body had been a shock to her relatively inexperienced eyes.

But his face held no judgment. No, as he stood there, still leaning against the trunk with his arms crossed, he looked to be calmly assessing her. When he continued to watch, she gave him a small, dismissive smile then simply turned and walked away. She felt his eyes following her, or perhaps it was her imagination, but as she moved away from the scene, she pushed his image from her mind.

Climbing up the hill, she tamped down her initial shock. Halfway to the top, she stopped to answer a crime scene tech's question, then directed another tech to take some extra photos of an area by the side of the road that looked slightly more disturbed than the rest. Before she'd even set foot on the road, she'd slipped back into her role as deputy chief of police.

Up by the vehicles, she paused for a moment and watched the activity. It was easier to focus on the tasks at hand than face what she knew she would ultimately need to face. She forced back a wave of sadness; now was not the time or the place. She knew that if she let the sorrow even so much as crack open a door it would leave an opening for the fear, panic, and utter confusion Carly knew was hovering in the far reaches of her brain, clamoring to be heard.

"Hey, Carly," Marcus said as he approached her, carrying a tire cast he'd presumably taken from one of the turn-out areas she'd sent him to scout. "I got one impression, but who knows if it will turn into anything useful. I hear the victim was cut up pretty badly, or it appears that way. One of the techs mentioned it to me on my way back. Any ID?"

She looked at Marcus, newly back on the job, almost back to his old self. She didn't want him here. But then again, she didn't want him anywhere else. He was the one person who would know exactly what it meant when she told him what she was about to tell him.

"Carly?"

She turned her gaze back to the primary scene. From where she stood, she could see the tops of heads—Vivi's, Daniel's, and

Ian's—along with those of a few techs moving around the hillside. A brisk autumn breeze touched her face and lifted her hair; the sun now hung high in the sky.

It was a beautiful day to find a body.

"It's Marguerite," she said.

CHAPTER TWO

CARLY UNDERSTOOD THE MOMENT OF stunned silence that followed her quiet announcement. At first, Marcus gaped at her, but when she didn't retract her statement he opened his mouth to say something, only nothing came out. Then he just turned and looked away, his mouth closing and tightening, his eyes shutting briefly. Finally, he crossed his arms over his chest and dropped his gaze to the ground.

She watched him struggle with the same series of feelings that had hit her when she'd first seen Marguerite's face—shock, denial, sorrow. She knew panic would come next. But then the memory of the code, the rules that had been drilled into them so many years ago, would claim a space in the chaos of his mind—demanding order, demanding obedience.

His body jerked once, then one more time. His fingers gripped his biceps and still she stayed silent, letting him find his composure. When he looked back up, his body appeared more relaxed. However, his jaw was clenched so tightly that she wondered if his teeth would crack.

"This is bad," he said after another stretch of silence.

"Master of the obvious, Marcus."

"Don't be flip about this," he snapped.

She took a deep breath and let it out. "I know it is."

"You didn't identify her?"

She shook her head and looked out toward the valley. "Of course not."

"And she has no ID?"

"Not that Daniel or Vivi could find right away."

"So, as of now, no one knows who she is."

They were both silent for several moments.

"We need a plan," Marcus said, his voice softening.

"I know," she agreed quietly as she turned back to him.

"We don't know what it means," Marcus said. "That she was killed here, I mean."

Carly gave a half-hearted shrug. "She wasn't killed here, she was brought here. But you're right, we don't know what it means. I think we're pretty safe in assuming that whatever it means isn't good, though."

"Do you want to leave?"

There it was. The question she hadn't allowed herself to ask. The question her mind had turned away from, even though her instincts had been subtly whispering the answer all morning. *Yes. Run.*

And, coward that she was, she did want to run. She wanted to run away so fast and so far that no one would ever catch her. But what she was running from, or part of it anyway, would follow her no matter where she went. Her own fear, her own guilt, were not going to be left behind.

Taking a deep breath and bracing her shoulders, she shook her head. "It won't solve anything and we need to take care of Marguerite first."

"Marguerite would want us to take care of ourselves," Marcus countered, not untruthfully.

"She would, but you can't deny we at least owe it to her to make sure she is identified and that Lorraine, as her closest relative, is notified. At the very least, we owe both Lorraine and Marguerite that."

She was right and Marcus knew it, although he only managed a tiny, almost imperceptible nod to show his agreement.

"Why don't I accompany the body to the lab?" she asked. "The first thing Vivi will do is run the fingerprints. Once Marguerite is identified, I have no doubt the right people will take over, and then we can be sure Lorraine will find out."

Marcus turned away from her. There were so many things they needed to talk about, so many things they needed to consider. But after what Marguerite had done for them, she deserved to be taken care of first. She deserved their help in making sure she did not stay a Jane Doe. Everything else could wait.

"Why don't I go?" Marcus asked.

Carly's knee-jerk reaction was to say no. Selfishly, she wanted to be the one there. She wanted to be the one that made sure Marguerite received the respect and attention she deserved. But other than that, other than her own control issues, she had no rational argument for going herself. And several for not.

Reluctantly, she agreed.

"Are you sure?" he asked.

She'd been closer to Marguerite than Marcus had and he knew just what it meant for her to send him in her place. But she answered, this time with more surety. "Yes, it makes more sense given your relationships at the lab—you've spent more time there recently, you know more people. And, given my position," she added on a sigh, "it makes more sense for me to go back to the station and start the paperwork. Ian will have to sign off on all of it, but I may as well get it started."

Marcus started to say something but cut himself off when Vivi and Daniel appeared, pulling a gurney behind them. With two techs and Ian handling the other end, the team had managed to get it up onto the road. Carly and Marcus watched the procession in silence, but when the body bag came into sight, she turned away. Marcus's gaze stayed fixed on the group as they loaded Marguerite into the ME van. He inhaled sharply when the van doors slammed shut—the only display of emotion he appeared to be allowing himself.

Carly cleared her throat. "We need to . . ." She let her voice trail off and gestured with her head to the others.

"Yeah, I know," Marcus answered. "Let's go do this."

Turning back to the van, she walked toward the team with Marcus a few steps behind her. "All set?" she asked, cringing internally at the lack of emotion in her voice.

"I have what I need," Vivi answered. "Of course, there will be a lot to do at the lab once we get her there, but I'm done here."

"And your team?" Carly asked Eric Waterson.

Eric, one of the techs who had helped bring the gurney up, led the evidence collection team. Tall and unnaturally skinny, the fact that he was so thin his face all but looked like a skull was an irony that did not escape her each time they worked together.

"We have a few more pictures we want to take and some mapping of the area left to do, but we should be finished in about four hours or so," he said.

She nodded her response and looked to Ian as she laid out her plan. "Marcus can accompany Vivi and Daniel to the lab and then help Eric's team with the evidence once they get there. I'll head back to the station and get started on the paperwork. Ian will you be in the office today?" When he responded in the affirmative she continued. "Good, then I'll e-mail my reports to you and you can sign off."

"And who should I send my reports to?" Vivi asked.

"Both Carly and me," Ian answered.

With marching orders confirmed for everyone, Eric rejoined his team and Marcus handed over the keys of the SUV to Carly. Within minutes, Vivi, Daniel, Marcus, and Ian were turning their respective vehicles around and driving back down Churchkill Road. After they had disappeared around a bend, she walked to the edge of the hill.

"Need a hand with anything, Eric?" she called down.

He answered that he had everything well in hand and she began to turn away when movement farther down the hill caught her eye. Ty and Drew were standing where she'd left them. She wondered what they were still doing there, what they could be thinking, then she realized she didn't really care, not now. She did however, want to see them safely gone from the scene.

Making her way down, she heard the murmured tones of their voices, but they stopped speaking as she approached. "I have a car if you'd both like a ride back to Kit's," she offered. She'd already told them they were free to leave and she felt as though saying it again would sound, well, rude.

"We'll walk," Drew answered.

"No ID?" Ty asked.

Wanting to put a name to a face was human nature. Sometimes it was to humanize the body, sometimes it was to help draw a line between them and us. For Ty, Carly suspected it was the former even though he lived several hundred miles away and would be unlikely to know anyone in the area.

She shook her head. "Not yet. They'll run fingerprints at the lab and take it from there."

"Any idea how she died?" Another question from Ty.

A twinge of exasperation must have flashed across her face and Ty looked suitably chagrined.

"It's an ongoing investigation," she said. "As a former cop, I'm sure I don't have to tell you what that means."

He smiled and pushed himself off the trunk. "You don't, but I had to try. Curiosity and all."

"Half the reason we become cops in the first place," she conceded. "Well, I'm sorry we met under these circumstances, but I hope the rest of your stay is more enjoyable. And thank you for your help today."

Ty smiled warmly. "Such as it was. I hope you get your guy, as they say."

"Me too," she said. More than he knew.

Turning to Drew, who hadn't moved from his spot, and hadn't stopped watching her either, Ty asked, "Ready?"

Drew's eyes left her for the first time and landed on his companion. Carly felt her heart trip a little panicked beat when Drew seemed to consider the question. But after a moment of silence lasting a breath or two too long, he stepped away from the tree. "Good luck," he said with a general nod toward the scene behind her.

"Thank you," she answered. "Have a safe trip home and we'll reach out to you if we have any additional questions."

Ty gave her a small encouraging smile and started back down the trail toward Kit's house. Drew lingered, then turned to join his friend. As she watched him leave, she acknowledged that something about him called on her curiosity. She didn't understand why that was and wasn't sure she wanted to. But looking away from where he'd disappeared down the trail and back over to the techs still crawling over the hillside, Carly knew that, for good or for bad, she had no time to figure it out.

Marguerite needed her.

• • •

"How'd it go this morning?" Vic Ballard asked as he leaned against the open door to Carly's office. She looked up at her boss, the chief of police, as she hit the send button that would provide Ian with all the necessary paperwork. They'd keep it for their files too, but for the most part, from here on out, it would be a county case. Legally, anyway.

"As well as can be expected." She'd called Vic and given him the basic details as she'd left the scene but he'd been on his way back from some conference or another and his phone had kept cutting out.

"With you and Marcus out there, who covered the other shift?"

"Carl and Teddy came on," Carly answered, naming two of their part-time officers. More and more they'd been relying on part-time help. Not long ago, the force had been her, Marcus, Wyatt, Ian, Vic, *and* four part-timers. But then Ian had left, followed by Wyatt, who'd joined the FBI. And Vic, never a very attentive boss in the first place, had seemed to take it into his head that he needed to attend every police conference on the eastern seaboard. In the past fourteen months, he'd been away from the office more than in it.

And then there was Marcus. Just over a year ago, Marcus had been nearly killed in an explosion while on duty. He'd only been cleared to return to full-time duty three months earlier. For many reasons, she was glad to have him back, but even with him, the force was down to two—her and Marcus. If she counted Vic, they could passably claim a force of two *and a half* full time officers, which was still half their previous size.

"And now?" he asked.

"They'll stay on until the end of shift. And with both Marcus and me on all day, I was going to put Lucy and Jake on the night shift again. They were both on last night too," she answered, naming the other two part-time officers.

"Good, that will give you the night off," Vic said. Despite his general hands-off approach to just about everything work related and frequent absences from the office, at least she could be grateful he supported her decisions. "You weren't on last night were you?"

Carly shook her head, then paused. "I wasn't on the roster, but I did get a call and go out last night."

Vic frowned.

"Mary Hanson and her husband were at it again. Or rather, he was at her again," she explained. Mary and Bill Hanson had been her landlords at her old apartment—a small one bedroom she'd rented above the appliance store they owned. She'd only recently moved, but during her time as their tenant she'd had much too close of a look into their relationship to walk away. Bill Hanson was not a nice drunk. And he was drunk more often than not.

"You could have let Lucy and Jake handle it."

Carly lifted a shoulder. "I could have, but Bill's brother owns the shop Lucy's husband works at. I didn't want to put her in the middle of something that could have a bad outcome for her husband."

Vic let out a sigh. "Of course. But you look wiped, why don't you head home after you finish the reports?"

"The reports are done. I sent them to you and Ian. I'm waiting to hear from Vivi or Marcus at the lab, but maybe I'll take you up on that later this afternoon." Marguerite's death had a lot of implications she and Marcus needed to discuss and having the option of taking some time to do it seemed wise.

"Good, do that. Speaking of the lab, any news yet?"

Carly shook her head. "No, we found no identification on her, but I'm sure Vivi, Dr. Buckley, and the rest of the team will do what they can." She glanced at the clock, it had been five hours since she'd left the crime scene. "I expect I should hear something soon," she added.

As if her thoughts had conjured him, her phone rang and Marcus's number popped up on her screen. "Marcus," she said to Vic as she picked up her cell without answering it.

Vic pushed off from the door. "I'll let you get to it. Let me know if I can help," he added, then closed the door behind him as he left.

She made sure he was out of hearing range before she answered. "Marcus?"

"Yeah, it's me."

"And?" she pressed without preamble.

"Her prints didn't show up in the system."

She wanted to scream, *What?* but she forced herself to take a deep breath and think.

"It can't be good," Marcus said.

"Are you . . . ?"

"No one can hear me." He answered her unspoken question.

"What do you think?"

"A lot of things, and none of them are good."

"Not helpful, Marcus."

He let out a long breath. "I think whoever killed her could have erased her prints from the system."

Carly wasn't much of a conspiracy theorist, but Marcus's thoughts mirrored hers, with good reason. It had been a few years since they'd seen Marguerite, but a cold case over a decade old that involved corrupt FBI agents is what tied her to them, and through them to Windsor.

If Marguerite had decided to re-open that case, those who had been investigated years ago, men and women who had probably risen in the ranks since that initial investigation, would have the power to do something like that—they would have the power to erase her existence.

"Maybe she was working on something that required her team to erase her from the databases?" she contemplated.

"And somehow her body ended up here? Come on, Carly."

Marcus was right and she knew better. The only tie between Marguerite and Windsor was her connection to Carly and Marcus. A yawning pit of guilt opened up in her stomach. She wasn't sure she would be able to live with the possibility that Marguerite had died trying to protect the two of them.

"Oh god," she said rubbing her free hand over her eyes.

"It was a warning. I don't think we can look at it any other way."

"But of what?" she demanded. "And why erase her prints then dump her where someone is sure to recognize her?"

"I don't know," Marcus bit out, "I don't know about any of it," he said, obviously sharing her frustration. "But we need to figure it out."

She had to bite her tongue to stop herself from making another snarky comment about his observations of the obvious. Forcing herself to slow down, she took a deep breath and let it out slowly. What mattered right at that moment?

Marguerite.

"Does Vivi know anything else? Did she do the autopsy?" Carly hated the sound of those words coming out of her mouth.

Marcus paused before answering. "Yeah, she did."

The crack she heard in his voice almost caused her own shell to fracture. Abruptly, she swung her chair away from her door and looked out the window as she fought the tears threatening to spill from her eyes.

"And?" Her voice sounded as weak as she felt.

Marcus started to speak, then stopped to clear his throat. On the other end of the line, he struggled to hold himself together. After a moment, he started again.

"She was tortured. Mostly with a knife. Likely a small, generic hunting knife. She was also beaten, five of her ribs were broken, and her torso," his voice broke again and he paused before finishing in a rush. "Her torso was bruised just about everywhere. Her femur was broken, there were cigarette burns on her breasts and inner thighs. The ultimate cause of death was internal bleeding from the beating."

Carly nearly threw up at the imagery Marcus's words had brought forth. Clenching her jaw, she took several deep breaths through her nose and willed the nausea away. She didn't have the right to be weak right now. Not after what Marguerite had suffered.

When she knew she could speak again, she did. "What is Vivi doing to identify her?"

"Facial recognition and DNA. But if she's been wiped from the fingerprint databases, it's likely the DNA, and maybe even any official photo identification records, will show up blank as well—and it will take some time to get those results," Marcus answered. "Do you still have those three burner phones we bought a while back?" he asked, changing the direction of the conversation.

She did, but it took a minute for her to remember where she might have put them during her move before she answered him. "Yes."

"Take one and call Marguerite's boss."

"Do you even know who Marguerite's boss is?" Carly asked. "I don't, and if we just get routed through to the tip line, it could be days before they follow up."

"Then one of us needs to contact Lorraine and tell her. *She* can call it in," Marcus snapped.

She agreed, but the uncertainties were making her cautious. "Whoever did this went to the trouble of erasing Marguerite's existence before leaving her body in Windsor as a message to us. Until we have a better understanding of just what that message is supposed to be, I don't want to make any moves, like leading them to Marguerite's family. Whatever you and I decide to do, we need to stay under the radar in case we are being watched."

She heard Marcus let out a deep breath—acceptance mixed with frustration. "What do we do then? If we are being watched, I get that we may not want to pick up a phone and call Lorraine or rush off to visit her in New Hampshire, but we can't let Marguerite remain nameless."

Carly sat motionless, as a plan began to form. "What if I do 'rush off' to see her, but I do it in Kit's SUV rather than my car?" she started. "She already told me I could use it to move the last of my boxes from the storage shed. Chances are, if someone is watching us, they'll be tracking us through *our* phones and watching *our* cars."

After a moment, Marcus made a sound of assent then asked, "And then from there? I assume you'll tell Lorraine and have her call it in?"

"Lorraine and Marguerite were always so close, I bet she knows who Marguerite's boss was. She can call it in and say someone contacted her and told her she needed to contact the state lab of New York about Marguerite. Once she does, it will at least bring Marguerite's own people into the investigation," Carly said. The plan had a number of steps in it but its complexity wouldn't increase the risk significantly.

"It's simpler than it sounds, isn't it?" Marcus asked. "And once Marguerite's people identify her body and take over—"

"Then we can focus on figuring out what this all has to do with us," she finished.

They were both silent for a long moment, then Marcus spoke. "I hate this."

She sighed. "Yeah, you and me both. But what choice do we have?"

"What choice did we ever have?" came his bitter response.

Carly had nothing to say.

"I'm sorry," he said after a moment. "It's just . . ." His voice trailed off.

"It's been a long, shitty day," she said.

"And one that isn't over for *you* yet," he pointed out.

"I'll bet it's not over for you either, since you're still at the lab, aren't you?"

She could almost hear his shrug. "I am, but I still have my place here in Albany so it's not a big deal. Vivi and the team were just organizing the evidence the techs brought in when I stepped away to call you. They were going to run a few preliminary tests this afternoon and begin fully processing everything tomorrow. I'll go through those preliminary reports when they come in and see if anything new comes up and then head home after that."

She wanted to ask him to call her if he learned anything, but in case their phones were being tracked, their quasi-elaborate plan included radio silence between the two of them until she returned to Windsor.

Again, she let out a deep sigh as she swung her chair back to her desk. "I'll call you when I get home?"

"Yeah, do," Marcus answered after a brief hesitation. "And Carly?"

"Yeah?"

"Be safe."

"I will," she said as they ended the call.

She stared at her phone for a long moment before pulling herself together. She'd have to go face Drew and Dani and Ty and any of Kit's other houseguests and make nice before being able to leave with Kit's Land Rover. She glanced at the clock again and took a deep breath. It would take her two and half hours to drive to Lorraine's home in Keene, New Hampshire.

For more reasons than just the drive, it was going to be a long night.

CHAPTER THREE

Carly's visit with Lorraine had been as difficult as she'd imagined. As she wound her way through the back roads, having opted for the long, quiet way home rather than the interstate, she still felt the sting of the tears she'd shared with the older woman, Marguerite's aunt. Carly hadn't doubted for a moment that Lorraine would agree to the plan she and Marcus had devised, but still, it had been heartbreaking to even have to ask.

Glancing at the clock on the dash as she stopped at a light in Williamstown, Massachusetts, she knew it would be well past ten o'clock by the time she pulled into her own driveway. After the night she'd had dealing with Mary and Bill Hanson and then the day that had followed, falling straight into bed, even if sleep eluded her, called to her like a siren song. But as she envisioned her pillow and quilt, her stomach reminded her that food was a necessity, not an option, in life.

Begrudging her own needs, Carly decided to make a quick stop by The Tavern to pick up some of Rob's butternut squash soup after she dropped the SUV back at Kit's house. She'd call Marcus while she ate and then, hopefully, climb into her king-size bed after that.

Realizing her day had seemed to consist of nothing but making and implementing plans, she let out a wry laugh in the darkness of her car. Ian's mentoring had clearly extended beyond just teaching her how to be a good officer.

• • •

Sitting with his family at The Tavern as they waited for their dessert and after-dinner drinks, Drew felt the air shift around him. The subtle and momentary drop in temperature told him someone had entered the restaurant, but a little prickling at his neck had him on alert. Glancing up, he saw Deputy Chief Carly Drummond looking quickly away from his table as she made her way to the bar.

His eyes tracked her as she walked across the restaurant. She had changed out of the uniform she'd worn earlier in the day—which wasn't surprising since it was well past nine in the evening—and now wore fitted jeans, dark boots with a small square heel, and a dark green sweater covered by an off-white winter vest. Her blonde hair, which reached just below her chin, had been clipped back when he'd seen her earlier. It was down now, curling around her face and, judging by the way she'd shoved the same few errant strands of it behind her ear twice in the last ten seconds, he'd wager she hated those curls—or at the very least, found them annoying.

Pulling up a seat at the bar, she started chatting with the bar-keep, who, if Drew remembered correctly, was named Rob and also owned the place. He waited until Carly had placed her order and a drink had been placed in front of her before he made his move.

"Excuse me," he said to everyone with a gesture of his head in Carly's direction. "Mind if I ask if she'd like to join us?"

The question earned him a few curious looks, but everyone immediately consented, so he rose from his seat and approached the bar.

A glass of what looked like whiskey with one ice cube had just touched her lips when he sat down next to her. "Deputy Chief Drummond," he said. The look that flashed across her profile before she turned to him almost made him laugh. If he'd had any previous doubts about whether or not she wanted to talk to him, he certainly didn't now.

She took a deep breath before she turned toward him. "Please, call me Carly."

He gave her a small smile. "Your day is finally over then, Carly?"

She raised her glass. "Almost. I'm picking up some dinner then heading home for the night. I dropped Kit's car back already."

"Come join us while you wait," he suggested, nodding toward the table where Jason and Sam sat across from Dani and Ty.

She shook her head. "Thank you, but I don't want to interrupt your dinner. And I'll only be waiting for a few minutes, I just ordered some soup to go."

"Then all the more reason," he insisted. He knew from the way she'd fixed her eyes on some point behind the bar that if she could find a polite way to say it, she would to tell him to go away. But he had great faith in the fact that it wouldn't do to have the Deputy Chief of Police, a public figure, act rudely toward tourists, even when off duty. He chose not to acknowledge that using this to his advantage didn't even cause a ripple in his conscience.

When she let out a tiny little sigh and looked down at her drink, he knew he'd won the mini-battle. Turning back to him, she said, "If it won't be an imposition."

"Not at all," he answered, sliding off his seat. As he pulled her chair back for her, his hand grazed her shoulders and her startled look almost teased a smile from him.

When they reached his family, he pulled a chair over for Carly while she said hello to Dani and Ty. Drew introduced Sam and Jason and they all settled themselves around the table, making room for the additional seat. When the shuffling of the chairs subsided and everyone was back in their spots, a beat of awkward silence passed before Ty spoke up.

"Did you get an ID on the woman?" he asked, as he raised his glass to take a sip of wine.

Carly pursed her lips. "No, we didn't. Not yet anyway. Her fingerprints weren't in the system."

Ty's brows shot up in surprise. "That's unusual. Is there anything you can tell us?"

"Not dinner talk," Dani interjected, softening the rebuke with a smile.

Ty rolled his eyes. "Right because we *never* talk about our work at our dinner table."

"This is not *our* dinner table and no doubt Deputy Chief Drummond has had a long day. And it's not as though you aren't familiar with the fact that, because it's part of an *ongoing investigation*, she likely couldn't tell you anything anyway," Dani responded without skipping a beat.

Drew watched Carly as her eyes bounced between the husband and wife. Ty leaned down and whispered something in Dani's ear. Dani responded by elbowing him in the side and muttering something that sounded suspiciously like "pervert" as she smiled. Carly looked away.

"Of course, my wife is right," Ty conceded. "But as one law enforcement to another, I do hope it's going well."

Carly's hazel eyes stilled for a moment as everyone's gaze landed on her, then she blinked. "Thank you," she said, dropping her eyes to her glass before looking up again. "And please, call me Carly." A few awkward moments of silence passed before she cleared her throat and spoke. "So twins? It must run in the family then?" she asked, looking to Sam and Dani. It was the right question to ask because the parents at the table seemed to take it from there, leading the conversation from pregnancy, to kids, to schools, to travel without kids, and everywhere in between. Drew didn't miss the fact that, with this topic, Carly had little need to participate in the conversation other than a response or question here and there.

He didn't have to wonder if the tactic was intentional. He'd known from the first moment he'd met her, when she'd walked into Kit's hospital room after the attack in Carly's parking lot, that she was more reserved than not.

Neither woman had escaped the attack unharmed, but when he'd tried to ask Carly how she was, she'd simply given him a long, assessing look before turning her back on him and brushing off the injuries she'd incurred while dragging Kit out of the way of a car intent on running her over with a two-word response, "I'm fine." And she hadn't been rude in their few subsequent meetings during the week that had followed, but she hadn't exactly invited conversation either—sharing nothing with him other than the bare necessities.

Still, he remembered that hospital visit with abnormal clarity. And, over the months, that fact had come to bother him, because there was no reason why those few moments he'd shared with Carly in Kit's room, should feel so poignant. He'd obviously been attracted to other women, and he certainly recognized the response when it came to Carly—he even understood that it was mutual, though Carly might not willingly make the same admission—but that didn't seem like enough to explain why she'd hovered in the periphery of his mind since that day they'd met in the hospital.

But even as he mulled it over again, his thoughts veered onto another track, one that caused him to shift in his seat. He'd seen her one other time, too. He'd been on a date in New York when she and Kit had walked into the same restaurant. He'd been struck by how different the two women walking into the restaurant had appeared from the two women he'd seen in the hospital several months earlier.

They'd been dressed up for a summer night on the town. Carly had worn a blue silk dress that looked like a long tank top. Only it hadn't been all that long, hitting her at mid-thigh and giving view to an impressive expanse of leg ending in nude heels.

And an anklet. A damned anklet that popped into his mind at odd, and unwanted, hours. A delicate gold chain with a small cross that dangled right over her anklebone. In that dress, with those heels, it seemed almost sacrilege to be wearing it. Still, months later, when he thought of her, he remembered that anklet, and just about the only thing he could think of then was wanting to see her wearing it and nothing else.

"Drew?" Dani's voice brought him abruptly back to the conversation.

Glancing at Carly, he noted that her hazel eyes were watching him. As they often seemed to be.

"Yes?" he answered, switching gaze to Dani.

"Carly's food is getting bagged up so we were saying good-bye," Sam said.

His eyes swung back to Carly, who was rising from her seat. Nice, he'd been the one to invite her over and he hadn't spoken a word. How suave of him.

"Why don't I walk you to your car?" he asked, standing.

"No, thank you, that isn't necessary."

"I insist."

Her eyes came up and held his for a brief moment, a question flashing through them. "Really it's not necessary. I just parked in the parking lot behind the restaurant."

His eyes narrowed. "Humor me."

• • •

Humor me. Carly knew she'd made a tactical error by mentioning the parking lot. She could tell by the way Drew's voice had become clipped and his shoulders had drawn back that he was remembering another dark night. After Kit's attack, she wasn't exactly fond of parking lots, either. But she was perfectly capable of walking herself to her car. There was also the fact that she had no interest in being alone with Drew just then. His eyes had been too observant for her liking all evening.

But even so, short of being overtly rude, she could think of no way to refuse his offer. So she turned a brittle smile on him and accepted. Offering a much warmer good-bye to his family and safe wishes for their travels home, she made her way back to the bar to pay her bill and pick up her soup.

Donning his jacket and gloves, Drew joined her as she waited for Rob to attend to a few other customers before running her credit card. "Did you get everything done that you needed to today?" he asked.

Her eyes flicked to his before returning to watch Rob mix drinks. She found it interesting that Drew hadn't just asked her if she'd moved all her boxes. It was as if he already knew she'd lied.

But of course, that was how it was with him—how it had always been, since that first moment she'd met him in Kit's hospital room. It was in his eyes, in the way he looked at her. He always seemed to have the answer to whatever question he had asked before he'd even asked it. And that made it seem like what he wanted from her, what he was really asking, was for something more. More from her, or maybe more *of* her.

It had unsettled her then and it unsettled her now.

"Yes, I did. Thank you." Rob stopped by with her bill, easing some of the tension she'd felt building in her shoulders. She signed the receipt, grabbed the bag with her soup, and turned toward the door. Beside her, Drew showed none of the discomfort she felt coursing through her body as he calmly held the door open for her.

As they walked in silence toward her car behind the restaurant, she listened to his measured steps as he matched her gait. Always so precise and efficient. She wondered what would happen if she ever had the courage to throw him off. She wondered what would happen if, heaven forbid, in the dark of the parking lot, she tugged his tidy shirt loose from his well-pressed pants and ran her palms over his skin. But as he came to a stop, exactly where he should beside her car to give her just enough space to open her door and slide in while still being close enough to protect her if needed, she knew she would never do it. His appearance of calm, his cool composure, was something she knew instinctively was hard fought and learned. And just as she knew that, she knew she wasn't equipped to handle whatever she might unleash in him with her touch. Especially not now.

"What happened today?" Drew's sharp tone brought her thoughts back from the wayward path they'd taken. Standing beside her car, hands tucked into the pockets of his cashmere coat, he studied her.

"I should think it was obvious. A woman was murdered." She turned from his scrutiny and unlocked her car door.

"I saw the color drain from your face when you saw the victim, Carly. I want to know why."

It was shocking, really, how quickly she could go from contemplating what it would be like to run her hands across his bare skin to debating just how to tell him to mind his own goddamned business. Had he asked politely, maybe expressed some concern for her, she still wouldn't have answered. But asking in the way he had, as if he were entitled to an answer, made her wish she wasn't a semi-public figure and could be more liberal with her language.

"How nice of you to be concerned. But I assure you, it isn't necessary." She opened her door and stepped around it. His eyes narrowed on hers.

"Something about that body scared you."

"I was shocked," she shot back.

She saw his jaw clench. "Carly."

"Good night, Drew. Thank you for walking me to my car. It's been a pleasure and I hope you have a safe trip back home." She slid into her seat and reached for the door. His hand came up to stop it from closing. She raised her brows at his high-handed method and gave him a look to let him know that releasing her door sooner rather than later would be in his best interest.

"You were scared," he said again. Only this time, his voice was quieter and she heard a hint of worry.

She let out a breath and counted to five. "I'm fine. Really. I just want to get home and go to bed."

He eyed her for a long moment and she had no doubt that he didn't believe a word of what she'd just said, except maybe the last part about getting home to bed. Much to her relief, though, he stepped back and let his hand fall away. "Take care of yourself."

She nodded and shut the door. As she pulled out of the lot, she saw him in her rearview mirror. Still standing where she'd left him. Still watching her.

CHAPTER FOUR

EARLY THE NEXT MORNING, AFTER passing through security, Drew followed an escort to Dr. Vivienne DeMarco's office at the state crime lab in Albany. Flipping through a folder on her desk, she looked up when the guard delivered him to her door.

"Come in, Mr. Carmichael," she said, rising to shake his hand.

"Please, call me Drew," he replied as he returned her greeting. She gave him a polite smile then sat down. Leaning back in her chair to look up at him, she quietly drummed a pen on its arm. He thought about sitting down across from her, but opted to stay standing instead.

"What can I help you with today?" she asked.

Rather than answer right away, he glanced around her office. Kit had told him enough about Vivienne DeMarco that it didn't surprise him to find that she'd been given a sizable office, despite being only a consultant for the lab.

"I understand you're the medical examiner for Columbia County."

"I am, yes."

"And for the state?"

"No," she said, her pen still drumming out a steady tattoo. "I do act as a secondary opinion for other county MEs, but I'm not the official state ME."

"Wouldn't that be a conflict of interest, if you were needed to consult on one of your own cases?" he asked, resting his palms on the back of the chair in front of him.

"I work for Dr. Sameer Buckley, here at the lab. He would

provide any secondary opinions on my cases, if needed," she answered, seemingly unperturbed by what must have seemed like a random line of inquiry.

"But I can't imagine you came here to discuss my work arrangements, did you, Mr. Carmichael?"

The leather of the chair under his fingers felt smooth and worn from years of use. He had a fleeting thought as to what Dr. DeMarco might find on it if she ever ran it through a series of evidence tests. "No, I didn't," he answered. He hesitated, then, going out on a limb, he spoke. "I'd like to be brought in on the case you're investigating from yesterday. The body of the woman found in Windsor."

The drumming of her pen stopped and she studied him openly. He'd heard tales of Dr. DeMarco's intelligence and he wondered how long it would take her to figure him out.

"You're CIA, aren't you," she announced.

Apparently, not long.

"What makes you say that?" he asked.

"You're obviously not any local law enforcement or you would have let us know yesterday. I also know you're not FBI—"

"How would you know?"

"You're old enough to have risen in the ranks, and with your air of superiority, I would bet you're used to giving orders. And while I don't know everyone in the FBI, if you ran in those circles, I would either know you or know *of* you," she answered.

Interesting. The comment about his age stung a bit. Sure, he was older than the doctor was, maybe by a few years, but not many. Unlike Carly—he had to be at least a decade older than she was. And, well, as to Dr. DeMarco's comment about his air, she wasn't the first person who'd called him arrogant.

Taking a seat, he gestured for her to continue.

"You're not the NSA type," she said, which he took as a compliment. "And as far as everyone knows, you're a businessman from New York. There are very few agencies that could or would set up that kind of cover, and usually when they do, it's not really a cover at all but holds enough truth to it to be mostly real. The DEA would, but only the CIA would keep the cover in place as long as I know yours has been. Or at least the only agency you would risk hinting to me about."

Kit had not been exaggerating about Dr. DeMarco's intellect. Impressed, he remained silent as she continued to study him.

Then she asked, "Why?"

He took a deep breath. "Because Deputy Chief Carly Drummond knows something she isn't sharing with the rest of you," he said, not having any idea how Dr. DeMarco would take his statement.

She arched an eyebrow at him.

"When you rolled the body over yesterday morning, you should have seen her expression," he continued. "It was clear to me that she either recognized the woman or recognized something about the way she had been killed. And based on what I heard last night, you still don't have an ID, so I'm assuming she hasn't shared what she knows."

"Last night?" Another eyebrow arch and Drew had a fleeting idea of what Dr. DeMarco's young son, whom he'd met at the fundraiser, had in store for him as a teenager some day.

"She borrowed Kit's SUV yesterday—ostensibly, to pick up some boxes from storage. I saw her at The Tavern after she'd returned the car to Kit's house—and it was much later than it should have been had she just stayed local like she said she was going to when she picked the car up. I think she went somewhere else, and after seeing her reaction yesterday, I think she needs to answer some questions."

"She's a grown woman, Mr. Carmichael—"

"Drew."

"Drew," she corrected. "It's entirely possible she had a valid reason for being out so much later than you deem appropriate."

Dr. DeMarco's allusion did not escape his notice and he sensed she had deliberately put it out there to check his reaction.

"You and the rest of the team are too close to her to see that she's hiding something. You need an outsider," he said.

"On the contrary. I did see her reaction. I also saw how you watched her. How your eyes tracked her every move."

Shit. He should have realized that Dr. DeMarco wasn't just book smart.

"Carly is hiding something," he insisted.

"Carly hasn't told us yet," she countered.

He shot her a look of disbelief.

Vivi set her pen down with a sigh. "I agree. She knows something we don't. But unlike you, I trust her. I trust that if she is keeping something from us, she's doing it for a good reason. And I also trust that when she feels she can, she'll tell us."

He didn't hold back his bark of cynical laughter. "That's quite a leap of faith you've taken there, Dr. DeMarco," he said, feeling every bit as jaded as he sounded.

She picked her pen back up and started drumming again. "I've been doing this a long time, and I don't like to boast, but I have a pretty good sense of what goes on inside people's heads. She'll tell us when she feels she can."

Dr. DeMarco's calm surety hit him like a slap in the face. The idea that someone with her background and experience *still* maintained trust and faith in people left him nearly speechless—or perhaps envious. Because any kind of trust or faith was getting harder for him to maintain with each passing day.

"Have you ever been wrong?" he asked, both curious and wary of her answer.

"Yes," she said softly. "I have. But I'm not about this."

Again, that surety, not just in what she thought but in *someone*. He paused, realizing he'd counted on her to be just as cynical as he was. This discussion wasn't going the way he had intended.

Deciding to try another tack, he conceded. "Perhaps. But I have unique expertise to bring to the table."

"No offense, but I doubt it," she said. Vivi DeMarco did not cut a man a break and he kind of respected her for it. But he did have something to offer.

"She was cut wasn't she? Several times and in patterns of five, a center piercing surrounded by four slices. Most of the patterns were probably centered on her stomach, but there were likely several scattered across her body," he said, pulling out what he hoped would be his trump card.

The pen stopped.

"And how would you know?" she asked.

"I saw the spots seeping through her clothes when we first came across her body. I recognized the pattern."

"And what does it mean?"

"It's the symbol of the Pen Royal Group, an organized crime conglomerate, for lack of a better word, that formed in the late eighties and operates out of DC."

Again, she studied him for a good long while before speaking. "Your information is accurate but old. They were formed in the DC area and operated out of there for several years before moving their primary headquarters to Dallas a few years ago. I guess with the growth of Russian and Chinese organized crime, DC got a little overcrowded," she added, the first hint of humor he'd seen from her.

"Or maybe they're getting old and wanted to live somewhere warm," he said, hopeful that even though she seemed to already know what he'd told her, she'd warmed up to him enough to allow him to join her team, if only temporarily.

She rolled her eyes at his comment, but a small smile touched her lips. "There are much easier ways to show a woman you're interested in her than this, you know."

"Do you know if what she knows has put her in danger?" Drew asked, ignoring her comment.

He could almost see her calculating those odds. But what he'd suggested did have some truth to it. Maybe Dr. DeMarco was right. Maybe Carly had an excellent reason for keeping her secret.

But just because she had a reason didn't mean there couldn't still be a monster lurking under her bed.

Finally, the doctor sighed and leaned forward. "Fine, assuming we get interagency approval, I'll request your participation in this investigation solely as an expert on the Pen Royal Group. At least they're an international group, so agency involvement won't look too fishy."

He let out a breath he hadn't realized he'd been holding. It had been a long time since someone had put him through his paces the way Dr. DeMarco had. "Thank you," he said writing down the contact information of his boss, Rina Ahmed.

He'd called Rina earlier and left a voice mail detailing his request. Knowing she would have seen through him in a heartbeat, almost as fast as Dr. DeMarco had, and then called him to the carpet and ordered him home, he'd been glad to only get her answering service. But with the request coming in from the state lab and from a doctor well respected in her field, Drew had at least a fighting chance of not having Rina tear him a new one when he returned to the office.

Of course, if she did, he would deserve it. Jurisdictionally, the case was gray, and even he knew there would be little to no return on his investment. Not even politically since, on the off chance they were to find something on PRG, the FBI would take over given PRG's US headquarters.

Dr. DeMarco took the paper he slid over and looked at the information before leaning back in her chair. "I'll call this in now."

"I appreciate it, Dr. DeMarco."

"Call me Vivi," she said, reaching for her phone. "We'll meet in the lab in an hour," she added. "Go talk to Ruben Allende in security, he'll get you set up with access."

He nodded, took that as his cue to leave, and rose. But as he passed through the door, she called him back.

"Drew?"

"Yes," he said, turning to face her.

"To be clear, next time I expect you to just ask her out."

• • •

Much to Carly's surprise, Vivi stood waiting for her in the lobby of the lab when she arrived for their morning briefing—a briefing she hoped would be short given the plan she and Marcus had implemented.

"I'm so glad you're here," Vivi said, rushing over to her as soon as she'd passed through security.

"Everything okay, Vivi? You look a bit harried." Vivi didn't get ruffled very often. Sure, *Carly* had been feeling unsettled since finding Marguerite, but she could see no reason why this case would affect Vivi any more than any of her other cases.

Her friend gave her a lopsided smile. "I'm fine. I just got off the phone with my cousin Naomi, and the family wants to throw Jeffery another birthday party. Apparently the small one with twenty guests wasn't big enough for his first birthday."

"Jeffery's birthday was three weeks ago," she said, speaking of Vivi and Ian's son.

"My family would celebrate it all year if they could," Vivi countered, speaking the truth. And though it seemed like overkill, Carly knew why. After having lost both her parents and her only brother on the same day over three years before, Vivi's huge extended family took extra care of their orphaned girl. Her wedding to Ian had been tasteful but lavish, the baby showers had seemed never-ending, and Jeffery's christening? Well, Carly'd had to bring on two part-timers to handle traffic control.

"So what's the problem?" Carly asked as they stepped into the elevator to the fourth floor briefing room.

"He already has enough toys. I don't mind the party so much, but the toys are going to be out of control."

"Have your family donate to a charity instead."

"I love that idea. And my family would too. But then they'd bring gifts anyway."

Carly let out a small laugh. She could imagine that happening. "Why don't you tell them you'll accept toys but you'll be donating them in both the Jefferys' names to Toys for Tots in December?" Vivi and Ian's little boy had been named after Vivi's brother, a Special Forces soldier who'd been killed while on duty in Afghanistan.

Vivi paused then smiled. "You know," she said as the elevator doors opened and they stepped out, "that might work. I think I'll run it by Naomi. It's a great idea, but Jeffery's birthday isn't actually why I came downstairs to meet you," Vivi said, turning toward her and putting a hand on her arm to stop her. They stood in the hallway around the corner from the briefing room.

Carly looked questioningly at her friend.

"I've brought someone else into the investigation. An expert of sorts," Vivi said.

She frowned. "That's your call, Vivi."

Vivi cleared her throat and her eyes darted away.

"Was it not your call?"

"No," Vivi answered, drawing the word out. "It was. But I'm not sure you're going to like it, so I wanted to give you a heads-up before we walk into the briefing room."

Carly couldn't see why she would care, but Vivi's behavior had her curious. "Why wouldn't I like it?"

Vivi took a deep breath and answered quickly, "Because it's Drew Carmichael."

Carly blinked, unable to process what Vivi had said. Then she reared back. "What!"

"He came to see me this morning and, believe it or not, he's law enforcement," Vivi said in a rush. "Well, of sorts," she added with a small frown.

"No, he's not. He's a businessman from New York City. His family owns some ridiculous number of companies."

She expected Vivi to argue with her, or support her, or say *something*. But silence answered her comment. Rather than tell her she was wrong, or tell her it was a joke, Vivi just stood there and held her gaze. Carly's stomach sank.

"I, I have a hard . . . I don't know what to say," she managed. "What agency or department . . . or . . ." Her voice trailed off; she still didn't quite believe it.

"I think he should tell you," Vivi answered, her voice soft with concern.

Concern? Vivi shouldn't be feeling concern for *her*. It shouldn't matter to Carly whether or not he was in law enforcement. Well, other than the fact that he hadn't said a word about it. And that he'd likely been critiquing her leadership skills the morning before—he had a few years on her, after all. Thinking about it, she realized that if he had been in law enforcement his entire career, he probably had more experience than any of the officers at that crime scene the day before—except for maybe Vivi, who had started at such a young age. In any event, he was certainly more experienced than she was.

The deeper the truth sank into her brain, the more she realized that perhaps Vivi did have cause to be concerned. "What agency?" she asked again.

Vivi's eyes darted around the hallway. They were still alone, but probably wouldn't be for long; Dr. Buckley would be arriving soon. Vivi's eyes met hers.

"He's with the CIA," Vivi said.

The small statement hit Carly so hard that she took a step back. "No," she said automatically.

Again, Vivi said nothing. And just like that, small memories came sifting through her mind. How it had seemed odd to her how comfortable Drew had been inserting himself into the investigation of Kit's attack, and how he'd been completely unruffled by the sight of the body on the trail. Grudgingly, she had to admit that she should have seen it earlier. She might not have guessed the CIA, but she should have figured out that he had *some* law enforcement knowledge or experience.

She sighed. None of this should matter to her. If *he* didn't matter, then where he worked or whom he worked for shouldn't matter either. But there was no doubt that the news of his profession had raised a strong emotion in her—an irrationally strong emotion if he truly meant nothing to her. And *this* revelation, more than the fact that he was CIA, sat uncomfortably in the pit of her stomach. She also didn't like that Vivi had seen her discomfort.

"Thank you for telling me, Vivi. I appreciate it," she said. And she did. She wished she'd had a better hold on her reaction to the news, but if she couldn't prevent wearing her emotions on her sleeve, she preferred that it had happened in the hallway with only Vivi there to witness it, rather than in the briefing room with Drew.

Vivi still studied her, the concern now showing in her eyes. "Really, Vivi," Carly said. "It was unexpected and," she paused, looking for the right word but unable to find it. "It was just unexpected," she repeated. "I'm glad you told me out here rather than letting me find out in there."

Vivi's expression changed to one of understanding, but she said nothing more about it. "Shall we then?" she asked with a gesture of her head in the general direction of the briefing room.

She nodded in reply and the two started down the hall.

"Hey," came Dr. Sameer Buckley's voice from behind them just as they reached the door to the briefing room. Carly turned to see Sam walking quickly in their direction. "Sorry I'm late," he said. "I got caught up looking at budgets and all, are we ready?" he asked, not bothering to wait for a reply.

Sam had been one of Vivi's first students, when she had been a PhD student herself. A bit of a savant like Vivi, he had started working with her on his own PhD three years before she finished the residency requirements of her joint PhD MD. When they'd finished in the same year, Vivi had been twenty-eight and Sameer twenty-three. They were two peas in the same brain-pod. Now, a little over seven years later, he officially held the title of the youngest director ever of the state lab of New York.

"Ready," Vivi said, following him into the room. She cast a smile in Carly's direction. Sam rarely, if ever, stopped moving.

When Carly stepped in herself, her gaze immediately landed on Drew. His eyes met hers, as they often did, and held. She thought she saw a flash of regret, or at least some emotion, on his face, but before she had a chance to recognize it, it disappeared. Of course it did. He'd be good at hiding things.

She looked away, then smiled when she saw Daniel seated at the table, already ensconced in a report. He had been another one of Vivi's students—smart enough to get into the program, but not in the same savant category as Vivi and Sameer. Still, the brilliant young man more than made up for that by being more committed to his profession than any young person ought to be. She almost laughed at that thought. Daniel wasn't much younger than she, maybe only two years behind her in age, but he seemed a lot younger—not because of the quality of his work, but because of the eager, almost fanatical way he approached it.

But because Carly knew the reason behind his attitude, she had nothing but respect for him. He'd lost his twin sister when they'd both been quite young. She had been kidnapped, and search after search had turned up nothing. Years later, when he was a teenager, Daniel had come across an article on Vivi and her work. He'd reached out to her to see if she could help find his lost twin.

Vivi had found his sister, who had been killed not long after she'd been kidnapped. The story had been awful and tragic, but finding her had, at the very least, given Daniel and his parents answers. From that day, Daniel had dedicated his life to forensic science and planned to someday focus solely on cold cases like his sister's.

But in order to do that, he needed as much experience as possible. After having worked with Sam during the serial killer case involving Vivi, the two men had become friends. When Daniel graduated the previous spring, Sam had offered him a job. So here he sat.

"You must be Drew," Carly heard Sam say. Not one to wait for introductions, Sam had kicked off the meeting. She watched as the two men shook hands. Drew's eyes met the director's but then flicked back to her.

"Vivi told me you'd be joining. A bit unusual, I think, but,"

Sam ended his statement with a shrug. "So what do you have, Daniel?" he asked, turning to the young man.

Daniel held up a paper from the file he'd been looking at. "She was likely killed in an industrial space. Her clothes had traces of machine grease and several different kinds of cotton fibers and the soles of her feet also had bits of glass, concrete, and some kind of chemical we are still running a trace on," he answered.

"Any indication of what kind of industrial space?" Vivi asked.

Carly had given Drew a curt nod of acknowledgment and then taken a seat beside him. She knew she wouldn't be able to completely suppress her reactions, she just wasn't that good at that sort of thing, so she figured it was the safest place to sit. If she'd sat across from him, he would have been able to read every expression that crossed her face. Now, listening to Daniel, she didn't doubt that she'd done the right thing. The imagery his words conjured made her heart crawl into her throat. Imagery that would not be easily forgotten.

"Nothing conclusive. If I had to guess, I would say maybe an abandoned fabric or clothing mill, but we'll know more once the next set of tests come back," Daniel said, answering Vivi's question.

"And location?" Drew asked.

Daniel shook his head. "No. There were some spores on the soles of her feet and on her hands, but we haven't identified them yet. When we do, which should be later today, it might help us narrow it down."

"Any more insight in to the pattern of the cuts?" Sam asked. "I know you were going to look into it yesterday, Vivi."

Vivi cast a quick look at Carly before replying. "Yes, I've traced the pattern and Agent Carmichael is here to tell us more about what they mean. But I'd also like his opinion on the other injuries we found on her body, as they seem incongruent with the detailed cuts."

"Do you have photos of the body?" Drew asked, sitting forward. Like Vivi, he too glanced at Carly as the photos made their way from Daniel's hands to his.

She looked down at the table as he started going through the images. Thankfully, as he finished, he slid them to his right, away from her line of sight.

"The pattern is the calling card of the Pen Royal Group," he said. "They formed in the late eighties from five different organized crime factions. Each on their own was a fairly sizable operation, but they created this co-op, for lack of a better word, because each faction had started warring with the others. That's not uncommon, of course, but they had the foresight to realize the more they fought with each other, the more they opened the market to other groups."

"So they banded together?" Daniel asked.

"They did. They operated out of DC for a long while but recently moved to Texas. Each cut," Drew said, singling out a picture, "represents one of the groups."

Carly forced herself to look at the image. It had been taken with a strong zoom lens, or perhaps just magnified, and showed nothing other than a skin-toned background with five cuts on it. If she tried hard she could pretend it wasn't a body she was looking at, let alone that of Marguerite.

"The center stab, and it's always a stab, is for the Botham family. Their specialty is bribery and corruption of public officials. They're kind of the administration of the PRG. One cut stands for the Rioto family and their specialty is drugs, another is for the Al Almidean family, their specialty is trafficking in anything that isn't drugs. The third cut is for the Mettinger family—they do financial crimes, cyberterrorism that sort of thing." Drew paused and pulled out another picture. He studied it, but didn't hold it up for the others to see.

"And the last cut?" Carly brought herself to ask.

He looked up at her. "That's for the Smith family," he said. "Believe it or not, that's their real name. They're the enforcers."

"Enforcers?" Vivi asked.

Looking away from Carly and letting his gaze land again on the image in his hand, Drew answered. "Yes, the enforcers. Anytime anyone in the group needs help making a point, the Smiths are the family to see."

Sam let out an annoyed sigh. "Interesting," he said. "But it doesn't help us identify her, does it? Perhaps she was involved in the PRG, but if she was, that will make it all that much harder to identify her."

Carly opened her mouth to protest any PRG involvement; thankfully, Drew responded first, cutting her off and preventing her from giving away the secret she held.

"But I don't think she was involved with them," he said. "And honestly, I don't think they had anything to do with it."

Carly snapped her mouth shut.

"Can I see the report of her injuries?" Drew asked.

Daniel handed him a file and he sat for a moment, quietly flipping through the information. Carly watched his efficient review of the details and wondered just what he was seeing, what he was thinking. He had a wealth of experience she knew nothing about. Had he seen a killing like this before? Assuming he had some ties to DC, had he known any of Marguerite's colleagues? As the questions flooded her mind, his lie of omission grew heavier, and more sour, in her stomach.

She looked away, hoping to also turn away from a truth she'd just acknowledged: Drew Carmichael affected her in ways she couldn't control. The attraction was there, and the curiosity, to be sure. But there was something deeper she couldn't escape from. Staring down at the fabricated grains of the laminated tabletop, she reminded herself that when the plan she and Marcus and Lorraine had put into place started to unfold, Marguerite would be identified, the investigation would be taken over by another agency, and Sam, Vivi, and Daniel would move on to their next case. Then she and Marcus would be left alone to figure out what the hell they were going to do, and Drew would no longer need to stay. He'd leave Windsor and go back to New York, or DC, or wherever he lived.

Drew cleared his throat, which brought Carly's eyes back to

him. "I think whoever did this," he said, pointing to the picture of the five cuts, "was copying the PRG. And the reason I say that is because this looks to be a case of straight, old fashion torture. They tried one thing, and when that didn't work, they tried another, and then another. It looks like there were at least four distinct types of torture methods employed here. That's not something the PRG does. It would undermine their impact if it appeared, in any way, that they weren't able to get what they wanted from whomever they were torturing on the first try."

"One and done kind of scenario?" Vivi asked.

"Exactly," he responded. "If whomever the PRG is questioning doesn't give them what they want with their one method of extracting information, they are simply killed."

"They might miss the opportunity to get information from people who are able to hold out longer," Sam said.

"But if word on the street is that the PRG only asks once, that alone is a pretty effective form of coercion," Daniel countered.

"So, if not the PRG, then who?" Vivi asked as her phone vibrated on the table. Picking it up, she looked at the number. "Just a second, guys," she said before answering the call.

Carly watched as Vivi spoke to the person at the other end of the line in short, single-word answers. Beside her, she felt, more than saw, Drew's desire to pull her aside and say something to her. Stubbornly, she kept her eyes on Vivi.

When she finished the call, Vivi set her cell down and seemed to contemplate it.

"Vivi?" Sam asked. "Is everything okay?"

Vivi looked up and landed her gaze on Carly. "I don't know, Sam. But we have visitors."

• • •

US Supervisory Deputy Marshal Mikaela Marsh entered the briefing room trailed by two more deputy marshals. Deputy Marsh reminded Carly a bit of Alfre Woodard, only about three inches shorter and seemingly nowhere near as nice. Pausing at the head of the table, she scanned the room. Her eyes lingered on Carly, then returned to Sam and stayed there.

"Dr. Buckley?"

"Yes?" Sam said but made no move from where he stood, unusually still, at the other end of the table.

"I believe you have one of my deputies in your morgue," she announced.

Vivi shot Carly a questioning look, then rose from her seat. "I'm Dr. Vivienne DeMarco. If you're referring to the woman who came in yesterday—late-forties, good physical shape, with long brown hair—then I'm the ME who performed the autopsy."

Deputy Marsh gave a single, sharp nod.

"If you'll come with me, we can view the victim, and if you could provide an ID, we would greatly appreciate it," Vivi said.

By some unspoken agreement, only Vivi and Sam accompanied the marshals down to the morgue. Carly, Drew, and Daniel stayed where they were.

"Carly?" Drew said from beside her. "We need to talk."

She let out a quiet, cynical laugh. The marshals were there, they'd take over the investigation. "No, I don't actually think we do. Now, if you'll excuse me, I need to make a call." Before he could stop her, she stood and walked out, dialing Marcus's number as she left. Stepping into an empty room around the corner from where Drew and Daniel sat, she closed the door as Marcus answered.

"It worked," she said.

"They're there?"

"Yes, a Supervisory Deputy Mikaela Marsh and two others she didn't introduce. They're down in the morgue with Vivi and Sam identifying the body." She could hear Marcus letting out a deep breath.

"At least we know Marguerite will be taken care of now. I'm thinking the marshals aren't going to take the murder of one their own lightly," he said.

She flashed back to the expression on Mikaela Marsh's face. "No, they most definitely aren't."

"Good. Once they're gone, we should talk. We need to figure out what to do next."

"Whatever we do, we have to be careful," she said. But what exactly she meant by "careful," she didn't have a clue. "We'll talk later?" she asked. When Marcus agreed, the two hung up.

Taking a deep breath, she exited the room, but because she wasn't quite ready to go back into the briefing room with Drew, she walked the halls until she came to the kitchen.

Pulling out some change she bought a chocolate bar from the vending machine, ignoring the fact that the clock had barely hit ten a.m. She had just finished four squares when Drew walked in, coming to an abrupt stop at the sight of her.

For a single, brief moment, she wondered if he planned to apologize to her. But then reason set in. What did he have to apologize for? Doing his job? *That* didn't make any sense. And she couldn't have expected him to go around announcing what he did for a living to everyone he met. He certainly hadn't owed her that honesty, they barely knew each other.

"The coffee's not bad," she said with a gesture toward the machine that made individual cups. He hesitated for a second then moved toward it. Eyeing him, she popped another square of chocolate in her mouth and went to pour herself some water.

"No coffee?" he asked.

She shook her head as she filled a disposable cup. "Not with chocolate—that would be bad news for everyone."

"Too much sugar and caffeine make you sick?"

She smiled and took another bite. "No, not sick, but jittery, unfocused. It's not the most helpful state to be in while working."

He leaned against the counter with his fresh cup of coffee. "No, I don't imagine it is."

"I assume they aren't back yet?" she asked, taking a few steps toward the hallway without, she hoped, appearing too eager to leave.

He shook his head but kept his eyes on her. For a moment she paused, and his eyes held hers—a small, quiet moment.

And then she forced herself to break eye contact and take another step away. "Thanks for your help this morning. I have a feeling the case is going to be transferred over to the marshals. If the woman is one of theirs," she added, not wanting him to think she already knew the answer to the question.

"Probably. I wonder how they found out, though. Don't you?"

She popped the rest of her candy bar into her mouth and shrugged. "Maybe they'll tell us," she said. Then, with a small wave, she turned and made her way back to the briefing room.

Drew had rejoined her and Daniel when Vivi and Sam led the three marshals back into the room. If possible, Deputy Marsh looked even more displeased with the situation.

"Our victim is Marguerite Silva," Vivi announced. "She was a US Marshal based out of DC."

Carly swallowed nervously when Deputy Marsh's eyes landed on her. "Are you the lead officer?" the deputy asked.

Carly shook her head. "I was the responding officer, the lead officer is Sheriff Ian MacAllister."

"And is he here?"

Carly drew back at the barked question, then shook her head. "No, I'm the senior local law enforcement here."

"Good," Marsh said, turning toward the door. "We need to talk. Where can we talk?" She didn't wait for an answer, nor did she wait to see if Carly would follow her. But Carly did. Pushing back from the table, she rose and then walked into the hallway in time to see Marsh enter a room two doors down. Thirty second later, she and the marshal were facing each other behind a closed door.

CHAPTER FIVE

CARLY SPENT WELL OVER AN hour talking to Deputy Marsh, but it took even longer to escape the lab after their meeting. When they'd finally returned to the conference room, the marshals had announced that they were officially taking over the investigation and then left to make arrangements to have all the evidence, including Marguerite's body, transferred to DC. After their departure, Drew had lingered, still attempting to find a moment to talk to her. In order to avoid him, she'd sequestered herself in one of the labs, where she'd helped Daniel package up the evidence for transport.

She felt relieved once she was finally back at her desk in Windsor, several hours later than she would have hoped, reviewing the week's schedules. The plan she and Marcus had put in place had worked. They still had a lot of unanswered questions, but at least Marguerite had been identified.

She'd just finalized the preliminary schedule when Vic walked in and took a seat. "I'm going to start the process for filling our open positions," he announced without offering a greeting.

She switched her gaze from her computer screen to her boss. He looked terrible. She frowned, realizing she hadn't seen much of him recently—since her schedule had been hectic and he'd been in out of the office so much. His eyes sat above dark circles and his cheeks looked sallow. Glancing down, she saw that he'd also lost some weight—never a big man to begin with, he now bordered on scrawny.

"Everything okay?" she asked.

He shook his head. "You and Marcus are working too many hours. The overtime I authorized this month was the highest yet." He raised a hand to stave off her defense, "And before you object, I'm not concerned, we have the money, given we're down two officers, but I am concerned with how much you two have been working. I know Marcus doesn't mind so much—working off his demons the way he is," he added under his breath. "But I'm guessing you might not mind a day off here and there."

She wouldn't mind, but she wasn't going to say as much. She had a job. One she mostly liked. And with no family or hobbies that needed her attention, she had the time to work.

"Well, let me know if I can help," she said instead.

Absently, he nodded. "Speaking of work," he continued after a brief pause, "How did things go up in Albany this morning?"

It took her ten minutes to brief him on the case, the arrival of the marshals, and the fact that Vivi and Sam had turned the investigation over to the federal agency. Vic didn't bother to hide his relief at not having his only two officers drawn into what would no doubt be a lengthy investigation. Promising to start looking into candidates and setting up interviews, he rose to let her get back to work. Carly watched him leave, then sat staring at the empty doorway for a moment. She had no idea where his sudden urge to fill roles that had been open for nearly a year had come from, but she also knew not to look a gift horse in the mouth.

After confirming the availability of the all the part-time officers, she finalized the shifts and closed out of the scheduling program. Debating about what to tackle next, the budget or the annual equipment inventory, she sat back in her chair and eyed the file cabinets.

Her thoughts shifted to what had happened that morning and what needed to happen next. She'd spoken to Marcus after leaving Albany and he knew about the marshals taking over the investigation, but he'd been out on a call when she'd returned to the station, so they hadn't had a chance to discuss anything else.

Carly sat, thinking about what constituted the "anything else" they needed to discuss—they needed a plan, or course, but a plan to do what? Before her mind could start down the dark path of everything they *didn't* know and *shouldn't* do, she heard the door of the police station open and Marcus greeting Sharon, their receptionist. Ten seconds later, he appeared at her door.

"How was it?" he asked, closing the door behind him and taking a seat across from her. She didn't have to ask him what he meant.

"Talking to Marguerite's boss was weird, really weird. I don't like keeping what little we do know from Vivi and the others, but Deputy Marsh agreed that it's probably for the best right now, until we have a better idea of what's going on." Carly paused, reflecting on her conversation with the deputy. "It seems so long ago. But then to hear her talk about it . . ." Her voice trailed off.

"Do you think we can trust her, the deputy?" he asked.

She mulled the question over before responding. "Yes. She told me Marguerite had worked for her for over a decade and I think that says a lot. I just," she paused again and turned to look out her window. "Never mind," she said with a little shake of her head. "It was a long time ago and we can't change the past."

"No, we can't," he said, knowing where her thoughts had been headed, and knowing just as well that it was a path not worth taking. "So, what now?" he asked, letting out a breath.

Carly relayed a summary of the conversation she'd had with Deputy Marsh, including a warning she'd issued about the possibility of electronic surveillance—given what had happened with the fingerprint database—and a plan they'd made to touch base again in a few days, once the marshals had looked into the situation further. Marcus couldn't find any flaws in the strategy, even though, like her, he didn't like the fact that it meant they'd more or less have to sit on their hands and do nothing for a few days. But not wanting to do anything that could bring unwanted attention to them or Windsor, waiting was perhaps the better part of valor.

"I hate this." He ran a hand down his thigh as he spoke, the thigh on which he'd had the skin graft just over a year ago.

Occasionally, she still saw him take a misstep on his other leg, on which he'd had knee replacement surgery. Thinking back to that time, when he'd been airlifted to a hospital in New York City after being trapped in a building with an exploding bomb, Carly swallowed. She'd been terrified then, but only recently had she come to understand, or allow herself to understand, how close she'd come to losing the one person who mattered most to her.

"Yeah, I hate it too," she conceded.

"And I wish I knew more about computers," Marcus said, oblivious to her train of thought. "I picked up a lot of things during my time at the lab, but I don't know enough about how to spot, let alone avoid, some of the electronic surveillance type stuff the deputy probably had in mind when she gave you that warning."

"Me neither. Naomi could do it, I'm sure," Carly thought out loud. What Vivi was to bodies and criminal investigations, Naomi was to computers. "But I wouldn't even know where to start."

"Wyatt would know more than we would," Marcus suggested.

And Wyatt lived closer. He'd been an officer with them up until about two years ago when, thanks to Vivi, he'd been offered a spot in a special program for local law enforcement at the FBI. They'd liked him and he'd liked them, so when they'd made him an offer to join the bureau, he'd accepted—his only condition of acceptance being that he be able to return to the Windsor area. Since Albany wasn't one of the hotspots agents vied for, they'd been able to place him in the local office just over three months earlier.

"Maybe we should talk to him," she said. "Just to get an idea of what kinds of things we would want to look for—not that I'm going to look," she added as Marcus opened his mouth to protest. "I feel like, well, I feel like I should be doing *something*, even if that something is just academic."

Marcus took a deep breath and let it out in a huff. "I get it. I can't do it tonight or tomorrow, though. I have a few physical therapy appointments this week."

"How's it going?"

"Fine, better than dealing with what we're dealing with now," he said, dismissively. He had been like this ever since he'd left the city and come back up north. He worked hard to rehab himself, but he didn't like talking about any of it.

"Maybe I'll call Wyatt and see if he can meet me tonight. It's not like I'm going to learn anything that will change what we're doing. Or what we're *not* doing."

Marcus made a vague gesture with his head that she took for agreement.

"If I learn anything interesting, I'll give you a call when I get home. If not, get a good night's sleep and we can talk tomorrow," she said.

Marcus let out a laugh as he rose from his seat, moving more stiffly than he would have the year before. "Yeah, call me. But between the two of us, if anyone needs a good night's sleep, it's you."

She raised her eyebrows at him. "You're not daring to tell me I look worse than you, are you?"

He laughed again. "I wouldn't dare. You are my boss, after all."

The comment could have been snide, but she'd heard the hint of affection. With a smile, she picked up the phone and dialed her old friend.

● ● ●

Drew walked into Anderson's restaurant in Old Windsor, intent on ordering one of his favorite meals for dinner. He'd been to the establishment with Kit many times before and he knew their flat iron steak would satisfy. Scanning the room—with its round wooden tables, hardwood floors, and deer heads mounted on the walls—he made a beeline for a stool at the end of the bar. A seat that offered a view of Carly. With a man.

Even though she continued talking and kept her gaze fixed on her companion, he could tell by the small pause her hands made as she gestured that she'd seen him come in. Other than that small arrested movement, however, she did not acknowledge him.

As the bartender chatted with another customer, Drew took the opportunity to have a good leisurely look at her. She wore jeans and boots again, but of a completely different sort. She hadn't dressed up—Old Windsor wasn't really that kind of town—but her jeans, rolled to well above her ankles, were that contradictory kind some women could pull off—they looked relaxed and casual, but fit in such a way that left no doubt about the wearer's awareness of, and comfort with, her body. Her boots were also different; ankle high with three-inch heels, their chocolate-brown color went well with the tan sweater that fell loosely off one of her shoulders as she leaned forward to say something to the man sitting across from her. As she did so, her blonde hair fell forward onto to her face. She tucked it behind her ear, as she always seemed to do, but here, in this setting—and apparently this company—the gesture was relaxed and easy, not one of frustration.

Interrupting his perusal, the bartender came by to drop off a menu. He already knew what he wanted so he went ahead and placed his order for the steak and a beer. When his drink was delivered, Drew pulled out his phone, trying not to spend his entire evening staring at Carly. But even as he scrolled through his e-mail, his mind strayed back to her. Begrudgingly.

She was a beautiful woman, a beautiful *younger* woman. Contrary to popular belief, not all men liked younger women. He found that with the life he led, the things he'd seen, he didn't really click with women who didn't have a fair bit of life experience. And while age didn't always equate with experience, he found it often did.

He had to admit, though, that he didn't know much about Carly or her life experience—they'd probably exchanged no more than a total of an hour's worth of conversation since he'd first met her seven months earlier. Then again, it wasn't as if he didn't know *anything* about her.

He knew her to be good at her job. He'd watched her the day before and he'd seen the way the other officers and techs had treated her with respect—not something he'd likely see if she hadn't earned it. He also knew she was brave—after all, she'd pulled Kit out of the path of a moving car, then brushed off her own injuries to focus on helping track down the perpetrator.

Based on the way Vivi trusted her when it came to keeping secrets about Deputy Marguerite Silva, she also inspired loyalty in her friends. And though he hadn't seen much evidence of it as it pertained to her interactions with him, she liked to have a good time too—after Kit and Carly had said their hellos and left him to his date that summer night in New York City, it seemed the only thing he could hear over the din of the restaurant was the sound of her and Kit laughing and enjoying themselves.

So she was intelligent, brave, loyal, fun, *and* beautiful—his attraction to her shouldn't be a surprise. But what did feel like a surprise, or more like a puzzle, was the fact that what he felt for her seemed to be more than the sum of those parts. And being a man used to knowing his own mind, it bothered him that he couldn't figure out why, just that it was.

When the bartender placed his steak in front of him, Drew glanced at the time on his phone and realized he'd been staring blankly at it for about twenty minutes. With a sigh, he slid the device into his pocket and began cutting his food as his eyes went back to Carly, and lingered. She and her companion were finishing their meals and whatever they were discussing seemed quite serious.

Drew didn't know whether or not what he was observing constituted a date, but the man certainly had her attention as he spoke. Every so often, he'd gesture and she'd nod, but he did most of the talking. *Who was he?* Drew wondered. Judging by how comfortable they seemed in each other's company, he'd bet they knew each other at least reasonably well. Maybe as friends, maybe as more. He had to admit to himself that, age-wise, they were better suited for each other than he and Carly would be. But still . . .

He took a few bites of his dinner as he continued to watch the pair talk about who-knew-what. Finally, it looked like they'd finished and a waiter brought their bill. As the man reached for it with one hand his phone must have buzzed, because he brought both his phone and his wallet out of his pocket. Carly started to protest, which made Drew think maybe it wasn't a date, but the man just grinned and answered his phone, using it as an excuse not to engage in a debate about who would pay.

Carly sat back and waited while her dinner date answered his call. As she looked around the restaurant, her eyes landed on Drew's. He considered looking away, but then a sick little part of him wondered how long it would be before she did. Not five seconds had passed when her eyes left his.

The waiter returned with their check and her companion signed it, even as he made to leave, juggling the call he still hadn't ended. Frowning, Drew thought that if the two *were* on a date, it wasn't ending well, at least not for Carly.

Saying something to Carly, who waved him on, the man rushed out of the restaurant, jacket in hand, phone to his ear. She rose at a more sedate pace and slipped on a beige wool peacoat. He didn't have to wonder long whether or not she would acknowledge him on her way out, as she was suddenly beside him, leaning against the bar.

"Drew," she said.

"That was a rather abrupt end to your evening," he responded with gesture of his hand toward the door.

She lifted a shoulder.

"I hope it wasn't a date," he added shamelessly. "Bad form and all."

Carly didn't respond. Instead, she looked at his nearly finished meal then, after a moment, back at him. "Now that the marshals are taking over, are you headed out?" She sounded rather more hopeful than he would have liked.

Buying himself some time, he bit into one of his fries then took a sip of beer and shrugged. "Maybe, we'll see. Call me curious, but I saw the way you reacted to the body and I'd still like to know what you aren't telling the rest of us."

To her credit, she managed to keep her face free from any conscious reaction. Unfortunately, for her, she hadn't yet mastered her more unconscious responses. He saw her spine stiffen and watched her pulse, visible in her neck, quicken. And when he saw her nostrils flare, he knew that, in an attempt to slow her now rapid heartbeat, she was struggling not to suck in a breath.

A good fifteen seconds passed before she spoke. "What I may or may not know is irrelevant now. The marshals are taking over and the rest of us can get back to business as usual. Now," she said, pulling her purse strap over her shoulder, "if you'll excuse me, it's late and I want to get home."

She didn't bother to wait for his reply, so he watched her over his shoulder as she walked away. She'd just confirmed what he'd suspected from the beginning. She knew something, something she hadn't told anyone. He didn't like secrets. And he found that he particularly didn't like her keeping secrets from him.

CHAPTER SIX

NOT THIRTY MINUTES LATER, DREW sat in his car down the street from Carly's house, trying to convince himself that he wasn't behaving like a stalker. He didn't plan to loiter about and take pictures of her or anything like that, but he *was* sitting in his car in front of her house—well, just down the road from it—debating about whether or not to go in and talk to her.

It wasn't out of the realm of possibility to think that the two women's lives could have crossed paths professionally, but the reaction he'd seen from Carly when Marguerite's body had been rolled over had seemed more personal. And as he sat in the dark of his car dissecting what he remembered, one thought settled into his head. Yes, she *had* been shocked, but the fear he'd seen—the fear she hadn't admitted to—had been real too.

That, more than anything, gave him the excuse he wanted, needed, to go talk to her. He didn't like the idea of her being afraid, and he didn't like the idea of what her fear might drive her to do. With a sigh, he started his engine and drove the remaining two hundred yards to her driveway.

Her new home, a renovated carriage house set back from a large restored Victorian, had been easy enough to find using the little bits of information Carly had dropped into the conversation she'd had with Dani when she'd come by to pick up Kit's SUV. And as he exited his car, he was gratified to see the porch light on, taking it as a sign she was not just home, but awake too. However when he knocked, no one answered. Much to his chagrin, this caused a small explosion of panic to burst through him and he knocked harder. He even called her name. Finally, the door cracked open.

"Drew?" she said, confusion clear in her voice.

Great, he'd interrupted her shower. Her hair, still wet, hung to her shoulders and she wore nothing but a robe. "We need to talk," he said.

"It's past ten o'clock. Can we talk tomorrow?"

"No."

She drew back at his terse reply, then responded. "There isn't anything we need to talk about. The investigation is closed, as far as we're concerned. You can go back to New York, or DC, or wherever it is you call home these days."

"Carly." Her name. That was all he said, because he knew part of her reluctance to be with him stemmed not from the investigation but from other, more personal reasons.

Several seconds passed. Finally, she sighed and stepped back, opening the door and gesturing him in without a word.

He stepped over the threshold.

"Let me go change. I'll be right back down."

Both a curse and a blessing—he would have liked to appreciate her in that robe for a bit longer, but he was wise enough to understand that they would both be more comfortable if she got dressed.

As she headed upstairs to change, he took the opportunity to examine her new home. The front door opened directly onto a small foyer and a staircase that divided the building into halves. Looking to the right from the front door, a tastefully decorated living room ran front to back. To his left, he saw an eat-in kitchen, with its cabinets and appliances anchored against the back half in an "L" shape. Walking through the kitchen, he noted another entrance to the living room behind the staircase. There was also a door with a small shaker-style window pane that appeared to lead out onto a small porch.

He was standing in front of a large fireplace in the living

room, admiring the renovation, when he heard her come back down the stairs.

"Drew?"

"In here."

She paused when she saw him standing in the middle of her living room. Then she cocked her head, "Why don't we have a seat in the kitchen?" She'd changed into yoga pants, a Boston College sweatshirt, and a pair of thick wool socks. They'd only just hit the middle of October, but fall did bring chilly nights.

He thought the couch looked cozier, but he also thought he was treading on thin ice already, so he followed her to the table and took a seat. When she sat down across from him, she gave him an expectant look.

"What did you want to talk about?"

He took a deep breath and thought about all the things he should say to her—instead, he said, "You knew Marguerite Silva, didn't you?"

To her credit, she didn't even blink. She did, however, let out what he'd call a long, suffering sigh. "None of this matters anymore. The case is no longer in our jurisdiction. The evidence has been sent to DC, as has the body. It's not our concern," she reiterated.

"That may be the case, but when you recognized her yesterday, you looked afraid, worried about something. I know I said the same thing last night, but I didn't say it well. I don't like loose ends, and I don't like that finding her body here in Windsor might mean something to you that you don't feel like you can share."

For the first time that night, she met his gaze and held it for a good long while. Unfortunately, he didn't see that as a good sign. She looked to be contemplating what to do with him, much like his mother had done when he was a child.

She sighed again, and rose from her seat. He began preparing an argument to counter the dismissal he saw coming, but then stopped himself. It appeared that she wasn't kicking him out after all; she was reaching for a bottle of whiskey—a rather nice one, he noted—and two glasses. In silence, he watched as she poured the whiskey and then added a single ice cube to each glass.

"Let's go sit outside," she said. It seemed cold for that, but he rose, took the glass she offered, and followed her out the back door onto a porch that held two Adirondack chairs. On the way, she grabbed two blankets, tossing him one as they sat. He placed it on his lap, but she unfolded hers and tucked it around her body, saying, "This is one of my favorite places to be."

Drew pulled his eyes from her form to follow her gaze out into the darkness—only it wasn't actually all that dark. With a full moon hanging above them, the sky faded from a bright sapphire to a much darker midnight as it collided with the horizon. The stars shone the way they do in cooler temperatures—somehow seeming a bit sharper, a bit brighter. A hill on the far side of a small lake rose like a dark shadow and the lake, a deep inky blue, held the brilliant reflection of the moon above—the water so still that, had the hill not been there to provide perspective, the moon and its reflection could have been confused with one another. To say the least, it was beautiful.

"I can see why." He heard, more than saw, her head roll toward him. But he didn't turn to face her. This night, this view, this land, meant something to her. And so he absorbed it. The changing, fading light. The crisp air that carried the hint of smoke from some fireplace nearby. A night owl hooting in the distance.

In companionable silence, they sipped their drinks. And after a long stretch, Carly surprised him by telling him what he'd come to find out, her voice quiet in the night.

"Yes, you're right, I did know Marguerite," she said. "Long ago, our paths crossed. Circumstances put us both in the middle of an investigation into corrupt FBI agents. And, yes, I knew the kind of work she did, I knew she was with the marshals," she clarified, then paused before continuing. "I *was* stunned when Vivi and Daniel rolled her over and I saw her face. Our town is big, but not *so* big. It wouldn't have been a huge surprise if the victim had been someone I knew from town and I had braced myself for that. But seeing someone I knew from DC was something I hadn't been prepared for and it was more of a shock than it might have been otherwise."

She stopped talking but he knew she had more to say. "Why didn't you say anything?"

He could hear her swirling the ice in her glass, then taking a sip. When she'd brought her glass back down to rest on the arm of her chair, she answered. "Like I said, I knew she was a marshal. But I haven't seen her in years, and I didn't know what she was working on when she was killed. I didn't know if she was undercover or not. I thought it best to keep her identity a secret until I had more information."

"And the marshals? Were you the one who gave them the tip?"

This time he looked and caught the tail end of her nod. "I did. I know her aunt and I arranged it with her that she would call it in. I figured that way there was less chance that *if* Marguerite had been working on something, we would call unwanted attention to it. A quiet tip seemed the most effective and efficient way to get her superiors involved."

"So you're done then? You're going to let it go?"

She lifted a shoulder. "There's not much I can do anymore," she said. And the sense of relief he felt at her words far outweighed what it ought to. He worked with a lot of women in law enforcement, a lot of highly capable women whom he at times both relied on and who relied on him. But never had he felt such relief at knowing the danger he feared for one person, one woman, was no longer a threat.

"I'm glad to hear that," he said. He thought about saying more, but didn't know what that "more" would be. And so they continued to sit in silence beside each other for a good long while, even after they'd both finished their drinks. When an owl swooped across the sky, startling them with his call, they each let out a small laugh. The moment they'd been sharing disappeared.

Rising from his seat, he took his glass in one hand and the still folded blanket in the other. She rose too and, throwing her blanket over her shoulder to free a hand, opened the door. He laid his blanket back down where she'd picked it up earlier and she tossed hers on top of it then took his glass and placed it in the sink with hers.

Drew didn't stop as he made his way through the kitchen, fearing that if he did, it would be much harder to leave. Following him to the front door, Carly opened it and he stepped out onto the front porch. He turned to say . . . what? Good-bye? Thank you?

But she beat him to it. "Drew?"

"Yes?"

"What is it you want from me?"

The question didn't shock him, but it did catch him off guard. Partly simply because she'd asked it, but mostly because, put so bluntly, he didn't actually know. Over the past two days, he'd made up all sorts of reasons to see her, talk to her, be with her. There was an easy answer, of course—they were two consenting adults obviously attracted to each other—but it wasn't an answer he was willing to give because that wasn't the question she was really asking. What she was really asking was if he wanted something more than the obvious. A question he truly didn't have an answer for. And though he hated to admit it, he said just that.

"I don't know." He held her gaze with his. In her steady regard he read no censure or judgment. Despite the doubts he'd seen in her eyes since she'd learned what he really did for a living, she seemed to see, and accept, the truth he now offered her.

"Good night, Carly," he said quietly.

For a moment, her head rested against the edge of the door, then she straightened and offered him a small smile.

"Good night, Drew."

Much later that night, as he lay in Kit's guest room replaying their conversation, he realized she hadn't actually agreed to let the investigation go.

• • •

Carly glanced out the window of Frank's Fed Up and Fulfilled Café. A drizzly weather front had moved in overnight and settled in for the morning. The streets were damp and the air looked thick and gray. But the tiny drops of water drifted down from the clouds so gently that the leaves would stay in place and the brief system wouldn't shorten the fall colors.

"It's way too complex," Marcus said.

She turned back to her breakfast companion and let out a deep breath. "Yeah, I know. As much as I don't want it to be, it is," she said before taking a sip of her mocha. Frank's mochas and a fall morning were pretty close to her idea of a perfect way to start the day.

"Based on what Wyatt was telling me last night," she continued, "I'm worried that if there are triggers attached to Marguerite, or to us, I'd set them off before I even entered her name in the search engine."

Wyatt didn't come close to Naomi's computer expertise, but he had significantly more know-how than Carly or Marcus. And what he'd explained to her—trap doors, warning flags, ghosts, and all sorts of other tricks and snares—had pretty much shot down any last hope she'd had of trying to look into Marguerite's death, or the past case, herself.

"No kidding. I'm hearing it secondhand from you and *I* may never look at a computer the same way again."

She gave him a look of commiseration and they both returned to their food, or what was left of it. She picked at the last piece of her egg and bacon bagel, Marcus scooped up the last of his yogurt and granola.

"I bet Naomi would know how to get through, or at least spot some of the things Wyatt talked about," she said without looking up. She wanted to test the idea with Marcus. She'd given it some thought herself, but involving Naomi had its risks. Because Naomi was Vivi's cousin, Carly knew that anything she asked of Naomi might get back to Vivi. But she could deal with the grapevine of gossip. What truly concerned her was the possibility that Naomi's actions would be traceable, and could bring repercussions back to her in Boston.

"Yeah, she could," Marcus agreed slowly. "We'd have to manage the situation with Vivi though."

Carly noted his lack of caution. In order to see if his expression matched his tone—if he was truly considering it—she looked up. And caught a glimpse of Drew watching them. With her back to the door, she hadn't seen him come in. Standing to the side of the line of people waiting to order, he appeared to be waiting for his food. Watching them from less than five feet away.

"Drew," she said in acknowledgement.

"Carly," he responded.

"You remember my partner, Marcus Brown," she said.

The two men nodded to each other, but neither made to shake hands.

"I hope you got a good night's sleep after I saw you last night," Drew said.

That was a surprise volley. She glanced at Marcus, who was looking back at her. She thought about saying that she'd simply run into Drew at Anderson's, but if she didn't mention that he'd come to her house afterward, Drew might.

"I did, thank you," she said, as Frank called Drew's name.

His eyes lingered on her for a moment before he mumbled a good-bye and went to collect his breakfast—which he'd thankfully ordered to-go. She watched him walk out of the café, bag and coffee in hand.

"*Last night*? What the hell?"

She took a deep mental breath and cursed Drew. "I saw him at Anderson's was all," she said. "He was there when Wyatt and I were having dinner."

Marcus eyed her for a good long moment. "Is there something going on between you two? I saw how he was looking at you—"

"Stop," she cut him off with a raised hand. "There is nothing going on between us. We've seen each other a few times over the past few days is all. Remember, he was one of the ones who, well, he was one of the ones who called the body in on Monday. He was there, too, at the site. You didn't see him since you mostly focused on the roads, but he and his friend Ty Fuller were there all morning."

"And?" Marcus pressed. Carly gave a fleeting thought to telling him to mind his own business, but then, judging by the look on his face, decided that it wouldn't go over well.

"And, it turns out he's some sort of law enforcement. Vivi would have to tell you what kind," she said, dodging that bit of information. Since she hadn't known he worked for the CIA before yesterday, she didn't want to say anything, assuming he preferred that information to remain on a need-to-know basis. She also didn't want Marcus to point out that the CIA wasn't technically law enforcement. "He was helping a bit yesterday at the lab, too. He has some sort of expertise in torture and Vivi brought him in to help us understand the different . . ." Her voice broke a bit and she looked out the window to blink away the moisture from her eyes. What had happened to Marguerite still felt so raw and brutal that it seemed ridiculous to be sitting there in that café, explaining herself to Marcus.

She cleared her throat. "Anyway, he didn't have much of a chance to weigh in, since the marshals showed up. Now, can we talk about whether or not we reach out to Naomi?" she asked, bringing the topic back around to something worthwhile.

Marcus narrowed his eyes at her, but then conceded, to an extent. "Yeah, let's talk about Naomi, but I'm sure I don't need to tell you that now is *not* a good time for you to be getting involved with someone."

She and Drew were so far from involved that she rolled her eyes, not bothering to respond. "Do you think we should ask her?"

"Do you think she'll tell Vivi?"

Carly thought about it before answering. "I'm pretty sure I could get her to keep it from Vivi for now, but I am concerned about putting her in any kind of danger."

Marcus bobbed his head. "Is there any way we can tell her what's going on without actually telling her?" he asked, his cryptic question making perfect sense to her.

Again, she mulled his question over. "I think we probably could. We could tell her enough about the situation, about the fact that someone knew enough about computers to be able to erase any trace of Marguerite from the official databases before killing her. That would probably give her some indication of the risk she could be taking if she agreed to help."

"I hate bringing someone else in . . ." Marcus's voice trailed off.

"But neither of us loves the idea of everything being in the marshals' hands either," Carly said. "It's one thing to leave the investigation of Marguerite's death to them, but they don't have the same concerns we do about what kind of message was being sent. If we don't understand the message, we can't play by their rules."

"And if we don't play by their rules, or at least appear to be, more people we care about could get hurt," Marcus said, finishing her thought. They both sat in silence for a few moments, contemplating their situation.

"We could run." Marcus made the suggestion again, only this time much more halfheartedly.

She inhaled deeply as she met his eyes. Running held no appeal to her and, to give Marcus credit, she didn't think it appealed to him either.

She shook her head.

He leaned back in his chair then confirmed her thoughts. "I know, I don't want to run either. Whatever happened all those years ago is bubbling to the surface. Maybe this time we can stop it."

"Once we know what 'it' is," Carly added.

"Exactly."

And they needed Naomi in order to figure that out.

"I'll call Naomi later this morning to see if she can meet with me tonight. I'll take my own car this time, but park outside the city and take the T in."

Marcus nodded, signaling both his approval and the conclusion of their breakfast meeting. They both stood and cleared their dishes. She slid on her police jacket as they stepped outside and when Julie from the quilt shop across the street waved, Carly waved back. Acting to all the world like the day was business as usual, when inside, she knew that, after that day, "usual" might take on a whole new meaning.

• • •

Drew took a sip of coffee as he stared out Kit's kitchen window. Pure laziness had driven him into town to pick up breakfast and he was glad it had. As he took in the riot of fall colors that dipped into the small valley before him, he thought about what he'd overheard of Carly and her partner's discussion.

His fingers tightened on his cup and the paper buckled in his grasp. Irritated with himself, he set the cup down, grabbed a mug from the cabinet and dumped his coffee into it. He didn't even try to relax.

She and her partner were *not* planning to let things go. With a wry smile he acknowledged what he'd realized the night before— she had said only that there wasn't much she could do, not that she planned to do nothing. And apparently she now had a plan to do *something*. Something involving someone named Naomi. Someone named Naomi who had some connection to Vivi.

What the hell could she be looking for? he thought. Sure, a lot of folks in law enforcement were in the field precisely because they were incessantly curious, but he sensed that she had more at stake than just nosiness.

And as he stood before the window, his bagel sandwich getting cold on the counter, he considered how the interests of Carly and the marshals might overlap. They would both want to know what had happened to Marguerite, and no doubt both would want justice. But where their interests diverged is where his thoughts lingered. If he were a marshal, he'd want to know why Marguerite had been killed and by whom. But if he were Carly, he'd want to know *why Windsor*. Why had the body of a US marshal been left in their town when it was clear she hadn't been killed there?

The marshals would be interested in that too. But it would be more urgent for Carly. It involved her town, her friends, her people.

He let out a frustrated breath and dumped the rest of his now cold coffee down the drain. Digging into Marguerite Silva held too many risks, he had no jurisdiction to investigate the death of a federal agent, but maybe he could find out more about this Naomi person. Of course, if Rina ever got wind of his plan, his ass was toast. Politically, investigating Marguerite would be worse, but to Rina, investigating *any* US national within US borders required not just a sign off from her, but a damned good reason, too. He was pretty sure his personal interest in Carly wouldn't make the cut.

But his plan didn't *really* include investigating Naomi. He just wanted to know who she was and if the help she provided, if any, could put Carly in any danger. The question as to why he cared enough about her safety to risk a good set down from his boss would remain buried in the darkness of his mind for the moment. The mystery of Naomi was a much easier problem to tackle.

After two hours and a couple of favors called in, he sat at the kitchen island staring at his computer. He had a pretty good sense of Naomi DeMarco at this point. She and her twin brother had made quite a name for themselves in certain circles. Hired by all the major agencies, including his own, to test the security features of the vast network of computers and communications that connected the agencies to everything from each other to agents deep undercover, Naomi and Brian were known to be the best. Their IQs weren't as high as their cousin Vivi's, but only by a couple of points—margin of error, really. Knowing that Carly would be dealing with the best, no matter what she and Naomi discussed, gave Drew some measure of comfort.

But what, specifically, did she want help with? Was she looking for some trace of whoever had had the access and knowledge to erase Marguerite from the system? Or did she want information on Marguerite herself? Or the investigation the marshals were conducting?

Drew shook his head as he reread the information a contact

had forwarded. Carly would want it all. Not only had she made an oath to protect and serve her town, but he knew that oath held more meaning to her than just words. And because of that, she'd want to know everything about Marguerite Silva. *That* would take some digging. Digging that someone like Naomi DeMarco would excel at.

Sitting back, he ran a hand over his face as her question from the night before ran through his mind. What *did* he want from her? A date? For some reason, they seemed beyond that stage. Dates were for getting to know someone and, though he had no real reason to, he felt like they already knew each other quite well. Sex? Maybe, yes. But even he couldn't let his mind go there—because it wouldn't be just sex with her. No, he knew beyond a doubt that if they crossed that bridge there would be much more to it than just physical pleasure. And what lay beyond that bridge was a dark, dangerous place he needed to be sure of before entering. The phrase "This way there be dragons" came to mind.

But did he want a relationship? He laughed out loud at that thought. He liked the concept, sure. But he hadn't been able to maintain a real relationship with a woman since college. There were a lot of reasons he could throw out as to why—his career being first and foremost. His erratic schedule made it difficult to make plans, but more to the point, the fact that he couldn't talk about what he'd seen or what he'd done or even where he'd been ninety percent of the time tended to limit conversational topics. Not to mention what keeping those secrets did to him. And with each passing year, the effects on his *own* psyche from this forced silence were becoming harder to ignore. In the past few years, he'd become poor company.

So what did he want?

Time, he thought. Time was the only thing he could admit to wanting from her now. He wanted time to be with her and do the simple things in life—things he didn't usually get do because his job wouldn't let him or, when it did, he didn't have anyone he really wanted to do them with. He wanted to sit on her porch with her like they had the night before, to cook and eat a quiet meal together, and maybe go for a walk or curl up and watch a movie, just the two of them. He just wanted to *be* with her.

Of course, she might not be interested in giving him any time, but at least he now had an answer to her question. An answer he planned to share with her when she returned from Boston that night.

CHAPTER SEVEN

Carly exited the Park Street T station, cut over to Beacon Street, and started heading west into Boston's Back Bay. At just past seven, darkness had fallen hours before. The vintage street lights cast shadows as she walked toward Naomi's home, a beautiful brownstone near the Public Garden that fronted Beacon Street and had a view of the Charles River from the back. The building had six floors: two that Brian and Naomi used for their business—the garden and first—two for Brian's living quarters—the second and third—and two for Naomi's—the fourth and fifth.

Standing on the stone stoop of the historic structure, she rang the buzzer. Moments later, the lock released and she pushed open the heavy door. Once she'd taken the elevator to the top floor, the doors opened directly into Naomi's apartment. A kitchen and dining room lay to her right, a large inviting family room to her left, and the stairs down to the bedrooms in front of her. The family room featured picture windows looking out onto the river and a large fireplace, presently roaring with warmth. Carly smiled, it wasn't quite like fall in Windsor, but it was still fall.

"Carly," Naomi spoke, as she came up the last few steps from the floor below and enveloped her in a big hug. "It's so good to see you."

"Naomi," she said, returning the hug. "It's good to see you too. Thanks so much for agreeing on such short notice."

"Nonsense," Naomi brushed her off. "As you can see, I had big plans for the night," she said with a laugh, gesturing to her leggings, bulky wool sweater, and fuzzy slipper boots.

Carly laughed too, but not because of Naomi's outfit. With nearly flawless skin and hair with hints of red that made her green eyes stand out, Naomi could go out wearing a pillowcase and still look better than most people.

"Here, come." Naomi motioned her into the kitchen. "I was going to pour myself a glass of wine, would you like one? Or maybe some tea or coffee?"

Carly glanced around the sizable kitchen and spotted a single-cup coffee machine. "Coffee, please."

Once they each had beverages in hand, Naomi grabbed her laptop and they made themselves comfortable in the family room—Naomi sitting at a small writing desk, her computer now plugged into a thick cable that disappeared into the wall, and she on a comfy upholstered chair.

"Okay, lay it on me, what do you need?"

Carly looked down at her cup and paused before answering. Then, because she had to, she told Naomi the truth. Well, part of it. She told her about Marguerite's body being found and the same story she'd told Drew about having worked with her before, years ago. She also added the name Joe Kincaid, a family friend who had introduced her to Marguerite, and Vince Archstone, one of Joe's colleagues. She didn't know if either of them had had anything to do with Marguerite's work, but they were all muddled together in her mind as being a part of that time.

"So, let me get this straight." Naomi leaned back in her chair. "You want to look into Marguerite Silva, and these Joe and Vince characters, because you're worried there is something going on that might affect Windsor?"

"I know it sounds a bit far-fetched—"

Naomi's frown cut her off. "No, it doesn't. I mean if you all knew each other back then, and then she shows up dead in your backyard but has no ties to Windsor other than you, I think you have the right to ask some questions," Naomi said. "But you don't trust the marshals?"

She wagged her head. "I do. I think they will be the best

agency to try to figure out what happened to Marguerite and I trust that they are motivated to do that. But they aren't as motivated as Marcus and I are to make sure that whatever happened to her doesn't have any effect on Windsor."

"Or on you and Marcus, since you knew her," Naomi added. Carly hesitated, then nodded, hoping Naomi wouldn't ask just how they'd known each other.

"And you say her identity was erased from the official systems altogether?"

She was about to answer "yes," then stopped herself. "Well we didn't have time to run it through the DNA databases, and I don't think facial recognition had been done either. But Vivi didn't find her in any fingerprint databases."

Naomi seemed to mull this over then she sat forward and started keying something into her computer.

"Not to make light of the situation, but this could be fun," she said, quirking an eyebrow at Carly before returning her attention to the screen. "I do have one more question though."

"Yes?"

"Why haven't you told anyone else about this? Or have you?"

Carly had expected this question and had prepared her answer. "Marcus knows I'm here, and technically we're the only police officers for Windsor. But I know that's not your question. I haven't told Vivi and Ian yet because Marcus and I agreed to look into it first. You know how Ian worries, and if it turns out to be nothing, then he doesn't need to be bothered."

"But if it turns out to be something?" Naomi asked, frowning at her computer.

"Then we'll bring in the others."

Naomi looked up, startling Carly with the intensity of her look. "Promise?"

Carly hesitated, then agreed. "Yes."

"Good, because I'm not sure what we're going to find, but it's going to be an interesting night."

Her stomach sank. "Why do you say that?"

"Because I've been online for less than three minutes and I've already found at least one trip wire."

"Trip wire?" she was pretty sure she knew what Naomi meant, if not exactly what she was talking about.

"Not a real wire, of course, but the technical equivalent of one. If I'd gone bumbling through it, someone, somewhere, would know I was looking for information on Marguerite Silva."

Carly swallowed, suddenly unsure of the wisdom of her decision to go to Naomi. "You don't have to do this, Naomi. I don't know who these people are and I don't want to put you in any danger."

Naomi waved her off and concentrated for a few more minutes.

As the silence extended, she couldn't stand it any longer. "Did you get around it?"

At the question, Naomi looked up. Then smiled. "Go around it? Why would I want to do that? I'm going to follow it."

Oh god, Carly thought.

• • •

Three hours later, Carly crossed Route 128 heading west on the Massachusetts Turnpike on her way back to Windsor, a stack of papers at her side. Naomi had been able to find some reports and information, most of which she'd e-mailed to Carly, but there had been a few things they'd printed up for her to look at later—mostly reports about Marguerite's last movements, credit card expenses, and phone usage. Carly planned to identify Marguerite's patterns and then see if there had been any deviations in the days before she'd been killed.

But she had other papers too. Before leaving Boston, she'd stopped by an Internet café near where she'd parked her car and ran a few searches she didn't want anyone, not even Marcus, to find out about. There were other people she'd known from that time, people she wanted information on without anyone else knowing, and being in Boston had given her the opportunity she'd needed to do a little of her own digging.

As the city and its suburbs faded away, she glanced at the files on the seat beside her then let her mind drift to the question of Joe. She had hoped to find a connection between Marguerite and anyone named Joe Kincaid, but she and Naomi hadn't found a thing—not even a phone call. Naomi had then done a deeper search, and while they'd found several Joe Kincaids, none had been the man she remembered. It didn't make any sense to her. Joe had been the one who had introduced her and Marcus to Marguerite. Didn't it follow that they would have had some traceable connection to each other?

In the dark of her car, Carly released a frustrated breath and shook her head. She knew so little about that time, about what had really happened. And now that Marguerite was dead, and they'd had no luck finding Joe or his colleague Vince, she wondered if she would ever know the truth about the events that had brought them all together.

But they *had* to find out. She and Marcus deserved to know the truth. So she'd given Naomi a physical description of Joe before she'd left and her friend had promised to keep looking. It was a long shot, but she hoped Naomi would find something. In the meantime, she at least had some reading material.

As she started to climb the gentle winding road into the Berkshires, Carly's thoughts turned toward getting home, pouring a glass of whiskey, and sitting on her porch for a bit to peruse her files. It would be late by the time she arrived, after midnight, but it would give her some time to calm her brain before going to bed.

As the idea of curling up alone on her porch wended its way through her mind, thoughts of the night before crept in—of sitting there with Drew, talking about some things, but also not much of anything.

She still didn't know what to make of him, but that shouldn't be a surprise, since he didn't seem sure about what to make of her either. She laughed quietly at that. Drew seemed like someone who knew exactly what he wanted at all times. She'd never seen him behave indecisively before. And she had a hard time dismissing that little bit of confusion she'd seen in his expression—it had made him more human and may have even been a bit endearing.

But despite that hint of boyish charm, there was still something about him, about his intensity, that left her feeling unsettled.

Then again, at this point, how she felt about him—how he made her feel—probably no longer mattered. With the investigation handed over, he had no reason to stay in Windsor.

Well, perhaps not *no* reason. She acknowledged that *she* might be a reason he'd stay. But since he didn't seem to know what he wanted from her, she didn't know what weight to give that possibility. Although a tiny part of her wondered what would happen if she asked him to stay. It wasn't a good idea, of course, so as she pulled into her driveway, grateful to be home, she dismissed it from her mind.

But as she passed the main house, her headlights swept over a car parked by her front porch, then landed on Drew, sitting on her front step, forearms resting on his knees.

Waiting for her.

•••

Drew felt a twinge of remorse for having put a tiny tracer on Carly's car earlier that day when it had been parked in downtown Windsor. "Sneaky" and "beneath him" were two phrases that came to mind when he thought about his behavior. And if she ever found out, she'd have every right to go ballistic. But when she stepped safely from her car, bag in hand, the relief that flooded through him washed away any regret.

From his position on the porch, he watched her pause then walk with measured, but confident, strides toward him. The peace offering he held rocked slowly in his fingers. Neither of them said anything when she stopped in front of him and her gaze dropped to the bottle in his hand. He held it up for her to see more clearly.

Her eyes came up with it, then moved farther up until they landed on his.

Without a word, she reached for the bottle with one hand and pulled her house key out with the other. Handing her the rare bottle of single malt whiskey he'd found at a shop in Great Barrington, he stood and stretched his legs as she opened her door. He walked in behind her as she tapped in the alarm code, then he turned to shut the door.

She'd left the heat on in the small house and after sitting outside for the past few minutes, the sudden change in temperature felt stifling to him. But since she hadn't bothered taking her coat off, he didn't either. He had an idea of where they were going.

Dropping her purse on the table, she made her way to the cabinets and pulled out two glasses. As she poured their drinks, his eyes drifted to her bag and the file he could see sticking out the top. He couldn't read the papers inside, but he did see a URL address and in it the search criteria "Sophia Lamot Davidson" printed across the top of the page. He didn't know the name but he filed it away.

He turned as Carly held out his drink. Without a word, he took it and followed her out the back door, grabbing a blanket for her on the way, and onto the same porch on which they'd sat the night before.

When she'd settled into one of the Adirondack chairs, he took her glass and held it while she wrapped herself in a blanket. He then handed her drink back to her, took his own seat beside her, and waited.

And waited.

"You make me uncomfortable, unsettled," she said.

He was glad he'd swallowed the sip he'd just taken because her statement hit him straight in the gut. He glanced over, wondering what she'd meant. Was she *afraid* of him? Even the chance that she could be afraid of him caused something to sour in his stomach. But she shook her head and seemed to read his thoughts.

"Not in that way," she said. "I'm not scared of you. I'm not worried you are going to do something to me without my consent or act violently."

He let out a long breath and turned his eyes back to the blackened lake. Once the fog from his initial reaction had cleared from his mind, he let her statement sift through it. And he found he still didn't like it—in a different way of course, but it still didn't feel good.

"It's because we're attracted to each other," he said, trying to give a simple answer to what they both knew wasn't a simple situation. When she didn't immediately respond, he turned to watch her profile. She appeared to be mulling the statement over.

"No," she said. At the possibility that she would deny the attraction, he had to bite back a reaction. But then she corrected herself. "I mean, no, I don't think that's it," she said thoughtfully. "I'm thirty years old, Drew, I've been attracted to other men and had other men attracted to me."

He turned away. At least she hadn't denied their attraction to each other—only that it wasn't the cause of her discomfort. "Then why do you think it is that I make you uncomfortable?"

She lifted a shoulder. "I don't know. Maybe it's the age difference."

Great, he thought. Something he couldn't change.

"No," she sighed, "that's not really it either. Or it's not entirely that, anyway. The truth is, more often than not, I can't tell what you're thinking. Some of that is probably just a part of who you are, but now that I know what you do for a living, I think some of it is due to the training and years of practice you've had too. I can *feel* the way you watch me. I know there's chemistry between us, maybe even something more, but I can't tell how you feel about it—if you welcome it or just wish it would go away. And to be fair, I'm not really sure where I stand, either."

When her voice trailed off, he didn't rush to fill the silence. She sounded more curious about the situation than anything else. And though he hadn't ever intended to hide his thoughts from her, he could see how she might have ended up feeling that way—he was a master at holding things close to the vest, sometimes to a fault.

He could tell her that he liked her, respected her, and found himself more drawn to her than any other woman he'd ever met. He could say a lot of things. But saying them didn't mean she'd believe him. No, in order for her to believe him, she needed the same thing he had already decided he wanted.

"Time," he said.

He felt her gaze turn to him.

"Last night you asked me what I want from you. I want time."

"Time?" she repeated.

"Yes. Time with you," he clarified to be sure she understood.

"Uh, why?"

He turned a somewhat disbelieving look on her. "You really need to ask why?"

She looked a little chagrined at his comment. Running a hand over her face and through her hair, she let out a deep breath. "No," she admitted, much to his relief.

"Will you give me that much? Will you give yourself that much?" He felt her eyes on him but he kept his gaze forward. His heart rate kicked up with every second that passed.

Finally she spoke. "Yes," she answered, quietly. "Yes, I'll give you time."

He let out a long breath. It certainly wasn't as though he didn't want the rest of things that came with a relationship, but wanting and needing were two different things. And right now, he knew that what they both needed was simply time.

"How was your trip tonight?" he asked, purposefully changing the subject. They could beat a dead horse, or they could move on to what it meant to spend time together.

She paused before answering. "It was good. I went to Boston to see a friend."

"A long trip for one evening."

She shrugged. "It was. But I wanted to talk to her about Marguerite."

That surprised him. He hadn't thought she would talk about her real reason for going. "I guess you decided not to leave it alone. Did you learn anything?"

"The marshals aren't as invested as Marcus and I are in making sure there aren't repercussions on Windsor from Marguerite's death, but I didn't want to go bungling into an investigation, so I went to talk to my friend who is a computer expert."

"Seems you'd need to be more of an expert to know what to look for, and look out for, in this situation."

"Naomi and her brother are computer security experts. Really good at what they do."

As she spoke, as they began to have a relatively "normal" conversation, Drew began to relax.

"And did she find anything?"

Carly nodded slowly. "She did. A lot of things that don't give me the warm fuzzies."

"Like what?" he asked, taking another sip of his drink.

For the next half hour they talked about the kind of electronic surveillance Naomi had found and what it might mean. They discussed the reports Carly had brought home and how she intended to study them and look for patterns. The conversation was flowing almost like it would between good friends, until he asked how she thought what she might find was connected to Windsor. He suspected that she already knew the answer, but she only lifted a shoulder in response. "I'll have to see where the paper trail leads and take it from there. Mostly I want to figure out if Marguerite did anything unusual before her death. If I find that she did, *then* I'll try to figure out if it means anything."

Sensing she had kept quite a bit to herself, at least on that last point, Drew took the last sip of his drink, swallowing his disappointment in the fact that she hadn't shared everything.

"Well," he said, rising from his seat with her eyes tracking him. "I'll let you get to it then."

She rose as well. The blanket she'd wrapped around her fell when she stood and he reached out to catch it. Warm from her body, the blanket's heat curled around his hand. He stilled, watching her watch him, not eighteen inches away. Her eyes darted to his lips.

He could have leaned down and kissed her.

He thought about it, he did. But he forced himself to step back. He'd asked for time and that was all he was going to ask of her until *she* felt comfortable enough to take the first step further. He moved toward the door, away from her warmth. Without a word, she followed, took his glass with hers, then placed them both in the sink.

"This is a nice bottle," she said, picking up the whiskey he'd brought and handing it back to him.

He shook his head. "It's yours, keep it. I kept you up tonight and, who knows, maybe we can share another drink tomorrow night."

She didn't say yes but she didn't say no either. He took that as a good sign and his cue to leave.

"Sleep well," he said as he stepped off her porch a minute later. "And don't forget to put the alarm on."

She didn't answer immediately, but he thought he heard a quiet "good night" before she shut the door.

CHAPTER EIGHT

CARLY MANAGED TO HAUL HERSELF out of bed and into work by eight the next morning. When she arrived, she was surprised to find that Vic, closeted away in his office, had already started his day. Coffee in hand, she sat down at her desk, pulled up the incident reports from the night before, and started going through them. With Windsor's low crime rate, her review never took too long, but she liked to do it as soon as she came on shift in order to stay up-to-date on the goings on in her town.

Vic knocked on the frame of her door twenty minutes later, just as she finished logging the reports into the computer system. Behind him stood a woman wearing a suit, her dark hair tied in a knot at the nape of her neck. Her serious expression gave Carly pause. *Had someone caught Naomi?* The woman looked to be all business and not afraid of a little confrontation.

Carly's heart sank.

"Carly," Vic said, stepping into her office. The woman trailed behind him, her eyes darting around the room, taking it all in. "This is Josie Webb. She's a recent graduate of the police academy and here to interview for one of our open spots."

Carly felt a smile disproportionate with the information she'd just been given spread across her face. "Hi Josie, I'm Carly Drummond, Deputy Chief of Police," she said as she stood and shook the woman's hand.

"I know I didn't give you any notice," Vic said, "But I was hoping you wouldn't mind spending a little time with Josie?"

"Of course not," she answered as her phone rang. "Excuse me first though, if you don't mind?"

Josie shook her head and stepped back in to the main office area with Vic, giving her just a little space.

Carly was thankful for the privacy, but once she'd hung up, she didn't bother to stifle the several curses that formed in her mind and flew from her mouth.

"There a problem?" Vic asked, popping his head back in.

Carly let out a long breath. "Mary Hanson is in the ER again down in Riverside. The nurses are trying to get her to talk to the sheriff's deputy, but she says she won't talk to anyone but me," she answered as she stood and began pulling on her jacket.

"What is it this time?" Vic asked.

"Broken wrist and nose." She zipped her coat and reached for her keys.

"Mary's husband isn't a nice drunk," Vic said to Josie.

"Or generally nice at all," Carly added. "But we do what we can. How do you feel about a ride-along?" she asked Josie.

A flash of excitement and surprise crossed the young woman's face as she darted a look at Vic for approval. He nodded and three minutes later, Carly and Josie were in one of the police cruisers headed down to Riverside.

The two women spent the drive down to the hospital chatting about Josie's brief military career, her short-lived marriage to a man with political ambitions, and her decision to leave him and enter the police academy so that both he and she could lead the lives they truly wanted.

Carly learned that, much like her, Josie was a small-town girl and had only applied for positions in towns like Windsor. By the time they reached Riverside, Carly found herself selling Windsor, the community, and the department to the young woman.

On their trip back forty-five minutes later, however, the optimism she had felt at a potential new colleague was dampened by the frustration that crawled through her. Mary Hanson had had to leave her daughter with a neighbor that morning in order to take herself to the ER. But, once again, she had refused to press charges or even consider leaving her husband. The only reason she'd asked for Carly at all was because the well-meaning sheriff's deputy had kept pushing her to press charges.

Mary's situation seemed to weigh on both Carly and Josie as they made their way north. The potential recruit asked a few questions about Vic and the other officers, but other than that, their ride back to Windsor was silent.

After arriving at the station and sending Josie on her way, Carly stopped by Vic's office to give her report. Leaning against the doorframe, she said, "I like her."

"I do too."

"She told me some of what she accomplished at the academy, she's a bit of a go-getter, assuming it's all true."

"It's all true," Vic said. "I talked to a couple of her instructors and even some of her classmates. She was clear about wanting to be in a small town, so none of her classmates felt competitive with her and were willing to talk."

"And I assume the references align with her résumé?"

Vic nodded.

"I say hire her then, before some other town does. I think she'd be a good fit."

"Good, I agree."

Carly turned to head back to her office, but Vic called her back.

"How long has it been since you've had a day off?"

"I don't know, three or four weeks, maybe. Maybe a bit longer."

Vic's eyes narrowed. "Go. Take the rest of the week and weekend off," he ordered. "Then Monday and Tuesday too, since those are supposed to be your regular days off anyway."

She shook her head. "I appreciate it, but then I'd have to reschedule everyone, and it's not worth the effort." While the idea of having five-and-a-half days off appealed to her, having to adjust the schedule, one of her least favorite jobs, did not.

"I can do it."

That brought her up short. She eyed her boss, looking for any sign that something might be wrong. He hadn't done scheduling in well over a year.

He sighed. "Don't look at me like that. I know I haven't been much of a chief lately, and I'm not going to bother making excuses. The least I can do is pick up some scheduling duties. I do know how, you know."

Again, she eyed him. He seemed utterly serious. Maybe even like he needed to do it, like he needed to get back to something familiar. The idea of a few days off began hold more appeal. Not only would she be free to focus on Marguerite, she might even be able to finish unpacking.

"You sure?"

He waved her off, "Yes, I'm sure, go. Go home and nap or unpack or whatever it is you do on your albeit limited free time."

Carly didn't need any more encouragement so she said thanks, signed out, and headed home, where she promptly undressed and crawled into bed for a two-hour nap.

After waking up and having lunch, she debated getting back into bed for another nap or maybe to watch some movies, but six boxes sitting in the garage attached to the main house were calling to her. And the fact that if she fell asleep again, she'd never sleep that night.

Pushing aside the thought that maybe that wouldn't be a bad thing—considering Drew's late-night visits—she traipsed out to the garage and started hauling her belongings back to the carriage house.

Setting them down in the family room, she opened the first and started to wade through the items. Smiling at some of the things she'd decided to save, like an old wool sweater, her prom dress, and her school yearbooks, she started dividing things into piles—things to keep and put away, things to throw away, and things to give away. The dress and sweater, which were still in surprisingly good condition, went in the latter pile.

Halfway through the third box, a box of books, she picked up one of her old favorites—*The Black Stallion*. She'd inherited the horse-loving gene from her mother and she remembered begging her mom for the book when she'd been about seven or eight years old. For a long moment, she sat and looked at the familiar cover, remembering not just the day she'd received the book but the day she'd gotten her first pony, the day she'd gone to her first show, the day she'd won her first blue ribbon. She didn't remember her first day riding though; she'd started so early, she couldn't remember a time when she *hadn't* ridden.

With a sigh for the life that was gone, she placed the book on the pile of stuff to keep and put away. But she'd placed it too close to the edge of the stack of books already in the pile and the hardback tipped and fell. And out came a picture.

Carly sucked in a breath. Slowly, she picked up the photo. In it, she wore her black riding jacket and white shirt as she stood next to her riding instructor holding a tri-colored championship ribbon. She remembered that day well. It wasn't the first time she'd won a championship ribbon, but it had been the first time she'd done so on a horse born and raised on their family farm. The petite mare had been one of her mother's favorites.

Unbidden, tears came to her eyes and a wave of longing pressed down on her. Gently caressing the photo, she knew she should put it away. After one last look, she went to slide the picture, and the memories it had invoked, back into the book, but something else in the image caught her attention. Wiping her eyes with her palms, she held it back up.

In the background, but clearly visible, Joe Kincaid stood smiling. The sight gave her pause and on a whim, she hurried upstairs to her computer. Scanning the image, she cropped the photo so that only Joe's face showed. Opening up her e-mail, she typed up a quick note to Naomi and attached the image. She didn't know whether Naomi could run facial recognition or not, but on the off chance that she could, the image would help.

Within seconds, Naomi responded, saying she had a few other things to work on but would run the image through her programs while she worked and would let Carly know if she found anything. Wishing she could have an answer right away, but knowing how unreasonable that was, Carly made her way back downstairs to finish her unpacking. She had barely gone through one more box—one more box of mainly things to give away—when her phone rang.

Hoping to hear Naomi's voice, she answered before looking at the number.

"Hello?" she said.

"Carly Drummond?"

Not Naomi, but a voice that did sound familiar. Only she couldn't place it.

"May I ask who's calling?"

"It's US Marshal Mikaela Marsh. Is this Carly?"

Carly, who had stood up to answer her phone, sank down into the upholstered chair in her living room.

"Yes, it is. Do you have any news for me?"

Marsh paused on the other end of the line, then started speaking. "We found where Marguerite was killed."

Carly felt a sharp stab in her heart. "Where?"

"An old abandoned textile distribution building."

"In DC?"

"Yes."

"How did you find it? Did it give you any information?"

Deputy Marsh let out another sigh. "I take it from your questions you weren't the one who called the tip in, or arranged to have it called in?"

That gave Carly a pause. "Someone called in a tip?"

"Yes."

"Interesting. But no, it wasn't me. Where did the call come from?"

"The phone it was called in on was traced to the DC area, but we couldn't get anything more specific than that."

"Because there wasn't enough time to trace it, or because the data was being obscured?" Given what had happened with Marguerite's fingerprints and what Naomi had found even in her initial searches, Carly assumed that obscuring the origins of a call would probably be considered child's play by whomever was involved in this.

"Not enough time or data. The call lasted about forty-five seconds, but by the time the person receiving the call realized the potential validity of the information, there were only about fifteen seconds left."

"Not enough time to get a trace," she muttered over the last part of Deputy Marsh's statement. "And who received the tip, Deputy Marsh?"

"Call me Mikaela, and it was me," the marshal added on an exhale. "I don't know how they got connected to me. There hasn't been any PR about this at all."

"So it was probably someone who knows something." Stating the obvious made her feel a bit like Marcus. On the other end of the line, Mikaela said nothing.

Finally, Carly asked what she wasn't sure she wanted to. "Was there any evidence, any . . ." She let her voice trail off.

Again, Mikaela let out a deep breath. "Yeah, there was lots of evidence that she'd been there. Blood, fluids, a shoe. We're still sorting through it all, but so far, no evidence of anyone else."

Carly let the images that information brought forth sift through her brain. She didn't want to but she needed to because it should have been close to impossible to have been able to do the things that had been done to Marguerite without leaving a trace.

"No cigarette butts?" she asked, remembering Marcus's report to her.

"No."

If they hadn't left those, then they probably hadn't left the knife or whatever they'd used to hit her either. "There were indications that she'd been bound, right? Did you find any rope?" she asked, thinking maybe there could be transfer DNA from whoever had tied her up.

"She was, but there wasn't any rope either. It's like a cleaning crew came through and swept the area clean except for the blood, fluids, and her one shoe."

Again, that information gave her pause. To only *half* clean a crime scene? That didn't make sense. "Do you think it was staged?"

"It crossed our minds, but the state of the evidence confirms it's been there since her time of death."

"What the hell?" she said, earning her a dark laugh from the marshal.

"Yes, our sentiments exactly."

The two women remained on the line in silence. Hesitantly, Carly asked another question. "And have you discovered anything else? Anything about how this might be tied to the FBI investigation?"

This time Mikaela paused before answering. "We haven't yet. I did dig through Marguerite's paper files though, and I came across the name of Anton Perelli—he was a deputy director at the bureau at the time of the investigation."

"Was?"

"He died of a heart attack about a month ago."

"Um, I hate to ask this and sound like a conspiracy nut, but was it suspicious?"

"No, it wasn't. Heart disease ran in his family. With the stress of his job, his lack of fitness, and his cholesterol numbers, it came as a surprise to no one."

Carly let out a sigh. "So, basically, you have nothing."

It wasn't a critique and Mikaela knew it. "We certainly don't have as much as we'd like to have, given that we have her body and the crime scene. We do have one last internal lead, though. Marguerite's former boss at the time of the investigation. He's due back in town from his vacation in a few days."

"And you think he might know something?"

"Hard to say, but since Marguerite was working for him when she became part of that investigation, we need to ask."

Maybe he knew more, but they wouldn't know one way or the other for another few days.

Carly let out a long breath. "Well, thanks for calling," she said. "I appreciate the update."

"You're keeping your promise?" Mikaela asked. Carly didn't ask which promise. But she also didn't want to lie to the woman who'd just shared what she'd shared.

"I took your warning to heart, Mikaela, about the computer searches, and I don't have the knowledge to do that smartly. I don't want to put myself, Marcus, or anyone here in town at risk by calling attention to ourselves. In fact, I've been given a few days off and am at home unpacking," she answered without answering.

"Good," Mikaela said. "If anything happens up there, you'll let me know?"

"Yes, I will. And thank you again for calling. Marguerite went above and beyond the call of duty when she met Marcus and me. It's been a few years since I last saw her, but she meant a lot to both of us."

Mikaela murmured something that sounded like "you're welcome" then promised to call if she heard anything more. After hanging up, Carly took a look at her two remaining boxes and decided to take a break.

After making herself a cup of tea, she grabbed a blanket and went to sit out on her back porch to watch the evening descend. Wrapping herself up, she sipped her drink as the sun dipped behind the hills, casting the scattered clouds into brilliant hues of pink and orange. She gave a moment's thought to the last few times she'd been out on this porch with Drew. He'd enjoy this sunset. She didn't know him well, but she imagined he would.

As she sipped her tea, she stilled her mind and let the evening unveil itself to her. When darkness took over and her mug was long empty, she stood, stretched her legs, and returned to the house. She was placing her mug in the sink when her phone rang again. Her short break had returned some much needed calm to her perspective, but that all went out the window when Naomi's number appeared on the screen.

"Naomi?" she answered.

"Carly?" Naomi's voice sounded strained and anxious.

"Yeah, it's me."

Naomi took a deep breath and let it out. "I don't think you're going to like what I just found out."

CHAPTER NINE

DREW SAT IN HIS CAR on the side of the road about a quarter of a mile from Carly's driveway. He wasn't hesitating to visit her this time, but he thought he'd seen the headlights of her car driving toward him—more like speeding toward him—and he'd pulled over out of instinct.

Sure enough, it was her. He watched as she blew past him, not slowing a bit. Her car disappeared in his rearview mirror as he pulled out his phone. Opening the app that corresponded to the transmitter he'd left on her car, he sat and watched the little red dot make its way toward town, then north onto the Taconic Parkway. Eight minutes later, the Berkshire Spur of the Massachusetts Turnpike took her west. Frustration weighed on his chest as he turned his car around and headed back to Kit's house. He knew her destination—Albany, to see her partner.

Drew dropped his phone on the kitchen island when he returned to Kit's and made his way to the picture window over the sink, where he stood. He didn't let himself think anything, he didn't let his mind process any thoughts because he knew he wouldn't like them. Jealousy, frustration, and desire weren't emotions he was used to feeling in any prolonged capacity.

But then, as he watched the moon, brightening the valley before him as it rose in the night sky behind the house, logic managed to wend its way into his brain. Carly was a cop, through and through. Her speeding just didn't make sense. Not when looked at in the vein of being on the way to meet a man. Especially not a man she saw every day at work.

This train of thought didn't make him feel any better

Because the only reason he could fathom for her to speed off to see Marcus Brown was Marguerite Silva. Before that thought had even completely registered in his mind, he had his phone in his hand, an e-mail from a colleague filling his screen. Two minutes later, the phone rang at the number included in the message.

"Hello?" came the voice at the other end.

"Hello," he said. "Is this Naomi DeMarco?"

She paused. "May I ask who's calling?"

"This is Drew Carmichael. I'm a colleague of your cousin Vivi and a friend of Carly Drummond's."

She made a 'hmmm' sound on the other end of the line. He should have expected her to be more circumspect than most. He could have pulled rank and called in favors, but that would have taken time. So instead, he laid it all on the line.

"You have no reason to trust me, but if you call your cousin, she'll vouch for me. But before you do, let me tell you what I know and what I need from you."

On the other end of the line, she gave a small chuckle. "You're a bit presumptuous aren't you?"

"Yes," he agreed. "I am even under normal circumstances, but this circumstance is far from normal, so bear with me." When she didn't say anything, he continued, laying out everything he knew about Marguerite and what Carly had told him the night before—well almost.

"An interesting story, Mr. Carmichael, do continue."

"I also know she was looking into someone by the name of Sophia Lamot Davidson, but I don't know if those were her searches or yours."

"Sophia Lamot Davidson?" Naomi repeated.

"Yes. What she has to do with anything, I don't know. But I do know Marguerite Silva is of primary concern to her." Drew took a moment and let what he'd said sink in. Naomi didn't speak but he could hear the sound of her keyboard clicking away in the background.

"And what do you want from me?" Naomi asked.

"Have you talked to her recently? Have you given her any new information?"

"And why would you ask?"

It dawned on him that Naomi DeMarco had yet to confirm she'd even spoken with Carly, but still he persevered. "Because I saw her driving away from her house a short time ago and, judging by the way she was driving, she was agitated and distracted by something. I'm concerned about her."

Again silence fell across the line. He didn't have much more to add, so he just silently hoped that maybe Naomi would believe him—or would believe him enough to at least call her cousin to confirm his identity and make sure that it was okay to talk to him.

"Ah, shit."

His chest tightened. "Ms. DeMarco?"

"Hold on. I'll call you back."

He stared at his phone for a long moment after she'd hung up, then set it down. He drummed his fingers on the countertop and willed it to ring. Five minutes and twenty-two second passed before it did. He answered before the first ring ended.

"Yes."

"Drew?" Naomi asked.

"Yes." He didn't like the anxiety in her voice.

"I think we may have a problem."

• • •

Drew leaned against the porch railing as he waited for Carly to come home. The app on his phone told him she would be there in less than six minutes. He wished he could be waiting for her inside her house, with the lights on and the fireplace lit, not out there on her porch in the dark. Not after what he'd learned.

The headlights from her car swept over him as she pulled into the parking area, momentarily blinding him. He closed his eyes and took a deep breath. The air, cold enough to hold almost no scent, chilled his face and lungs. When he heard the engine switch off, he opened his eyes and watched as she opened her door and unfolded from the driver's seat.

Her blonde hair fell around her face and she tucked a strand back even as she pulled her jacket tighter around her body. Shutting the car door, she started toward him.

He pushed off the railing so she would see him.

She hesitated at his movement, then continued. "Drew?" she said, coming to a stop in front of him. "Is everything all right? You don't look," she paused and cocked her head. "Well, you look like something is bothering you. Is everything all right?" she repeated.

He regarded her hazel eyes for a long moment as question after question came spinning through his mind. But only one thought made it out.

"I don't think it is—is it, Carolyn Davidson?"

He knew she was going to run a split second before she did and when she turned to bolt, his arm snaked around her waist and he pulled her back toward him. His action hadn't been well thought out and she slammed into him with more force than he'd anticipated. His other arm immediately went around her, holding her in place.

And based on the wild look in her eyes, he had about ten seconds to make her trust him before she started fighting.

"Carly, it's me. It's Drew. I've been Kit's friend for fifteen years and have been coming to Windsor long before you even moved here. I've been with the CIA for nearly twenty years, I have never been with the FBI. I was twenty-five and stationed overseas when your mother was killed. Carly, look at me. You know me. You know I would never hurt you. I'm not one of them."

She didn't really know him, not in the usual sense anyway. But he did believe she knew him in a way that mattered in this moment.

He could feel her shaking in his arms.

"Carly, look at me," he pleaded.

Slowly her eyes came up.

"It's me," he said quietly. "You know I wouldn't hurt you."

After a long moment, she gave a jerky nod.

"It's," her voice sounded thin but at least she could speak. "It's just been a long time since I've heard that name."

Gently, he reached up and tucked some of her hair behind her ear. "I'm sorry, I shouldn't have called you that, not out here, not out of the blue. Are you okay?" He had his head tilted down, trying to maintain eye contact with her. Her body still shook in his arms. He didn't want to let her go.

Again, she nodded. Then took a deep breath and bobbed her head one more time.

"Let's go inside and we can talk," he suggested. Rather than agree, she started to look around. He'd heard her drop her keys when she'd started to run so he slipped one arm from around her and slid his other hand into hers, taking a firm grip. Spotting the keys, he leaned down and scooped them up, then led her to the door.

After opening it and hanging the keys on the hook where he'd seen her put them, he waited for her to plug in the alarm code. When she finished, he pulled her over to the table, took her jacket, and motioned for her to sit. After draping both of their coats over the backs of chairs, he made his way to the kitchen.

He went directly to the cabinets where the glasses and whiskey were kept and poured them each a drink, handing Carly hers when he returned to the table. And because he couldn't help it, as he moved to take his own seat beside her, he ran a hand over her hair then drew it down over her cheek.

She looked up as he sat down and he could see the questions in her eyes. So he decided to answer them to the best of his ability.

"I'll start with what I know, then what I think I know, and then we can talk about what I don't know," he said. Carly said nothing but her eyes watched his and he took her silence as assent.

"I know your mother and uncle were killed fourteen years ago and you and your brother, Michael Davidson, now Marcus Brown, were taken into protective custody. I know the media reported that your uncle was being investigated for financing a few terrorist groups and I know their deaths were blamed on him getting into business with the wrong people."

"He wasn't," she said. "He wasn't doing business with terrorists."

He reached over and took her free hand even as she took a sip of whiskey. "I believe you. That's why I noted that was what the media reported. I also know that, just prior to his death, your uncle began spending time with two men, Vince Archstone and Joe Kincaid. And I know that, just tonight, you learned that Joe Kincaid is really Joe Franks, an FBI agent who, based on the fact that he was in your lives with an assumed name, was probably either undercover himself or lying to your family about who he was. He may also have been the subject of the internal FBI investigation you told me about the other night."

Carly gave a small nod, not even questioning how he knew this. At least not yet.

"And here is what else I can guess," he continued. "I can guess someone thought—and seems to still think—you or brother might know something about what was being investigated at that time, which is why you were both put into the witness security program. It's not a far leap to assume Marguerite Silva was your handler, wasn't she?" He asked the question gently, knowing how hard it must have been for her and Marcus to find her body here in their hometown, if he was correct.

She stared at her drink, but then gave a small nod. Conflicting emotions battled inside him; he was relieved she seemed to be coming back to him but anxious about what he now knew.

"So when her body showed up here the other day, you and Marcus, rightfully so, in my opinion, believed it to be a message from someone—someone involved in the murder of your mother and uncle and the investigation of the corrupt FBI agents. You think it was a warning to keep whatever it is you might know to yourselves, don't you?"

Carly continued to stare at her drink, rubbing her fingertips down the sides. Several minutes passed, before she spoke. "Yes, we do. And we also think Marguerite probably died trying to protect us."

Her voice cracked on that pronouncement and he rubbed his thumb over her palm, giving her the only reassurance she would accept in that moment.

"And when I learned who Joe Franks was, or really, who he *wasn't*, it, well, it shook me up." Her glass rattled as she set it down.

"I imagine it would."

She shook her head. "No, you don't understand. It's not just that he wasn't who we thought he was, or wasn't who *I* thought he was. He was in love with my mother. And she with him. Or so I believed," she finished.

Drew let this sift through his mind before finding the logic, and when he did, something in his chest constricted. "And you think maybe that was all an act too, that maybe your mother died being betrayed by someone she trusted with so much."

Carly's only response was a tightening of her hand under his. He didn't know what to say. He understood how she would find that revelation hard to stomach, and nothing he could say would make it any better.

"What kind of warning do you think Marguerite's body was? What have you and Marcus talked about?" he asked instead.

She looked up at him and blinked. Then answered. "That's what's so frustrating about this. We have no idea. We don't know what it means because neither of us knows anything, or anything important anyway, about what happened nearly fifteen years ago. I can see how, if we *did* know something, Marguerite's death could be an effective warning—a 'we know you know something and we know where you live so keep your mouth shut' kind of thing. But we honestly don't *know* anything. I didn't even know Joe was FBI until tonight. He certainly never said anything. Even after my mom and uncle were killed and he introduced us to Marguerite, he acted like he was doing it as our family friend, not as anyone official."

Her voice had risen and her hand clenched again in his. Without letting go of her, he sat back and took a sip of his drink.

As he did so, she pulled away and ran both her hands over her face, burying herself behind them.

"That's what's driving me crazy. I don't know what to do to fix this. I don't know who is involved. I don't know what they want from us. And if I don't know any of that, I don't know how to protect my friends and their families either. Because if they went after Marguerite, why would they hesitate to go after one of our other friends if we don't play by whatever rules they've set out—rules that we're not even aware of?"

Her frustration came at him in waves. It didn't hurt that he knew a thing or two about how she might be feeling. Not exactly, of course, but he'd been in his fair share of situations that made the phrase "between a rock and a hard place" seem quaint.

After another long stretch of silence, Carly took a final, big sip of her drink and stood. He did the same and, after taking their glasses to the kitchen, he rinsed them at the sink and set them out to dry. As he did so, she came and leaned against the counter beside him.

"How did you know?" she asked, her arms braced across her stomach. He had known that question would come.

"I overheard you and Marcus in the café the other day talking about someone named Naomi who was associated with Vivi. It shouldn't come as a big surprise that all this, that you," he emphasized, "are of concern to me. So I looked her up and figured out who she was. From there it wasn't hard to sort out what you might have gone to her to ask for help with. And then, of course, you confirmed you'd done just that."

"But my name, who I really am?"

"Who you are isn't a name, Carly. Who you are is who you choose to be. Who you are, in my view, is a capable, caring, loyal woman who is in a difficult situation—but I know that's not what you were asking," he rushed as she opened her mouth to, no doubt, point out he wasn't answering her real question. Drying his hands, he turned and leaned his hip against the counter, facing her.

"I saw you leave the house today, on your way to Marcus's.

You were driving fast and a bit erratic, like something was bothering you. At first, I'll admit, I thought you were running off to meet another man—Marcus," he said with a self-deprecating smile. "Which, if you are wondering, did not make me feel good. But that's neither here nor there," he added when she frowned at him.

"It took a few minutes, but I realized the most likely reason for you to act so out of character, or what seemed like out of character to me—driving that way—was if something had happened with the case. I knew it meant more to you than you were letting on, so I took a gander and guessed that whatever had you bothered had to do with Marguerite. And since I knew who Naomi was, I called her."

Again, Carly frowned. "And she told you?"

"Not exactly. I told her what I knew and I also told her I had seen some papers of yours with the name Sophia Lamot Davidson on them."

"You saw my papers?"

"They were sticking out of a folder when you dropped your purse on the table after getting back from Naomi's," he answered. "I didn't see the actual papers, but the tops had the search string visible and I read the name."

Her brow furrowed at this, but when she said nothing more, he continued. "Eventually, she called Vivi, verified who I was, and then she and I had a long chat."

Carly's eyes went wide and she went a little white. "Oh god, does Vivi know?"

Drew shook his head. "No, she doesn't. It turns out that as soon as I mentioned your mother's name, Naomi had started digging. She'd put two and two together before calling Vivi and before she'd told me. She's aware of the sensitive nature of the situation and assured me that while Vivi may not let it drop, she has accepted Naomi's request to let she and I handle things for now."

"That's not going to last long," she muttered.

"I know, it probably won't," he said. "But it should give us enough time to figure out what to do."

She looked up. At first she said nothing, but he waited for the question he knew would follow.

"How did you know I was at Marcus's and, come to think of it, how did you know when I'd be home these past few nights? I can't imagine you've been waiting hours for me."

Okay, not the question he'd expected. He'd thought she would ask about his statement, about them figuring out what to do together. Then again, her actual question didn't surprise him entirely.

He ran a hand over his face, then met her eyes. "I placed a tracker on your car before you went to Boston. I knew there was more to this case than you were letting on and I didn't like the idea of you going at it mostly alone."

She stared at him for a long moment. "You bugged me?"

He shook his head. "I didn't bug you. I can't hear anything you've said in your car, there's no audio on the device. In fact, it's not even inside your car. But I wanted to be able to know where you were in case something happened."

A beat passed again. "I see you're not rushing to offer to remove it."

"I will if you want me to," he said. But no, he didn't plan to make the offer.

"Do you think I'm in danger? I know that sounds stupid to even ask, but since this whole thing started I've only been able to talk to Marcus, and neither of us is a dispassionate observer in this whole mess."

He shook his head. "No you aren't a dispassionate observer, but neither am I. Not really." He paused and let those words sink in, then continued. "But yes, I think you could be in danger. I know you and Marcus have been worried about your friends and their families and yes, maybe even a little about yourselves. But I would wager that, given what happened to Marguerite, it's your friends you are worried about most. I get that, but I also wouldn't underestimate the danger both you and your brother might be in."

He waited for her to respond and when she did, she surprised him once again with her train of thought. "It's weird to have someone else refer to him as my brother," she said. "It's been so long since anyone has and when we were put into custody we were told we even had to stop thinking of each other that way. Sometimes I wonder if we were too successful."

"Carly, don't," he said, reaching out to brush his thumb down her cheek. "You and your brother did what you needed to do. But the game has changed and you don't have to do it alone anymore."

When she turned to look at him he could see the debate in her eyes, but then, one more time, she surprised him. Without a word, she stepped close to him and wrapped her arms around his waist. Instantly, his came around her and pulled her close. Resting his cheek on her hair, he wondered how long it had been since someone had hugged her, had told her she wasn't alone. Then again, he couldn't remember how long it had been since someone had just simply hugged him.

Feeling a bit bowled over by the realization, by the fact that it had been so long since he'd offered and received this uncomplicated, yet powerful, comfort, his arms tightened around her. She burrowed against his chest and adjusted her own arms. And for a long moment they stood there.

But then, slowly, Carly pulled back. Stepping away from him, she shook her head.

"I'm sorry, I don't . . ."

"Don't," he cut her off. He didn't want to hear her apologies or her excuses. She held his gaze and seemed to understand that he'd needed the contact as much as she had. She pursed her lips, then looked away.

"I should be going," he said with a glance at the clock on the microwave. He and Naomi had agreed to talk again in the morning, but he had some calls he wanted to make that night. He should tell Carly. He *would* tell her, but he'd do it in the morning. Maybe this way, she'd get a good night's sleep without thinking about some of the things he and Naomi had decided Naomi should look into.

A good night's sleep without him.

He cleared his throat and stepped away. Picking up his coat from the chair, he slid into its comfortable warmth. She'd followed him to the table then proceeded him to the door.

"Thank you, Drew," she said as she opened it.

He turned to look at her. Then he dipped his head and brushed a light kiss across her temple.

"You're welcome. We'll talk tomorrow, and don't forget to set the alarm after I leave." Something about the statement caused her to give him a small smile. He responded with his own then, before he knew it, found himself seated in his car.

When he pulled into Kit's driveway fifteen minutes later, he let a small smile tug at his lips. He realized she hadn't asked him to remove the tracker from her car.

CHAPTER TEN

To say Drew woke early would be a lie, since he hadn't really gone to sleep. Throughout the night he'd drifted off for a few minutes here and there, but with what he'd learned from Naomi and his most recent conversation with Carly floating in his head, he was, simply put, worried.

He rolled over in bed, looked at the time, and accepted that sleep would be elusive to him until he figured out how to fix things—figured out how to solve this problem. Carly and Marcus were doing a good job on their own and he didn't belittle their plans or any actions they'd taken so far, but, well, he was a guy. When someone he cared about had a problem, he had to fix it. Whether they wanted him to or not.

He tucked an arm under his pillow and gazed out the massive windows of the guest room in which he lay. Floor-to-ceiling windows had been installed in nearly every room on the southwestern side of Kit's house. He still remembered how exposed he'd felt the first few times he had come to visit, as if anyone could be looking in at any moment.

But over time, he'd come to enjoy the view they offered. And he'd come to realize that with the house set so far back on her property, the beauty they let in far outweighed the risk of someone spying.

With an annoyed groan, he rolled onto his back and stared up at the ceiling. Gazing out the window wouldn't accomplish anything. He needed a plan. But what kind of plan could he put in place? He had no jurisdiction, and given that he'd been part of the investigation for all of ten minutes before the marshals had taken it over, the request for interagency cooperation that Vivi had initiated now meant nothing.

He needed help. Not something he ever readily admitted to.

Turning his head, he glanced at the clock again. Seven for-ty-five. She'd be awake. Before he could second guess himself, he grabbed his cell and dialed a familiar number.

"Drew?" Dani answered.

"I didn't wake you, did I?"

She laughed. "Not hardly. TJ has decided he's a morning person. Luckily, so is his dad, so those two are out for a run while I'm enjoying my breakfast."

He paused at the domestic image she'd painted. It wasn't what he had ever expected of Dani, but he had never seen her happier. He also hesitated because, now that he had her on the line, he wasn't sure what to say.

"It's about Carly Drummond, isn't it?"

He sighed. "Was I that obvious?"

"I worked with you—sometimes night and day—for over ten years. For good or for bad, we're pretty damned good at reading each other."

Her words carried a lot of truth, but as he heard them now and imagined her sitting in the kitchen of her Portland home—six-months pregnant with twins, her husband and young son out for a run, and her happy about it all—they rang false. Like he hadn't known her at all.

"I wasn't always so good at reading you, Dani."

She let out a sigh herself. "I changed, Drew. You were always good at reading me, sometimes too good. Do you remember how mad I would get at you when you wouldn't let me do things? It was only because I knew you were right. You were right to stop me or push me. But this, this life I have now, wouldn't have been possible without you. Not without the support and encouragement you gave me after my parents died, not without the mentorship you gave me when I was with the agency, and not without the chance you took getting us on that mission in Maine. Now, before you start to argue, why don't you tell me why you called—because I know you didn't call to hear me sing your praises, your head is already big enough. What's going on with Deputy Chief Drummond?"

"She's in trouble," he said, before he gave himself the chance to stop.

A beat passed. "What kind of trouble?"

"Not that kind of trouble. She hasn't done anything bad," he said, then he told her. All about what Carly had told him, what he'd seen in his short time at the state lab, and everything Naomi had shared with him. When he finished, Dani remained silent for a long moment.

"Um, wow," she said. "Witness security?"

"Hmm."

"That's a bit of a surprise."

"Understatement, but yes," he agreed.

"Why don't you call Rina and ask her to set up a task force?"

"Under what premise? There is no possible way we can claim any jurisdiction here."

"True," Dani conceded. "But that was the case when we went to Maine too. When she 'loaned' us out to the DEA," she said, referring to the case that had brought her and Ty together and helped them to find the man who had killed her parents.

"We had a bit more to go on there," Drew said. "The drugs and weapons were traveling internationally."

"But our main target was an American. And besides, how long have you been working for Rina?"

He had to give it some thought before answering. "Just over eighteen years." He'd gone straight from graduate school to her division and had been there ever since, rising in the ranks as she did.

"And how many favors have you asked her?" Dani pressed.

"That's not how it works, Dani. We sign up to do a job and we do it. We don't get to ask for favors from our employers."

"Bullshit. You did it for me. When we went to Maine."

He started to protest then stopped himself because it would

sound hollow. He *had* asked Rina for a favor in setting up the arrangements that had let them do what they'd done in Maine. But the favor had been for Dani so, for some reason, it had felt different.

"But that was for you," he said. "I've been making excuses and exceptions for you since you joined my team," he added, hoping to make light of the situation.

Dani let out a deep breath before speaking. "While I don't doubt that's true, given some of the things I probably put you through, you still asked for a favor and Rina came through. Do you not *want* to ask her?"

To not ask would mean sitting back and playing a passive role in the situation. Something he couldn't do, not with Carly at the center. So then, why was he having such a hard time doing what he needed—and wanted—to do?

Dani waited patiently on the other end of the line, silently letting him sort through his thoughts. When finally he came to a conclusion, he didn't like it one bit. "I don't want to ask Rina because I don't want her to say no," he said quietly. The honesty in his statement said more about his feelings for Carly than anything else. He couldn't sit this one out, not a chance, even if Rina said no. And going against his boss would have repercussions he didn't want to contemplate.

"It's real, then, is it?" Dani asked. He let a ghost of a smile touch his lips at her question. She hadn't asked if what he felt for Carly was *serious*—she'd asked if what he felt was *real*. A much bigger question for people like him and Dani, people who didn't have a lot of *real* in their lives.

"Yeah, it is," he said on an exhale.

"Then you have no choice, you need to ask Rina. It seems to me, you have enough people to put together a small task force. You, Carly, her brother, Dr. DeMarco, Naomi, and maybe those marshals too. Maybe Dr. DeMarco, with her FBI connections, can bring in another trusted colleague, because if you're going to be looking for someone inside *those* walls, you're going to want people you can trust."

"I know," he said. And he did. Not surprisingly, what Dani suggested echoed what had been bouncing around in his mind since leaving Carly's the night before.

"Should I talk to her before I talk to Rina?" he asked, hardly believing he had asked the question. A few years older, he'd always been Dani's boss, the one she'd come to with questions. Sure, he'd asked for her opinion before, but never concerning his personal life. Honestly, he wasn't sure he'd ever asked for anyone's opinion on his personal life.

"Uh, yeah?" she answered, sounding like a teenage girl.

"What?"

"What do you mean 'what'?"

"I mean, you said that like I asked a dumb question. It wasn't a dumb question."

"Yes, it was, Drew. Think about it. The woman had her life turned upside down when she was sixteen. She's been keeping a secret ever since then—not a little secret, but a huge one. Then, suddenly, she finds the body of one of the only other people who knew the secret in her hometown, and she doesn't know how it happened, who did it, or, most importantly, why. She doesn't know who she can talk to and she's worried that, if Marguerite was targeted, whoever did this might start targeting her other friends. I'm thinking she's probably feeling a little bit out of control right now. If you go and form a task force without talking to her first and suddenly bring in all these people to 'fix' things for her, my guess is it might send her over the edge. Not that she'll go crazy, but, well, you might regret it, is all I'm saying."

"Put that way, you have a good point," he said.

"Yes, I do."

"I see Ty's been able to work on your modesty over the last few years."

She laughed. "Ty likes me cocky."

"God help him," he said with a small laugh of his own as he rose from the bed. He paused by the windows and looked out again, remembering the look on Carly's face when she'd stopped to take in the view as they'd walked up the trail nearby not even a week ago. He'd noticed her almost awed expression at the time, and while he'd tucked that experience into his mental file, he hadn't given it much thought since. Now, as he looked out over the valley, he found he could almost understand it. He could easily stand there all morning, absorbed in the colors and the wildlife.

But he had things to do.

"Dani?"

"Yeah?"

"Thank you," he said.

"You're welcome. And when you get this all settled, why don't you guys come up for a visit?"

"Presumptuous, Dani," he responded. He liked the idea, but he had no idea where he and Carly would end up when the situation was over. He liked to think they'd be together in some fashion, but he still couldn't get his mind to even contemplate what that might look like. Mostly because he had no experience in it.

"Maybe," she conceded. "Even so, give it some thought, and promise me one thing?"

"Yeah?"

"Be careful."

He let out a deep breath. She wasn't talking about the situation with Marguerite. "Thanks, I will."

"And Drew?"

"Yeah?"

"I love you, you know that, right?"

Her statement seemed to hit him in the solar plexus with the strength of a two-by-four. Not because he didn't know it. Not because he didn't consider Dani and Sam his family and he theirs. But because they hadn't ever said it. Not he and Dani. Not once. And to hear it from her seemed to break something inside him. Things were changing and he'd been trying so hard to not let them, trying to keep a neat and tidy world that he only had to look at from his one perspective.

But to hear Dani, one of the toughest, most contained women

he'd ever met, say those words so easily changed everything for him. How, he wasn't sure—not yet. But he knew then, with those few words, he couldn't stop it even if he wanted to. And he didn't even want to.

"I love you too, Dani. Now go take care of yourself, and that toddler and husband of yours, and I'll come and visit as soon as I can."

She paused for moment, then in Dani-fashion made some comment about how he'd better come up and visit or he'd be sorry and hung up.

Smiling to himself, Drew glanced back at the clock. He wanted to call Carly, but since she had the day off, he thought she might be sleeping in. Between him showing up at her house the last several nights and her own worries, as well as work, she probably hadn't slept much.

Opening the app on his phone, he found that she was not at home. Her car was parked in front of Frank's Café in town. He debated on what to do for five seconds, then went to the duffel bag he still hadn't unpacked and pulled out his running gear. If Carly wanted a leisurely breakfast at Frank's, she deserved it. Besides, the conversation he wanted to have couldn't happen over coffee in a café anyway. So, he opted to go for a good run to kill some time and maybe clear his head a bit before seeing her.

Five minutes later, he locked Kit's door behind him and headed up the trail he and Carly had walked a few days before. Only this time, with no reason to stop, he headed straight to Churchkill Road, where he turned left toward the dead end. The road, damp from the recent drizzle, muted the sound of his feet, and for a good long while all he heard was his own breathing. Because it was still slightly overcast and there was a definite chill in the air, running, which was never one of his favorite things to do, was a little easier to deal with. The peaceful quiet of the road, the smell of the fallen leaves, and the distant scent of a fire burning in someone's fireplace didn't hurt either.

Spotting the end of road about a half mile ahead of him,

Drew caught sight of a woman. Dressed in dark pants and a thick sweater, she looked up from where she stood on Churchkill Road as he approached. Probably in her early seventies, she appeared to be collecting her mail. He glanced down the driveway near where she stood and recognized that it must be the Kirby farm Carly had mentioned.

Slowing his jog, he came to a stop about fifteen feet in front of her. His breath formed puffs of fog in front of him.

"Everything all right?" the woman asked, holding what looked like a bunch of magazines or catalogs.

He smiled. "Yes, fine. I'm Drew Carmichael, a friend of Kit Forrester and Garret Cantona. I'm staying at their place for a few days while they are away."

The woman nodded but said nothing.

"I was up here the other day with someone and she was mentioning that the road by your farm used to go all the way through to another hamlet where there is a church and a swimming creek."

The woman smiled. "Yes, it's a lovely hamlet. One of the oldest in the area. The church is still standing, although now it's more of a town hall than anything else."

"And the creek and swimming area?"

"It's still there and still popular. The town maintains it now and in the summer different local groups sell drinks and snacks from the old church to raise funds."

As she spoke, he let his eyes travel down her driveway and toward where he imagined the old road would go. As he did, a car, a state trooper, came up the drive and paused.

"Everything okay, Judith?" the driver, a man who looked to be in his mid-thirties, asked.

"Yes, Craig, everything is fine. This is Drew Carmichael, a friend of Kit and Garret's," she said. "Mr. Carmichael, this is my son-in-law Craig Neil. I was telling Drew about the old church and swimming hole."

The man gave him a good once over. "I'll be going then," he said. After rolling up his window, he continued down the road.

"He and my daughter and their two girls live on the farm," the woman said. "By the way, I'm Judith Kirby."

Drew held out his hand, then cast her an apologetic look when he realized how sweaty it was, and pulled it back. "It's nice to meet you. I hear your farm is famous for its beef?" He shouldn't be standing around. He needed to keep running or his muscles would stiffen up. But the question had just popped out.

Judith laughed. "Yes, we are, I suppose. Locally, anyway. My husband and daughter, Meredith, Craig's wife, run the business now, but it started with my husband's grandparents. Craig, of course, is a state trooper, but he helps out when he can."

"That's a nice legacy, and it's nice your daughter is interested in continuing it."

Judith laughed a little. "She is, she loves it. Strange as it might sound, but she does. Now, if you want to see the old church, feel free to go across our property. Follow the driveway down—it will turn left toward the house, but keep going straight. After about twenty feet or so, you'll see where the old road used to be. It runs along the south side of one our pastures and there is a bridge when you get to the end. It's old, but it will hold you if you want to cross."

His eyes traveled the path as she spoke it. He couldn't see all the way to the creek and the bridge, but he could see a little break in the tree line where the road must go.

"You wouldn't mind?" he asked, suddenly feeling the need to explore.

"Of course not, dear. And if you want to come back this way, you can, or you can continue on through the hamlet and meet up with the county road. If you do, turn right and about a mile down the road, you'll see Lancaster Road on your right. If you follow Lancaster—"

"It will meet up again with Churchkill and then I can take the trail back to Kit's," he finished, remembering what Carly and Marcus had said about Lancaster and Churchkill roads meetings.

"Exactly," Judith said with another smile.

He paused, his fists on his hips. Then he smiled himself and looked back to Judith. "Thank you, if you really don't mind, I think I will."

She stepped back and waved him on.

He thanked her again and began jogging down her driveway. Her directions had been simple and he made his way toward the creek without difficulty. When he came to the bridge, he slowed to a walk. The wooden structure had no railings and had so much dirt and grit accumulated in all its nooks and crannies that it had the overall appearance of packed earth. Drew walked about halfway across and looked out over the edge.

In his mind's eye, he could see the summer swimmers. The creek, about eight-feet wide, flowed into a much wider area on either side of the bridge, creating a swimming hole about fifteen-feet across. The shores were sandy with enough rocks to give the kids who were interested in climbing a place to explore. And the banks were grassy and dotted with trees.

On the other side of the bridge from the Kirby farm stood the church Carly had told him about. The single-aisle white clapboard building with small stained glass windows lining the sides brought to mind every picture postcard of historic Northeast towns he'd ever seen.

Inhaling a deep breath of the clean, cool air, Drew turned his attention, and his body, toward the hamlet itself. Picking up a jog again, he passed the church on his left and continued on toward the main road that traveled through the quaint village. Most of the houses he passed looked to have been built in the late seventeen hundreds or early eighteen hundreds. Several had porches and most were painted either white or some sort of pale yellow. Almost all of them had gardens that he imagined were lovely in the summer.

Leaving the hamlet, and his sense of having traveled back in time a few hundred years, Drew hit the main county road both Judith and Carly had mentioned. Turning right, he ran about another ten minutes before hitting the intersection with Lancaster Road. Heading up the hill on the dirt road back toward

Churchkill, he pushed himself hard, knowing he'd have the relative flat of Churchkill and then the downhill back to Kit's house ahead of him.

By the time he reached Kit's house his breathing had slowed, but he knew he'd be sore the next day from the climb up Lancaster. Coming to a stop in the driveway, he gave himself a moment to cool down and stretch before reentering the house. As he did so, he paced some circles and took in the area around him. It *was* beautiful, he'd give Kit and Carly that—they'd picked a spectacular place to live. And as he paused at a point in the driveway where he could see around Kit's house to the view that lay to the west, it dawned on him that it had been a long time since he'd taken the time to explore, to do something or go somewhere without a plan.

This thought followed him inside as he showered and changed. Even as he sat down to do a bit of work before heading over to Carly's house to talk to her about his growing idea, the same thought bounced around in his head. What had happened to him over the years?

As a kid, he and Jason had constantly explored new places— much to their parents' chagrin. He remembered being fourteen and Jason twelve when they'd taken the skiff and tried to sail to Maine. From Long Island. They'd made it about three miles away from home before their dad, who'd caught up to them in a motor boat, had found them in a cove where they'd stopped to swim.

And then there had been the hike he'd taken by himself through the Scottish Highlands. Nineteen at the time, already planning to join the CIA, but still playing with his own freedom. He'd spent the entire summer on that hike. It had been part fun, part contemplative, and part grueling. And he still remembered the freedom of the uncertainty of each day. At that age, each day had felt like an opportunity to learn something new, to have a new experience.

As he wrapped up the last of his e-mails, he realized that it had been well over a decade since he'd had that feeling, that feeling of excitement about the endless possibilities a day could bring. Now, if he didn't know exactly how a day or mission would turn out, he experienced nothing but a sick feeling in the pit in his stomach. Sure, he improvised. He didn't necessarily schedule every minute of the day. But every day, every mission, had an objective.

Sitting in bucolic Windsor, that statement felt dramatic, but when it came to his job, the sentiment held a lot of truth. And for the first time in forever, he began to wonder what that kind of perspective did to him. Knowing people's lives rested on his shoulders with nearly every decision he made, what did that do to him—to his body and to his mind? Did it make him a better agent? A better person? Or had it stunted him?

With a deep sigh, Drew closed down his computer and his rambling thoughts and turned his attention to Carly and her situation. Fixing her life was much easier to think about than fixing his own.

• • •

Thirty minutes later, he pulled up to Carly's house. After knocking on her door, he took a step back and eyed his surroundings. His gaze fell on the main house and he wondered when, or if, the owners would be up for the weekend. His eyes traced the elaborate roofline of the three-story Victorian. Taking in the details of the small, round stained glass window in the house's turret, he realized he'd been standing there for several minutes.

With a frown, he turned back around and knocked on her door a second time. Again, he heard nothing. Wondering if perhaps she'd gone back to bed or was taking a walk, he stepped off the porch and started around the building. He'd just come around the corner and turned toward the lake when Carly's figure appeared coming out of the woods.

He watched as she approached and noted the exact moment she spotted him. Her head came up, dropped down again for a brief moment, then came back up, her eyes meeting his. Dressed in exercise clothes, she'd been doing the same thing he had less than an hour earlier.

"Have a good run?" he asked.

She bent down, resting her hands on her knees, to catch her breath. After a moment, she looked up and smiled, then made a face.

"As good as a run can get," she answered, making him smile too.

He followed her into her house and watched her walk to the sink and fill a glass of water before she turned and leaned against the counter.

"So what brings you here?" she asked, eyeing him with curiosity.

"I was hoping to run something by you. An idea I have." He wasn't her boss, she wasn't part of his team, and he couldn't dictate a plan. He'd have to convince her. And not just her, but Marcus too.

She set her glass down and pushed away from the counter. "I can take a wild guess what this is about, but I'm feeling pretty grubby right now. I'd like to take a shower first if you don't mind."

Drew shook his head, knowing her request probably had more to do with giving herself some time to prepare to talk about Marguerite and the situation again rather than getting clean. "That's fine. But can you call Marcus and have him come over too? I think he needs to be a part of this. I assume you told him that I know?"

She tilted her head and studied him, then slowly nodded. "I told him some of what we talked about last night. He knows you know who we are. I'll call him from upstairs and we can talk more when he gets here. In the meantime, can you make some coffee? I'll want some when I come down. Marcus probably will too when he gets here. Feel free to make some for yourself, as well. All the stuff is there," she said, waving to a cabinet behind her before heading upstairs.

As he measured the coffee and the water, he heard her mumbled voice, presumably talking to Marcus, and then the sound of the shower running. Of course, an image of her in the shower flashed in his head and he acknowledged that he wouldn't mind being up there with her.

But even as the thought entered his mind, another even more disconcerting thought followed: what made him long to be up there with her at that moment wasn't sex. He did, of course, want to be with her in that way at some point—of that there was no doubt—but at that moment, well, at that moment he found himself craving the *intimacy* of that type of situation more than the situation itself.

He wanted that connection to Carly, that sense of belonging and ease he'd seen between couples he knew—Dani and Ty, Jason and Sam. He wanted to be able to stand in the doorway of the bathroom as she showered and talk with her. He wanted comfort and companionship and trust. He wanted things with Carly that he'd never desired or sought with any other woman.

As the coffeemaker sputtered out its final drips, this realization settled, unfamiliar and uneasily, in his mind and he didn't quite know what to do with it. Thankfully, he noticed Marcus's police cruiser pulling in beside his car, giving him a distraction. Through the kitchen window, he watched Marcus climb out of the car. Pausing as he stood, the young officer cast his gaze around, then stretched and flexed his injured leg.

Opening the door before Marcus had a chance to knock, Drew greeted the man he had at one time viewed as a potential rival. Knowing better now, for right or wrong, he felt more charitable toward him. A feeling that did not appear to be reciprocal.

"Carmichael," Marcus said, stepping into the house. "What are you doing here?"

Having thought Carly would have mentioned that he was there, Drew paused before answering.

"Well?" Marcus demanded, walking over to the coffeemaker and helping himself to a cup.

"I wanted to talk to you both about an idea—"

"We don't need your help," Marcus cut him off as he sat down at the kitchen table. "We'll do fine on our own."

Looking at the belligerence in Marcus's eyes, Drew considered that perhaps Carly wasn't the only one feeling a bit out of control. What Dani had said about the situation as it applied to Carly could apply to Marcus as well.

"Oh, Marcus, you're here," Carly said after she'd jogged down the stairs, stopping Drew from saying any more.

"I am," Marcus replied. "You didn't tell me Carmichael was here."

"Coffee?" Drew asked Carly.

Her eyes bounced between the two men before she replied, "Yes, please."

Drew poured her a cup and then one for himself before taking a seat at the table where Carly had joined her brother. He slid a cup of black coffee over to her and, with a mumbled, "Thank you," she took a sip.

"So what do you want to talk about?" Her voice came out almost jocular and Drew's gaze honed in on hers. Her strained expression told him that, even if she had doubts as to where this conversation would go, she wanted to hear him out. And she wanted to make sure her brother did too. If she hesitated, that would be reason enough for Marcus walk away. Any sympathy he might have felt for Marcus vanished, Carly did not need to be carrying the burden of Marguerite *and* managing her brother's moods.

"We don't need to talk to him about anything," Marcus interjected.

"Marcus," she reprimanded him with a glare. They held each other's gaze for a long moment.

Finally, Marcus jerked his eyes away and muttered, "Whatever."

"Drew?" Carly said, turning her eyes back to him. He let his focus go to Marcus, who was staring defiantly out the window, before returning his attention to her.

"I think you need some help. From inside the bureau," he said. And before either of the siblings could object, he continued.

"Based on what you know, you believe your mother and uncle were involved in an investigation into a corrupt agent or agents. We also know Joe Kincaid is really Joe Franks and that he is currently a deputy director with the bureau, but we don't know if he was part of the investigation or the subject of it."

At this point, Marcus turned an accusatory glare on his sister. "You told him all this?"

"I learned about Joe from Naomi DeMarco," Drew said, fighting an urge to reach across the table and smack him upside the head for acting like such a petulant teenager. "But what *I* know isn't as important as the fact that someone connected to your mother's death and your placement in the witness security program knows where you live. And even more important, they don't appear to mind killing to get what they want."

"Tell us something we don't know," Marcus said.

Drew's eyes narrowed on the younger man. Marcus was making it very hard to like him. "So now, in addition to whoever that is, I now know who you are, and so does Naomi."

"So?" Marcus demanded.

"Marcus," Carly reprimanded again.

"So, secrets like the secrets you two have been living with are like a tapestry. Once one of the threads comes loose, the whole thing can unravel, if it's not handled properly."

"I didn't take you for much of a seamstress," Marcus said.

Drew sighed and looked back at Carly, who seemed to be considering what he'd said. "Has that been your experience? Really?" she asked.

"What the hell? He's a *businessman* from New York. What does he know about these kinds of things?" Marcus asked, coming out of his chair.

"Don't be an ass," she shot back, rising to go toe-to-toe with her brother. "May I?" She gave Drew a quick glance then turned back to Marcus.

"Please." That she'd had the forethought to ask pleased him.

"I told you he was law enforcement of some sort, but he's

actually intelligence," she said, holding her own with her brother. "Drew has been with the CIA for, how long?" she asked not taking her eyes off Marcus.

"Just over eighteen years."

"Over eighteen years" she repeated. "I would wager he knows a hell of lot more than you and me combined about *these kind of things*."

Marcus looked about to contradict his sister but then seemed to pull back his frustration and let what she'd said sink in. After another moment, his eyes flitted to Drew. Marcus's posture hadn't changed, but Drew thought he might have seen a shadow of hope flicker in his eyes.

"Is that true?"

"It is. I joined the agency right after I finished my masters. I was an active agent for about twelve years, working mostly in Eastern Europe and North Africa before coming back to the home office. Now I run a team of agents that work in the same area."

After several tense moments, Marcus seemed to capitulate and he sank back into his seat and let out a deep breath. Drew didn't harbor any illusions that Marcus welcomed him into this situation, but again, he thought he caught a glimpse of hope in Carly's brother's eyes. That maybe he *could* help them.

"So what is your idea, Carmichael?" Marcus asked.

"You need to handle this properly, which means you need help from inside the bureau. You have someone you trust already, use her," he said.

Marcus looked up and blinked at him, possibly surprised he hadn't suggested that *he* take over the investigation. His potential involvement needed to be discussed eventually, but he wanted to at least get them to consider, if not commit, to bringing in *someone*.

"You mean Vivi," Carly said.

"Yes."

"But she doesn't work these kinds of cases," Marcus said.

"Vivi has been working with the bureau for many years and I have no doubt she is both well-liked and well-respected. I suspect that if you told her what you know about your past, as well as what Naomi has been able to dig up, she'd be able to help," Drew said.

"Help with what, though?" Carly pressed. "We don't even know what to do ourselves."

"You know how capable she is," he said. "My guess is that once she has the details, she'll be more than able to help come up with a plan to determine exactly what was going on back then and we can use that to figure out what is happening now. Her background with cold cases will come in handy as well, I would bet," he added.

Both Carly and Marcus sat back in their chairs. Carly took a sip of her coffee, but Marcus kept his arms crossed over his chest. After a moment, their eyes met.

Drew could feel the tension coiling in his body as he waited to hear their verdict. Had they been on his team, he would have simply issued an order. But with the way Marcus teetered on the edge of anger and acceptance, any show of force on Drew's part would shut the conversation down.

Carly looked at him. He felt a glimmer of hope that they'd agree, but suddenly her cell gave a shrill ring, making them all jump, and he knew he'd have to wait.

"It has promise," she said. "But let me get this first and then we can talk."

At least she hadn't said "no," but he wanted that phone call over with and the both of them on board with his idea before they had any second thoughts. Unfortunately, listening to Carly, he realized that finishing their conversation would have to wait.

"When? At the house? Is anyone there yet? Yeah, okay, I'll be right there," she said, then hung up.

She set her phone down, paused, then looked at Drew and her brother. "I have to go." she said. "That was Carl, one of our part-time officers," she explained to Drew. "There were reports of gun shots being fired at Mary Hanson's house."

"Why the hell did they call you and not me?" Marcus rose from his seat but paused when she waved him back down.

"They're on their way already and Vic is with them, along

with Jake. They have enough police power. Carl wanted me to know, well, because, you know," she said, giving her brother a meaningful look.

"I don't know," Drew said.

"Mary and Bill Hanson were my old landlords."

"At that place you lived in above the appliance store?" he asked, not bothering to keep his opinions on her former apartment from bleeding into his impression of the owners.

"How do you know where she used to live?" Marcus demanded.

"He helped in the investigation when Kit was attacked," Carly said to her brother as she crossed the room. Turning to Drew as she spoke, she related a too common story of domestic violence while she pulled on a pair of boots and rummaged in the coat rack for her jacket.

"So now you're on call every time something happens to Mary?" Drew asked, again not bothering to hide how he felt about the situation.

She stopped and eyed him. "Yes, I am. She has a two-year-old daughter and she's a woman who's been isolated from everyone else other than those whom her husband lets her see. I've been a friend to her for a long time. If there's a possibility that one of these days she will finally listen to me and get help, then, yes, I'll go every time they call."

For the third time that day, a disconcerting thought had set him off balance. First, he'd realized that he'd stopped exploring life. Then, he'd found that he wanted intimacy, real intimacy, with a woman for the first time he could remember. And now he was coming to understand that he'd, apparently, turned into a cold-hearted bastard.

"You're right, of course, but do you at least have a vest or something?" he asked, not having any idea if Windsor police even *owned* Kevlar vests.

She shook her head. "I'm not going to go near the house until the others have cleared it. I will grab my weapon and badge from upstairs in a second, but I'm there as a friend."

Drew said nothing more, but Marcus seemed about to protest. Carly quelled him with a single look before she bounded upstairs to get her gun and badge. Two minutes later, she stood at the door, sliding her weapon into her hip.

"Marcus, stay here and work with Drew, hear him out. It's not a bad idea and you know it."

"I should be there," Marcus said.

"There are four on-duty officers there now. If they need you, they'll call," she said before walking out the door and leaving him with her brother.

A brother who looked even less happy now than he had fifteen minutes earlier.

"You're going to let her go?" Marcus demanded, looking him in the eye.

"Even if I wanted to stop her, I couldn't."

"You don't *want* to stop her from heading to a scene where shots have been fired?" Marcus asked, disbelief sounding bitter in his tone.

"Of course I want to stop her, in a theoretical way. But it's her *job*. A job she does well. And more than that, what she's doing for Mary is part of who Carly is. She cares about this community and the people in it."

Marcus grunted and sat back down. "Sometimes I think too much."

Drew didn't agree with that assessment so he said nothing. He could see, every day, how much she loved her community. But given what had happened to her, in his mind, she hadn't yet let herself fully embrace Windsor as home. She still rented a house when she could buy one—a small one to be sure, but still a place for her to put down her own roots. She also hadn't invested anything in making this new rental a home. Oh, it was cozy and had all the right furniture, but it held nothing personal—no pictures of her with her friends, no paintings or prints, not even a throw pillow on the couch.

"So, what do you think of my idea?" Drew asked, bringing the conversation back to his original train. Carly had appeared to have given Marcus decision-making authority, so he shifted his tactic a bit and prepared a few new arguments if needed.

"I think Carly likes it," Marcus said after a moment's hesitation.

"And you?"

Again, Marcus hesitated.

"Do you trust Vivi?" Drew asked.

"Yes," Marcus answered immediately.

"Then?"

Marcus let out a deep sigh. "Then nothing. It does make some sense. You have to understand that, after all these years of keeping our past a secret, it doesn't come easy to suddenly be out in the open about it."

Drew did understand and he gave the younger man credit for his astute observation. "I get that, believe me, I do. Secrets have a way of taking on lives of their own sometimes."

"There's more, isn't there? Your idea involves more than just Vivi, doesn't it?"

This time, Drew let out a deep breath. Taking a sip of coffee to buy himself some time, he found it lukewarm. Rising from his seat, he dumped the remaining contents out in the sink. "Yeah, there's more," he said as he poured a fresh cup. He leaned against the counter to face Marcus. "I'd like to ask my supervisor to have an inter-agency task force set up so I can participate."

For a moment, Marcus did nothing but blink, then he managed to say, "There is *nothing* about this case the CIA has any jurisdiction over."

"Your uncle was accused of funding terrorist groups, some of which operated in North Africa." This was an argument he'd cultivated after talking to Dani.

"That was a lie! He wouldn't have done anything like that!" Marcus countered, coming up out of his seat in protest. When his injured leg seized he went crashing back down with a litany of curses.

Drew knew he had two choices: to look away, pretending

he hadn't seen anything, or face Marcus's condition head on. But even if he could pull off the former, he found he didn't want to. Marcus's body had been wrecked and nearly destroyed when he'd tried to save a woman and her child. And now, with the body of Marguerite Silva being dumped in his backyard, he was in mental turmoil too. And he couldn't ignore the fact that Marcus was someone who cared about Carly. He deserved Drew's respect and acknowledgement, though not his pity.

"Need anything?" he asked from his position at the counter.

Marcus glared up at him, even as he rubbed his thigh. He looked to be working out a cramp.

"Does that happen often?"

Marcus's mumbled reply contained more than a few curse words.

"Fine," Drew said, moving back toward the table. "If you don't need anything for your leg then we can get back to the conversation."

Marcus looked up and gave him a you-gotta-be-kidding-me look, but Drew continued. "I happen to agree that your uncle was most likely set up. But the thing is, working in the areas I've worked in, I've become pretty good at following money trails. If there was any data planted in his accounts, chances are, between Naomi and me, we'll be able to figure out not just that it's there, but probably where it came from and also where it went."

That seemed to pull Marcus's attention away from his leg. His hand still rubbed it, working the muscle, but he focused on Drew. "So you think Naomi should be part of this task force too?"

"Along with Mikaela Marsh and maybe one or two of her trusted marshals, yes."

"And Sam," Marcus added, which Drew took to be a good sign.

"Dr. Buckley?"

"Yes, he has an eye for things like you wouldn't believe."

"Okay, so we have you and Carly and Vivi. Then we have the marshals, Dr. Buckley, me, and Naomi," Drew summed up.

"And Wyatt."

"Who's he?"

Marcus told him about their former colleague, now an FBI agent, and mentioned how Carly had already talked to him a bit about electronic surveillance. Hearing this, Drew guessed that Wyatt was the man he had seen at Anderson's with Carly.

"You trust him?" he asked.

"Yes," Marcus answered without hesitation.

"Then I think we have a good team."

Marcus said nothing but gazed out the kitchen window, his hand still on his leg. "I'm not entirely comfortable with it, but if it will make this all go away, then I think we should do it and you have my support. What are the next steps?"

Inside, Drew felt a band of tension release in his body. "Good," he answered. "As for next steps: I'll call my supervisor and start the conversations, but before we finalize anything, I want to talk to Carly to make sure she's on board."

"What's going on between you and my sister?" Marcus asked.

Drew studied the man sitting across from him then lifted a shoulder. "I'm not sure," he answered honestly.

Marcus's eyes narrowed on him.

"But it's not anything . . ." Drew paused in his effort to reassure Marcus that his intentions were good. He ran a hand over his face, then leaned back in his chair and shook his head. "I don't know," he repeated. Absently, he noted that the genuine confusion he heard in his own voice would not have reassured him had he been in Marcus's position.

But oddly enough, what he'd said, or how he'd said it, elicited a chuckle from Marcus. "It's like that, is it?"

"Like what?" Drew's own eyes narrowed.

"You've met Ian, Dash Kent, and David Hathaway, right? And I know you know Garret."

"Yeah, so?"

Rather than answer, Marcus gave him a flat look then shook his head as he stood and slipped his jacket on. His leg held this time and Drew watched as Marcus checked his weapon and pulled his keys out of his pocket.

"You know how to lock up?" Marcus asked.

"I know how to set the alarm but I don't have a key."

"Good, I'm glad to hear that. Set the alarm on your way out. You don't need to lock it. If anyone comes in, the alarm will let everyone know."

With that, Marcus left.

And in the silence of Carly's kitchen, Drew continued to wondered just what Carly's brother had meant. *It's like that, is it?*

CHAPTER ELEVEN

WHEN CARLY TURNED ONTO HER road, the sun hadn't yet set but somehow the light seemed tired, softer in some ways. After the last several hours, she didn't feel much like laughing, but the sight of Drew standing on her porch when she pulled up to her house did bring a small smile to her lips.

Idly, her mind flitted to the tracking device he had put on her car. She hadn't asked him to take it off. Under normal circumstances she'd be furious with him for having done something like that. She also knew him well enough by now to know that, under normal circumstances, he would never have *done* such a thing.

Looking at him leaning against her porch railing, his black coat hanging open, she wondered what would happen if she walked up to him, wrapped her arms around his waist, and kissed him. No, scratch that, she had a pretty good idea what would happen: in less than two minutes he'd be backing her up the stairs to her bedroom.

Years ago, when she'd been a little girl on their horse farm, one of the grounds workers had told her that the shock from the electric fence came when you let go—not from touching it in the first place. She hadn't ever tested that information, but when she thought about Drew, she thought being with him would be a little like touching an electric fence. If she decided to reach out for him, she better plan to hold on because, instinctively, she knew that letting go would hurt like hell.

"Everything okay?" he asked, knocking on her driver's side window, making her jump. She hadn't even noticed that he'd left the porch.

"Yes, fine," she said loudly as she turned to grab her jacket and purse.

"You look a little tired," he said, holding the door open for her as she exited the car.

She lifted a shoulder. "I didn't do much today, but because it wasn't the day I had planned for when I woke up, for some reason I do feel tired." She rummaged on her key chain for her house key.

"You don't need a key. It's not locked," Drew said. She looked up at him. "Your brother left before I did. I didn't have a key to lock up, but I did set the alarm," he explained.

She blinked at him. "You know how to set my alarm?"

He hesitated, then answered. "I have a good attention for detail."

She studied him. His blue eyes met hers, unblinking and unapologetic. Of course he'd have a good eye for detail. She doubted anyone lasted in the CIA for nearly two decades without having a good eye for detail.

She cleared her throat. "You should have let yourself in."

"That would have been presumptuous. Just because you left me here with your brother five hours ago doesn't mean you'd want to come home to find me sprawled out on your couch."

She couldn't help the not-so-little twitch her lips made at his comment. It was so like Drew to be so conscientious of propriety. But, she wouldn't have minded finding him sprawled on her couch, not that she thought he ever actually *sprawled* anywhere.

His eyes narrowed on her, so rather than keep fighting the smile that tugged at her lips, she turned toward the door. "Please come in," she said, entering her house and leaving the door open behind her.

She heard him follow and shut the door as she typed in her security code. He was in her kitchen by the time she hit the last button.

"You look like you could use a drink." He was more right than he knew. She also wouldn't mind a little down time on her back porch and maybe a chance to watch the sunset.

She smiled her agreement and draped her jacket on the back of one of her kitchen chairs. A few minutes later, Drew held both their drinks as she wrapped herself up in a blanket and sat. Once she'd settled, he handed her a glass and took a seat beside her.

They sat, not saying anything, watching the evening activity—the sun began its descent, a few evening birds made an appearance, and two ducks came back to the pond. A few times, she took a deep breath, inhaling the comfort of Windsor in the fall.

"Did you catch up with Marcus?" he asked after several quiet minutes.

She shook her head. "No, what did you decide? I think what you were suggesting is a good idea, and we all trust Vivi."

He agreed then updated her on his conversation with Marcus as well as his subsequent conversation with his supervisor.

"So you think she'll be able to put a task force together?" Carly asked. She knew the murder of a federal marshal and the possibility of a compromise in the witness security program would, more likely than not, be the primary reason to authorize such a task force. But to her, because Drew had been the one to ask, it felt like something everyone was doing for her and her brother.

"If anyone can do it, Rina can. The question really depends on how much energy she wants to put into it."

"Do you think she'll blow you off?"

Drew lifted a shoulder and took a sip of his drink. "Rina's an interesting woman. She holds a lot close to the vest. I like her and I trust her, but I don't always know what's going on in her mind. Which, I admit, is probably a good thing."

"So you think she might not come through?"

He tilted his head one way and then the other. "At this point, I think it's fifty-fifty. She said she would try to see what she can do, and she's done things like this before—put things in place based on a personal favor—but I guess it depends on whether or not something else comes up that requires her attention." Drew sounded like someone hoping for the best but preparing for the worst.

Carly mulled this over. If his boss didn't come through, at least she, Marcus, and Drew were all in agreement that Vivi and Wyatt could still be brought in. And with Vivi could come Naomi. So, even if Rina didn't come through with the authorization, the only people they'd be missing from their group were the marshals. And Drew—in his official capacity. Because even if his supervisor didn't come through, she knew he wouldn't be stopped from doing what he could. What repercussions that might have for him professionally, she didn't know, and that might be the "worst" that he was preparing for.

They sat in a comfortable silence as the sun dipped behind the hills. Carly took another sip of her drink and let her head rest against the back of her chair as the liquid flowed down her throat and warmed her body.

"Do you like your job?" Drew asked suddenly.

Carly lifted her head and looked at him. She heard a depth of interest in his question that she didn't often, if ever, hear when other people asked her that very same thing. Drew didn't seem to be asking to make idle chitchat and the curiosity in his tone gave her pause—like maybe he'd been asking himself the same question.

Slowly, she turned her glass in her hands as she thought about how to answer, as she thought about whether or not revealing some of her own frustrations, questions, and truths might help him with his. After a long pause, she spoke.

"Today was supposed to be my first full day off in weeks. Don't get me wrong, I like working and I'm glad I have a job that I enjoy and am good at, but it can be draining."

"Aren't you only supposed to work a certain number of hours a week?"

Under her blanket, she lifted a shoulder. "Firefighters are held to stricter hours than we are, but we're understaffed and someone needs to work. I've been earning a lot of overtime, which is great, but I'm glad Vic, our chief of police, is finally getting serious about hiring some new people."

"But," he prompted.

She let out a sigh. "Honestly, it's not the hours that are

draining. We deal mostly with things like theft and minor assaults around here, but then there are people like Mary."

"What about people like Mary?"

"I told you I've known her for years, and for about as long, I've known that her husband abuses her. She's isolated from most people, has no friends—it's the classic situation. Because I got involved once, when I first moved in, I'm kind of her go-to-girl when it comes to dealing with law enforcement."

"And?"

"And she talks to me, she tells me everything. But she doesn't want me to help her. She just wants me to get other officers, or sheriff's deputies, off her back. I took on the role at first because I thought I might be able to get her to trust me and eventually let me help her help herself. But she doesn't want help. Or is too scared to ask for it, or get it, or doesn't trust herself. Or maybe just doesn't see herself as worth it."

"Or, a combination of all those things."

"Most likely a combination of all those things," she agreed. "But she has a kid now. *They* have a kid now. The two-year-old I mentioned. Emily. And while there isn't ever an excuse for what goes on in that house, it seems like, after all these years, maybe Emily should be enough to give Mary the motivation to get help."

"But she hasn't, has she?"

Carly shook her head. "No, Mary is still insisting on staying with Bill. And Bill is still beating her. To my knowledge, he hasn't touched Emily yet. We've tried to get CPS in there but lies and secrets come easily to Mary and Bill, and there's nothing CPS can do."

"People can't always be helped."

"And they can't always help themselves, either."

"Not unless they want to."

A few minutes of silence passed as she let her mind drift over her day and even her career. Then she let out a deep breath. "So, yes, there are things I like about my job. I like helping when I can and I like the occasional challenge. But there's a lot that is hard for me to accept—I don't like that I can't do more to help some folks. Mary might not want my help, but then for each situation where someone doesn't want our help, there are situations where people do need a hand, but because of my official role, I can't give it. Or I can't officially give it, I should say."

That seemed to get Drew's attention and out of the corner of her eye, she saw his head turn toward her.

"Thomas Rutledge had a drinking problem and was going to lose his farm," she said. "He was a good man who sank into depression after his wife died from cancer about three years ago. I helped him get help and get his farm back running." Carly hadn't told anyone this story. Not even Marcus.

"And how did you do that?"

He probably wouldn't approve. Hell, *she* didn't even really approve of what she'd done, but it *had* worked out. "I got him into a rehab and helped cover his loans for a few months. It bought him enough time to get sober and get his land back to production. And before you ask, yes, it was a loan I made to him and, yes, he is already paying it back."

Beside her, she could feel Drew's disbelief. Or maybe she felt her own doubts bouncing off of him and coming back at her.

"There are more, aren't there?" he asked, his voice quiet in the falling dusk.

There were more. Not as many as she would have liked, but there were more. A young woman she'd sent to Naomi for a fake ID so she could escape her abusive father. A young man she'd helped get into the military with the hope that he'd have a better life than his crack-addicted mother could offer him. And Anne Kramer, the little girl with Downs syndrome—her parents loved her dearly but couldn't afford all the treatments and classes, like physiotherapy, that the doctors recommended. Carly hadn't exactly abused her position by convincing local doctors and therapists to help the Kramer family, but being the deputy chief of police—and a good friend of the county sheriff—hadn't hurt.

She shrugged and waited for Drew to say something, to question her decisions or judge her actions. But beside her, all she heard was a chuckle.

Surprised she looked over. "What?"

He met her gaze with a lopsided smile. "Earlier today I was thinking you hadn't really settled here at all. Your walls have no pictures, you rent rather than own, and while your home is cozy and I like it—a lot—there is very little of *you* here. I thought it was because you hadn't allowed yourself to settle in. But now, my guess is that's because most of your spare cash and time go to helping others. Am I right?"

She looked away, feeling embarrassed. "It's not like I have *that* much to give—or loan—away. I do only make a cop's salary," she said, rather than answer his question directly.

"I think it's crazy, Carly, I really do, but I also think it's pretty amazing. Look at me, my family has more money than we could spend in the next four generations, and while we do make significant contributions to a lot of charities, we don't get on the front lines like you've done. Like I said, crazy but pretty amazing."

She recognized his underhanded praise, but his honesty meant more to her than the actual words.

"What about you, Drew? Do you like your job?" She'd offered him a lot of truth in the last few minutes and she wondered if he would offer the same in return. She hoped he would.

His long hesitation told her more than he'd probably intended. She knew a lie could roll from his lips sweet as candy. But the longer he took to answer her, the more certain she became that his eventual answer would be the truth.

He took a deep breath, let it out, then started speaking. "I do like my job."

"But," she prompted, because she heard it coming.

He paused again, took a sip from his glass, then set it down gently on the arm of his chair. "I took a run this morning. I went up the trail to Churchkill Road, then toward the Kirby farm. I met Judith Kirby who was out getting her mail—and her son-in-law drove by as well."

"She's a nice woman," Carly said, interested in where this was going.

"She is and she let me run through their property to the creek and church and hamlet you told me about that day we hiked up the trail to where we found Marguerite. I followed the old road, saw it all, then came back up Lancaster to Churchkill and down the hill to Kit's.

"When I got back to Kit's, it occurred to me that the little journey I'd just taken had been the first thing in recent memory I'd done without an objective, without an end goal."

She frowned at this. "I imagine in the world you work in, having an objective is pretty important."

At this he turned and gave her a rueful smile. "Yes, objectives and goals are the life blood of the agency. Maybe they are just information or intelligence. But often they are more than that. But the thing is, I used to be pretty adventurous as a boy and a young man," he added, then went on to tell her about trekking across Scotland as a nineteen-year-old and a road trip he'd taken with a college friend around India.

"And now?"

He let out a sardonic chuckle. "Now as adventurous as I get is getting permission to run through someone's property to see a creek and a church."

Carly let out a little laugh as well. Put that way, he did sound a bit stodgy and boring—two words she never would have thought to use to describe him before this conversation. The words intriguing, caring, possibly pigheaded, and sometimes tightly wound came to mind. But intelligent, efficient, and kind were also on the list, and closer to the top of it.

"So how does this relate to your job?" she asked, suspecting the answer.

He lifted a shoulder. "I like my job. But the thing is, I used to *love* it. I loved the travel and the adventure, and while I didn't seek danger, there's no denying the high that comes from a successful assignment. I was a good field agent, but at some point I made a decision, a decision I'm not even sure I was conscious of, and I began taking on roles with more and more leadership responsibility. Roles that gave me teams to manage and responsibility for entire geographic areas."

"And your job changed," she said, taking a sip of her drink.

"And my job changed."

"Do you want to go back?" she asked, immediately wishing she hadn't. If he'd loved being a field agent, then she had no right to judge if he wanted to go back. And if he did, she would encourage him. But the thought of him being back in that world—a world she admittedly didn't fully understand—didn't sit well with her.

When he hesitated, she looked over at him. He shook his head. Taking another sip of her drink, she turned her eyes back to the pond.

"No, I've been out of it for too long, but honestly, even if that wasn't the case, I'm not sure I'd want to go back. It's a bit of a young man's game. There are agents who are older, but I," he paused again, as if searching for the right word. "I just don't think it's the right fit for me anymore. Maybe it's age, maybe it's ability . . ."

"Or?"

He let out a deep breath. "Or maybe my heart isn't in it anymore. You know, when I was a field agent, it seemed like we had some breathing room on occasion. Like if we pulled something off or were successful at something, we had a little bit of down time after. We could have a drink with colleagues, maybe pat ourselves on the back a bit, and maybe even have a little time to catch up with family and friends."

"And now?"

He ran a hand over his face and to her, the gesture revealed how spent he was. "I don't know if it has always been like this or if I see things differently now that I have the role I have. But it seems like before one assignment is even over there's another one waiting in the wings. All of them urgent, of course. It's like this never ending series of shit storms we have to get involved in, manage, and hopefully survive. Just one after the other without any break."

That level of mental and, most likely, emotional engagement *did* sound exhausting—and it made burning out seem likely. But she didn't think he was completely burned out. He might be struggling now, but she found his struggle to be much deeper than just whether or not he liked his job.

"So what is it about your job that you enjoy?" she asked, hoping to help him think of a few things so that he could figure out what exactly he wanted from his position and then perhaps start to redefine what he did.

He tilted his head in thought then, as a flock of late migrating Canada geese landed on the pond, he answered. "I like watching the agents who report to me grow and develop. I like training new agents and teaching classes at The Farm," he said, referring to the CIA training grounds. "I like making sure they're prepared and ready to handle new assignments. In every way."

"In every way?"

"Yes. Mentally, physically, emotionally. Agents aren't like fighting machines. The CIA isn't like the military—though some people would say otherwise—and shock and awe isn't our thing. The CIA is all about subtlety and secrecy and discretion. And while I don't agree with everything the agency has done in the past, I do think the intelligence it has gathered—intelligence that agents have gathered—has done a lot of good that most people won't ever know about."

"So, the new agents?"

He turned and flashed her a grin, acknowledging that he'd climbed onto a bit of soapbox without answering her question.

"Agents need to be ready for whatever assignments they get. Sure, that means being physically ready, but most important is being mentally and emotionally ready, because so much time is spent thinking and observing before acting."

"And you like getting them ready for that."

"I do. I like seeing agents who are confident about their abilities—not arrogant, but confident. It's good for the agency, but mostly it's good for them. If an agent starts to have doubts—and we all do at some point—if they have a good sense of self and a belief in their abilities, it can help them cope when situations don't go as planned or take a turn for the worse."

"And how often do you get to work with agents on this kind of stuff? How often do you get to teach?"

Again he let out a deep breath. "Not often enough."

The tone of his voice warned her that he was nearing his limit for how long he could talk about this. She recognized the pattern—the kinds of questions Drew seemed to be asking himself were big, and if this was the first time in his career he'd started asking them, he would need to take it slowly. And because she honestly believed he should be asking himself all these questions—what he liked, what he didn't, how he felt about his job—she wanted to respect the space he seemed to need.

"Are you hungry?" she asked, dropping the subject altogether—and surprising him, if she read the look on his face correctly. She grinned. "I haven't eaten since this morning. Between waiting for my colleagues to clear the Hanson house and then waiting at the ER for Mary to get bandaged up once again, I didn't have a chance to grab lunch."

He stared at her as if not quite sure whether her change of subject was to be trusted. Then he smiled too. "We can't have that. What are you craving?" he asked as he stood and took her glass.

"Pizza," she said definitively. "But I don't want to go out."

"I can go pick it up."

"Or better yet," she said, hauling her blanket-wrapped self out of her chair. "The place in town just started to deliver out here three weeks ago."

"Yep, even better," he said as he followed her inside.

CHAPTER TWELVE

DREW ROLLED OVER IN BED, looked at the clock, and acknowledged that this week had been filled with a lot of firsts for him. It was close to nine a.m. He hadn't slept so late since college.

He shifted onto his back then rolled his head to the side and looked at the empty spot beside him. He had left Carly's house fairly early the night before when her friend Matty had stopped by, along with her husband, Dash, and their four-month-old twins, Daphne and Charley. That they were all close friends had been obvious from the way Carly's face had lit up when she'd seen their car pull onto her drive. And they'd certainly been nice enough, but the scene had felt too familiar for him to stay and be a part of.

Having just finished their dinner together, his leaving had seemed natural. But as he gazed at the empty sheets beside him now, he knew that it hadn't been. After his realization earlier the day before, when he'd recognized the type of intimacy he wanted from Carly, witnessing it in her friends Matty and Dash had made him feel distinctly uncomfortable. As he got up and began to dress for another run, he didn't have to think too hard to know why he'd fled—a strong word, but truly what he'd done. He had been afraid that Carly, or worse, her friends, would see what he wanted written all over his face.

Which was also something that hadn't happened in years. Carly had been right when she'd commented that part of his ability to hide his thoughts was just who he was—even as a kid he'd been able to keep his face more or less unreadable when the situation called for it. And she'd also been right about the impact his training and career had had on the skill—he'd essentially perfected it over time. In fact, he sometimes wondered if he could express emotion at all anymore.

At least he knew the answer to that quandary now—some silver lining to the situation, he supposed.

His cell phone rang on the bedside table as he tugged on a shoe. Leaning over, he picked it up then checked the number.

"Rina," he said, answering.

"It's all in place," she said without preamble. "I spoke to Deputy Marsh this morning, she's expecting your call. I've also authorized Naomi DeMarco and her brother, Brian, if needed, as well as Ian MacAllister, Dr. DeMarco's husband. With Dr. DeMarco, Agent Wyatt Granger, and Dr. Sameer Buckley, you'll have the FBI, CIA, the sheriff's office, the Windsor police, two freelance consultants, the state lab of New York, and the US Marshals. With that kind of firepower for this kind of problem, I expect you to wrap it up quickly."

Drew was speechless. The task force she'd put in place told him more than she ever would about just what she thought of him. If she didn't respect him, if she didn't *like* him, she wouldn't have gone to such lengths. He thought about saying something along those lines, saying he appreciated her faith in him, but knowing she'd view the acknowledgment as a waste of her time, he decided not to. All Rina would want was a simple thank you and a promise to get the job done. Followed, of course, by him actually getting the job done.

"Thank you," he said.

"You're welcome, now get to work."

He muttered, "Yes, ma'am," but suspected she didn't hear it when his line cut off. Without missing a beat, he dialed Carly's number.

She sounded out of breath when she answered and he wondered if she'd been out for a run already.

"Everything okay?" he asked.

"Yes, everything is fine. I spoke to Vivi earlier this morning and we are going to meet her and Wyatt at her house at around noon, which will give Naomi time to get here. I was going to call you, but it was early so I decided to go for a run first. Will you be there?"

"Yes, I'll definitely be there—and Rina, my boss, came through. There is an official interagency task force now, and in addition to Naomi, she's also authorized Naomi's brother, Brian DeMarco, if we need him, along with Vivi's husband. Rina also spoke with Mikaela Marsh, who is now expecting our call as well."

"Really?" she asked after a few beats.

He smiled. "Yes, really."

"All for my mom and uncle. And, of course, Marguerite?" she asked more out of surprise than for any clarification.

"Yes." There were likely more factors that Rina had taken into consideration, but he gave her the simple answer.

"Ooh-kaay," she drew out. "What now?"

"Well, it sounds like you already have Naomi on her way, so maybe you should call Vivi and you both can decide whether or not you want to bring in Brian, Dr. Buckley, and Ian MacAllister. I can call Deputy Marsh, fill her in, and see if she wants to fly up here or call into this first meeting at noon. How does that sound?"

"Sounds good. I'll let Marcus know, too."

"Sounds like a plan, then."

Carly murmured her agreement and then an awkward silence followed for a few beats. Clearing his throat, Drew spoke, "I'll call Deputy Marsh right now and then head out for my run. Can you text me Vivi's address and I'll see you there?"

"I'll do that as soon as we hang up," she said then hesitated before speaking again. "Drew?"

"Yes?"

"Thank you," she said.

Never in his life had those two words caused such a reaction in him. The soft sincerity in her voice coupled with the underlying hint of nervousness about what might come next made him want to gather her in his arms and tell her everything would be okay. It made him want to reach for her and not let go. It made him want to end this thing, so that she could go back to being too helpful to her community and live the life she wanted without all the fear and secrets.

The first two weren't an option, not right now—they didn't know each other well enough for that quite yet and both actions implied promises he didn't know if he could keep. But as for the third, as for ending this thing, well, *that* he could most definitely work on.

"You're welcome," he said softly back. "I'll see you in a few hours and I promise you we'll get this all worked out."

"Promise?" she asked after a split second of hesitation. But this time, he heard a teasing smile in her voice.

He smiled back. "Yes, I promise."

• • •

A few minutes after noon, Drew turned onto a long, gravel drive-way that climbed a gentle slope to a charming bungalow with a large front porch and several flower gardens that looked to have been put to bed for the coming winter.

Pulling up past the right side of the house, he parked his SUV beside Carly's car and noted the number of other vehicles, two of which he recognized: Marcus's cruiser and the sheriff's SUV. Two other cars were also present, which he took to be Naomi DeMarco's and Wyatt Granger's, since he assumed it would be hard for Dr. Buckley to make it to Windsor in the middle of the day and he already knew that Mikaela Marsh planned to call in.

Climbing out of his vehicle he took a good look around yet another beautiful Hudson Valley location. Standing closer to the back of the house than the front, his view was somewhat obstructed, but he'd bet that from the front porch Vivi and Ian could see for miles.

Turning to the forest that lay about hundred feet behind the DeMarco/MacAllister home, the colors seemed to be vying for attention, each one more vivid than the next. As his eyes traveled to the house, he noted a smaller porch area where the back door stood that led to what looked like a newer slate patio. It held several chairs, a stone bench, and a fire pit and would be a perfect place to sit during a chilly spring or fall evening, have a glass of wine, and maybe roast some marshmallows.

"We're in here," Vivi called as she opened the back door. Her son perched on her hip and played with his mother's hair while a big, hairy gray dog bolted out to greet him. He stilled as the beast barreled toward him, came to a not-so-graceful stop, then started butting its head against his knees, all the while looking at him with yellow, wolf-like eyes.

"That's Rooster," Vivi said with a laugh at the dog as he shamelessly begged for attention.

"He's a big boy." Drew reached down, though not far, to rub between Rooster's ears.

"He is, but, thankfully, he's as gentle as they come," she replied.

Drew straightened away, much to Rooster's discontent. "It's a beautiful spot you have here," he said, walking toward her, Rooster trying to wend his way between his legs like a cat.

Vivi answered with a wide smile. "Thank you. We love it. Ian, of course, was raised here. This is the back forty acres of the close to three hundred his parents own. We've done a little work, like extending this back patio and adding the fire pit and may have to do a small addition at some point if we decide to have more kids, but it is our little piece of heaven."

"But you're from Boston, right? I thought I remembered Kit saying something about that," he asked as the entered the kitchen through a small room that held a washer and dryer, but also assorted boots, jackets, and outdoor apparel. Rooster must have caught a distraction as he made a beeline for something deeper in the house.

"I am, but I happened to come across Windsor one day as I was driving around the country. I was trying to escape some demons and happened upon this place. I've been here ever since and can't imagine being anywhere else."

"Drew." Vivi's husband, Ian, entered the kitchen with his hand out. "It's good to see you again, though I'm not sure why we're all here."

Drew said nothing about the reason for the meeting—figuring Carly had decided to wait so that she only had to tell the story once—and took the offered hand.

"Here let me take him," a voice came from behind Ian's shoulder.

Drew looked over at the person who had just entered the kitchen. Or, to be more accurate, he looked up at him. A man who was at least six-and-half-feet tall, with dark hair and dark eyes, came striding into the kitchen, reaching for Vivi's son. The toddler seemed to be on board with that plan and held his arms out as Rooster danced at the man's feet.

"Lucas, this is Drew Carmichael. Drew, this is Lucas Rancuso." Vivi made the introductions as she handed her son over. "For all intents and purposes, he's my brother in every way but blood, and hence, Jeffery's all-too-doting uncle."

Drew watched the man lift Jeffery high in the air, high enough that Jeffery's back pressed against the ceiling.

"It's nice to meet you," Lucas said, his eyes focused on Jeffery, who laughed and clapped his hands as Lucas made funny faces and bounced him in the air a bit.

"Lucas is also a detective with the Boston Police Department," Vivi said.

"But not today, I'm not. Today, I'm the 'manny' while you all have whatever meeting you are going to have. Jeffery and I are going to go for a long hike in the woods with Rooster, aren't we, Jeffery?" Lucas brought the toddler back down to his side and Rooster started prancing, presumably at the word "hike."

"Where's the backpack?" Lucas asked turning to Ian.

"In the pantry," Ian answered.

"Come with me," Vivi said as the other two men—and

dog—moved to find the item in question. "Do you want coffee or tea?" she asked, waving toward the pot and the kettle. "I know it's lunchtime, but between having a baby in the house and our jobs, we pretty much have coffee in the pot at all times."

Drew declined the offer and followed Vivi into a living room filled with people. He immediately spotted Carly standing with Marcus on one side of the room. She met his gaze and offered him a small smile. He wanted to go to her side, but judging by the look on both of their faces, she and Marcus were nervous enough. He didn't need to upset the balance between them.

So rather than veer off toward Carly, he continued to follow Vivi, who introduced him to both her cousin Naomi, whom he'd met over the phone but not in person, and Wyatt Granger, the young man he'd seen with Carly at Anderson's.

"Okay," Ian said, walking into the room sans Lucas, Jeffery, and Rooster. "Now, who is going to tell us what the hell is going on?" he asked, drawing all eyes toward him. The abruptness of his words were tempered when he waggled his eyebrows at his wife, who shook her head, fighting a grin.

Ian shrugged and smiled. "Just kidding. Sort of. Now do you two want to tell us what this is all about so we can figure out what we're all here for and what we're going to do about it?"

Carly's eyes darted to Drew, who took the hint and spoke. "Let me call Deputy Marsh and then we can get started." Everyone but Carly and Marcus found seats. Once he'd dialed and put the marshal on speakerphone, Drew looked toward the siblings. "We're all here now, why don't you go ahead and start?"

He watched Carly and Marcus each take a deep breath, but she spoke first. "Both Marcus and I want you all to know the deception we've been living was necessary." At that pronouncement, Drew saw Vivi and Ian share a look while Wyatt's brows dipped, his attention focused on his friends and former colleagues.

"As you know, Marcus and I are, and have always been, close. And for good reason. When I was sixteen and Marcus was nineteen, our mother and uncle were killed and we were put into witness security. From that day on, we haven't been able to tell a single person the truth about who we are, not our real names or the fact we are brother and sister. The names we were born with are Michael and Carolyn Davidson."

She paused, and by the way her eyes were darting between Vivi, Ian, and Wyatt, it was obvious she was anticipating that at least one of them would be upset about their secret. But to the credit of her friends, their expressions showed nothing but a mix of confusion and concern.

When no one jumped on the bomb she'd just dropped, Carly turned toward Marcus, who took up the narrative. Over the next ten minutes, he described what little they knew about the situation leading up the deaths of their mother and uncle, their subsequent placement in the witness security program, and Marguerite's role. The significance of Marguerite's body showing up in Windsor needed no explanation.

When neither of them had any more to share, the room fell into a deafening silence. For a moment at least, they had rendered everyone speechless. Deputy Marsh, who already knew the information that had just been imparted, also remained silent, letting Carly and Marcus's friends absorb what had just been shared.

Not surprisingly, Vivi was the first to speak. "First, I want to say how sorry I am for both of you. If anyone can understand what it's like to lose a parent to violence, it's me. Although, I suspect losing a parent in any way, at any time, if you are close, isn't easy."

Drew knew, from Kit, that Vivi's parents had been killed a few years earlier by a drunk driver.

"I think I speak for everyone in this room," she continued, "when I say that we will all do whatever we can to help. You just have to tell us, or we need to figure out, where to start."

Drew caught Carly's eye and made a subtle gesture with his head in Naomi's direction. He thought it might be time for someone else to talk. In response, her eyes went instead to the phone. When she looked back up at him for his reaction, he nodded in agreement.

"We've told you what we know, but on the line is Mikaela Marsh. She's been Marguerite's boss for ten years and knows all of Marguerite's cases, including ours. She recognized me at the state lab and she agreed to dig around, discreetly, and see what her team could come up with. Mikaela?" Carly prompted.

"The Davidson kids came onto my radar when Marguerite joined my team. She told me that an internal FBI investigation had gone bad and her former boss at the time, Thomas Richer, had directed her to place the siblings into protective custody. Her paper records are sparse, and with the exception of finding the name of Anton Perelli, a former deputy director at the bureau, I found little else in her files. Thomas is retired and unreachable in Thailand for a few more days, but when he gets back, I'm hoping he can shed some light on the situation."

"What about Perelli?" Wyatt asked the marshal.

"He died of a heart attack recently. We won't be getting any more out of him."

"There are no other files?" Vivi asked.

On the other end of the line, Mikaela hesitated. "I suspect there are. Somewhere. But I can't find them, and after my warning to Carly not to go acting like a bull in a proverbial technical china shop, I didn't want to do the same. I have one person on my team working on it, and she *will* find them, but it may take some time."

"I can help," Naomi offered.

Realizing Mikaela didn't know everyone in the room, Drew went ahead and made the introductions. When he got to Naomi, he included a litany of projects Naomi had worked on for various other agencies. When Naomi provided her security clearance, or at least the one she was allowed to disclose publicly, Mikaela let out a deep breath.

"Thank you," the marshal said. "We could use the help and it's starting to piss me off how buried everything is."

"I was able to dig some stuff up already," Naomi said, looking to Carly for direction on how much to reveal. When Carly nodded her consent, Naomi relaxed back in her seat. Her fingers keying away on her laptop the entire time she spoke, she told the room about FBI agent Joe Franks—aka Joe Kincaid—and Vince Archstone—also an alias, she assumed—whom she hadn't had a chance to look for quite yet.

"What is Joe Franks doing now?" Wyatt asked.

"He's a Deputy Director, based out of New York, assigned to one of the anti-terrorism teams," Naomi answered.

"I could look into him," Wyatt offered. "I'm a relatively new agent so if I go looking around at the profiles of seasoned agents, I can make it look like career research. That way, Naomi will have more time to look into whoever this Vince guy is and also help the marshals track down those files."

Marcus and Carly shared a look before Marcus spoke. "That sounds like a good idea. Anyone have any objections?"

No one did, so Naomi picked up her train of thought. "I can continue to look for Vince, but do you think either of you could give a sketch artist a decent likeness of him—at least of what you remember him looking like? That picture Carly had of Joe was what made finding him so easy."

"I can do that," Marcus said.

"Perfect," Naomi said. "Deputy Marsh, it would be great if you could put me in touch with your tech person. I also want to dig back and see what I can find about what Joe Franks might have been up to around the time he was seeing Sophia Davidson."

"What kind of records are you talking about?" Carly asked.

Naomi lifted a shoulder. "I'm thinking bank, phone, credit card records, those sorts of things." As every law enforcement officer, other than Drew, began raising objections, she added, "All legally obtained, of course."

"Deputy Marsh," Ian said, once it was clear Naomi had her marching orders.

"Call me Mikaela," she cut him off.

"Mikaela," Ian began again, "I know you are looking for regular files, but have you thought of checking property records?"

"Housing records?" she asked.

Ian shook his head. "No, records that track where witnesses' physical property goes. I'm not sure about the marshals, but I know sometimes the system that tracks the case files and the system that tracks the physical evidence are two different systems. If a case is really old or has gone cold, people sometimes forget the property files exist. If we can find some of the physical evidence from the case, it might help us get a better picture of what was going on."

"I hadn't thought of that," Mikaela said. "About eight years ago, most of the federal agencies updated their property intake and tracking systems, but I would bet any physical evidence the FBI collected fourteen years ago from the Davidson/Lamot home wouldn't have been updated in those systems. Now we have to find someone within the FBI we trust to go check."

"I have someone I can call right after this," Ian said.

"He does," Vivi said, confirming Ian's statement. "Ian can give his contact a call in a bit and we'll let you know, Deputy Marsh."

"And what about the property that wasn't taken into evidence?" Wyatt asked. "Like your house," he added. "Assuming you had one."

"We did. And horses," Carly answered.

Drew hadn't known the family had had a farm, and by the way her voice had caught when she'd mentioned the horses, he could tell that she'd lost even more in the events fourteen years earlier than she'd let on.

"I can look into that," Drew said. "With my business and professional connections, it's something I can do while Mikaela and Ian's contacts are looking into what's inside the system."

Carly eyed him. "Thank you."

"Now, it's my turn," Vivi said, her gaze focused on Carly. "I know you have probably gone over this at least a thousand times in your head, but can you tell me exactly what happened in the days leading up to your mother's death?"

"Why don't you both take a seat before you do?" Drew suggested, gesturing to the siblings.

"Oh, of course," Vivi said, rising. Ian waved her back down

before he and Drew went to the kitchen to retrieve two chairs, as all the others were presently taken.

Carly flashed him a grateful look and quietly whispered another, "Thank you," as he put a chair down for her. A few seconds later, she was seated and focused on Vivi, while Marcus, beside her, looked to be trying to conjure his own memories.

"I was horse-crazy back then. My mom and I bred and raised several horses and I spent about every waking hour that I wasn't at school, or doing homework, at the barn. Of course I remember Joe and Vince, and I remember my mom being so happy to have Joe back in her life. They'd known each other in high school."

"It was the happiest she'd been with a man in my memory," Marcus interjected.

"Did she date a lot?" Vivi asked, the sympathy in her voice making it a compassionate question, rather than a judgmental one.

Carly shook her head. "Not that I know of. I remember a few men over the years, maybe two or three?" She looked to Marcus to confirm and, after a moment, he nodded in agreement.

"So she was happy with Joe," Vivi repeated, prompting them to continue.

"I do remember some tension in the house at that time," Carly went on. "Not *between* my mom and Uncle Tony, but I think something was bothering both of them. But of course, they didn't say anything to me."

"Did they say anything to you, Marcus?" Vivi asked.

Marcus shook his head, paused, then shook it again. "No, they didn't. It seems like maybe if it had to do with any of the businesses we owned, I should have known about it. I'd been working at my uncle's side since I was fifteen. I mean, I'd gone off to college, but I loved business and he knew it, and my mom knew it, so I spent a lot of time with him early on learning about everything."

"But your uncle didn't say anything?" Ian asked.

Again, Marcus shook his head. "No, but I was only home from college for about three weeks before my mom sent us to Los Angeles. She said it was to visit her old nanny who was like family to all of us, but in retrospect, I know she wanted to get us out of the house because three days later she was dead."

Marcus turned his gaze down while Carly turned hers toward the window that faced out the front of the house. With her profile to him, Drew could see her blinking away tears and wondered how many times over the years she'd had to hide her pain. He almost called a halt to the meeting. He wanted to take her away and give her the space and freedom to mourn the death of her mother—probably for the first time since it had happened.

But Marcus cleared his throat and continued. "What I know is limited, since I wasn't living at home most of the time. And as for Carly, she was just a kid when this all happened, doing the things kids do, paying attention to the things kids pay attention to."

"We were all sixteen at some point, Marcus. I think we all remember what it was like and no one expects Carly to know things beyond what she's told us," Vivi said, making sure both siblings knew that no one faulted them for their lack of information.

"But what else *do* you remember, Carly? You remember tension in the house, you remember Joe and Vince, and you remember your mom and Joe being happy. Is there anything else?" Vivi asked.

Drew watched as Carly pulled in on herself, trying to recall days and moments from years ago. The task was almost impossible, but given that those hours were probably indelibly burned into her mind as the last times she saw her mother, he held some hope that she might remember something.

"We had a sick horse, a young mare we'd imported. The vet had been out. His name was Doctor Haney. My primary competition horse was getting ready to be shipped to Long Island for a big show I was going to ride in when I got back from Los Angeles. Two others I was slated to ride for someone else were also scheduled to be shipped, along with three sale horses."

"Did the shippers visit the farm?" Mikaela asked.

"No," she said with a shake of her head. "They didn't. They shipped for us a lot so were accustomed to our needs. They were scheduled to arrive five days after I left, so I spent most of my time before leaving for Los Angeles getting both the horses and the equipment ready. When they came, my mom and the barn manager would have just had to get everything loaded. Obviously, that didn't happen," she added, casting her gaze down.

"Was there anything else?" Vivi pressed gently.

Again, Carly seemed to withdraw to think. After a few moments, she frowned.

"What?" Marcus asked.

She shook her head then shrugged. "I don't know, it's probably nothing, but before we left for Los Angeles, Mom gave me a new pair of earrings. A small set of diamond studs. I've only worn them once or twice because I think she gave them to me to match the pin I wore on my jacket during competitions. I mostly just set them aside because I never rode in a competition again."

Vivi open her mouth to say something, but Drew spoke first. "But there was something different about them, wasn't there?" he asked. "Now you're thinking about them, what made them come to mind?"

Carly's eyes came up and locked on his. She was silent, then, keeping her eyes on his, she spoke. "It's probably nothing, but when she gave them to me, she said they were earrings Joe had given to her when they had been high-school sweethearts. She said that Joe had been her first love, and while her love for my dad was real and strong, she felt lucky to have been given another chance with the man the boy she'd once loved had turned into. She told me the earrings had been his grandmother's, but she wanted me to have them."

"Did she say why?" he asked. His heart began hammering in his chest as he waited for her answer. Thankfully, he didn't have to wait too long. When she spoke, her voice was soft and a hint of wonder had crept into it, as if surprised that she had one more memory of her mother to hold onto.

"She said they were for luck and for love. She said neither were predictable, but when they happened, we needed to ride the wave and be grateful for the time it carried us."

His gaze stayed locked on hers, then Vivi shifted in her seat, no doubt trying to bring their attention back to the room. After another beat, he broke eye contact and glanced at Vivi, whose eyes were fixed on him, a single eyebrow raised. He half expected her to point out that she'd clearly been right that day in her office when she'd called him on his attraction to Carly, but being more subtle than that, she turned back to Carly.

"So, you think they were given to you for sentimental reasons?" Vivi asked.

Carly looked at her friend, blinked then slowly lifted a shoulder. "I thought so at the time. I guess I still think so. Only then I thought they were for luck for the upcoming show and now I think they were her way of giving me a reminder of what she wanted for me: love and happiness." Her eyes darted back to Drew, but then just as quickly went back to Vivi.

"Okay," Ian said on a deep breath. "Here's where I think we are. Naomi is going to do her computer magic and see what she can find on Vince Archstone, Joe Franks's history, and any files the marshals might have on the Davidsons. Wyatt is going to learn all he can about Joe Franks now to see if he is the dirty agent they were investigating back then. Marcus, you're going to go up to Albany and work with the sketch artist. Mikaela, you're going to connect your tech person to Naomi and follow up on the physical property once I check with my contact. Drew, you're going to look into what happened to the house and horses—"

"And businesses," he interjected. "Marcus mentioned the family owned businesses, we don't know what happened to them. I'll find out," he added.

Marcus looked up. "We should talk about that."

Drew held his gaze, suspecting Marcus had more to offer than run-of-the-mill details. "Why don't we talk after you meet with the sketch artist," he suggested. Marcus didn't look thrilled with the idea, but he agreed and they both turned their eyes back to Ian, prompting him to continue.

"And so that leaves us . . ." he said, looking at his wife and handing the topic over to her.

Vivi took her cue. "I'm going to talk to John, the head of the behavioral science team at the FBI, about the psychology of dirty cops. It's not my area, but I want to hear what he has to say about why, after fourteen years, a dirty cop might suddenly reappear."

"And I have three more boxes of things to go through," Carly added her part. "Most of it will be things from when I lived with Lorraine, but some of it will be stuff Marguerite brought to me after our placement. I haven't opened them in years and I don't think they'll contain anything useful. But at this point," she shrugged and let her voice trail off.

"I'll help you," Drew said, earning a look this time not just from Vivi but from Ian and Wyatt too. Naomi didn't so much as look at him as try, unsuccessfully, to suppress a grin. "I'll need to spend an hour or two working later this afternoon, but I can help now."

"That would be great, thank you," Carly said.

"And so that leaves you, my dear," Vivi said turning to her husband.

"I'll keep everyone on task and watch Jeffery today, since Lucas has to leave. I figure that will leave you free to do what you need to," he said. "And, if we all want to meet again back here tonight, I can make sure everyone gets fed," he added, making his wife smile.

"That would be great, thank you," Vivi said to him. It did not escape Drew's notice that Carly had said those same words to him.

Not wanting to be subjected to another one of Vivi's inquisitive looks, he moved farther into the room and looked at Carly. When she met his gaze he spoke. "Are you ready?"

She held his gaze, took a deep breath, and nodded.

CHAPTER THIRTEEN

DREW TURNED HIS CAR AROUND, waited for Carly to pull out ahead of him, then followed her down Vivi and Ian's drive. In his rearview mirror, he saw Marcus and Vivi talking as they watched them drive away.

For a moment, he wondered if they were talking about him, then chuckled at the thought. They might be curious about him, but he was hardly the most interesting thing going on in Windsor.

He used his time in the car to call to a friend in the private security industry. There were few people he trusted more than Jay Alexander and his team, which included Dani and Ty, and asking Jay to ferret out what had happened to the Lamot/Davidson holdings would free him up to do whatever Carly might need him to do. He still wanted to talk with Marcus, but given that Marcus had only been nineteen when he'd lost the family holdings, Drew preferred to get the details from an experienced, less-involved party.

As he pulled up beside Carly in front of her house fifteen minutes later, he ended his call. He could hear her punching in the alarm code when he stepped onto the porch and as he closed the door behind him, he noticed that she kept her eyes averted from his as she silently reached out for his jacket.

"Hey," he said, as she moved past him. She draped their jackets on the backs of two kitchen chairs, then headed toward the stairs. "How are you?" he asked.

"Fine," she said as she started up the steps.

"Carly?" he said, not moving from where he'd stopped inside

the door. She could ignore him or she could stop; he thought the odds were fifty-fifty either way.

Pausing with her back to him, she hesitated, then turned.

"How are you?" he repeated.

She pursed her lips and looked away. But then looked back and met his eyes. "I don't know," she said. "Honestly? I think I'm still letting it all sink in. I have more questions than answers—about more than just what happened to Marguerite and why. But I don't have the time or the space I know I need to think about it, so I'm going to do the only thing I know I can do right now and that's work. I know I can't work this like any other case, I can't really stay unemotional about it, but I can follow the processes and procedures I've been trained to follow, and deal with the emotions as they come."

Drew looked at her for a long moment. She was entering the fray without hesitation and with her eyes wide open, well aware that she'd be dealing with her own memories and emotions and doubts as they navigated this investigation. He'd worked with some of the toughest women—people—in the business, and in his opinion, Carly held her own with all of them.

He gave a sharp nod, "What do you need me to do?"

She offered him a small smile. "Help me get the boxes down?"

"Of course, where are they?"

She waved a hand behind her, "In my closet upstairs."

Without another word, he followed her up. The staircase came to a small landing at the top before it made a ninety-degree turn to the right, which led to two more steps up before entering the bedroom.

As Drew stepped into the room, his eyes swept over the bed and landed on the set of wide French doors that led out onto another little porch. His gaze lingered there, it would be a great place to have a morning cup of coffee.

The wide plank oak floors, the kind that weren't seen much anymore, had rough-hewn edges and uneven coloring, lending themselves to the charm of the renovation. Painted a colonial gray and lined with cream-colored wainscoting, the wall colors went well with both the dark wood of the floors and Carly's Shaker-style bed. The simple elegance of the king-sized piece, capped off with a colorful quilt, created a warm and inviting space.

The room itself ran the full length of the house and sat on top of the living room. A doorway to his left looked to lead to a bathroom, and one to his right presumably led to the closet—both of which sat over the kitchen/dining area side of the house.

"Over here," she said, leading him toward the door to his right.

"It's a beautiful room," he commented, following her into a large walk-in closet. Carly hastily picked up a few items of clothing from the floor and tossed them into a linen basket.

"Thank you, the owners did as good a job up here, as they did downstairs, and I do love it. The boxes we need are up there." She pointed to three cardboard containers sitting on the top shelf of her closet. One sat on its own while two were stacked on top of each other. "I put them up there when I moved in. I've unpacked the rest of my things, but I put these away since I had no intention of unpacking them."

He reached for the two stacked on top of each other and began to slide them toward himself. "Why not?" he asked, placing them on the floor and reaching for the third, bigger box.

"Most of what will be in there are things I collected while I was living with Lorraine, and just a few things from my previous life. When I finished college and the academy and then got a job, I guess I figured I probably didn't have much use for whatever was in them, so I've kept them closed up."

Handing her the larger, but lighter, of the three, he hoisted the other two then gestured for her to lead them out of her bedroom— away from her inviting bed—and back downstairs.

"You don't sound like you're expecting to find anything." He set his boxes down on the coffee table as she set hers near the fireplace.

She took a seat on the floor beside her box and shook her head. "I think we need to go through them. After all, I did find the picture with Joe in it in one of my old books, but do I think we'll find a smoking gun or something that will explain what happened? No," she said, shaking her head.

He agreed, but dutifully, he sat on the sofa and opened the first of the two boxes in front of him. He wondered if she felt any sense of nervousness about having him go through her life like this, but when he looked up, she was already engrossed in her own box. Turning his eyes back to what lay before him, he pulled out two spiral bound notebooks.

Flipping through the pages of her notes from what looked to be two of her senior year classes—one for math and one for physics—he set them aside. Finding three more like it, he quickly dispensed with those as well. Glancing up at Carly, he saw that she'd pulled out a few items of clothing and a couple of framed pictures, one of which she held on her lap.

"What are those?" he asked.

She looked up with a start, as if she'd forgotten that she wasn't alone.

"Pictures?" he asked, glancing at the frame she held.

Silently, she held up an image of a horse standing alert and alone in a misty field—its head up and ears forward. The lighting suggested a warm, humid morning just starting to heat up and the full trees in the background pointed to summer. The beauty and the solitude of the herd animal had been captured in a startlingly vulnerable moment.

"Did you take it?"

"I did." Carly glanced at the photo again, then set it aside. "When we were put into the program, when we went to live with Lorraine, I had to give up horses altogether. Not only did I no longer have the money for it, but I was too well known in that world to show my face there. Even if I'd disguised myself, people would have recognized me."

"So you had to quit cold turkey?"

Her eyes darted away. "Yeah."

He considered asking if she ever thought about riding again as an adult. But maybe, having had to give up something she'd loved, it was less painful to give it up altogether than to try to keep hold of it with one hand.

Without another word, he went back to his box. There were more photos in the binder he'd pulled out. Slowly, he turned the pages of what must have been a senior project or portfolio.

The subjects were people doing everyday things—walking down streets, gardening, playing soccer, smiling with friends, swimming in a pond somewhere. But the lighting and composition gave each photo a life of its own. Looking at one in particular, a picture of an older woman in a garden, Drew could almost hear the conversation between the woman and Carly as Carly shot it. Whoever she was, she looked back at the camera with a smile on her face, a laugh hanging in the air. She carried a basket of flowers and the light caught the edges of her summer dress. It was simple, but the still image had more life to it than he saw in many living people.

"These are remarkable," he said as he continued to flip through the images.

When she said nothing, he looked up to find her watching him.

"What are you looking at?" she asked, unable to see what he held on his lap. He lifted the portfolio.

"Oh that. It was my senior project."

"You're very good."

She lifted a shoulder. "Thanks."

"Do you take photos anymore?"

She started to shake her head, then hesitated. "Not really. Occasionally, if there is an event in town, I'll help out the newspaper—take some pictures and give them the images if they need them. But generally, no, I don't."

Drew made a mental note to himself to ask her more about her photography when the situation had settled down. With one last compliment on her work, he set the collection aside and pulled out a small box.

"I can't believe Lorraine kept this." Carly's voice brought his head up. She held up a dress. A formal dress.

His lips tilted into a lopsided grin. "Prom?"

She laughed and turned the dress around so that she could look at it. The color of burnt orange, a color only someone with her skin tone and hazel eyes could pull off, the dress dangled in her hands. It had a V in the front and a deeper V in the back and looked to be something that would hug every one of her curves.

"Homecoming, hence the fall color. I can't believe I wore this," she said with a smile.

"What's wrong with it?" He had no problems picturing her in it.

She made a face. "It's a bit mature, isn't it? I mean, I was eighteen. This looks like something I'd wear to the policeman's ball *now*."

He blinked. "Maybe you should see if it still fits."

Her eyes shot to his and then she laughed. "Like it, do you?"

"It's a little more revealing than the dress you were wearing when I saw you in the city last summer, when you were with Kit." Although there had been something about that dress too, that had caught and held his attention. It had been looser than the one she held now—not a dress made to hug or cling, but one that would easily shift and slide with the gentlest of touches. "Do you still have the anklet you were wearing that night?" he asked, then wondered if perhaps he shouldn't have—the memory of that little piece of jewelry made his mind go all sorts of places.

"You noticed my anklet?"

"Not to put too fine a point on it, but I have mentioned a time or two that my attention to detail is extraordinary."

She stared at him as if wondering what other details he might remember, then abruptly set the dress down and reached for something else in the box. "Yes, of course I still have it," she answered, then added nothing more.

Drew felt his temperature spike a good ten degrees. But he'd made a promise to himself to let her be the first to make a move—when a move was to be made. So he turned his focus back to the wooden jewelry box he'd just pulled out of the box.

Opening it, he found a picture lying on top of everything else inside. Obviously, not one she'd taken—in it, Carly posed in the same dress she'd been holding a moment ago. A corsage decorated her wrist and one of her arms looped through that of a young man in a suit. Her hair, much longer than she wore it now, hung down her back, with pieces of it pulled up, giving her the look of someone in a period piece. She wore no necklace, but in her ears he could see a pair of diamond stud earrings. When he lifted the photo out of the box, he saw that beneath it lay those same studs.

"Are these the earrings your mother gave you?" Drew asked, holding them out to her.

Carly looked up sharply from a book she had been thumbing through. Coming to her knees and reaching across the coffee table, she held out her hand. He dropped the studs in her outstretched hand, then watched her examine the two pieces.

"Yes, they are."

"You look like you didn't remember you had them."

"No, I knew I had them, but like I said, I haven't seen them in years. I left them with Lorraine when I went to college and haven't needed them since. I guess I figured they were safer packed away than lying in my bathroom drawer somewhere."

Or maybe, he thought, she hadn't wanted the reminder. "Do you want to put them back in this box? The one with the picture of you and Mr. Young Stud in it?"

She stared at him blankly. He held up the picture. A smile started to spread across her face, one that turned into a laugh within seconds. "Oh my god," she said, reaching for the picture, "that's Luke Dunfey. He was a friend of my brother's. We dated for a bit during my senior year in high school and first year of college."

"Your brother let you date one of his friends?"

"Hey, your brother married one of your friends," she shot back, referring to Sam and Jason.

"Wait, *the* Luke Dunfey?" Drew asked. He'd been about to point out that Sam and Jason had grown up together but the comment died on his lips when he suddenly recognized the name.

Carly laughed again and set the picture down. "Yes, the very same. He was a good guy. I've followed his politics and it seems like he's *still* a good guy," she said. One of the few respected independents in congress, in some circles the thirty-five-year old senator was already being dubbed the next John F. Kennedy.

"I can't believe you dated Luke Dunfey," Drew grumbled as he handed her the jewelry box that had held the picture and the earrings. She slipped both back inside as she set it on the table.

"You dated Sierra Sloane," she said even as she went back to digging in the box beside her.

"How did you know I dated Sierra?" he asked, surprised. Three months earlier, he and Sierra, a woman who rightfully held the title of super model, had been on exactly four dates.

"Kit told me. I guess she knew Sierra from some parties they'd both attended in Europe and was not pleased to see pictures of the two of you," Carly said.

"We went on four dates. And why would that bother Kit?"

She shrugged. "I don't know. I didn't ask. She just said she didn't think someone so 'in the limelight' was the right person for you."

Drew had figured out the same thing after the first two dates, but the last two had been events he'd already agreed to go to with her, so he hadn't been able to break things off sooner. And now, looking at Carly sitting on her knees going through a pile of books and folders, he couldn't agree more—he had no interest in being in the limelight, on his own or with someone else.

"What's this?" He had reached back into his box and pulled out a DVD. It had the image of a riding arena filled with fences on the cover and a title that referred to a Long Island Classic.

"Oh, wow," Carly reached for what he'd found once again. "It's a collection of videos taken of my rides from the last time I competed at that venue. I took it with me to LA because I wanted to study it. This is the event I was supposed to ride at, the one the horses were being shipped to when my mom was killed."

"Do you have a DVD player?"

"Yes." As she bobbed her head, one of her curls fell into her face; she brushed it back subconsciously, her eyes trained on the DVD cover.

"Do you want to watch it?" he asked, wondering if it was a good idea.

She shook her head. "Or, not yet, at least. I want to get through all these boxes before we reconvene at Vivi's tonight. Maybe if there's time later . . ." She let her voice trail off.

Drew heard the hesitation in her voice so he let it go and turned back to his box.

Another hour passed as they thumbed through every book and notebook, examined the front and back of each photo, and did a thorough search of everything else, including all the pockets and linings of the clothing.

By about four o'clock, they had separated the contents of the boxes into two piles: items Carly wanted to donate, which included mostly clothes and a few books, and a pile of stuff to go back into a consolidated box and into her closet. Drew loaded up all of her portfolio pictures, along with her two yearbooks and a few other mementos, into the combined box. The earrings she kept out, but the picture of her with Luke Dunfey joined the other keepsakes.

By unspoken agreement, after tidying up and washing the dust off their hands, Carly poured them each a cup of coffee and they went to sit on the porch. They needed to be at Vivi's in a few hours, and a little quiet time together would do them both good.

But after only a few moments of silence, Carly spoke. "What do you think this is all about?"

Drew looked down at the dark liquid in his mug, feeling like his thoughts were about as clear. He shook his head. "I don't know, and that's what worries me."

"But why now? Why after all these years would someone track us down?" she asked.

"The obvious answer is that whoever is involved is going to start again. They think you know something and they want to keep you quiet."

"But we don't."

"That hardly matters if they *think* you do. And of the two questions—why and why now—I don't think why is the more interesting of the two."

"Meaning?" she pressed.

"Meaning, I think what's most interesting about this situation isn't that it's happening, but that it's happening *now*, nearly fifteen years later."

"Why was there such a long lapse of time and what has happened that would bring all this up again?" she clarified.

"Yes. I know Vivi is going to look into it, and I think if we can figure that out, we'll be able to figure out the rest."

"You mean like a triggering event with a serial killer? Figure out what the trigger is—what happened recently—and maybe it will lead us to whoever is doing this?"

He turned his gaze to the lake. "Maybe. Maybe it's happening now because whoever he is just got out of jail, or, since we think a fed is involved, maybe he has been stationed abroad for the past fifteen years and just came back. Or maybe someone just came across the case file and wanted to pick up wherever the corrupt FBI agent left off. Maybe it isn't even related to what happened fourteen years ago."

"It could be a hundred and one different things."

"Which is why we need all the data everyone is digging for today." He stood and reached for her now empty mug.

She eyed him, then handed it over and rose as well. "Whatever happens tonight—whatever we learn—thanks for going through all of this with me."

He nodded, knowing full well that what they were "going through" was just getting started.

• • •

Drew glanced out the window of his SUV and caught one last glimpse of the lights from the carriage house before the trees swallowed it from view. He didn't like leaving Carly alone, but he'd received a text from Rina shortly after they'd spoken that morning, making it clear she expected daily updates from him. He'd also received an interesting e-mail from Jay that he wanted to spend a little time focusing on, an e-mail best read in the privacy of his own—well, Kit's—home.

As soon he pulled into Kit's drive, he sensed that something wasn't right. He parked in front of the garage knowing no one needed access to it and sat in the quiet of his car, absorbing his surroundings. Within seconds, it came to him. Garret and Kit had taken one of their two cars to the airport when they'd left, leaving only Kit's SUV behind. But from where he sat, through a narrow window in the garage door, he could see the roof of a second vehicle parked next to Kit's.

The good news was that it wasn't likely to be that of a prowler. The bad news was, it was probably Kit's brother's. Not that he didn't like Caleb Forrester, but he had no interest in sharing his space with the man. Of course, Caleb wouldn't care one way or the other how Drew felt—with the exception of his sister, and maybe Garret, Caleb cared very little about anyone.

"Honey, I'm home," Drew called as he walked in the door. At least with Caleb he didn't have to worry about covering up his sarcasm or annoyance.

Caleb's head appeared from behind the open fridge door. Slowly he straightened up and, beer in hand, swung the door shut. "Carmichael. What are you doing here?"

"I could ask you the same. Your sister's party was last weekend, not this weekend."

Caleb shrugged and popped the top of his beer bottle. "I sent a donation."

"Not exactly the same thing," Drew said, feeling the other man watching him as he dropped his computer bag and folders on the kitchen island. When he looked up, sure enough, Caleb's golden eyes were tracking his every movement—eyes that even Drew found disconcerting every now and then, not that he'd ever admit it. "What?" he asked.

"I'm just passing through," Caleb said. "But you look like you're here on business. Is that company business or *business* business?" he asked with a gesture of his bottle toward the files.

Drew tapped the stack of files absentmindedly as his gaze went to the kitchen window. He didn't want to share Carly's situation with Caleb. But even as he acknowledged the thought, he knew he'd be crazy not to. Caleb had a wealth of experience to draw from and his analytic skills were just as strong as his physical ones. It was that combination of abilities that had Drew's own agency hiring him as a contractor on a near-regular basis.

"Does this have anything to do with the lovely Deputy Chief Carly Drummond?"

Drew's gaze landed sharply on Caleb.

Caleb tipped his head and Drew could've sworn he saw him smirk.

"I saw the way you looked at her when we were investigating the attack on Kit."

Drew's eye's narrowed and he had an overwhelming urge to tell Forrester to fuck off; instead, he slipped a file from the stack and held it out.

Leaning against the fridge, Caleb eyed the documents before taking a step forward and reaching for the file over the island. Drew pulled out his computer and turned it on as Caleb read.

"Well, hot damn. Witness security?" Caleb raised his eyes from the papers after a few minutes.

Drew nodded.

"I have to say, I didn't see that one coming." Caleb slid the file back.

"I think it's fair to say it came as a surprise to a lot of people."

"So what are you doing about it?"

As Drew entered in the series of passwords needed to access his company e-mail, he filled Caleb in on the task force and the upcoming evening meeting and meal. By the time he was finished talking, Caleb actually looked intrigued.

"That's a lot of firepower you have."

"Yes, it is," he said, bringing up an e-mail reply to update Rina. "You want to round us out? I'm sure Rina could get you assigned."

Caleb let out a snort. "Not on your life. Decision-making by consensus isn't my thing."

Drew looked at him over the screen of his laptop. "Ian's cooking."

"And that's going to be the best part of the night." Caleb finished his beer and moved to the sink to rinse the bottle. "I can tell you right now how your evening is going to go."

"Oh yeah?" Drew said, not bothering to look up from the report he was drafting.

"Naomi will have some crazy piece of information only she could dig up; Vivi will have some psych analysis that may or may not prove useful; Ian will suggest something so practical no one else will have thought of it; and Sam and Daniel will have a whole bunch of scientific things to contribute that no one but Vivi will understand."

Drew chuckled. "And what about the marshals?"

"Useless. The whole lot of them."

Drew didn't agree, but he also knew that Caleb was making a point just to make a point, and accuracy would only get in the way. "So you're saying you want to come? Because from what I'm hearing, it really sounds like you want to."

"Like I want an ice pick to the eye," Caleb said, heading toward the stairs that led down to the room where he always stayed when he was at Kit's.

"I'm sure Vivi would have a lot to say about your avoidance techniques."

Caleb gave him the finger as he disappeared down the stairs. Maybe having him around wouldn't be such a bad thing Drew thought, his smile lingering as he hit "send" on his report to Rina and then began downloading Jay's e-mail. But the smile faded quickly when Jay's report opened on his screen. Twenty minutes later, he was still neck deep in the content—he had no idea what it meant, but he knew for certain that he and Marcus would need to have a little chat.

CHAPTER FOURTEEN

RETURNING FROM ANOTHER RUN AT nine o'clock the next morning, Drew walked into a kitchen that smelled like coffee, sautéed onion, and even a little garlic. He hadn't forgotten that Caleb was there, Kit's brother was a hard presence to forget or ignore, but Drew had always imagined the guy subsisting on coffee and MREs—and maybe the souls of the damned—and he hadn't expected to find him making a full-on breakfast.

"Smells good." Drew walked to the sink and poured himself a glass of water.

"There's enough for two. Grab some coffee and a seat. It will take another fifteen minutes or so."

Not one to turn down a homemade meal, even if he wasn't entirely sure what the meal was going to be, Drew finished his water, grabbed a mug and filled it with coffee the color of tar, then took a seat. He eyed the computer he had left on the island when he'd returned from Vivi and Ian's the night before, but rather than open it, he opted to watch the show in front of him.

"So, tell me about last night. What shrinky-thing did Vivi come up with?" Caleb asked as he swirled what looked like cooked rice in a sauté pan. Facing the stove and with his back to the room, Drew only caught a few glimpses of the concoction Caleb was pulling together.

"Turns out corrupt cops are motivated by the same thing most criminals are. Money, power, and love."

"That seems like an underwhelming contribution from the girl-wonder."

Drew smiled. "We all agree that whomever we're looking for is motivated by power. The events that followed the killing of Sophia and Tony were too precise—too by the book—to lead us to believe that love or a lust for money were involved."

"And that gets you . . .?" Caleb flipped what looked like a piece of ham high into the air and caught it with the pan.

"Not far, admittedly, but we did also learn that, while corrupt cops who are in it for money or love have some unique characteristics that other criminals don't share, those in it for power more or less have the same psychology as a serial killer."

"So, basically, you're looking for a corrupt, murdering FBI agent that has sociopathic tendencies."

Drew ran a hand through his hair. "Yep, that about sums it up."

"What about Naomi? Surely she wasn't to be outdone by her cousin?"

Drew chuckled then looked around for his sweatshirt. His body had cooled from the run and he was beginning to feel chilled. Spying it hanging on the coat rack, he took a sip of coffee then rose from his seat. "She was not. Naomi found that the other person floating around the Lamot/Davidson house at the time, Vince Archstone, is actually Vince Repetto, a white-collar crime FBI agent. Based on the records she found—like receipts from restaurants where both men were present at the same time, that kind of thing—*and* those that she didn't find—like any official record of the investigation—we're thinking—"

"Counterintelligence," Caleb finished.

"We are, yes."

As Caleb poured eggs into a sizzling pan, Drew's stomach grumbled.

"But who was investigating whom? Was Repetto investigating Franks or the other way around? And how did Carly's family get involved?" Caleb asked, reaching for two plates out of a cabinet.

"We think Carly's family was targeted because, several years earlier, they had come on to the FBI radar, when her uncle was investigated for insider trading. Nothing came of that investigation—"

"But the FBI could easily use it to set up a new investigation by making it look like they were re-opening the original one."

"Exactly. And as to who was investigating whom, Naomi and Brian are working on that now."

"So that leaves Ian and the marshals. I can't imagine the marshals had anything to share, so what did the good sheriff have to say?"

Again, Drew chuckled. "Ian didn't actually contribute much other than dinner, but the idea he'd offered earlier in the day definitely bore fruit."

Caleb added rice to each plate. "Not at all surprising."

"He suggested that the marshals look for the physical property of the Lamot/Davidson's and not just the electronic records. He had a friend of his from the bureau help out, an Agent Rodriguez, since any files associated with the original investigation would be with the FBI."

"And I take it they found something?" Caleb added a slice of ham to each plate.

"Interestingly, they did." Drew paused to watch the plating.

When Caleb reached for the cooked eggs, he glanced back, apparently awaiting more information.

Drew continued, "It turns out that all the personal property from Carly and Marcus's home that was not taken into evidence was put into a private storage unit six years ago, and the key to that unit was found inside one of the boxes of evidence held by the FBI."

Caleb turned around with a plate in each hand, and paused. "You mean to tell me that six years ago someone approached the marshals and said 'Hey, we'd like to move the personal property of someone participating in your super-secret program and then hand the key to the FBI,' and the marshals let them?"

Drew reached for a plate. "We don't know if that's exactly what happened, but, yeah, something like that."

"That's fucked up." Caleb shook his head as he slid a fork over to Drew.

"Yep, Deputy Marsh wasn't too happy about it either."

"I told you. Useless. The whole lot of them. So where did you leave things?"

Drew took a bite of the unusual dish and sat back in surprise. "This is really good."

Caleb grinned. "I don't like to do things halfway. Of course it's good."

Drew rolled his eyes as he swallowed. "Vivi is looking into Franks and Repetto to see if she can help determine who is more likely to have the psychology of a killer. Naomi and Brian are doing more digging. The marshals are on their way up to Albany with the physical evidence and are also going to bring a few of Carly's personal things from the storage container. She and I are going to go through those this afternoon. And the rest of the team is going to keep doing what they do: Sam and Daniel will be working on the trace evidence as it comes in; Wyatt will see what more he can find out about Franks and Repetto through the FBI grapevine; and Marcus, well, he's working today, but he and I will be having a little talk soon."

Caleb finished chewing his bite then looked at his watch. "It took precisely fifteen minutes and forty-two seconds to tell me all that. How long was the meeting last night?"

"I left after an hour. The rest of them stayed for dinner."

Caleb's fork stilled halfway to his mouth. "You didn't stay for dinner?"

"No, I had some things I needed to do."

"Bullshit."

Drew's eyes came up from his plate to his companion. "You have quite the vocab today." Caleb wasn't generally one to swear all that much, at least not out loud. Hearing him do it twice in a conversation was notable.

"You were avoiding her friends." Caleb pointed his fork at Drew as he spoke. "That's why you didn't stay."

The look he gave Caleb told him to back off. But of course, he didn't.

"You don't want them to *not* like you, so you're not giving them the chance to form any opinion of you at all."

Drew cocked his head. "Is this about me, or about why you didn't come to your sister's fundraiser last weekend?"

Caleb glared at him for a long moment, then he dropped his fork to his plate and picked up his coffee. "All I'm saying is that Carly's friends are important to her. They should be important to you too."

Drew found that little piece of advice a bit ironic coming from Caleb, who rarely engaged in any social activity, unless Kit surprised him with it. Still, that didn't make it untrue. It also didn't make it something he wanted to discuss.

"Here," Drew said, firing up his computer and opening the report Jay had sent the day before. "Take a look at this." He slid the computer over and then turned his attention to finishing his breakfast while Caleb scanned the document. He'd just finished when Caleb looked up.

"Interesting timing."

"I thought so." He stood and reached for Caleb's empty plate, stacking it atop his before making his way to the sink.

"I see why you said you need to talk to Marcus. You going to do that this morning?"

Drew slipped the plates into the dishwasher. "I'm going to head over now, before I meet up with Carly." He reached for one of the pans—it was only fair that he clean up since Caleb had cooked—but Caleb waved him off.

"Go take care of this," he said, gesturing to the computer. "I can clean up."

Drew held the man's gaze for a moment, then nodded, closed his computer, and headed to his guest room.

• • •

An hour later, Drew parked in front of the Windsor Police Station. He planned to grab a couple of mochas from Frank's, and maybe even some pastries, but first things first.

"I was wondering when you'd find me," Marcus said from the doorway of Carly's office as soon as Drew walked in.

"We need to talk."

Marcus looked about as thrilled as Drew felt about the pending conversation, but he gestured him into the office. "It will be more private in here."

Much like Carly's home, the office said little about its inhabitant. Then again, he knew Marcus had been Deputy Chief before his sister, and that this had been his office. It would be like her not to touch anything when she'd temporarily moved in.

"Have a seat," Marcus offered, then walked over to the window and looked out. Drew thought about continuing to stand, but after a beat decided to sit, hoping it would ease some of the tension in the room, ease some of his own tension.

"You know what happened to the businesses, don't you?" Drew asked.

Keeping his back to Drew, for a long moment, Marcus remained silent. Then he nodded.

"Why haven't you said anything to Carly?" Drew asked.

Marcus ran a hand through his hair then rested it against the windowsill. "When I was twenty-seven, Marguerite arranged a meeting for me with Bill Wycoff, the chair of the board that oversees all the businesses," he started. "Carly was twenty-four at the time. I was out of the military, out of the police academy, and had just started my job here. She was getting ready to go to the academy after finishing her masters and I knew she planned to join me out here—either in Windsor, if she could, or somewhere nearby."

Marcus paused, tapped the wooden sill with his finger, then turned and took a seat behind the desk.

"Bill told me about the will my mom and uncle had left. He told me about how we both inherited all the businesses when I turned twenty-eight." Again, Marcus paused, his eyes focused on nothing in particular except maybe the past.

"He wanted to know what I wanted to do." He picked up his narrative again with a heavy voice. "He told me that all the horses had been sold, which was something both Carly and I figured had happened, since they couldn't very well take care of themselves, but the news about the will and the businesses surprised me."

"Did it?" Drew asked. Because he didn't believe it.

Marcus's eyes came up and a sardonic smile touched his lips. "No, I guess it didn't *really* surprise me. I guess I meant that I didn't ever give it any thought. If I had, of course I would have expected us to get the inheritance at some point. But it, well . . ." His voice trailed off.

"It wasn't something you had let yourself think about, was it?"

Marcus shook his head.

"And so you told him no?"

Marcus pushed away from the desk and stood again. "I told him no," he answered as he paced back to the window. "More specifically, I told him to set up a trust or power of attorney and keep the businesses running without me. That was six years ago. That's why all the property was transferred into private holdings at that time. Marguerite arranged it all."

"You said you wanted to go into the family businesses. You had a chance. Why did you say no?"

"Because of Carly, damn it." The window rattled as Marcus slapped his hand against the wall. "She was so young when it happened. You should have seen her." As Marcus spoke, Drew heard years of frustration in his voice. "She was shattered. Everything she knew was gone, everyone she knew was gone. All she had was me. And eventually Lorraine and Marguerite, but that was some time in coming."

"You lost everything, too."

Marcus paused, perhaps letting those words sink in. Then he let out a deep breath. "I did. But if I'd taken over the businesses and we'd come back out into public as ourselves, as Carolyn and

Michael Davidson, with whomever had killed my mom and uncle still out there, it wouldn't have been me they would have come after. It would have been Carly."

"And you couldn't have that," Drew finished.

Marcus looked up sharply. "Of course not. Who in his right mind wants to give his sister a death sentence?"

Drew regarded the younger man. Despite all his issues, Marcus wanted to do the right thing. At least when it came to his sister.

"You don't believe me?" Marcus demanded, taking his silence for something it wasn't—judgment.

"Of course I believe you, and obviously you were right to be concerned about Carly's safety, especially given what's happened recently. But you said you did it for her. I have to think maybe you did it a little for yourself, too, and that's a good thing. I believe you made the decision you did to protect her, but the thought of losing your sister wasn't one you wanted to contemplate either, was it?"

Marcus stared at him. Then he shook his head. "No, we don't have a lot left of our pasts, but we do have each other," he replied quietly.

Drew rose from his seat. "I'm glad you realize that. I'm glad you see your decision was as much for her as it was for you."

"Why's that?" Marcus asked, turning toward Drew, shoving his hands into his pockets.

"Because she's going to need to know that when you tell her."

"When I tell her?"

"She knows I'm looking into the businesses and horses. She'll expect some information. She *could* get it from me. But I think it might be better if she got it from you."

As Marcus stared at him once again, Drew could practically hear the other man's train of thought—moving from denying that he'd need to say anything, to protesting that he should, then finally to resigning to the fact that he would.

Marcus nodded.

"Soon?"

Marcus's mouth tightened, "Yes, soon."

"Good." He rose then showed himself out, leaving Marcus to decide the particulars.

Taking long strides down Main Street as he left the police station and headed toward Frank's Café, Drew made a mental note to mention Marguerite's role in the movement of the property to the private facility to Mikaela—that was one good thing to come of the conversation he'd just had, at least they had an answer to that question.

But even with a new piece of the puzzle in hand, restlessness plagued his body. Working in intelligence, he should be used to the snail's pace of an investigation, he told himself. This investigation should be no different. Only it was. There was so much more at stake than simply closing a case, and both his body and his mind seemed to feel the urgency.

Fifteen minutes later, he pulled up in front of Carly's house and parked his car next to hers. Taking a breath that in no way reduced his disquiet, he grabbed his offerings and made his way to her porch. Before he'd even had a chance to knock, she opened the door. He paused, taking her in, then handed her a to-go cup of coffee.

"Thanks," she said, taking it, but rather than stepping back to allow him in, she leaned against the doorframe and regarded him.

"Is everything okay?" he asked.

She tilted her head. "I *think* so."

"May I come in?" he asked with only slightly exaggerated formality.

"Why don't you like spending time with my friends?" she asked, not moving.

He drew back. "I beg your pardon?"

"Why don't you like spending time with my friends?" she repeated. "The other night, when Matty and Dash and the twins came over, you couldn't leave fast enough. Then again, last night, as soon as the update on the case was finished, you were out of there. And don't tell me it's because you had to write a report for your boss, because I know you did that *before* the meeting, and even if you wanted to *update* it, that wouldn't have taken more than thirty minutes."

Caleb's comments from earlier echoed in his mind. But Caleb had only touched on half the truth. Staring down at Carly, Drew seriously considered lying—or not really lying, but throwing her a soft answer. But he only thought about it for a moment.

"Because I'm not good at making friends," he replied. "I can count on one hand the number of friends I have that aren't related by blood or marriage. It's easier that way, in my line of business—there's no one to notice my erratic hours, no one to ask how my last trip went, no one to ask where I'm going or when I'll be back."

She blinked at him and he could tell his bleak assessment of himself hadn't been what she'd expected. Even *he* heard the dissatisfaction in his voice. And the honesty of that emotion gave him pause, making him question the true source of the frustration he'd been penning up—was it really the investigation, or was it his *life*?

"But you went to college, surely you have college friends or friends from growing up?"

He exhaled a deep breath. "I have acquaintances that were friends at one time. People I can go to dinner with once every few years or grab a drink with on a random night here or there."

Carly may have been forced to keep a big secret, but in her adult life, she'd managed to make friends—and good ones, judging by what he'd seen. He knew she saw some parallels in their two lives, and truth be told, he did too in some ways, but the fact was that they were different. A single big secret had put her life on a different track. But Drew, well, he switched tracks on a near-daily basis. Secrets and lies were a fluid constant for him, not a single defining event—and that lifestyle was clearly starting to take its toll.

"I see," she said, giving nothing away in the steady gaze she'd locked onto him. But then her eyes shifted over his shoulder toward a sound coming from behind him. He heard it too. A truck.

No, not a truck, a van, with Mikaela Marsh at the wheel and someone else in the passenger seat. Carly mentioned something about grabbing her shoes and within a minute she rejoined him in the driveway to greet the marshals.

"The storage locker with your personal belongings was better organized than had I anticipated, so it was easy to grab your things. I have nine boxes of yours, plus the fifteen filled with evidence that I want to get up to Albany quickly," Mikaela said with a pointed look at the coffee and bag of pastries Drew still held.

"Let me run those inside," Carly said, taking the bag and his cup. When she came back out, he and Mikaela's deputy already had the van open.

"Mario will need to stay with the evidence, but the three of us can carry the rest of the boxes in," Mikaela said as Carly joined them at the back of the van.

"Where do you want them?" Drew asked.

"In the living room," Carly replied, eying the contents of the van. "I moved my couch and chairs this morning, there should be plenty of room," she added, without a hint of concern about what he'd just told her—no pity, no attempt to make him feel better, no softness in her voice for him.

Fifteen minutes later, he and Carly stood on the porch and watched Mikaela and Deputy Mario Something-or-other back out and head up to Albany. When they'd left the drive, Drew turned to enter the house, but she held out her hand out to stop him.

"You should give it a try," she said.

His brows came together. "Give what a try?"

"Having friends. I happen to know you're a pretty good guy. A little elusive and maybe a little hard to read at times, but mostly a good guy."

"*Mostly* a good guy?" he repeated. She didn't seem to feel pity for him and his isolated existence—thankfully, since he seemed to be feeling enough of that for himself today.

She smiled at him. "Yes, *mostly* a good guy. If you were a *completely* good guy, there is no way you would have survived in the CIA for as long as you have. And since everything you've done is part of what has brought you here—and I happen to like that you're here—I'm glad you're only *mostly* a good a guy."

He shook his head but smiled at her logic. He'd never imagined that only being "mostly a good guy" could be such a good thing.

• • •

Drew eyed the last box as dusk rapidly approached. They'd gone through the others and, along with more videos, they'd found lots of pictures, books, ribbons from Carly's riding days, and a whole host of other things that would be found in a typical sixteen-year-old girl's room.

"How are you doing?" he asked as he placed another DVD on the pile they'd started.

Sitting cross-legged on the floor, she looked up from the photo album laying open in her lap. "Fine. "

When he raised his eyebrows at her in doubt, she opened her mouth to say something, then shut it, and the album, and stood. After stretching out her back, she took a seat in the chairs across from where he sat on the couch.

"Okay, I'm not fine. I'm not terrible either. I know that's what you're worried about, but it doesn't feel traumatic or anything like that. Honestly, it feels weird. Most people have a chance to outgrow things," she said, waving to some of the items scattered around her living room, such as two stuffed animals and her old bedside lamp with a shade she'd covered in stickers when she was a little girl.

"I didn't have that chance. It was there one day and gone the next. I feel dissociated from the person this girl was, so it feels a little like looking into someone else's life. I mean, I know I'm not," she said as she reached forward to pick up a photo in which a young version of herself stood beside a horse and held both a huge ribbon and a silver cup. "I know this was me. I remember the day this happened. But . . ." She let her voice trail off.

There were a lot of memories lying about her living room;

memories she hadn't let herself contemplate for years. It was going to take more than four hours for her to understand how she felt about it all—not the stuff, but what it represented, the extent of what she'd lost. "How about a break. And maybe a drink?" he suggested.

She smiled and put the photo back on the coffee table. "Perfect. And maybe a small snack too. I'm feeling a little peckish," she added as she stood.

Once they'd settled in the chairs on the porch, with cheese and crackers between them and whiskeys in hand, they sat in companionable silence for several minutes—until both their phones rang almost simultaneously. Drew cast Carly a curious glance, which was answered with one just as curious. They both answered.

"It's Marsh," Mikaela said on the other end of his phone.

"Mikaela," he said, to let Carly know who had called him.

"Vivi," Carly said into her phone keeping her eyes on him.

"I'm leaving the lab right now," Mikaela said, "but wanted to update you on the final autopsy results on Marguerite." Drew turned his attention back to the call.

"Vivi is talking to Carly right now," he said.

"I know. Vivi is going to walk her through what we found in the boxes. We didn't find any smoking guns, but there was a lot of data—Wyatt and Naomi are still culling through it. But I wanted to call you because the autopsy result isn't pretty."

"We didn't think it would be," Drew interjected.

"No, we didn't. But I figured I would tell you so that you can tell Carly."

Drew looked away from Carly, toward the north side of the pond, as he contemplated what Mikaela had just said. He'd had some idea of how bad the report would be, he'd seen the pictures. Apparently, it was only the tip of the iceberg.

"Talk to me," he ordered.

"She was hit on the head first. Not hard enough to kill her, but hard enough to knock her out."

"She must have fallen and picked up some trace evidence on her clothes at that point."

"She did. But it's not helpful. It was mostly dirt and gravel, and the chemical traces on it lead us to believe she was in a park about ten miles south of DC in Virginia. But where in that park, we don't know, though we do have people looking. We also have people reviewing street cams and local security videos to see if we can get a picture of her car entering or exiting."

"You haven't found her car have you?"

"No, and since we've had a BOLO out on it since we first identified her body, I'm thinking it's at the bottom of a lake or river somewhere."

Unfortunately, he agreed with that. They might find it someday, but unless they put a ton of resources into diving all waterways in the metro DC area, that "someday" was probably a long way off.

"I don't need to know the rest of the details. Just give me the highlights, anything new or different than what Vivi and Dr. Buckley found," he said.

"Two things," Mikaela started. "The first is that we think two people were involved. Based on an in-depth look at the faux gang markings cut into her skin, it looks like some were made by a person who was right-handed and some by a person who was left-handed."

Interesting. During the meeting at Vivi and Ian's the evening before, Naomi had said she thought only either Repetto *or* Franks was involved. Was she wrong? Or was yet another person involved?

"And what else?" he prompted.

"Well, the second thing isn't so much something we found in the autopsy, but a question raised by our examiner and seconded by Vivi. We know she was naked when she was tortured and killed. And before you ask, no she was not sexually assaulted. Surprisingly," Mikaela muttered. That kind of surprised him too. Tying a naked woman up, torturing her, and *not* sexually assaulting her had to say something about the perpetrator. Definitely something to ask Vivi.

"And?"

"And she was dressed before she was moved."

"Why go to the trouble of dressing the body before dumping it—if you've already mutilated it and shown no regard for it up until that point?"

"Exactly."

"I don't suppose we have any answers?"

Mikaela exhaled. "No, we don't. But Vivi is working on it. She called her friend John Levitt again and I know they were scheduled to talk tonight."

Drew glanced at Carly, he had no doubt that she and Vivi would make a plan to check in after that.

"Okay, so what are you up to now? Are you going back to DC tonight?" he asked.

"No, we're checking into a hotel in Windsor. Vivi and I thought it would be best for Mario and me to stick around for at least another day while we finish going through the evidence at the lab, plus it's possible Naomi will have something soon too. What about you? Did you two find anything in those boxes?"

"No, not yet. We have one more to go through, but for the most part, it's pictures and lots of videos of Carly's riding career—and things like books and yearbooks and mostly stuff you'd expect."

"Yeah, I didn't think you'd find anything, but it was worth a shot, and I'm glad she has at least some of her belongings back. Let me know if you find anything in the last box?"

"I will," Drew confirmed.

"And, last but not least, any recommendations for dinner around here?"

Drew smiled and directed her to The Tavern. The place held good memories for him; it was the first time he'd had more than just a glimpse of Carly outside of her work.

He ended his call with Mikaela at nearly the same time that Carly ended hers with Vivi. Resting his head against the back of his chair, he inhaled a deep breath of the fall evening air then rolled his head over to look at his companion on the porch.

"Lots of news, I take it?" he asked.

"Lots of potential news," she answered, staring out toward the pond. Then she turned to look over at him. And smiled. "Maybe the glass of whiskey wasn't such a good idea. You look tired," she said.

He smiled back. "Not physically tired, but frustrated. I was hoping they would find more."

"I know exactly what you mean." She began to unwrap herself from the blankets and stand up. "Come on. It's getting cold out here. Let's take our snack inside. I'll make some coffee, you can make a fire, and then we can fill each other in on the news."

He stood and picked up the platter as she gathered everything else and they headed inside—he to the living room, where he made some room on the coffee table for the platter then turned his attention to the fireplace.

He could hear Carly in the kitchen making coffee as he started the fire. When the kindling started to crackle and flame, he took a look at the woodpile. They had enough for now, but it wouldn't last too long into the night.

"Where do you keep your wood?" he asked as he came into the kitchen and paused by the back door.

"It's in a shed to the left of the—" Her voice cut off at the sound of a car pulling into her drive.

He knew of no reason why the hairs on the back of his neck should stand up. The car could be anyone. It could be Marcus or Ian or Vivi or even her friends Matty and Dash again. Intellectually, he knew that. But still, he stayed where he was, out of sight from the front door.

"Carly? Come over here," he managed to say.

She glanced at him, looked about to argue, then calmly walked toward him. The minute he could reach her, he grabbed her and pulled her against him.

"Do you think you might be overreacting?" she asked, pressed against his chest.

"Maybe," he conceded. They heard a car door shut and, despite her words, he could feel her body tense against his.

"It could be anyone. It could be Marcus," she said quietly.

"Could be."

"Drew."

Then there was a knock at the door. They both went still. Another knock. And then a voice.

"Hello? Hello? Carolyn? Are you here?"

Carly nearly shot out of his arms. He held her tight as she turned her eyes to him. He could feel his blood vessels expand as adrenalin flooded his system.

"Carly?" he whispered.

She'd gone pale, her eyes wild. "Oh my god, Drew. That's Joe Franks."

CHAPTER FIFTEEN

CARLY FELT EVERY MUSCLE IN Drew's body tense as his arms tightened around her. She watched his face change; the relaxed expression he'd worn all afternoon shifted to something altogether different. The man he'd been was gone, replaced by the seasoned agent.

"We need to call 911," she said.

He looked down at her. "You *are* 911. Do you have your weapon?"

She shook her head against his chest. "It's upstairs in the lock box." She didn't carry it in the house, had never had a need to. And in the five years she'd been working in Windsor, she'd only had to pull it out less than a half a dozen times and had never discharged it outside of the shooting range.

Franks knocked at the door again.

"Drew?"

What to do when a potentially corrupt FBI agent came knocking at her door wasn't something she'd been taught in the academy. Especially not when the agent was possibly the person responsible for her mother's death.

She could feel the blood pounding through her system, pulsing through her temples.

Drew released her a bit and squatted down. When he rose he had a small gun he'd pulled from his ankle holster.

"Call Ian first, since we know he's nearby, then call Marcus. He's probably still in Albany, but in case he's on his way back, we could use him," he said, taking his phone from his pocket and unlocking it before handing it over to her.

She took the phone. "What are you going to do?"

"I'm going to slip out the back door and come around behind him," he answered. "I want you to stay right here, though. Right here behind the stairwell where he can't see you."

She nodded, not taking issue with way he dispensed the order.

"Don't come into view until you hear me tell you to, okay?"

Again, she nodded. He gave her one last look, brushed his fingertips over her cheek, then slipped silently through the porch door and disappeared around the back of the house.

The knock came again and she backed as far against the stairwell as she could get. Without Drew standing beside her, she felt exposed. Franks couldn't see her in either position, but tucking herself against a wall as she dialed Ian's number made her feel safer.

"MacAllister," Ian said.

"Franks is here, Ian," she said.

As she listened for Ian's response, she heard Drew's voice come booming from the front of the house. "Joe Franks, put your hands where I can see them." And that, more than anything over the past two minutes, made her heart race. If Franks had a gun or a weapon, Drew could be in real danger.

"I'm on my way," Ian answered. "Leave the line on—put the phone in your pocket, if you can. I'm just south of town and can be there in five minutes."

Carly didn't say anything more; she was too focused on what was happening on her front porch.

"Now turn around slowly, you know the drill." Carly leaned against the wall, her heart thudding, and listened.

"Slowly lift the edges of your jacket," Drew said.

"I'm unarmed," Franks answered.

"You're a near forty-year veteran of the FBI, you're never unarmed."

"I'm not here as an FBI agent today," Franks said.

Judging by the lack of a follow-up order from Drew, Carly suspected Franks was complying.

"Carly," Drew called, making her jump. "I want you to come out now."

As she peeked around the stairwell and stepped out into the kitchen area, she could see Drew standing in front of the porch with his gun. Franks still must have been standing by the front door, as she couldn't see him at all.

"Franks, the door behind you is going to open," Drew said as she approached it from her side. "Don't turn around, don't move. Don't look, don't even think about it. Do you understand?"

Carly had her hand on the knob and she assumed Franks must have agreed when Drew spoke again. "Good, Carly can you come out now?"

Slowly, she opened the door, keeping her body behind it as best she could. Her eyes went first to Drew, who looked completely in control, as if he could stand there all day, and then to the back of Franks. He'd gone grayer in the intervening years, but he was still wearing the kind of clothes she remembered him wearing—work boots, jeans, a collared shirt, and a sports jacket.

"Carly, I need you to search him," Drew said. Her eyes went back to him. He didn't like asking her to touch the man who might be responsible for her mother's death. And, strangely enough, his obvious concern made it easier to do.

Setting the phone down on the arm of one of the porch chairs, she started at Franks's ankles. She did the most thorough pat down she'd ever done in her life, knowing not only her life, but possibly also Drew's, depended on it. When she finished, she stepped back and gave Drew a nod, indicating she'd found nothing.

He nodded back. "Why don't you step away. Come on over here." She heard a quick intake of breath come from Franks when she passed by him without looking. Reaching Drew's side she turned around and met the eyes of the man she'd been wondering if she'd ever really known.

"I'm here as a friend, Carolyn," Franks said.

She studied him for a long moment. Beside her, she felt Drew giving her the time and space to decide—he'd made sure they were safe, but now he was leaving it to her to decide what to do next.

She remembered Franks as having been an attractive man in the way older men were to young girls, and time hadn't changed that. His face held a few more wrinkles than she remembered, but his lean frame, dark hair streaked with a distinguished amount of gray, and dark brown eyes—eyes filled with concern—painted a familiar, and handsome, picture.

"My name is Carly now," she said, dimly aware of sirens in the background.

"Carly," Franks repeated. "You look so much like your mother." She knew emotions could be faked, but hearing the pain in his voice when he mentioned her mother reminded her of all the times she'd seen him watch Sophia Davidson. The happiness and love she'd seen on his face, and on her mother's, was hard for even the most self-involved teenager to miss.

"It's okay," she said, putting a hand on Drew's arm. Slowly, he lowered his weapon as Ian pulled into her drive. She felt the muscles in his arm tense, no doubt wondering if Franks would use the distraction to make a move. But she knew he wouldn't.

And he didn't. Joe Franks stood still as a statue as Ian joined them in front the house, his weapon in hand.

"Everything okay?" Ian asked.

"Carly?" Drew said.

She took one more long look at Franks and his eyes met and held hers. He seemed to be asking her to trust him, but he didn't say it. Like Drew and Ian, he was leaving that decision to her.

"It's not okay, but I think Joe is going to be able to clear a few things up, aren't you, Joe?" she said not taking her eyes off of him.

He held hers too, as if he was drinking in the sight of her. "Yes, I can do that," he replied.

She held his gaze for one more moment before turning to Drew. He'd put his gun down and, without her even noticing, had tucked her hand that had been on his arm into his, curling his fingers around hers.

He gave her hand a little squeeze. "Shall we go inside?"

Her eyes flitted to Ian, also standing beside her, calm and watchful as always. She had two good friends who had her back in more ways than one.

"Yes, let's go inside."

It was time to learn what had happened all those years ago.

•••

Drew shot a look at Ian—he didn't want the sheriff to let his guard down quite yet. They would follow Carly's lead, but not blindly. In response, Ian placed his weapon in its holster, but left the holster unfastened.

Drew picked up his phone as he and Carly moved into the house. Franks came in behind them with Ian trailing.

"I didn't call Marcus," she said to him quietly.

"I'll do it," he replied. Then, to both Carly and Franks, he said, "Why don't you two have a seat?"

Minutes later, both Marcus and Mikaela Marsh—who deserved to hear firsthand what Franks might have to say about the death of her deputy—were on their way.

Drew was pulling out a chair to sit down himself when the coffee maker beeped, reminding him that, just minutes earlier, they'd been doing nothing more exciting than making coffee, building a fire, and getting ready to go through one last box.

"Do you want a cup?" he asked, putting a hand on her shoulder to draw her attention away from Franks. The two were studying each other and neither seemed to know quite what to make of the situation.

She looked up then blinked. "Uh, yes, please. I made a lot in case we wanted more than a cup, so there should be enough for everyone."

Drew looked at Franks, who nodded and said, "Yes, thank you."

Predictably, Ian declined, no doubt preferring to keep his hands available should he need them.

After setting one cup down in front of Carly and another in front of Franks, Drew took his own and sat down between the two.

"You really do look like your mother," Franks repeated.

"I heard that a lot growing up," she said.

A moment of silence passed, then Franks looked over at Drew. "What do you want to know? Where should I start?"

"Marcus is on his way over, as is Marguerite Silva's former supervisor. We'll wait until they get here to start," Drew answered.

Franks took a moment to digest this then turned his attention back to Carly. "I know it probably doesn't seem like anything makes sense right about now, but I promise you I will do my best to explain what I can," he said to her. "I don't have all the answers and I hope that's where you all can help, but I will tell you everything I know."

Drew didn't need to look at Ian to know the sheriff felt as cynical as he did about that statement. Sure, stranger things had happened, but with Carly's life and happiness on the line, he wasn't going to start out by giving Franks the benefit of the doubt.

"Did you really love my mother?" Carly asked suddenly.

Drew watched Franks. It looked as though someone had sucked the air right out of the man's lungs.

Franks struggled to catch a breath for a moment before he responded. "Yes, I did. Very much. She was the first, and really only, woman I ever loved." Then he paused and turned to Drew, silently asking permission to talk about this subject before the others arrived.

He replied with a nod.

"You know we went to high school together," Franks continued. "I transferred in my junior year, when Sophia was a sophomore. I remember the first time I saw her. I was sitting in the registrar's office waiting for my class schedule and she walked in with a note from one of the teachers.

"She walked me to my first class and I think I've been in love with her ever since. Of course, I went off to college, and then she did too. We drifted—she moved to England after graduating and I was already working for the bureau at the time. She met your dad and we eventually lost touch."

"But you reconnected, obviously," she said.

Drew listened to what Franks said, but his attention was on Carly—because, of all the questions she could have asked, this was what she wanted to know first.

"Yes," Franks answered.

"And when you came back into her life, was that for show? Was any of that real?"

Drew understood her true question from the small hitch in her voice. Nothing about what had happened back then made any sense to her—nothing other than what she had witnessed between her mother and Franks. And she wanted to know if this one, simple—or as simple as love can be—thing had been true.

"For me? It was all real, every second of it," he answered. "But for your mother, I think it was different. The situation was difficult and we'll talk more when the others get here, but she wasn't sure whether to trust me or not and, honestly, I don't blame her. But by the end, it was all very real. What you saw between your mom and me was true. Had it not ended the way it had," his eyes dropped and he cleared his throat. "Well, we had been talking about getting married."

Carly sat back and took a sip of her coffee, letting his words hang in the room. They were all quiet for several minutes before the sound of two cars arriving fractured the silence.

"Ian?" Drew said.

"Got it," Ian answered, moving to the door. "It's Marcus and Mikaela," he said as he opened the door.

"Carly?" Marcus called as he hit the landing of the door a minute later.

"She's fine," Ian answered.

But even with his friend's assurance, Marcus walked straight to his sister. "Are you okay?"

"I'm fine," she said, echoing Ian then inclining her head in Franks' direction.

Marcus straightened and looked at the man from his past.

As he watched a myriad of emotions wash across Marcus's face—anger being the most prominent—Drew stood, hoping to defuse any tension. "Marcus, why don't you have a seat and I'll get you a cup of coffee?"

Marcus looked about to argue, but then looked at his sister and took a seat.

"Mikaela?" Drew asked. The marshal shook her head.

Drew retrieved Marcus's coffee as the rest of them settled, then took his seat again. He could feel the tension building in the room, both Marcus and Mikaela seemed to have ratcheted it up more than a few notches, so he thought it best to get started and hope what they were about to hear would distract them enough from their own thoughts.

"Franks," Drew directed.

"Call me Joe."

Drew thought not—not yet. "Why don't you get started?"

"Yes, how about you start by telling us if you killed Marguerite?" Mikaela demanded.

Joe's head reared back, then a look of sadness came into his eyes and he shook his head. "I did not kill her, but I know who did."

"Who?" Marcus demanded.

"Vince Repetto. And whoever else is working with him."

"Special Agent Vince Repetto? The man you worked with undercover when investigating Sophia Davidson and Tony Lamot?" Mikaela clarified.

"Yes, but we weren't investigating Sophia and Tony back then, we were investigating Repetto," Joe answered, confirming what they had all suspected—that the entire situation had been a counterintelligence operation.

"And how do you know Repetto killed her?" Mikaela pressed.

"Because I was tracking him. Or his phone, anyway." Joe took a deep breath and started to tell his story. "Repetto has been after Michael and Carolyn—"

"Marcus and Carly, now," Marcus interrupted.

Joe paused for a moment, then continued. "Repetto has been after the kids since they were first put into the program. I'll go into what happened back then in a minute, but I think right now you want to hear about Marguerite." When Marcus and Carly nodded, he continued. "She and I have kept in touch ever since the day she was assigned to your case. Not openly, mind you, but we had our ways of communicating so I could check in and see how you two were doing."

Marcus opened his mouth to say something but Carly silenced him with a look.

"A few weeks ago, she called me and told me she thought Repetto was back on the trail," Joe said.

"After nearly fifteen years?" Mikaela asked.

"Yes, after what happened to Sophia and Tony, Repetto's boss kept him under pretty strict watch. You see, we all knew he was guilty of a whole host of financial crimes, which is what we were investigating him for in the first place, not to mention the murders, but we didn't have enough proof to convict him. So Anton Perelli did the best he could and he kept Repetto on a pretty short leash these past fourteen years."

"But when Perelli died a few months ago . . ." Mikaela stated the obvious.

"Exactly," Joe said. "When Perelli died, Marguerite and I thought Repetto took that as a sign that he should pick up where he left off."

"Which was where?" Drew asked.

"Using his authority as an agent to manipulate local businessmen and financial markets for his own monetary gain," Joe answered.

"But Marcus and Carly were still a loose end," Mikaela surmised.

"They were, at least in Vince's mind. Why else would they be put into witness security unless they knew something, right?"

"And so he needed to take care of that—of them—before he could really get back to his old business," Drew said.

"He contacted Marguerite under the guise of looking into old, cold cases—which the murders of Sophia and Tony are," Joe continued. "He asked her a lot of questions, several about the kids."

"Wait," Carly interrupted. "How would he even know Marguerite was the deputy assigned to our case? Isn't that supposed to be confidential?"

Joe looked chagrined at the question. "That was probably Marguerite's and my fault. After she placed you with her aunt, she and I met for dinner one night so she could update me. I didn't want the details, I didn't want to know where you were or who you were living with, but I did want to know you were okay."

"Considerate of you," Marcus bit out.

Joe's eyes flicked to Marcus and then came back to Carly. "One of Repetto's friends happened to come into the restaurant at the same time and saw us. He told Repetto about it and Repetto asked me if she was the marshal assigned to the kids. I told him it had been a date, but I don't think he believed me. At any rate, she was his best lead to try and find you, and so when he was ostensibly researching the old case, it was her name he pulled out of his contacts to reach out to."

"So what happened? If you were tracking Repetto the night he killed Marguerite, how did he get to her?" Mikaela asked.

"Because he was tracking me too. I'd gone down to DC to meet with Marguerite. By then we had a system for communicating. She'd call my office line and ask if it was a different number. I'd tell her it was the wrong number but then I'd take the number she'd given me and find a place I could call her back from. The night before she died, we met at some packed college bar in Georgetown and she told me about Repetto fishing around. I'm glad she did, because I got a call from him the next day and he gave me pretty much the same story.

"I didn't tell him anything but agreed to meet with him since I was already in town. I wanted to see his face, hear him ask me in person." At this, Joe paused and his brows dipped. Then he shook his head. "Repetto is an interesting guy. He's not, well he's smart but he's one of those guys that's almost too smart for his own good. His ego gets in the way of what he's trying to accomplish."

"And?" Mikaela cut in.

Joe lifted a shoulder. "And I was right. When I talked to him in person, he was definitely not on the up and up about what he was doing. I left the meeting and knew he'd probably either follow me himself or have someone else do it for him. So in turn, *I* called in some favors and activated the tracking device on his phone. When he started to head down to the park that night, I knew it couldn't be good.

"That night, that night Marguerite was killed," Joe paused, then ran a hand over his face and closed his eyes for a long moment before he spoke again. "It took me longer than I'd hoped to find someone to take my place in my hotel room so I could sneak out without whoever was following me knowing. I had a friend dress like a hotel repairman. We switched clothes and he stayed in my room while I walked out. By the time I got to the warehouse where Repetto had taken her, it was already too late. She was dead and he was gone."

"Then how did she end up here?" Marcus demanded.

Again, Joe closed his eyes. Then he took a deep breath. "I brought her."

"You what?" Mikaela demanded.

Drew turned to get Ian's take on the story. The sheriff's only acknowledgement was a single raised eyebrow. It seemed he and Ian were in agreement that the tale was just bizarre enough to be true.

"I moved her here to Windsor," Joe repeated. "I know I shouldn't have, but I needed to let Michael, I mean Marcus, and Carly know. I couldn't call them out of the blue and, because Repetto was following me, I couldn't come here in person and talk to them, to you," he said, looking at the siblings.

"But you did come," Carly pointed out.

"I borrowed a friend's car, turned off every device that could possibly be used to track me, then yes, I did come. But I only had ten hours to deal with the situation, that was it. In the morning, Repetto was expecting to see me at the DC office in a meeting with his new boss to discuss how our two teams could work together. My stand-in worked in the hotel room, but he couldn't go to my meeting for me. Once Repetto knew I was gone, I was pretty sure he'd figure out a way to come after me. And then, if I was here, after you."

"So you brought Marguerite's body up here and threw her down a hill to what, warn us?" Carly's voice echoed in the room and didn't hide the horror and disbelief she obviously felt. They'd assumed that the body had been a warning, but one from someone already depraved enough to have killed Marguerite. Not one from someone who had considered her a friend.

"And how did you know to come here? I thought you said you didn't want to know the details of where we were living," Marcus said.

Joe blinked several times, but didn't back down. "I didn't throw her body down the hill. I laid her on the side of the road. I knew you both lived up here in Columbia County because Marguerite did tell me that much. I also knew you were both in law enforcement. I've done some work in Riverside and I knew neither of you worked there, so I picked the next biggest town in the county. When I got here, a state trooper drove by me and I followed him up that dirt road. It was shift change time, so I figured he was going home and if I laid the body out where he would see it, she would be found quickly."

"Generous of you," Marcus snapped.

"Look," Joe said as he let out a deep breath. "I know it probably seems callous, but I can assure you that Marguerite would have wanted me to warn you in any way I could even if it meant moving her body. You needed to know that what happened fourteen years ago wasn't dead and buried, and while I regret doing what I did, I did the only thing I thought I could do at the time."

"And you couldn't have bothered to tell us before now?" Carly asked.

"Like I said, I've been in DC for meetings and am supposed to be teaching a course at Quantico next week. I also wanted to keep an eye on Repetto while trying not to let him figure out that I know what he's done and what he's planning to do. But I still needed you both to be on alert."

"So then, why now?" Drew asked. "Why today?"

"Because I talked to one of my new agents yesterday and she started telling me about a colleague of hers who is based in the Albany office but had called her to ask about the team. We happen to have an opening so she was asking me if she should encourage him to apply. Of course, when she gave me his background, I knew he wasn't interested in my team, but that he was probably a former colleague of yours asking around on your behalf," he answered.

"You expected us to sit back and do nothing?" Marcus asked.

Joe dipped his head, acknowledging his mistake. "My intent was to put you on alert. Of course, I knew you would look into it, how could you not, but I hadn't expected you to have the resources you apparently do to have gotten as far as you have in this investigation. I thought I would have a little more time to figure out what Repetto's next move was and then figure out how to safely contact you both."

"How do you know what we've figured out?" Drew asked.

"You all knew who I was and, more importantly, no one asked who Repetto was when I started talking about him. Since Marcus and Carly," he still stumbled over the names a bit, "only knew him as Vince Archstone and me as Joe Kincaid, I know you at least know we were undercover fourteen years ago. You also didn't seemed surprised by anything I said regarding the investigation being about an FBI agent and not about Sophia or Tony. I don't know everything you know, but I know you've probably figured out more than I'd given you credit for."

Everyone sat in silence, absorbing the information and the new twist on the situation. At least it appeared they now knew who was responsible for the murders of Marcus and Carly's mother and uncle as well as that of Marguerite Silva. They would, of course, verify the story, but if pressed, Drew would bet Franks spoke the truth.

"How did her body get down the hill if you so carefully laid it out?" Mikaela asked, the suspicion still strong in her voice.

"The disturbed ground," Carly answered, surprising everyone. She turned to Marcus and continued, "Remember, I mentioned that an area on the road right above where we found Marguerite had been disturbed more than the area around it?"

Marcus nodded, but it looked like it cost him a lot to do it.

"My guess is that a wild animal came along, after Joe laid her out. A bear, probably, since they are opportunistic feeders. Plus, a bear would be big enough to inadvertently push Marguerite over the edge as it investigated," she said.

"And when Marguerite began to roll down the hill, the animal probably would have been startled enough to thrash around, possibly creating the disturbed area you saw," Drew finished.

Drew thought the explanation was as good as any—Franks had looked quite taken aback at the thought of Marguerite being found down a hill.

"So how do we know Repetto isn't on to you now?" Marcus asked. The words he used were an implicit sign that he was starting to accept what Joe had told them, even if his tone suggested otherwise.

"Because I have a cabin in Maine, and when it became known I wasn't feeling well, it made sense that I take a few days off to relax. I flew into Portland, rented a car, and met up with a friend who is now happily ensconced in front of the fireplace at my cabin. I took his car and drove down here. I've also left all my belongings, including my phone, computer, and clothes in my cabin, in case there were any tracking devices on them. My friend bought me a change of clothes, some toiletries, and new phone. I also have his credit cards so I can book a room down here if I need to stay."

"You've certainly thought of everything, haven't you?" Marcus muttered.

"I haven't," Joe said.

"You haven't?" Carly repeated.

He shook his head. "I haven't figured out how we're going to catch Repetto. I couldn't bring him down the first time and it nearly killed me to see the man who killed Sophia walk away. I'll be damned if I let him slip through my fingers this time."

Marcus and Carly were too involved in the case to make a decision about whether or not to trust Joe Franks, so Drew shared a look with Mikaela and Ian. Judging by the looks on their faces, they were all in agreement.

"Well, Joe Franks," the marshal started. "I'm sure you won't be surprised to hear a few of us in this room would like to verify your story."

"Of course," Joe said.

"In the meantime, I'd like for you to accompany my marshal back to the hotel we've checked into," Mikaela added.

He stood to leave, but his eyes lingered on the siblings, as if, now that he'd found them again, he didn't want to let them out of his sight.

"And if what you've said checks out," the marshal continued, "we can share what we've learned and then figure out together how in the hell we're going to bring that bastard down."

• • •

Drew didn't want to leave Carly, but he needed to talk to Ian. He followed the sheriff, Mikaela, and Joe out to the porch. Ian and Mikaela were deep in discussion, so, rather than interrupt, he left whatever would come next in the hands of the sheriff. Keeping an ear to the house, where he could hear Marcus and Carly moving around, he watched Mikaela climb into her van as Mario, who'd been standing guard outside, slid behind the wheel of Joe's car with Joe in the passenger seat.

Ian came back up and stood beside Drew on the porch as the two cars turned around and left. He'd just started to ask Ian about the plan when Marcus opened the door to join them. Carly's brother glanced at Drew and Ian then turned his back on them and promptly walked to the edge of the porch. Seeing the rigid set of the younger man's shoulders, Drew knew his own questions would have to wait.

"Do you believe him, Ian?" Marcus asked, not turning around.

Ian shot Drew a quick look before he leaned against the porch rail and answered. "Mikaela will get some additional details from him when they get back to the hotel, and we'll have Naomi check out the story, and Brian if we need him."

"That's not what I asked," Marcus said. "I asked if you believe what he told us?"

Neither Drew nor Ian underestimated how important Ian's answer was to Marcus. Marcus was looking for someone to blame and wanted to know if he'd found his man.

"We don't have any evidence to back up his story yet, but yes," Ian said. "I believe him."

Marcus's hands formed fists over the porch railing as he leaned against it. And for a long moment, he remained silent. Then abruptly, he turned. "Evidence. It's all about the evidence, isn't it?"

The rhetorical question went unanswered.

"If he's telling us the truth, we *know* who killed my mother and my uncle. Or at least who had them killed. And we know who killed Marguerite. But we're not going to be able to do a damned thing about it until we have evidence, isn't that right?"

Ian paused before speaking. Drew suspected that the sheriff already had a ready answer, but took a moment because he knew how important his answer might be. Marcus was on the edge of spiraling into a dark place where revenge takes hold of humanity and destroys it.

"We'll find it," Ian said.

Marcus shot him a disgusted look then turned his attention to Drew. "I wish I lived in your world right about now," he said, no doubt alluding to the commonly held notion that the CIA operated outside the law.

"We have our own rules too."

"Marcus, we'll find what we need to," Ian repeated.

"After nearly fifteen years?" Marcus asked with disbelief. "If they haven't found anything yet, they sure as hell aren't going to find it now."

"They haven't been looking," Drew said.

"And they didn't have people like Vivienne and Naomi," Ian added.

Marcus glared at them both for a long moment before shaking his head. "I can't . . . I'm not going to deal with this right now. I'm going back to the lab," he added, then pushed between them and made his way to his car.

Drew looked at Ian, who was already pulling out his keys.

"Don't worry, I got this," the sheriff said. "I'll call Vivienne and we'll all meet him at the lab."

"What about your son?" Drew asked, wondering how they'd find a sitter on such short notice.

Ian gave him a ghost of a smile. "My folks live half a mile away and like nothing better than to take him in whenever Vivienne and I get called in."

Though Drew thought that sounded pretty appealing, he said nothing. He could hear Carly moving boxes around in her living room and wanted to get back to her.

"You should go in," Ian said with a nod toward the door. "I'll touch base with you both later tonight," he added, then made his way to his SUV.

He was already walking through the door when he heard the sheriff's engine start. "Carly?" he said, closing the door behind him.

Sitting on the living room floor again, she appeared to be sorting through the items they'd already looked at and dividing them into piles.

"I'm going to give a bunch of this stuff away," she said, without looking up.

He watched her for several moments, then moved to sit down.

"Don't," she said.

He froze. "What?"

She closed her eyes and her hands, holding a stuffed hippo from her childhood, dropped into her lap. She took a few deep breaths and as she did, he stood still, uncertain what to do.

She opened her eyes and met his gaze. "I need to be alone right now."

"Carly," he started to disagree, but she cut him off.

"Please don't, Drew. I know you mean well and I know you want to be here and that means something to me. But right now, I just need to be alone—and I need you to *let* me be alone, because I don't have the energy to fight you on this. So please . . ."

She wanted him to go. He didn't want to. He hadn't even considered leaving her alone, not after what she'd just heard. But when he looked at her sitting alone on the floor and felt the slow thud of his heart in his chest, he wondered if perhaps he was being selfish. He wondered if his reason for staying was for her benefit, or his. If it was for hers, why should he second-guess what she'd just asked of him? And if his reasons were more selfish, well, his feelings hardly mattered at the moment, did they?

Either way, he should go. He should do what she asked even though he was loathe to do it. He didn't like how the thought of leaving her seemed to punch a hole in his gut. Nor did he like the distant, efficient look in her eye. And he wasn't happy that, when he thought she most needed someone, when she most needed a friend, she was pushing him away.

But it was what she had asked of him. And she had asked so little that, even though this didn't seem to be the right time to ignore his instincts, he was going to do just that. He nodded.

Seeing her shoulders drop in something that looked like relief did not make him feel any better. He turned and walked to the kitchen. Retrieving his jacket, he paused by the door. She still hadn't moved.

"You'll call if you need anything?" he asked.

She nodded.

He hesitated.

"Please," she said again cutting off any question he might ask.

He swallowed. "You know how to reach me."

He left before he could listen to logic and change his mind.

CHAPTER SIXTEEN

THE NEXT MORNING, CARLY WATCHED her small living room fill with people. She had no idea how they had coordinated their arrival, but Vivi, Ian, Wyatt, Naomi, Mikaela, Mario, Joe, Marcus, and even Brian—who must have come over from Boston the night before—filed into her home, one after the other. The only person missing was Drew.

Her stomach sank a little at the realization. Actually it had been pretty low ever since he'd walked out the night before. She'd asked him to go, yes, and he'd struggled with the decision, then ultimately done only what she'd demanded. But the second the door had closed behind him, she'd wanted him back.

She hadn't wanted to talk about anything, just simply wanted him there. She knew he would have given her that, his undemanding presence, if only she could have brought herself to ask for and accept it.

"Where's Drew?" Vivi asked, coming up beside her.

While everyone else was making themselves comfortable into the living room, Carly had come into the kitchen to put on a second pot of coffee. "I don't know. I imagine he's on his way," she answered. She *hoped* he was on his way. Even though she knew he hadn't been happy with her when he'd left, she didn't think it would keep him away.

Vivi started to say something, but just then Joe Franks walked into the room.

Carly turned and watched him approach. Mikaela had called earlier to confirm that Joe's story had checked out. They now had a primary suspect in the murders of her mother and uncle, as well as Marguerite—Vince Repetto. She still felt somewhat numb about it all.

"Carly," Joe said, coming to her side.

When Carly glanced at Vivi, her friend reached out to give her arm a small squeeze before leaving her alone with Joe.

She looked into the eyes she remembered so well—better than she thought she had. With him appearing back in her life, she remembered more—about him and her mom and what had happened back then—more than she was ready for.

"Coffee?" she asked, turning away.

When she didn't look up at him and began gathering more mugs instead, he spoke. "I loved your mother very much. I know I said it last night, but now that you know I was telling the truth, that I *am* telling the truth, I want you to hear it again. And it wasn't just her that I loved. It was you too. And to an extent, Marcus, though I was just getting to know him. But still, he was a part of the two of you, and so he was a part of me too."

She didn't know what to say, so she said nothing as she filled a mug with coffee and handed it to him.

"Are you still riding?" he asked, changing the subject.

She shook her head. "No, we didn't have that kind of money when we lived with Lorraine, but more to the point, I was too recognizable in that world."

"Well, maybe you can once we get this wrapped up once and for all."

As she opened her mouth to question just how he thought they were going to wrap it all up, Drew knocked on the door and walked in.

Holding her coffee mug close to her chest, she watched him close the door, look into the living room, and pause. He'd see what she'd done the night before—the piles now all put away in boxes, her riding videos—they'd found several—stacked neatly by the television, and the vacuum tracks on the throw rug. Yes, in her efforts to keep busy, at two in the morning, she'd pulled out her vacuum cleaner and vacuumed the entire house. She was glad her landlords hadn't decided to come up for the weekend or they might have started to doubt the sanity of their tenant.

When his eyes turned and caught hers, they briefly flitted to Joe, then came back to her. His unreadable expression studied her; she had no idea what thoughts might be going through his head. She wanted to talk to him. She wanted to apologize for sending him away the night before. But rather than come into the kitchen to talk to her, he simply said, "Good morning," and joined the others in the living room.

"Is everything okay?" Franks asked.

Carly's heart sank into her stomach. "It's fine," she said. Because that was what she always said. "Maybe we should bring the coffee in and get started?"

Without a word, he helped her carry several mugs and the coffee pot, as well as some sugar and a pitcher of half-and-half, into the living room. People moved aside as she and Joe deposited everything onto the coffee table. Naomi immediately took over as hostess, pouring coffee for those who wanted it. Drew declined, and moved to the far end of the room. Leaning on the frame of the window that looked out toward the back of the house, he stood apart from the rest of the group. Again.

She wondered how often he had done that—been a member of a group while somehow staying outside of it. She thought probably quite often. At that realization, her heart sank a little further. He'd been trying, like she had, to be more for her. He'd been honest with her—she knew that—about his life, his career. And she also knew his honesty wasn't just important because of *what* he'd said to her, but also because he'd said it all. In more ways than one, he'd been trying since day one of this situation, to be a part of something with her.

And she'd pushed him away because she hadn't been strong enough to let him in. Seeing him standing on the outside now, she knew it wasn't just his nature that put him there, it was her doing as well.

"Let's get started," Ian said, calling everyone to attention. With one last look at Drew, Carly sat on the edge of her sofa and let Ian do his thing.

"I think it's pretty clear why we're all here today. We now believe FBI agent Vince Repetto is responsible for at least three deaths, including those of Carly and Marcus's mother and uncle. Deputy Director Franks, Joe," Ian said with a gesture to the man, "was involved in those events and is here to walk us through what happened. Everything that's not in the records."

"I know it's been a long time, a very long time, in coming," Ian continued with a look at Carly then Marcus, "but we have more resources now than they did when this first happened, including Naomi and Brian—who we all know have talents we're better off not knowing about—and, of course, Vivienne, with her background in cold cases. So, now I've set the groundwork, Joe, do you want to take over?"

Joe stood as he began to speak. "Vince Repetto is an agent in one of our white-collar crime divisions. About sixteen years ago, a routine check on employees showed two financial transactions that raised red flags with the auditors and they handed his files over to my team to investigate."

"But you're anti-terrorism, aren't you?" Marcus asked.

Joe wagged his head. "We are, primarily, but several people on my team, myself included back before I was deputy director, act as a sort of counterintelligence within the agency when needed."

"How does that even work?" Carly asked, setting her coffee down, unable to stomach it just then.

Joe lifted a shoulder. "It's a bit of an unusual arrangement, but because our anti-terrorism activities encompass so many disciplines—from money to weapons to intelligence to murder—our group is uniquely set up to loan agents out to other divisions under the guise of investigating potential terrorist threats."

"But really, you're investigating agents," Naomi clarified.

Joe responded to Naomi. "We are, again, only when needed. If we see a situation, like Repetto's, where it looks like something is going on that shouldn't be, we create a back story, send an agent to the team, partner them up with the agent we want to investigate, and see where it leads us."

"In our case, it led to the deaths of my mother and uncle," Marcus said.

"Why were Tony and Sophia chosen?" Vivi asked, attempting to keep the conversation on track.

For a moment it looked like Joe wanted to say something to Marcus, but then he gathered himself in and answered. "When the auditors handed Repetto's file over to us, we dug into his life and realized that not only were there those two questionable transactions, but a history of them. Most of them were smaller than the two that had raised the flags, but taken together they added up to quite a bit of money. Based on what we were seeing, we suspected he was dealing in insider trading of some sort.

"We ran an analysis of the companies and learned that many of them, though not all, had some sort of nexus with Tony Lamot—sometimes there were people Tony knew on the board, sometimes the contacts were social. There were all sorts of different connections."

"Tony wasn't involved in insider trading," Carly said, cutting off anything more Joe might say.

Joe's eyes lingered on hers, then he answered. "No, Tony wasn't. Quite the contrary. He thought he was helping the government investigate *other* people for wrongdoing."

"You're being vague, Joe," Naomi broke in. "It's not useful and it won't help us get to where we need to be."

Carly watched as this uncharacteristic comment from Naomi elicited the first reaction she'd seen from Drew all day. His lips tilted into a small smile.

"You're right. Okay, here's the bottom line. We can talk particulars as needed, but here are the facts. Four years prior to our investigation, Tony Lamot was, in fact, investigated for insider trading. Nothing came of that investigation and there was no evidence to suggest any involvement on his part. But what the investigation did was bring Vince Repetto into Tony's orbit—Repetto himself wasn't involved in the investigation, but his partner was.

"What we ultimately learned in our investigation of Repetto is that about six months after the original investigation into Tony ended, Repetto approached him and asked if he would be willing to help the FBI investigate other insider trading claims. Your uncle was a good man." Joe paused to glance at both Carly and Marcus. "Of course, he said yes. So, for the next few years, Tony Lamot gathered bits of information and passed it on to Repetto. The information flowed both ways as well, and occasionally, Repetto would ask Lamot to drop a piece of information in the ear of one businessperson or another. Tony was told this was to test the flow of information and to see if a specific businessperson would use the information provided to make illegal trades."

"But that wasn't the case," Naomi said, reaching to refill her brother's coffee mug.

Joe shook his head, but Brian piped in as he held his mug out for his sister. "Tony wasn't helping the FBI, was he? He was helping Repetto himself manipulate the market."

The question didn't require an answer but Joe nodded.

"How did you figure this out?" Carly asked.

"Because when the information first came to me and I saw the nexus to Tony, I knew I could reach out to Sophia. It gave me an excuse to do something I'd wanted to do for years," he added quietly.

"Anyway," he continued on an exhale, "the FBI knew nothing about what I just told you when I contacted your mom and uncle the first time. The three of us met for several hours and when it became clear to your uncle that he hadn't actually been helping the FBI, as he'd been told, he was more than happy to fill in the gaps for us. We'd suspected what was happening, of course, but it wasn't until we talked to your uncle that we knew *how* he was doing it. Tony was horrified, naturally, and both he and Sophia wanted to help."

"And so you involved civilians in your investigation?" Marcus said. "Despite the dangers."

Joe sighed. "It's a poor excuse now, but we didn't think Repetto could be dangerous. His crimes were all white collar. His role in the FBI didn't even require that he ever use his gun. He was certified to carry one, but given what he did, we all looked at him as a bit of a desk jockey. A smart one, but not someone we thought would get violent."

Marcus stood and began to pace, unable to sit and listen passively.

"So why didn't you take the information my uncle and mom gave you and arrest him?" Carly asked.

Joe ran a hand through his hair and met her gaze. "I wish we could have done that. You will never know how much I wish we could have done that. Your uncle wanted to help, he really did, and he gave us the information we needed to understand how Repetto was operating, but he wasn't the most organized person and certainly didn't have any ready records of his encounters with Repetto. Especially since Repetto had told him, under the auspices of keeping his involvement a secret, not to keep records."

"It was going to take time to gather what you needed, wasn't it? The actual proof and not just my uncle's word," Carly said.

"And then your mom suggested that, while she and Tony gathered the data, maybe they could help with the active investigation," Joe replied.

"And you didn't argue." Again, Marcus cut in.

"Actually, I did," Joe said. "I didn't want her involved any more than she already was. But she was adamant. She didn't like how Tony had been used and didn't like that someone with the kind of authority Repetto had was taking advantage of people. It was her idea to try to catch him in the act. So to speak."

"So what did that mean?" Ian asked, setting his empty mug down on the coffee table.

"It meant that we set up an operation where it looked like my anti-terrorism team was going to investigate Tony for funding terrorists. When we did this, my boss arranged with Repetto's boss, Anton Perelli, to have Repetto partner with me to investigate the claims."

"The bogus claims," Carly clarified.

"Yes, the only people who knew they were bogus and that the true target of the investigation was Repetto himself were me, my boss, Perelli, your mother, and your uncle. Repetto obviously had no idea and probably took his being brought into the investigation as verification of just how clever he'd been in his own dealings."

"So, as part of this operation to investigate Repetto, you both went undercover together," Vivi said.

"Yes, we did. The story we'd set up was that we were businessmen with interests in the Middle East who were, eventually, looking for someone to help us funnel money to groups that were on the terrorist watch list but who would help us conduct business in certain regions."

"And how was that supposed to catch Repetto in the act?" Brian asked.

"We wanted to put Repetto into Tony's orbit more often than he was," Joe answered.

"And hope he would use those opportunities with Tony in the same way he had in the past, but this time you would have a record," Naomi finished.

"That was the plan," Joe answered.

"Did it work at all?" Mikaela asked.

Joe bobbed his head. "Yes, but not quickly enough."

"Why not?" Carly interjected.

"We think Repetto got nervous about having me, another agent, around and it took him a lot longer than we had anticipated to take the bait—unfettered time with your uncle—that we'd dangled. He did eventually, of course, because a guy like Repetto couldn't resist, but it takes time for the kind of racket he was running to play out."

"So when my mother and uncle were killed, you think there

was something in play but that it just hadn't played out enough for you to act on it?" Carly asked.

"Exactly," Joe said, and in his voice she heard years of regret. "And then they were killed and the false information your uncle had fed to Repetto wasn't acted on."

"And you had nothing," Marcus said. "After all that, you had nothing."

Joe looked at Marcus for a good long while before answering. "Your mother was collecting data for us. She was remarkable." His voice broke. "Incredibly smart and significantly more organized than your uncle. She told me she was working on gathering all the information we would need regarding Repetto's interactions with your uncle."

"And I assume, since we're all here now, you never got that information?" Vivi's voice was gentle.

Joe shook his head. "No, we had plans to meet up. She was going to hand over what she'd gathered to me. She was excited about it. I think," he paused and cleared his throat. "I think she liked thinking she was going to be the one to give us what we needed to bring Repetto down. I tried to get her to give me what she had, but she wouldn't. She wanted it all organized and wrapped up with a damned bow or something before she handed it over." Joe didn't say it, but in the guilt Carly heard in his voice, she knew he still struggled with the fact that, had he been a bit more persistent and not given into her wishes, Sophia and Tony might be alive today. "She was killed before she could give me the information," he said quietly as he sat down. "And we never found it."

Silence fell over the room at that statement. Joe had shed a lot of light on what had happened fourteen years earlier, but what he hadn't done was provide any information that gave them any direction, any lead to follow.

"And you think he's back to his old games now that his old boss is dead?" Mikaela asked.

Nodding, Joe replied. "Like I said, Perelli knew everything. He didn't like the idea of having a dirty agent on his team and he did what he could to keep Repetto contained. It was the next best thing, since we couldn't arrest him."

"Which is why Repetto hasn't moved roles or ranks in the past fourteen years," Wyatt said.

"Perelli's death is the only thing Marguerite and I could think of that would set him off again."

"And, as you've said before, in doing that he needed to tie up some loose ends," Vivi said with a pointed look toward Carly and Marcus.

"As far as I can tell, he thinks they know something," Joe said.

"But we don't," Carly interjected.

Joe shrugged. "He seems to think you do."

"This is all very interesting," Marcus said, "but we have nothing more useful now than you did fourteen years ago."

Again, a long moment of silence fell across the room.

Finally, Drew spoke up. "You said Sophia was smart and organized. Would it have made sense for her to have made a back-up copy of the data she'd gathered?"

Everyone looked his way, but he seemed unaware of the sudden scrutiny; his eyes were fixed on Joe, his stance casual.

"I thought of that and, yes, it would have been like her to do something like that. But when I couldn't find the originals, I didn't have much hope that we'd find any back-up she might have created. That said, we did go through everything we could, even the barn and all the kids' stuff."

"What about what they took with them to Los Angeles when she sent them there?" Drew asked.

"We went through all that as well."

That was news to Carly. She glanced at Marcus and, judging by the frown on his face, he hadn't known about it either.

"What about the earrings?" Drew asked, causing Carly's gaze to shoot back to him.

"What about them?" she asked tentatively. And for the first time that day, his eyes held hers.

"She gave them to you before you left. She also made a point of telling you they had belonged to Joe's grandmother. She probably thought that if anything happened to her, you would try to give them back to Joe. After all, it would make sense, even to a sixteen-year-old girl, that Joe might want something to remind him of the woman he loved. Especially if it was a family heirloom."

She gazed at him for a good long moment as his words sunk in.

"Carly did try to give them back," Joe said. "Not right away, but about six months later. She asked Marguerite to get them back to me. I told Marguerite I wanted her to keep them."

"But they're just earrings," Carly said. "You've seen them."

"They are and maybe it's nothing, but I have seen diamonds used to transfer data. A few years ago, a man used a laser to inscribe launch codes he'd obtained onto diamonds and then sold them. Again, it might be nothing."

"But it might be worth checking out," Naomi said, clearly as intrigued as everyone else in the room appeared to be.

Carly sat, stunned at the thought that she might have been holding the information needed to arrest Repetto all along. After a moment, she rose and headed upstairs to collect the jewelry.

When she came down, she didn't know who to hand them to. Vivi set her coffee down and reached out to take them, saying, "We'll run these up to the lab and see what we can find. In the meantime, we still have a few more things to go through in Albany and I want to make some calls to the doctor who performed Marguerite's final autopsy and whoever ran the tests on the trace evidence found on her clothes."

"Now that we have a better idea of who was supposed to be involved in what, Brian and I will run some more queries to see if we can find anything that *wouldn't* fit the pattern," Naomi chimed in.

"And I want to take a closer look at the financials," Brian added.

"We'll go with you, Vivi," Mikaela said. "If there is anything we can find out from Marguerite's body, I want to be sure we find it."

And, like that, everyone was gone—off to the lab, off to their computers. Everyone except Drew.

When Carly walked back into her house after watching the last of the cars drive away, she found him in the kitchen, his sleeves rolled up, washing coffee cups.

She watched him, his tall, lean frame somewhat hunched over her sink. She wanted to go to him, but wasn't sure if he would welcome it.

"Do you really think the earrings might have something?" she asked.

In response, he shrugged and placed a cup on the drying rack.

"I'm sorry, Drew," she said before she could stop herself. "I shouldn't have asked you to leave last night. I thought it was what I wanted, but then, after you left . . ."

The only response she got from him was a slight stiffening of his shoulders as he started to wash the coffee pot. She took a chance and approached him. But rather than get too close to him, like she wanted to, she picked a spot near him and leaned against the counter so that she could get a good look at his face.

"You did what you needed to do," he said. "I'm not angry with you."

She laughed. It probably wasn't the best reaction, but she couldn't help it. He looked up sharply as he set the pot in the drying rack.

"What?" he asked.

"You *are* angry with me. I can see it in your posture."

His jaw ticked. After a few beats of silence, he stepped in front of her, crossing his arms as he studied her. "I'm not angry."

"You are."

"Why would I be angry with you?"

"Because I pushed you away when you wanted to stay. Because I second-guessed your instincts. Because, when I asked you to leave last night, I made you do something you didn't want to do. I can imagine there are any number of reasons you might be mad at me," she said, somewhat aware she was baiting a bear.

She watched his arms come down and his hands land on the counter behind her, bracketing her between them.

"You *asked* me to leave, you didn't *make* me to do anything."

"You're right," she said, suddenly feeling her heart rate kick up. "I didn't *make* you do anything. But the fact that I asked you to go, after everything we've talked about this past week, after all the time we've spent together, pissed you off."

She could see his jaw tensing again as he leaned even closer to her. She had to lean back a bit to maintain eye contact.

"I still make you uncomfortable," he said, noticing her movement.

She looked into his blue eyes and wondered where he was going with that comment, but she owed him the truth.

"Yes," she replied. Not in the same way as he had when they'd first started spending time together, but she still had the sense that being with him wasn't a decision to be taken lightly.

"Why?" he pressed as he leaned a bit closer.

"I don't know, but I might point out that, right now, you're using your size to intimidate me," she shot back.

"I'm not."

"You are."

"I'm a decade older than you," he said, his eyes dropping to her lips.

She thought of all the things he must have seen in his life, in his job, and everything he must have had to do.

His eyes came up and she held his gaze.

"In probably more ways than one," she responded.

He stared at her for a beat—a beat in which she felt her heart thudding in her chest—and then his head dipped and he kissed her.

He kept his hands on the countertop by her sides, but his lips came down firmly on hers and she realized in that moment how long she'd been waiting for this. Exactly this. She tipped her head up and tilted it, to give or get better access to him—which it was she wasn't sure and didn't care, since all she knew was she wanted more.

And more.

But apparently he didn't. Abruptly, he ended the kiss and pulled back. His face only inches away, his eyes staring into hers.

"I didn't want to do that," he said.

She raised her eyebrows.

"Okay, I did want to do that," he conceded. "But I made a promise to myself when you first told me I made you uncomfortable that I wouldn't be the first one to make a move, physically. I wanted you to do it so I could be sure that, when it happened, if it happened, it would be something you wanted."

She studied him for a long moment. It was just like him to make such a promise to himself.

"I'm not sure I'll ever be entirely comfortable with you. But I'm beginning to think that could be a good thing for me." She clasped her hands around his neck and pulled him back down to her lips. Back down to where she wanted him.

His arms came around her instantly and within seconds he had her seated on the counter, his hands now buried in her hair as he kissed her. She'd known from the first moment she'd met him that being with him would be like this—this wasn't just a kiss, but a demand for something more from her. And knowing he wouldn't settle for anything less had made her hesitant before. But not now. Now her legs wrapped around him and pulled him closer as her hands went to his waist, tugging his shirt free of his pants.

Her fingers encountered his skin and, at her touch, she felt heat shoot through his body. He inhaled sharply and deepened the kiss even more as one of his hands came down to her lower back, pressing her harder against him.

As his hand made its way under her shirt and spread across her back, she leaned away, letting him trail his lips down her neck. She tugged his shirt up more, running her hands up his sides, craving the touch. Craving everything. Deeply.

And then she heard it. Drew's lips paused below her ear; he heard it too.

A car.

They stayed where they were, chests rising and falling as they each strained to catch their breath, cursing the interruption—or at least she was. Drew raised his head, brushed his thumb across her lips, dropped one more kiss there, then stepped back.

"Do you want me to go see who it is?" he asked with a nod toward the driveway.

She held his eyes, not wanting to turn away, but after a beat she did. From her position on the kitchen counter, she could see out the front window and to the car now parking beside Drew's.

She frowned.

"Carly?" he asked, instantly alert to her response.

"No, it's fine." She slid off the counter and to her feet. "It's Vic, my boss."

He said nothing as she straightened her shirt, stepping aside as she made her way to the door. She hesitated before opening it, but then swung it open as Vic climbed out of his car. The look on his face told her she was going to regret his arrival for more reasons than one.

Five minutes later, she walked back into her house, her suspicions confirmed. It didn't appear that Drew had moved much; he stood waiting for her with his hands resting on the back of one of her kitchen chairs, though he had tucked his shirt back in. She paused and looked at him. It wasn't a stretch to remember what she'd been feeling mere minutes earlier.

"Is everything okay?" he asked.

She blinked, then let out a long exhale. "No, I mean yes, everything is fine. Sort of. I guess."

"Sort of?"

She took a deep breath and joined him at the table. Like Drew she didn't sit; she didn't have time.

"I had two more days off, today and tomorrow, but Vic said something's come up in Boston and he has to head out of town."

"So he needs you to come back to work."

"Mmm hmm. But the good news is we agreed to extend an offer to a job candidate, so once she starts, assuming she accepts, we'll only be down one full-time officer." It would help a bit, but it still left her with all the tasks of the deputy chief of police.

"How are you—" he started, then cut himself off. *How are you going to manage the job and the investigation,* was what she assumed he was going ask. That was pretty much what had been going through her mind since Vic had told her he needed her to come back early.

"How can I help?" he asked instead.

He couldn't help, but just the fact that he'd offered meant a lot to her. Funny how a small act of kindness could bring her nearly to tears.

She lifted a shoulder. "I don't know. Maybe head up to the lab and keep me posted on what's happening up there? I was going to go myself, but, well . . ." She let her voice trail off, then added, "I know Marcus is up there, but he's, well, he's not in a great place right now."

"Of course." He pushed himself off the chair. "What time will you be off shift tonight?" he asked as she handed him his coat.

"I don't know. I'll know more when I look at the schedules."

He slid his coat on. "I'll call you as soon as we learn anything."

"Thank you," she said quietly.

He stopped in front of her and she wondered if he was going to kiss her again, but then he stepped back. "Call me at any time."

She nodded. "Oh, Drew?" she said as he opened the door.

He turned back. "Yes?"

"Find him, will you? Repetto. I know Joe said he's in DC, but if he thinks someone might be on to him, I don't want him to run. Not now that we finally know what happened."

Drew studied her, then dropped his hand from the door and took the two steps back toward her. This time he did kiss her. Just briefly. Then he said, "I promise you, Vince Repetto will not get away this time."

She had a fleeting thought of what a trained CIA agent could do to ensure a promise like that, but she was pretty sure that wasn't what he'd meant to imply. *Pretty* sure.

"Drew," she said, wanting to be sure.

"Go do your job. Call me if you need me. You know where I'll be and I'll certainly call you," he said then stepped away. He closed the door behind him before she could say any more.

Several moments passed as she stood there in the silence of her kitchen. Her mind toyed with the idea of letting what she'd learned in the last twenty-four hours filter through her thinking, but if she started to let it process, she wouldn't be able to stop. And between Vic bringing her back to work, learning who killed her mother and why, and knowing they needed to bring him to justice but not knowing how they would do it fourteen years later, Carly could feel herself teetering on the edge of being swept away by how overwhelming it all was.

For a fleeting moment, she wondered what it would be like to break down, to truly fall apart. She hadn't ever let herself. Maybe because she was afraid of seeming weak—if only to herself. Or maybe because she was afraid of what she might find out about herself if she gave herself permission not to stay strong, not to power on.

She sighed and started up the stairs to change into her uniform. Maybe someday she'd give herself permission. But today was not that day.

CHAPTER SEVENTEEN

DREW STARED INTENTLY AT A photo of Vince Repetto that Joe and Vivi had tacked to a whiteboard in the lab conference room they'd co-opted for their purposes. Behind him, Naomi and Joe were huddled around one computer going through Repetto's life history while Brian and Wyatt were huddled around another looking into the electronic traps and backdoors that had been set up to monitor searches of Marguerite, Sophia, and Tony. Repetto was smart, but not smart enough to have set up the kinds of things Naomi had found when she'd first started looking into him, nor did he have the ability to remove Marguerite from the fingerprint databases Vivi had used when the body first came in. Clearly, he had an accomplice or two. Even though his career had stalled out under the supervision of Perelli, Repetto had been on the job for over twenty years—a man could make a lot of friends in twenty years.

Turning around, Drew took in the room's activity. Vivi, Daniel, and Dr. Buckley were deep in conversation about something—a report that Vivi held and they all scrutinized. Mikaela and Mario were looking at a map of DC, using the information Naomi was digging up and trying to track Repetto's movements in the weeks prior to Marguerite's death.

And then there was him. Standing there on his own with nothing to do. He wasn't well versed in this type of investigation. He didn't have the expertise to read an evidence report on the trace elements found on Marguerite, nor did he have the technical abilities of Naomi and Brian. There were a lot of good people trying to resolve the situation, and for that he was very pleased. But he was feeling more and more useless by the minute.

"I have those financial reports you printed, Naomi," Ian said, entering the room with a stack of papers in one hand and several bags clutched in the other. After leaving a meeting in Albany and before heading to another back in Riverside, he'd stopped by to check in and run a few errands for the team—which included picking up lunch from a local deli and, apparently, the documents from the printer down the hall.

Finally, a report Drew could sink his teeth into. "If you're still doing your searches, Naomi, I can read through the financials. See if anything comes up," he offered.

Naomi didn't move her eyes from her screen, but gave him a wave as if to say "Carry on."

He glanced at Vivi to get her take—she'd become the natural leader of the group—only to find her watching him. "Does that work for you?" he asked her.

"Of course," she said, handing Daniel the report she'd been holding and approaching Drew. When she'd reached his side, she asked, "You okay?"

"I'm fine," he said, eyeing the papers Ian had placed on the table with the sandwiches before walking over to talk to Wyatt. When she didn't say anything in response, he turned his gaze to meet hers and felt a bit disconcerted by her scrutiny.

"Should I not be?" he asked.

Vivi tilted her head and studied him. "This isn't easy for you, is it?"

Great, the last thing he needed was to be subject to a shrink, especially not in front of everyone else. "It's fine," he said, adding a note of insistence to his voice. "I'll just take these." He reached for the papers. But she put a hand on his arm. He glanced up, catching the look Ian shot in their direction.

"Come get some coffee with me," Vivi said.

Drew thought Ian might try to save him from her meddling,

but no such luck. The sheriff gave a tiny shrug and turned his attention back to Wyatt.

"Fine," he said and followed her out. "Have you found anything in the reports?" he asked as they made their way down the hall.

"A few things we're following up on. It would be easier if we could figure out what items were used to cause all the different types of damage to Marguerite's body and then find those things, but we're working on it."

He started to ask her what she thought those items might be, but she continued. "I'm worried about Carly," she said, which was not even close to what he'd thought she might want to say to him. "And Marcus, of course."

He considered his answer. Vivienne DeMarco was leading him into a trap. Although, what that trap might be and why she would feel the need to lead him into it, he hadn't a clue. "I think you have a right to be concerned about them."

"Has she said anything to you? About all this?" Vivi asked as they rounded the corner to the small office kitchen.

He lifted a shoulder. "Not specifically, no."

"What do *you* think about everything?"

He leaned against the counter as she made herself a cup of coffee. "I think the same thing that probably everyone else is thinking: we need to find a way to bring Repetto in."

"What do you think our options are?" she pressed, also leaning against the counter, but turned toward him.

"Not sure I understand what you're asking."

Vivi took a sip of her coffee, then crossed an arm over her chest. "I mean, what do you think our chances are and what do you think the best way to pursue him is? The murder charges? The white-collar crimes? Tax evasion? There are any number of legal avenues we can pursue when it comes to bringing him to justice, do you think we're better off with one over the other?"

Drew eyed her for a long moment. His gut told him this was some sort of test because he knew, as of this moment, they were pursuing every avenue.

"I'm not sure."

She arched an eyebrow at him. "You've been in law enforcement for nearly twenty years and your gut isn't telling you anything?"

He felt his jaw clench. "I'm not in law enforcement. I'm in intelligence," he corrected. "The kind of law enforcement you practice is different from what I do."

"Hmm, it is, isn't it?" she replied. Then looked at him expectantly.

"What?"

She let out sigh, as if he should know better. "What we're doing in that room is very different from what you do, and yet you feel like you should be as competent and as capable as you are when you're in your own realm. And because you don't feel that way, you're starting to feel doubt and guilt and probably a bit superfluous is my guess."

"Do you 'shrink' everyone, or is this just my lucky day?" He'd meant the question to sound light, but it hadn't.

"Let's walk," she said, pushing off the counter. "And yes, I do it to everyone, all the time. I don't always talk about it or mention it, but it's part of who I am, at this point, so you'll just have to deal with it."

He pushed off the counter as well, and they made their way back to the hallway. "I'm not sure who to feel sorrier for, you or your friends."

"Me, probably," she offered, then shrugged. "But maybe not. My point is, ninety percent of what you know isn't relevant in that room in the same way ninety percent of what my husband knew when he left the Rangers wasn't relevant to his current role. It's not a projection on who you are, just what you've been trained to do."

"Thank you, Dr. Phil-lis."

"No need to get snippy," she said as they turned down the hall leading them back to the conference room. "Because you do have something this investigations needs."

"What's that?" he asked. Perhaps a bit sarcastically. Perhaps.

"Certainly, we want you to look over the financials. Between your intelligence training and the businesses your family owns, you probably have the best eye for reviewing those."

"Thanks."

"But," she paused at the door to the conference room and, with a hand on his arm, stopped him from entering. "The most important thing you can do is to be there for Carly."

He stared at her, taken aback by the personal nature of her comment. On the verge of telling her to mind her own business, Drew stopped himself. She wasn't making the suggestion to make him feel useful. By the look in her eye, he could see that this was something Vivi, as Carly's friend, *needed* him to do. She needed him to look out for her friend, to make sure Carly stayed okay. So that the rest of them could focus on what they had to in order to bring this whole situation to a resolution.

"Please," she added.

He nodded. "Of course."

He didn't miss the look of relief that crossed her face. "Thank you," she said quietly.

They both stood there for a moment, then she took a deep breath and gestured with her head toward the door. "Back to the lion's den. You going to come in and start with the finances?"

He paused. "In a minute. I want to call and check in with Carly first."

She gave him a smile and then, much to his surprise, rolled up on tiptoe and kissed his cheek.

"Thanks," she said again, turned, and was gone—swallowed up by the investigation before her.

And there he was, holding his phone and dialing a now quite familiar number.

• • •

Drew hit "send" on the update he'd just finished for Rina, leaned back in his chair at Kit's kitchen island, and stretched his arms over his head. After a long day, he was now at a little bit of a loss as to what to do. Carly was still at work, out on a call, and though Vivi had mentioned that Ian and some of his friends were getting together for dinner that night at Anderson's, he wasn't sure he wanted to join them.

"How goes it, Romeo?" Caleb asked, jogging up from his downstairs domain.

"What are you still doing here?"

Caleb chuckled. "That good, huh? Where is the lovely Deputy Chief tonight?"

Drew thought about telling Caleb where he could shove his question, but when Caleb opened the fridge and slid him a beer, he changed his mind.

"Working," he answered.

"It must be killing her to have everyone else focused on the case when she has to keep working."

Twisting the top off his bottle, he took a sip before answering. "It is. She hates it. But she's hanging in there."

"So what is the update?" Caleb leaned against the counter and crossed an arm over his chest, taking a sip of his own beer.

Drew glanced at his laptop, as if the summary he'd just sent to Rina would come to life and answer for him.

"Abbreviated version?"

Caleb rolled his eyes. "Dear god, please."

Drew's lips tipped into a small grin. "Okay, here goes. Vince Repetto, whose father-in-law is US Senator Buzz Laturna, has a gambling problem and an expensive wife."

"Add a mistress into the mix and he'd have the trifecta of clichés."

"Ha, not that we know of. But we think he may have been using at least nineteen other people in the same way he used Tony Lamot. Naomi and Brian are continuing to look into that."

"Of course they are."

"And the bullets that killed Sophia and Tony weren't from Repetto's gun. Of course, we weren't expecting them to be," he said, cutting off Caleb's running commentary. "I know this will come as a shock, but the actual bullets are magically missing from the evidence, so all we have to work from is a digital image of them. Even though we know the bullets didn't come from Repetto's gun, Daniel's resourceful. He's going to try to clean up the image, then run it through the system again to see if it matches any evidence from other crimes. None of us are holding our breath that it will be the key to solving this, but it's worth a try."

"So, is there any good news?"

"Actually, two good leads," he graced Caleb with a hold-your-horses look. "Repetto recently rented a yacht moored at a marina on the Potomac."

Caleb frowned. "It's almost November—weird time to rent a boat. Are you thinking it might be where he's stashed whoever he's working with?"

Drew nodded as he took another sip of his beer. "We are. Naomi and Brian are looking into that as well. Checking the utilities, CCTV, that kind of thing."

"And the second lead?"

It was Drew's turn to frown. "We don't actually know what it means yet, but the earrings Sophia gave to Carly just before she left for Los Angles were inscribed with the string 411SB58. And before you ask, yes, we think it's important, but, no, we have no idea what it means. Wyatt is running the number through every database he can think of and has come up blank so far. If you have any ideas, feel free to share."

"Gun registration?"

Drew shook his head.

"Airplane registration?"

He started to say no, then paused. "I actually don't know if he's run them through the FAA database. I'll text him and see."

"See, I'm sometimes good for something," Caleb said, raising his bottle in a mock cheer.

"I'll withhold judgment until something comes from it."

"Has anyone ever told you you're a hard ass?"

Drew laughed. "More than once."

"So what are you doing now? I know you weren't ruminating on the case when I came in. You didn't have that look you get when you're in Agent Carmichael mode."

The only thing that kept him from giving Caleb the finger was the fact that the guy was probably waiting for it. "I'm doing nothing."

"Wrong answer. You're brooding over Carly."

Drew glared at Caleb, even though he knew the younger man was trying to get a rise out of him. "I don't brood."

"Fine. You were analyzing, assessing, deconstructing—"

He cut Caleb off. "Vivi told me that Ian, Dash Kent, and David Hathaway are getting together for dinner tonight at Anderson's."

"Ah, and now you don't know whether or not you should go. Even though I bet the good doctor strongly recommended it, didn't she?"

Drew picked at the label on his bottle. "She didn't exactly *recommend* it."

"Maybe not in so many words."

He inclined his head. "Maybe not in so many words, no."

"So are you going to go? Spend a little time with Carly's best friends' husbands?"

"You make it sound so . . ."

"Normal? Like something a normal guy would do if he was interested in a woman—get to know her friends?"

"You're really annoying—you know that, right?"

Caleb lifted a shoulder. "Doesn't mean I'm not right."

Whether Caleb was right or not was something he decided he didn't need to contemplate. But he did need to eat. And Carly wasn't home yet, so he could kill some time at Anderson's. It certainly sounded better than spending any more time with Caleb, a man that Drew now realized was annoyingly more astute than he had ever suspected. He threw Caleb one if his more imperious glares then, without a word, drained his beer, grabbed his coat, and walked out.

Dash called Drew's name as he'd stepped into the restaurant.

He glanced around to find the man sitting toward the back of the room with David Hathaway. He gave a small wave of acknowledgement and made his way toward them. It appeared that Ian hadn't yet arrived, so whether he'd be invited to join them, he didn't know.

Dash stood and shook his hand when he stopped by their table. "Good to see you," he said. "You remember David from Kit and Garret's party?"

He said hello, reaching out to shake David's hand. Despite the fact that the two men were married to two of Kit and Carly's good friends, he knew very little about either of them—only that Dash was one of the area's local veterinarians and David was an arson investigator and firefighter.

"Join us?" Dash asked. "We just ordered drinks and are waiting for Ian before we order some dinner."

"You don't mind?" Drew asked, feeling a bit awkward.

"Of course not," David said as a waiter stopped by to place two beer mugs on the table. "The two sodas go to the pool room," David added, speaking to the server. "My stepson, James, and his friend Chelsea are here too," he said, turning back to Drew.

"Can I get you anything?" the waiter asked as Drew removed his coat and took a seat.

"I'll have whatever local you have on tap," he said to the waiter, who nodded and moved away. He looked back at the two men. "But no wives?" he asked in response to David's comment about his young companions.

Both shook their heads.

"Jesse and Emma flew to Seattle today to visit her parents for a few days," David said.

"And Matty is at home with the twins, but her mom is up visiting," Dash said. "Her mom and my mom are good friends so, together, they're taking care of Charley and Daphne—and Matty is getting some much-deserved sleep."

David shrugged. "Then again, this is kind of a guys' thing

anyway. We try to get together about once a month on our own," he added, echoing what Vivi had told Drew earlier.

Drew supposed their "guys' night" was a good thing. He hadn't ever been so entwined in another person's life that he'd needed to carve out his own time. If anything, his life had been the opposite—he'd actually needed to carve out time to be with other people or he would have stayed heads down in Langley all hours of the day and night.

He was about to ask when Ian would arrive when the front door opened and in walked the sheriff. Drew noticed Ian's lack of surprise at seeing him there and guessed that Vivi had told her husband that she'd mentioned the outing to him.

"Drew, glad you're joining us," Ian said as he sat down. The bartender called over and asked Ian if he wanted his usual; Ian replied with a prompt, and definitive, yes.

He had an urge to ask Ian how Marcus was doing, but since neither Dash nor David knew anything about that whole situation, and didn't need to, he bit his tongue. Then he wondered what he would talk about without work to discuss.

He'd been on plenty of dates and attended enough business meetings to fill a yearly planner, but when was the last time he'd hung out with friends—or in this case, potential friends—with no agenda, no plans, and pretty much nothing in common? He took a sip of beer, or several, while the other three caught each other up on their wives and kids and, as he listened, wondered what he had gotten himself into. It wasn't that he was disinterested, he just didn't have anything to add, for obvious reasons. Well, if nothing else, he'd at least enjoy a good burger.

"You like football?" David asked him suddenly. Drew felt his heart sink a little. He was *not* looking forward to an evening of talking football.

"More of a basketball fan," he answered.

"And how do you feel about politics?" Dash asked.

"At this point, a necessary evil."

"How do you like Windsor?" David followed up.

Drew cast Ian a questioning look, but the man didn't look interested in shedding any light on the conversation—not judging by the glint in his strangely colored eyes.

"It's nice," he answered slowly. "It's beautiful—small, but pretty."

"Think you'll be sticking around?" Dash volleyed.

On that subject, Drew intended to stay close-lipped. He saw their intentions were good—they were scoping him out—but *he* had no intention of saying anything that might get back to Carly without first saying it to her.

He shrugged in response. "Did any of you watch that Knicks game two days ago?" he asked instead. It was apparently the right question, as the three men at the table promptly launched into a "discussion" about the state of basketball, their favorite teams, and, of course, who would win the title. As a bit of a basketball junkie himself, *this* was a conversation in which Drew could happily participate.

As he drove to Carly's a few hours later, he realized he'd had a good time. There was a lot about that realization that bothered him. It seemed to highlight how few "good times" he'd had lately. But the night had also driven home the point he'd made to Carly a few days earlier about how few friends—real friends—he actually had. Not that David, Dash, and Ian were now his bosom buddies, but they could become friends and, more importantly, he saw what good friends they were to each other.

But he'd chosen his life all those years ago. And he didn't regret it. Not truly. At least not often.

With that somewhat dispiriting thought, he turned into Carly's driveway. The lights streaming from her porch and kitchen came as no surprise, he'd known she would be home, but they were a welcome sight.

"Come in," she called when he knocked.

"You didn't lock your door?" As the door swung open under his touch, he walked into what appeared to be an unoccupied house. He had heard her clearly, but he couldn't see her. Light from the television flickered in the living room, casting the room into ever-changing blue hues.

"I've only been home for about fifteen minutes. I figured you'd be by sooner or later. If you hadn't shown up in ten minutes or so, I would have locked it," she replied from the couch.

Drew closed the door, locked it, and walked into the living room to find her lying down. She'd changed from her uniform and was tucked under a blanket with her head on a pillow and a remote in her hand.

"What are you watching?" He removed his coat and took a seat in the upholstered chair. The video obviously had something to do with horses, but beyond recognizing that someone rode an enormous animal as it hurled itself over jumps that looked at least as tall as he was, he knew nothing about what he saw on the screen.

"That's me," she said softly.

His eyes focused to watch Carly and her horse jump another fence that looked impossible to clear. But clear it they did, and when a score flashed up on the screen—numbers that meant nothing to him—it appeared that her trip around the course was over.

He let out a little sigh of relief, which was stupid. She'd obviously survived that long-ago ride, since she was sitting right next to him. But then, to his distress, she rewound the DVD and pressed play again.

"Is that really you?"

She nodded against her pillow. "Yes. This is one of the DVDs from the boxes Mikaela brought. Practically my whole riding career was caught on tape. Or DVD, to be more precise."

"Those jumps look twice your size, at least." He managed to choke out the words as he watched her sail over something that looked like two pickup trucks backed up against each other, only instead of truck beds there were round poles.

She laughed. "Not quite. This was a four-and-half-foot jumper course."

Next, he watched her fly over something that looked like a brick wall. "Is that as high as they go?" Dear god, he hoped so.

She shook her head. "No, grand prix events have fences over five feet tall and can be wider than six feet, in some cases. This was a big class for someone my age, but not the biggest."

Drew watched her clear the last fence again and this time she let the video continue on to another event. In this one, she was riding a big gray horse. Carly wasn't petite, but she looked tiny perched on the beast's back. And from the first jump, he could see the difference in this animal versus the one he'd just watched. The first horse, big and brown, had seemed focused and calm. This massive gray beast looked like a teenager who would rather be out partying.

As he watched, the horse let out a buck after the first fence. The move had his heart rate kicking up; he glanced at Carly. She was smiling at the sight. He frowned. Horses were a different world, but he had a hard time believing she could be smiling about almost being dumped from an animal that clearly had more important things on its mind than its rider.

His eyes turned back to the screen to see Carly sitting up in the saddle trying to wrangle the horse through a turn. The horse's head came up and its body seemed to be bouncing up and down more than moving forward. But somehow she managed to get the beast focused on the next fence and they both made it over.

Unfortunately, the next jump had different results. Drew watched Carly pick up speed as she headed toward a fence that didn't look very big. He didn't know why she would need so much speed for something that didn't compare, height wise, to what she'd already jumped, but the move was clearly intentional, she had a plan. Only it was a plan the horse didn't seem to agree with. About six feet in front the fence, the gray simply stopped. Physics and gravity took over and Carly went sailing over the animal's head.

As he watched her land in a heap on the dirt of the arena floor, Drew felt as if the air had been knocked out of *his* lungs. Transfixed, he stared, willing her to get up. Again, he knew it was ridiculous, but still, watching her lie helpless on the ground was not how he'd planned to spend the remainder of his evening.

After what felt like an eternity, she rose. Dusting the dirt from her white pants, she watched as someone brought her horse back; the cheeky animal had gone for a run around the arena once its rider had been dislodged. Carly and the helper shared a few words, then she raised her hand and acknowledged someone, a judge maybe, and led her horse from the arena.

He turned to look at her again. "You could have been killed."

Again, she smiled. "Yes, that wasn't one of my more graceful dismounts, but Athena was worth it."

"Athena?"

"The mare I was riding. That was a water jump. They're very wide, which is why I picked up so much speed. She'd decided that day that water wasn't her thing. But when she was on, she was really on. She was one of the most talented jumpers I ever rode."

"Um, she didn't look like it." He found it hard to believe that the beast was anything other than a killer waiting for an opportunity.

"She was moody," was all Carly said. He watched as a soft smile stole across her features, the kind of smile he hadn't seen from her before. He stared at her, at the look of raw joy and memories reflected in her eyes, then he turned his attention back to the screen.

For several minutes he watched her younger self take another round over a series of jumps, again on Athena. But this time, the horse looked completely different. The gray, light on her feet, looked intent on attacking every fence, and even he could see how tuned in to Carly she was—turning corners, taking smaller strides or longer ones, speeding up, and slowing down. The round was entirely different than the first one he'd watched. And when her score flashed on the screen, the video cut right into another round.

"This is the jump off," Carly said.

"The what?" he asked as Carly and the mare circled on the screen.

"The jump off. For the riders who go clean—meaning, we didn't knock any rails down or have time penalties—we go into a jump off. It's a much shorter, tighter course and the fastest time with no rails wins. Or if there aren't any clean rounds, the person with the least penalties wins."

Her explanation hadn't taken more than a few seconds, but by the time she'd finished, she was clearing the second jump. For the next forty seconds—according to the ticking clock on the screen—he watched the pair make seemingly impossible turns, launch over fences, and gallop around the arena. When the round was over, a score of first place flashed on the screen.

"You won."

"I did," she replied softly. He could her the pride still lingering in her voice, even after all these years. She rewound the DVD and played it again.

"You loved this, didn't you?" he asked as he watched her start the same round.

"I did," she said. He rather suspected she should have answered "I do."

"It was like flying. No, that's not entirely true. There's something, well," she paused. "That day, that round," she said with nod toward the screen, "Athena and I were of the same mind, we wanted the same thing, we were speaking the same language. Do you have any idea how powerful that is? To have that kind of connection with something? It's nearly impossible to find with another person, someone who speaks the same language, but then to find it with an animal? It changes you, it changes the way you see the world. There's a rush in it to be sure, but beyond that, having that kind of trust between two animals is a bond that can't be broken and that feeling is something we riders seek over and over again, almost like a drug. Yes, we want to win, but more than that, I think, in all our hearts, we want that indescribable *feeling* of being connected, of being part of a team."

Her eyes hadn't strayed from the screen as she spoke and when she finished he glanced back to the image on the TV as well. Her score flashed again and the round was over. Looking back at Carly, he saw that she was still smiling, still remembering that day all those years ago. Watching her, sitting not four feet from where he sat, he had no doubt that she remembered exactly what she'd felt that day.

He wondered if she might ask him if he had ever felt anything like what she had described, but studying her face, he realized her own memories, memories she probably hadn't let herself experience in years, had drawn her to a different place. A place that had nothing to do with him. And he was grateful for that.

Because he hadn't. He hadn't ever felt the kind of freedom and connection and power she talked about. Yes, he'd had some good moments, moments when he'd pulled off something that seemed impossible and, yes, he'd experienced an adrenaline rush. But he hadn't ever felt anything like what she'd described, especially knowing that words, as powerful as they could be, probably didn't even begin to describe her actual experience.

For the next hour or so, they sat in companionable silence and watched. He watched her riding different kinds of horses, even some ponies. Some of her rounds were high and fast but some were slower paced with lower fences and seemed to be focused on something other than speed—though what that was, he didn't know. Someday he'd ask, but for now, he was content just to share the evening with her.

After the DVD ran out, he looked over to find her asleep. With a small smile, he rose, climbed her stairs, and pulled the comforter off her bed. After coming back down and laying it over the throw blanket she'd already draped over herself, he turned off the television and all the lights but one, and slid into his coat.

With one last look at her, he set the alarm and quietly left.

CHAPTER EIGHTEEN

CARLY AWOKE WITH A START the next morning. It took her a moment to realize she was on her couch with her comforter sprawled on top of her. She glanced at the chair where she'd last seen Drew to find it empty. She had no doubt he'd set the alarm behind him when he'd left.

As she sat up, her eyes fell on the horse competition DVD cases sprawled in front of the TV and something niggled at her brain. She sat quietly to see if it would form into a full-fledged thought. Before it had the opportunity though, her phone rang.

Picking the device up from the table, she sighed when the number popped up. One of the part-time officers—no doubt calling to check in after her night on duty. Carly gave a little prayer of thanks that Vic had decided to make an offer to Josie and made a note to herself to ask him when she would start. Pushing aside dreams of less-busy days, she hit the answer button as she made her way upstairs to shower and change for work.

Forty-five minutes later, she hung her jacket on the back of her desk chair and took a seat. With the two night-duty officers signed out, and Marcus and one other part-time officer on for the day, she pulled out the incident reports from the night before as well as those from the few days she'd been out.

"Hey," Marcus said as he walked into her office. "Did you get a good night's sleep?"

She knew that he was really asking if Drew had kept her up, so she shot him a look before motioning for him to shut the door. He shut it then sat down in the chair across from her.

"Have you heard anything new?" she asked.

"You haven't talked to anyone today?"

She shook her head. "No, is there something I should know?"

"Not that I know of. I was asking because I haven't heard anything either."

"So, we're waiting to find out if the bullets will tell us anything, Naomi is still checking on Repetto, and they're digging into the boat rental," Carly said, mostly to herself, as she sat back in her chair. She didn't bother hiding the frustration hounding her.

"And the number," Marcus added. "Also, there's something we need to talk about." He shifted in his seat.

"Number?" she asked, ignoring the second part of his comment for the moment.

"The number Wyatt found on the earrings," he reminded her.

And then it hit her—not what the numbers meant, but the thought that had danced in her head earlier. It had just come at her full force.

"What?" Marcus asked, obviously sensing her change of focus.

"I don't know, it might be nothing."

"It's not as if you're going to be wasting my time by talking about it. I'm not going out on patrol for another thirty minutes."

"The number. I think it might have something to do with horses," she said.

"*Horses?*" He didn't hide his skepticism.

"Yes, think about it. What did mom's life consist of? Us, horses, and her friends. If the number doesn't have anything to do with us, maybe it has something to do with horses, something she thought one of us might recognize if we saw it."

"You think it was a message to us? Or you, to be more precise, since my knowledge of what you guys did in the barn was limited to noticing how attractive the female working students she hired were." For the first time in a long time, Carly caught her brother giving a glimpse of a smile for a good memory from back then.

"I think it's a possibility. Don't you?"

"I suppose, but you don't recognize it, do you?"

She shook her head. "I don't. But I've been out of that world for a long time and have intentionally forgotten most of it. If I'd seen the number back then, it may have been different."

"So, what do you propose?"

She rose and reached for her jacket. "Let's go up and talk to Trudy White. She might know."

"She manages a racing barn," Marcus pointed out, but rose as well. "Racing horses is a completely different thing than what you and Mom did."

Carly smiled as she slid her arms into her jacket and grabbed her keys. "See, you remember more than you think about our horse operation. And you're right, it is different. But remember, until she moved up here, Trudy spent most of her time on the same circuit I used to ride. She's closer to it and may recognize the numbers."

Marcus gave her a non-committal response but followed her out to her cruiser. Once inside it, she flipped on the wipers as they headed west of town. A cold front had moved in, along with rain clouds, and in just a few day's time the brilliant colors of fall had faded almost entirely, turning a monochrome yellow. Within the next few weeks, those leaves that were still clinging to their branches would fall onto the green fields before being covered by snow after a month or so—assuming there was snow at Thanksgiving this year. Even with the muted colors, she found beauty in the rolling hills and appreciated the way the land seemed to be preparing itself, much like people did, for the change in season.

"Have you ever been up to Trudy's barn?" Marcus asked.

Keeping her eyes on the road, Carly nodded. "A few years ago they had a break-in, but I haven't been up since." She made a left turn onto a hard-packed gravel road heading up a hill toward the farm. Within seconds it felt like they'd been transported back in time—as it often did around Windsor—with nothing but rolling hills, a gravel road, and an occasional home or barn visible down a long driveway. If she'd seen the hunt ride by—and they did have an active hunt in the county—the only thing that would have reminded her what era they were in would have been the fact that the women now wore britches and no longer rode side saddle.

"You?" she asked.

Marcus shook his head. "No, not to the barn. I've met Trudy in town a few times, though. She introduced me to John Green Sr. and John Green Jr., the owner and his son."

Carly smiled.

"What?"

"I guess I never realized they were Trudy White and John Green. I wonder if there is a Colonel Mustard or Miss Scarlet involved in the enterprise too."

Marcus chuckled. "I hadn't ever thought of it that way either. But, with everything else going on, maybe we shouldn't be looking for similarities to a game of unsolved murders."

Carly gave a small laugh as she turned onto the driveway of Birch Hill Racing. "No, you're probably right."

However, as the road climbed a gentle hill and the massive owner's house came into view, she heard Marcus suck in a breath. Because even in an area that hosted many large summer and weekend homes for the wealthy of New York, Birch Hill was quite a sight. Sitting off to the right of the drive and up another hill, the massive stone home, with a grand staircase leading to its wrap-around veranda, looked more like something to be found in Newport, Rhode Island, than Windsor.

"But, then again," Marcus said, letting the rest of his comment hang. Birch Hill would be the perfect location to shoot a sequel to the movie *Clue*.

"I know," she said, acknowledging the overwhelming nature of the building. "But we're not headed there. Trudy's place is on the other side of the barn and, chances are, that's where she is."

They made their way past the drive leading up to the main house and toward the large whitewashed barn. Horses grazed in the fields to their left, and in the distance they could see one bend of the practice track that lay behind the main barn and to the right.

It was perfectly situated for the owners to be able to watch the training through binoculars from their porch.

Giving a wide berth to a semi-truck-sized horse trailer, Carly pulled into a spot next to a newer-model diesel pick-up. As she climbed from her car and shut the door behind her, she paused to take in the trailer. She hadn't seen one up close in years, but she knew well that it was getting prepped to ship horses somewhere warm for the coming winter. It would be loaded with hay, grain, supplements, buckets, water, blankets, and tack. The horses would be bundled, wrapped, and, depending on their temperament and what they were going to be doing when they arrived at their destination, possibly given a mild sedative. Then they would be tucked into their stalls, the ramp lifted, and the door shut before the truck began its journey south.

She'd forgotten how many times she'd done the same thing with her own horses. She'd forgotten how much she'd known about every horse ever loaded onto her trailer. She'd forgotten what it was like to feel the excitement of opportunity—wondering if the show would be successful, if she would win, if her young horse would have a good experience. No matter how many times she'd loaded a trailer for a trip, she'd always had a sense of hope, of wonder.

"You okay?" Marcus asked, coming to stand beside her. She blinked, realizing she must have been standing there for a while.

"Yeah, I'm fine," she said as she turned away from the trailer and led Marcus toward the barn.

"Carly, Marcus, over here!" Trudy's voice called from what looked like a hay shed.

Carly glanced at her brother and they followed Trudy's voice.

"Sorry, I'm in the middle of getting some of this hay sorted for the trip," Trudy said once they'd found her atop the stacked bales. She turned away to give directions to one of the barn hands, directing him to take several bales to the trailer and several to the main barn.

Jumping down, she wiped her hands on her jeans then held her right one out to shake both their hands. "Sorry for the chaos.

We're getting ready to ship our yearlings down to northern Florida to start their training in the new year."

"No problem." Carly couldn't help but smile as she shook Trudy's hand. She knew just how much work organizing such an endeavor required, and even so, she'd heard affection in Trudy's voice when she'd mentioned the yearlings—like she was referring to her own children. And in that subtext, Carly recognized a kindred spirit—horse-people were born, not made.

"What can I help you with? And do you mind if we walk and talk? I need to get the trailer loaded so they can head out by noon." Trudy didn't bother to wait for an answer and started toward the main barn.

"Everything going okay?" Carly asked as she and Marcus followed.

Trudy turned her head and flashed a sardonic smile, her long brown ponytail swinging with the motion. "Ever try to wrangle nine thoroughbred yearlings into a trailer? They are pretty well mannered, considering, but a few of them have egos and take exception to being told what to do."

Carly smiled, she was well acquainted with the egos of horses. "Not thoroughbreds, but I do know what you're talking about."

They stopped at a stall and Trudy pulled a blanket off a rack on the door. "I didn't realize you were a horse person," she said, sounding more curious about why she hadn't known than surprised at the fact itself.

"It was a long time ago," Carly said, reaching into her pocket for the piece of paper on which she'd written the numbers Wyatt had given her. "So long ago that I can't recognize this string of numbers. I was hoping maybe you could."

Trudy stopped folding the blanket and reached for the piece of paper Carly held. "A tattoo number?" she asked, referring to the tattoos given to racehorses before their first race.

Carly shook her head. "I think it has something to do with the hunter-jumper world."

Trudy glanced down at the numbers then promptly handed

them back. "You're right. Well, they aren't racing numbers, and are not limited to the hunter-jumper world either. It's an FEI passport number."

Of course. Now that Trudy had identified it, Carly was stunned that she hadn't seen it sooner. The FEI was the international body that governed the higher levels of competition. Not only that, it also issued equine passports. Every horse she and her mother had imported or exported had had one—people needed passports, so did horses.

"Do you recognize it?" Marcus asked.

"Is that from a horse of yours?" Trudy pulled another blanket off a stall door.

Carly shook her head. "I don't recognize it, but it could have come from one of our horses."

Trudy stopped folding the blanket and looked at her. "You used to ride? Not just ride, but compete too?"

"It was a long time ago," Carly said again, pulling out her phone in a rush to call Naomi and Wyatt so they could run the number through the FEI database.

"Well, if you ever want to ride again. Stop by. Not this week, but things should quiet down after next week," Trudy offered. "We have all these race horses, of course, but I have a few jumpers that are retired or recovering from various injuries up here with us too."

"Thanks, I may take you up on that," Carly replied, surprising herself. "Would you excuse me? I need to make a call." She held up her phone.

"Please," Trudy said, "go ahead. Would you mind giving me a hand?" she asked, turning to Marcus.

"Of course not," he replied, after a brief hesitation. Trudy promptly handed him a stack of blankets. She pulled three more down from three different doors then led Marcus out of the barn, leaving Carly alone to make her call.

As she waited for Naomi to pick up, she breathed in deeply. The scents of leather, hay, and horse filled her senses. It had been so long, too long, since she'd had the pleasure of experiencing those comingling smells.

Naomi answered on the third ring and Carly filled her in quickly. Through a stall door that had a window onto the yard, she watched Trudy and Marcus making their way toward the trailer. Naomi assured her they'd get right on it and, even though Carly wanted Naomi to look the number up right away, she knew Marcus would want to listen in as well, so they agreed to touch base again once Carly and Marcus had returned to the station. It was the right decision, but one that left her feeling anxious.

Until a big bay horse stuck its head out of a stall door and gave her a nudge, drawing a soft laugh from her. Carly slipped the phone into her pocket, and reached out to rub the horse's nose. Obviously a cuddler, the bay's brown head dropped into better reach and she gave it a good scratch between its ears before its head came up and rubbed against her side. Carly laughed again as she braced herself against the push of the horse then wrapped her arm around its nose and dropped a kiss on its muzzle. The feeling of regret that washed through her when she realized she had to leave, that she couldn't hang out with Trudy, this horse, and all the other horses, was a strong one.

With one more rub between the bay's eyes, she stepped away and kept walking, a bit worried that if she stopped to notice any of the other horses she might not get out of there for several hours. As she rounded the barn toward the car, she found Marcus and Trudy walking down the ramp of the trailer empty handed. After thanking Trudy again, she and Marcus climbed into their car and headed back to the police station.

When they arrived, Sharon, the station's receptionist, handed Carly a stack of messages, old school style, then she and Marcus headed into her office. Thumbing through the messages as she removed her coat, she noticed a call from Josie and made a mental note to call their new recruit back, hoping she would be able to start sooner rather than later.

"Did you meet her?" she asked, holding the slip of paper up for Marcus to read as he sat down in the chair across her desk.

"Yeah, she seems like she'll work out. It'll be nice to have a little more help around here. Not that I'm the one taking the brunt of the heavy lifting."

Carly glanced at his face as she sat down and noted his narrowed eyes. But rather than probe into the reason for the sarcasm she'd just heard, she placed the slip of paper aside and began dialing Naomi's number on her desk phone. When the line picked up, Carly hit the speaker button and Naomi's voice filled her office.

"We found her," Naomi said.

"Who?" Marcus asked.

"The horse the number was referring to."

"Who is it?" Carly felt the adrenaline kick in. This could be the lead they so desperately needed.

"A mare you and your mom imported from Holland. Her name on the passport is Seraphina KM."

Carly sat back as an image of a three-year-old chestnut mare filled her mind. She remembered Sera well. All the horses they'd imported had good minds, some were quirky to be sure, but Sera stuck out for her unusual temperament. She had been a young horse with the soul of a kindly, wise old woman. They'd had her for a year before the murders, and in that year she'd come a long way. Carly had been getting ready to take her to her first show when she'd left for Los Angeles and never seen any of the horses again.

"She went on to have a very successful career," Carly said. "She won several big grand prix events and represented the US in the World Cup and the World Games." When she felt Marcus's eyes on her she looked up. And realized what she'd revealed—to the extent that she could, she had secretly followed the careers of all the horses that had ever come through their family barn. She may not have been able to ride any longer, but obviously her heart hadn't let her give it up so easily.

She glanced away, out the window with a view onto the alley

behind the station. The day, cloudy to begin with, was starting to darken, and the look of winter hovered in the air.

Naomi cleared her throat. "Well, yes. We know she's living in Florida now. She was bred for a few years, but now she appears to be retired."

"At eighteen, that makes sense," Carly murmured.

"But here's the interesting thing. The day after you two were sent to Los Angeles, your mom called your family vet out to the farm. I pulled those records and your mom had a microchip implanted into Seraphina."

"But that's a common practice," Marcus interjected. "All the horses were chipped, even I knew that. It prevents fraud and such."

Carly frowned in thought. "That's true, but Sera was chipped before she was imported. Unless there was a problem with the original, there would have been no reason for Mom to have had another one implanted in her."

"And since you weren't showing her, you wouldn't have had any reason to even know if there'd been a problem with the original." Marcus picked up her line of thought.

"So whatever Mom had implanted in Sera, it wasn't likely anything Sera would have needed. It would have been something different," she said.

"But would Mom have known how to get data onto a chip?" Marcus asked, looking at Carly.

She shrugged.

"Bob Weston," Joe Franks' voice answered.

"Bob who?" Carly asked.

Marcus sat back. "You're right. It wasn't Bob so much as his son. Bob Weston was married to Sue Karol Weston," he said, directing his comment to her. "Sue and Uncle Tony used to play tennis together. Tony was starting to do some business with Bob when he and Mom were killed. Bob was helping their son start a microchip company."

"Kenneth Weston's company is a huge manufacturer of GPS chips now," Naomi said picking up the narrative. "They are based out of the Boston area. Drew just left to talk to him to see if he ever did any work with your mom."

At the sound of Drew's name Carly couldn't help but glance up at her brother. A quick look of disapproval crossed his face, but he said nothing.

"We thought it might be better to have someone talk with him in person. Drew has some business acquaintances in common with Kenneth, so he volunteered to go. He's also going to stop by Lorraine Silva's house on his way back, to check in on her," Vivi added.

"I've cleared him to tell her a bit about the investigation," Mikaela said. "We felt that, as Marguerite's last of kin, she deserves to know what we can tell her."

At the thought of Lorraine, a shard of panic lanced through Carly. "Do you think Repetto knows about Lorraine? Do we need to be worried about her?"

Vivi chuckled. "Turns out Drew's had people keeping an eye on her since we first identified Marguerite and figured out Lorraine's role in raising you and Marcus. He has a friend who owns a private security company."

For the moment, Carly opted not to ponder the strategic but thoughtful action Drew had taken. "Do we know anything else?" she asked.

"What about the guy on the boat?" Marcus prompted.

"Ah yes, that guy," Brian said.

"He's a pain in the arse," Naomi interjected.

Brian murmured his agreement then elaborated. "So we tracked the utilities like Drew suggested and, sure enough, there is a disproportionate amount of electricity flowing to the boat Repetto rented. We took a look at the security footage at the marina and saw one of our favorite hackers boarding the boat one night."

"A hacker?"

"Yep," Naomi answered. "A particularly gross one too. In every sense of the word. He's not the good kind. Not like us. But he hasn't ever done anything straight up illegal, either."

"Does he have the skills to erase Marguerite from the system?" Carly asked.

"Most definitely," Brian answered.

"Isn't *that* illegal?" she wondered aloud.

"Hacking into the federal system is illegal. But it's possible he didn't hack into it."

"So you're saying Repetto somehow got him legal access into the system?" Carly had no idea how that was even possible.

"I know," Naomi said, responding to Carly's disbelief. "It sounds crazy and we agree that it sounds crazy. But we're looking into it. We're looking into secret injunctions, search warrants— those kinds of things—that Repetto might have gotten, or might have forged, that would make Jason Moran's—that's the hacker's name—access at least appear legal."

"If it's fake, wouldn't Moran notice?" Marcus asked.

"Yes," Brian answered. "But if the forged or fraudulent document that granted the access *looked* real enough, he'd have a solid defense if it were ever called into question."

"Which is why you guys are keeping an eye on him—it's possible that he doesn't care whether or not something is *illegal*, just whether or not he can get *busted* for doing it," Carly said.

"Like I said, he's never done anything illegal, but with loyalties like his, it would be easy to slip over to the other side with the right incentives and protections in place," Naomi responded.

"Okay, so that's the hacker. Anything else? What about Repetto himself?" Carly asked.

"He flew up to Boston this morning on an investigation," Joe weighed in. "We've been monitoring his calls and he's reached out to some interesting people."

"Such as?" Marcus prompted.

"He seems to be picking up where he left off. He's placed calls to two people who were involved in investigations conducted by his team that ultimately yielded no charges," Joe said.

"And you think he's going to try to do to them what he did to Uncle Tony," Marcus suggested.

"We think he's testing them out," Vivi answered. "And before you ask, yes, we're following up on this as well."

"What about the bullet?" Marcus probed. "Any leads there?"

"That's been interesting," Sam cut in. "I was able to clean up the image and we got two hits. The same gun was used in a robbery/homicide in Los Angeles about four years after your mother and uncle were killed, and then again in a homicide in a small town on one of the San Juan Islands in Puget Sound."

"But no leads on who is using it?" Carly asked.

"No," Sam said. "Neither case resulted in an arrest, but we've requested the files from both police departments and they should be here sometime today. We'll see what we can find once we have those."

Carly had started to ask Vivi what they hoped to find in the police reports when there was a knock at her office door.

Without waiting for Carly to respond, Sharon popped her head in and said, "Josie Webb is here."

Carly gave her a blank look.

"Her first day is today," Sharon went on in answer to the unasked question. "She left a message saying she'd be in right after she picked up her uniform and got her paperwork done."

"I'll be right there," Carly said, her eyes flicking to Marcus in question. Clearly he'd also missed the memo about today being Josie's first day. Sharon nodded and shut the door again.

"It sounds like you need to go?" Vivi said over the speakerphone.

"Yeah, I guess we do," Carly answered. "You'll keep us updated?"

"Of course," Vivi replied. "And you can call anytime."

They disconnected and Carly looked up at her brother, recognizing the wary look in his eyes.

"I don't want to train a new recruit," he said flat out. "And besides, I still need to talk to you about something."

Whatever he needed to talk about could wait—if it had been urgent, he would have already brought it up. "That's too bad," she answered. "I need to stay here and go through files, the budget, scheduling, and all."

"Carly, I'm not so good with people right now," he managed to say.

"Yeah, I noticed. And while I'd like to be sympathetic—I *am* sympathetic—the fact is, I can't do anything with her today. Nothing I'm doing is anything she needs to train on. We need her out on patrol as soon as possible. We need her to be comfortable enough to eventually *lead* patrols. And I don't have the time to do that with her, so, whether you want it or not, the job is yours."

Her words had been practical, but she *needed* him to do this, and she needed him to do it without complaining.

His lips tightened but he gave a curt nod. "I'll take her around today, then maybe one of the part-timers can take her tomorrow?"

Carly let out a breath and agreed to the compromise.

"If you hear anything today, you'll let me know?" he asked.

"Of course."

She watched as he stood and grabbed his coat from the back of the chair. When the situation with Marguerite and Vince Repetto was over, she and her brother were going to sit down and have a long chat.

"Thanks, Marcus," she said as he moved out the door. He didn't answer but raised his arm in response. When the door closed behind him, she looked down at her desk and computer. Paperwork and budgets would make up most of her day. While her friends were out trying to find out who had murdered her mother, she would be reviewing budgets. While Drew checked on Lorraine and talked to Kenneth Weston, she would be scheduling.

Never in her adult life had she felt so frustratingly futile.

CHAPTER NINETEEN

DREW LEANED AGAINST THE PORCH railing waiting for Carly to come home. He'd talked to her a few times throughout the day—on his way to Boston, after leaving Ken Weston's office, and during his visit with Lorraine—and he'd found himself wanting to hear her voice more and more as the day had gone on.

But as he stood in the cold, his hands shoved into his jacket pockets, he recognized that if the kiss they'd shared was anything to go by, getting involved with Carly would be like diving into a churning sea where forces stronger than he could fight or control would take over. And while there was something awe inspiring about such power, the thought of yielding to it did not rest easy with him, yet.

However, when her car pulled into her drive and her headlights swept over him, he realized that when he saw her most of his hesitancies fled. When he saw her, as he did now, what he wanted most was to feel her lips on his, her legs wrapped around him, and her hands, well, anywhere.

When her door opened, though, and Carly climbed out, Drew knew that the memory of their kiss hadn't been foremost in her mind. Her body jerked like a poorly controlled marionette as she exited her car. Her hand shook as she wrapped it around the door handle. Pausing, she turned to look at him over her shoulder. Her mouth was tight and she gave a little shake of her head before reaching for something inside her car.

"Carly?" he asked as she straightened up.

"It's been a long day, Drew, I need to be alone tonight," she answered, holding her coat in front of her.

Her words echoed what she'd said a few nights earlier. The night he'd left and regretted it. The night he'd left and *she'd* regretted it. He wasn't going to let it happen again.

"Why don't we go inside and talk about it?" he asked, shoving off the railing.

She started toward him, toward her front door, swerving around him as she passed. "It's not a good night. I know I said it before and then said I didn't mean it, but I really do need to be alone tonight." She kept her back to him as she unlocked her door.

"Too bad," he said as the door swung open and he reached over her head to hold it for them both to pass through. She looked at him over her shoulder again. He hadn't a clue what had happened, but the weary frustration on her face—frustration that seemed to have her close to tears—rocked him.

He swallowed. "Your alarm," he said as the beeping picked up speed to indicate that it was headed for a full-on blast. She stared at him, then abruptly moved to the device and keyed in the code.

Drew locked the door behind them and moved into the house where he waited for her to turn around, but she didn't. Instead, she kept her back to him as she tossed her coat onto one of the kitchen chairs.

"Look Drew, please. I'm not in the mood for company tonight, and I can't," she paused, maybe looking for the right word. "I can't be bothered with any niceties. I really can't."

He could tell from her voice that she was speaking the truth—and it was a truth, a place, he'd been before. "Then don't."

She turned. And when she did, he noticed that her uniform was stained. Barely visible on the dark material, it was more the telltale stiffening of the fabric than any color that gave it away. It was soaked with blood.

"Jesus, Carly," he managed to choke out. "You're covered in blood." He didn't move toward her. The logical part of his mind told him it wasn't hers. He *knew* this to be true for any number of reasons, not the least of which was that she wouldn't be walking around if she'd been injured enough to warrant that much blood. Still, he held back because he felt his own hands shaking and he didn't trust himself to go to her.

"It's not mine," she said, her voice faded in fatigue.

"I can tell," he responded. "What happened?"

She opened her mouth, then closed it. Then she opened it again and spoke. "Look, I can't do this right now. Right now, I just need to shower and be alone. It was a shitty day. I really need some time to myself."

"Too bad." The words were out of his mouth before he'd had a chance to think. He'd said them before, outside moments earlier, but now—after seeing her, hearing her—they seemed to take on a different meaning. A meaning not to be so easily brushed off.

Carly narrowed her eyes at him. "I'm asking you to leave," she repeated.

"Too bad," he said for the third time. Thankfully, he outweighed her, so she couldn't physically kick him out. What she could do mentally was a different issue, but physically, she didn't have a choice. He wasn't wild about the fact that he was using his size as an advantage over her, but he believed—no, he *knew*—that she should not be alone.

She pursed her lips, shoved a piece of hair behind her ear, then crossed her arms over her chest. Still, he didn't move. Finally, after about a one-minute standoff, she threw her hands up.

"Fine, you can stay, but only because I can't force you to leave short of using my weapon as a threat. Don't expect *anything* from me tonight, though. Don't expect me to talk or have dinner with you, or even acknowledge you're here. I honestly can't deal with anything tonight. Nor do I want to."

He hesitated, then nodded.

She eyed him for another beat, then turned and headed up the stairs to her bedroom. A few minutes later, he heard the shower start. Covered in blood as she was, as her clothes were, he anticipated she'd spend a good long time under the spray of the water, trying to wash away whatever had happened. From experience, he knew it wouldn't work, but she'd have to learn that herself.

On a sigh, he removed his jacket, hung it on the back of one of the kitchen chairs, and took a seat. He thought about pulling out his phone to see what he could find in the local news about whatever had caused Carly to be covered in someone else's blood, but in the end he decided he'd leave it for her to tell him. *If* she told him.

He was still at the table a half an hour later when she came downstairs. Her hair was damp and she wore a robe. A short white silk robe.

The sight of her bare legs and the knowledge that she very likely wore nothing beneath the thin fabric hit him like a sucker punch in the gut. Blood rushed to all sorts of places it shouldn't, especially considering she didn't want him anywhere near her and was doing her best to ignore him.

She didn't acknowledge him as she entered the kitchen and headed straight to a cupboard in the back. When she reached up to one of the higher shelves where kept the bottle of whiskey he'd given her, her robe rode up the back of her thighs almost to the point where he could see the curve of her backside.

Itching to touch her, he crossed his arms tightly over his chest to stop from reaching for her.

She got ahold of the bottle and moved to grab a glass. All the reaching, however, had pulled her robe askew, and it now gaped open when she turned toward the cabinet with the glasses—toward him.

He shifted in his seat.

"Carly?"

She looked up from the amber liquid pouring into her glass.

"What are you doing?" He tried to keep his gaze from dipping to her chest and the way the silk fell, barely covering her breasts.

"Making dinner."

She put the bottle down and, thankfully, turned away from him to recork it. He managed a few breaths when she didn't bother to put the bottle back in the cupboard. He shouldn't be feeling the way he was feeling; he shouldn't be wanting what he wanted from her at that moment. He knew that. But when she opened the freezer drawer and bent down to grab a cube of ice for her drink, he stopped breathing entirely. Her robe hung open and he had a perfect view down its front. He saw everything.

Fierce desire roared through his body, leaving him shaken and inexplicably angry. He felt the muscles in his arms tense from restraining himself. He'd swear his body was vibrating.

As if sensing this change, Carly looked up as her fingers closed around an ice cube. Ever so slowly, she straightened, dropped the ice in her glass, and closed the freezer drawer.

Without a word, she turned and walked back upstairs to her bedroom.

He heard a door open and shut. A few minutes passed before his brain was his again, before he could think clearly. He took a few more moments to breathe deeply, thinking about Carly, what she had asked of him, and what she needed.

When he felt capable of being himself, of being in control, he rose from his seat and climbed the stairs. Looking into her bedroom, he saw her through the window, curled up on one of the chairs on the balcony. She had a blanket, but it looked thin. He pulled the comforter off her bed as he walked by, opened the door, and stepped out.

She glanced up at him as he shut the door, then stared back out into the darkness. She'd hardly touched her drink. Lifting the comforter, he tucked it around her nearly naked body, then sat beside her on another chair in silence. Pushing his own desires aside, he recognized what she was doing as she sat there, gazing at nothing. He'd been there before.

Whatever had happened that day was something too big to process all at once. He knew that, consciously or not, Carly was attempting to empty her mind of all the images, thoughts, doubts, and emotions that were crowding in around her. And when her mind was clear, she'd go back to the beginning, to when there was nothing there—no story, no players, nothing. And then, and only then, could another story be built. Maybe one in which she could make sense of whatever had happened.

Pieces of the past would be filtered through and selected to build the new story. She would remember moments where things could have been different or could have gone a different way, and it would be those moments that would be the hardest to cope with. Because, in the new story her mind would build—a story without all the messiness of real life—those moments would become so prescient, so obvious, that she would wonder how she could have possibly missed them and let this thing that had happened happen.

But she wasn't there yet. So they sat.

After a few minutes, he tuned out the cold and focused on listening to the woman next to him. Her breath came in and out in a steady rhythm. Every once in a while, she'd sniffle a bit or take a sip of her drink, but other than that, stillness weighed heavy on the night. Even the creatures of the dark that he knew were out there hid silently in the shadows.

Finally, she stood, grabbed the comforter as it fell from her lap, and moved into her room. All without acknowledging him. He didn't mind, just simply rose and followed her in. He watched her toss her comforter on her bed and disappear into the bathroom. Not knowing quite what to do with himself, he wandered to the other side of her bedroom and lingered in front of the open door of her closet. He could see her uniform lying on the floor inside, crumpled, discarded in haste. He knew that feeling too. He couldn't count the number of times he'd wanted nothing more than to rid himself of whatever stench he wore. And it wasn't always the clothing that carried it.

Listening to Carly brush her teeth, he slipped his hands in his pockets and waited for her to emerge. When she did, he could see that fatigue was taking its toll. From her unyielding expression, he could also see that she hadn't changed her mind about his presence.

"I'm going to bed," she said. She'd turned the bathroom light off and now the only light filtering through her room came from a small lamp on her bedside table.

"What happened today?"

She shook her head. "I don't want to talk about it. Not right now. I won't be able to sleep if I do."

"And you think you'll be able to sleep if you don't?" He knew the answer and suspected she did too, but whether or not she'd admit that sleep was a long way off was something else entirely.

"I don't want to talk about it," she repeated.

"It's not going to go away."

"I'm well aware of that," she shot back. "But *you* need to go."

"No," he answered. "You're not going to be able to shove it into a dark corner of your mind, you know. Not even for tonight. Trust me, whatever happened is going to stay with you and the longer you try to keep it tucked away, walled off from every other part of you, the bigger it will get and the more power it will have over you." He'd revealed more about himself than he'd intended, maybe more than he had even recognized, but he spoke only the truth.

Carly gave a dismissive laugh. "Power? You think this is about power?"

He opened his mouth to say that the power he was talking about was different than the power she referred to.

But she continued, cutting him off. "I have none. That's part of the problem. With everything." She threw her arms up in an all-encompassing gesture before crossing them over her chest. "None, Drew. I have no power in anything and I'm tired of it. I know I can't change it, but I can't deal with it right now either. I don't want to talk about it, I don't want it thrown back in my face, but the fact is, I can't do *anything* right now. I can't bring Marguerite's killer to justice, I can't bring my mother's killer to justice. I can't convince my boss to give Marcus his job back as deputy chief. I can't keep kids from drinking and driving and doing dumb things, and I can't make women in abusive relationships leave."

She paused and took a deep breath and, in that space of time, he wondered if there had been an accident that night involving kids, or perhaps another incident with that woman, Mary, that Carly had mentioned before.

Carly shook her head. "I'm the *police*. I'm supposed to have some sort of power, right? But I have none. Not where it matters. So don't talk to me about power. Don't talk to me about strength. And don't talk to me about *talking* about things, because right now, right now in this room, I feel like I have nothing. No power and no strength to fight. And talking about it will do nothing but remind me of that."

Drew studied her, noting the bleakness in her eyes, even as her chest rose and fell with the argument she'd put forward.

"You're stronger than you think, and power isn't always about exerting it over other people. Sometimes it's about finding it for yourself. If you feel you can't do anything for other people, what can you do for yourself?" he asked.

She regarded him for a long moment. Then her head cocked a fraction of an inch.

And he realized his mistake. "Carly," he said in caution.

She ignored his tone and walked toward him.

"This isn't what you really want," he said.

She stopped not twelve inches in front of him.

"You asked me what I can do for myself. *This* is something I can do for myself."

Slowly, she began pulling his shirt from the waistband of his pants.

"This wasn't what I meant," he said, but even as he said it, his body called him a liar. As her cool hands made contact with the skin at his waist, every ounce of need and want he'd felt in the kitchen earlier came roaring back.

"Too bad," she said, echoing his words as she slid her hands under his shirt and up his chest.

"Carly," he managed once she'd slid her hands back down and drew them away. But then they came back and began unbuttoning his shirt. He closed his eyes.

She didn't need this, which should be reason enough to stop. But everything she'd said about having no power, about feeling helpless and useless, was too familiar for him to turn away from.

And in her truth, he had glimpsed a brutal reality of his own. His own frustrations and fears were starting to slip into this night, into this moment.

He should stop this.

He should stop her.

"Jesus," he said as she slipped his shirt off and ran her lips across his chest.

He didn't make a single move as her hands guided his sleeves off his arms or when they untied her robe, letting it drop to the floor. Or when her hands curled over his belt and her fingers slipped between his skin and the waist of his pants. She pulled him against her, feeling his body's reaction to her, and looked up at him with her hazel eyes.

"I'm happy to do all of this myself, but it would be more fun if you joined in," she said, unbuckling his belt and releasing the button and zip of his pants. Holding his gaze, she slid his pants and boxers down over his hips.

He watched as she began to kneel. And digging his hands into her hair, for good or for bad, they dove into the abyss. Together.

• • •

Drew awoke tired, sore, and having no idea what to expect from Carly in the morning light. Her frustrations had unleashed his own and, between the two of them, years of pain, loss, and even anger had come out in the night. Being together hadn't been sweet, it hadn't been beautiful. It had been raw and furious and, at times, ugly.

But it had also been honest. More honest than he'd ever been with anyone. More honest than he'd ever been with himself. In the dark hours of the night, the cost of his own helplessness, the price demanded of him in order to toe the line in his type of work, came pouring out in every move he made. Much of what he had done over the years, he stood behind. But there were things, things he couldn't speak of, things he couldn't change, not then and not now, that had cost him a part of his soul. And it wasn't just those events that had cost him, but also the silence he'd had to keep.

"You're awake," Carly's voice came from the direction of the bathroom. He opened his eyes to see her standing in the doorway, showered and back in her robe. Despite how they'd spent the past several hours, his body reacted in a predictable way.

"Yeah," he said, sitting up and reaching for the water they'd brought up at some point in the night. He glanced at his chest as he put the glass down and noted the marks she'd left on him. Looking back at her, he realized that she probably had a few marks of her own. "Come here," he said, holding his hand out to her.

She eyed him. "I need to get to work in a few minutes," she said, even as she moved toward him.

"Tell me what happened yesterday?" he asked quietly.

She sat down beside him and paused before answering. He took her hand and held on, even as her gaze went to the windows. "Do you remember me telling you about Mary and Bill Hanson?"

"The woman in the abusive relationship?" He knew that if he had it right, the story wasn't going to be a good one. Not with all the blood on Carly's uniform the night before.

She nodded. "We got a call at around five reporting a couple of gunshots. It was," she paused and absently played with his fingers which were entangled with hers. "It was awful," she said, opting not to give him the play-by-play. "He finally did it. He finally killed her. Then shot himself. When we got there, Emily, their daughter, was sitting next to her mother—in a pool of her mother's blood." Her voice caught as she relayed the last bit. He tightened his fingers on hers.

"I picked Emily up. I needed to," again Carly's voice choked. She cleared her throat. "I needed to get her out of the blood."

"I'm sorry," he said, sitting up a bit more.

She continued to play with his fingers, holding them in her hand. "I tried so many times to get her help."

"I know." He didn't bother to point out that successfully helping people depended more on the people actually wanting the help than on the quality of the help being offered. Instead, he pulled her into his arms and onto his lap.

They sat that way for a long time. She didn't cry or break down, but they shared a quiet moment as he rubbed her back and held her. He brushed a kiss across her hair as she slid her arms around his bare chest.

"I hate that I couldn't help her," she said, looking at him. Then she buried her head against his shoulder.

He held her as she finally did cry, her body rocking against his. "I know," he said quietly.

CHAPTER TWENTY

FINALLY READY TO LEAVE FOR work, Carly had her hand on the handle of her car door when yet another car pulled into her drive. After Drew had left that morning, Joe had made an unexpected visit. And now it seemed that Caleb was doing the same. Glad to have a chance to catch up with her friend's brother, she smiled and walked toward his black Range Rover as he parked and climbed out.

"Caleb, it's good to see you. Drew mentioned you were in town, but I wasn't sure if I'd get to see you."

He dropped a kiss on her cheek. "It's good to see you too, though I'm sorry to hear about what's going on."

She lifted her shoulder and gave him a wayward look. "One of the worst things about it is that I can't really do anything to help, since I have to work."

They shared a look of commiseration. If there was one thing Carly knew about Caleb, it was that he was a man of action. Being in her position, being unable to participate in everything the others were doing, would make him shrivel into nothing but a shell of himself.

"So, how are you?" he asked earnestly.

Touched by the sincerity in his voice, she paused before she answered. "I'm okay. Really, I am," she repeated when his brows shot up. "I feel like I'm on a roller coaster of highs and lows. I can't stop it, so all I can control is how I react to it."

"And how are things with Drew?"

That question surprised a laugh out of her. "Are you looking out for his virtue, Caleb? Wanting to make sure my intentions are honorable?"

"It's hard for people like us. People like him and me."

The seriousness of his response gave her pause and she didn't need him to elaborate any further.

"I know," she said softly.

"He's not going to be very good at it, at . . ." He waved his hand at her.

"A relationship?"

"Probably not at first. But you won't meet someone more committed to trying."

She knew that too.

"Then again, I noticed he didn't come back to Kit's last night, so maybe he's better at it than I thought." He waggled his eyebrows at her, no doubt attempting to lighten the mood after he'd made his point.

She gave him a playful shove and started back toward her car, then stopped and turned back around. "Are you going to stick around? We have another meeting at Vivi and Ian's tonight, if you'd like to join us."

He chuckled. "Like I told Drew, not a chance. But if *you* need anything, just call. Have there been any updates? What about the numbers on the earrings?"

Carly smiled and relayed what Naomi had told her about Seraphina the day before, then she told him about the subsequent decision made by Joe earlier that morning to send Marcus down to Florida with Trudy to talk to Sera's current owners.

"That's good news," he said, leaning against the side of her car as they talked. "What about Repetto himself?"

She shrugged. "We don't know much more than we did yesterday."

"But there's something else, isn't there?"

Carly took a moment to answer. "Joe Franks stopped by this morning. We talked about some stuff, the past, that kind of thing. But . . ."

"But, what?"

She dipped her head. "It's probably nothing, but it just seems like, when I hear Joe talk about Vince Repetto, I have a hard time picturing the man Joe is describing actually doing what we know he did. The financial crimes, sure, but the murders? I don't know. Like I said, it's probably nothing, but something just doesn't feel right."

"Like what? Tell me what Joe has told you."

She glanced at Caleb and his serious expression told her he was interested, truly interested, in hearing her thoughts. She took a deep breath. "He was born in Canada," she said, "not that that has anything to do with it, but raised mostly by his dad in Alabama. Good family and all, but Joe said he always seemed out to prove himself, and that he also had a tremendous sense of entitlement."

"Was he capable?"

"Joe's words were that he was smart enough to get into the academy and keep his job, but beyond that? He said Repetto always seemed more interested in projecting an image than having any substance. Big ego, tiny id."

"And planning and executing three murders doesn't really align with someone whose life sounds pretty superficial."

Carly shook her head. "It doesn't. Not to me. Especially when we keep hearing from Joe how unexpected the violence was. But what do I know? I'm hearing this all second hand, of course, from Joe."

"Do you think Repetto had a partner?"

She zipped up her jacket, it was getting chilly standing around outside. "I asked Joe. We know he has one now, but Joe said that he didn't think he did back then. He thought that Repetto's ego was too big for a partner."

Caleb wagged his head. "Egos are a funny thing, in my experience. We all have them and we all need them. And while they can be a major source of strength, they can also be a major source of weakness."

She had never thought of egos that way—she usually thought

of the impact a person's ego had on others, not on the person with the ego.

Caleb straightened away from the car. "You're getting cold. Why don't you head into work." Then, with a teasing smile, he added, "I'll keep Drew on task."

She widened her eyes in mock surprise. "Does that mean you're going to join our team of capable crime solvers?"

He laughed and opened her car door for her. "Not a chance."

• • •

Carly pulled her car up at Vivi and Ian's just as dusk began to take hold. Unable to help with the investigation, she had spent most of the day walking Josie through the Windsor police systems, catching up on paperwork, and figuring out who could fill in for Marcus.

With the exception of the call from Marcus and the few updates from Drew, it had been one of the most painfully quiet days of her recent life.

Marcus's call. Carly's mind recalled it as she turned off her car's engine. She thought he'd been calling to check in before leaving for the airport. Instead, he'd unloaded what he'd been trying to tell her for the past few days—that several years ago he'd had the opportunity to take over the family businesses and he hadn't done so. Because of her.

He had told her that he hadn't wanted to risk her life by going back to his. She knew he'd told her the truth, that he hadn't wanted to risk losing her, but to her it felt like just one more thing for her to feel guilty about. Logically, she knew she shouldn't feel guilty— she would have made the same decision in his shoes—but still . . .

Exhaling a deep breath, she forced her mind back to what she'd learned from Drew's updates throughout the day. The ballistics reports and files had arrived from LA and Washington and he'd spent a chunk of his time reviewing those. He'd also told her that Naomi and Brian were working on gathering additional information on Moran. She expected to hear updates from everyone else once she went inside.

A little smile played on her lips when she emerged from her car and caught the scent of the grill coming from the back of the house. She paused and inhaled deeply as she took in the scene. She recognized Drew's car, but there were several others there as well. Good, she hoped she was the last one to arrive so she wouldn't have to wait for dinner *or* the updates.

"Carly," Vivi called from the front porch as Rooster came darting out to greet their visitor. "Come in," she added, waving her over.

"It's getting cold out there," Vivi said as she ushered her inside. Rooster squirmed in delight at all the people in his house, nudging the latest arrival's hand for a good rub.

"The price we pay for having such a beautiful fall," Carly responded, removing her coat and hanging it on a hook by the door before complying with Rooster's demand.

"The men are all out by the grill, but come into the kitchen and join the rest of us for a glass of wine," Vivi directed. "I'm throwing the salad together."

Rooster got one last pet from her then she followed Vivi to the kitchen where Mikaela and Naomi, who was making faces at Jeffery, were lingering.

"How are you?" Mikaela asked as soon as she entered the kitchen.

"Frustrated, oddly exhausted, and wanting this all to be over," she replied.

"I don't blame you, for any of that," Naomi said, crossing her eyes and sticking her tongue out at the baby, which caused him to laugh.

Carly smiled.

"You may not be out running a physical marathon right now, but it's certainly a mental one, not to mention emotional," Vivi said. "Which could explain why you're tired. And, by the way, I was very sorry to hear about Mary and Bill Hanson," she added, giving Carly's arm a squeeze with one hand as she poured a glass of red wine with the other.

The crimson liquid swirled in the glass when Vivi handed it to her. "Thank you," she said. "Their daughter, Emily, is with social services now, and Mary's sister has come to town. Both families want custody of the little girl, but if the paperwork checks out with Mary's sister, I'm hoping she gets it. I don't think it would be good for Emily to be anywhere near Bill's family. They're still blaming Mary, saying if it weren't for her, Bill wouldn't have done it."

Vivi made a sympathetic sound, just before Jeffery let out a howling laugh—startling both women. Carly watched Vivi's eyes travel to her son, who was playfully pushing on Naomi's puffed out cheeks and causing her to make raspberry noises. All four women watched Jeffery's antics for a few minutes, then Carly turned back to Vivi.

"Can I help with anything? Please?" she asked.

Vivi smiled, understanding her need to do something, even something mundane, and handed her a sweet onion. "Here, you can sit down there and chop this," she said with a gesture to the kitchen bar. Carly took the onion, the cutting board, and a knife, then took a seat on a stool and began slicing.

The men came marching in a few minutes later, making Carly smile. Men often made fun of women for going to the bathroom together, but she was pretty sure it didn't take Ian, Lucas, Joe, Sam, Brian, Wyatt, Daniel, *and* Drew to put a few steaks on the grill.

"I'll need to flip them in about five minutes," Ian said to Vivi after he'd greeted Carly. "Should I get out the plates and stuff?"

Vivi murmured a response but Carly's eyes and attention were focused on Drew. She watched his expression shift and some of the tension leave his body when his gaze met hers. He didn't come over to kiss her hello or make any overt gestures, but she could see the intent in his eyes.

Never in her life had she had a night like what she and Drew had gone through the night before. In her anger and frustration and her feelings of impotence and helplessness, she'd pushed him.

She'd pushed them both beyond their breaking points. And in those dark hours, he had shown her what she'd always known: that he had his own demons, his own questions, his own doubts. It wasn't easy for either of them, at this stage in their lives. But despite the explosive, and sometimes aggressive, night they'd spent together, for the first time in a long time, she felt like she wasn't alone, struggling to stay afloat in a stormy sea. How, or even if, they would emerge from the tempest remained to be seen.

"You okay?" he asked, his fingers brushing her lower back as she set the salad on the table a few minutes later.

"It's been a long day, but yeah, I'm better—certainly better than I was last night. I didn't know Lucas was back." She began stacking napkins near the silverware Ian had brought out. They were setting everything up buffet style on the kitchen bar.

"Apparently, he came up late last night," he replied as he separated the forks from the steak knives. "Said something about planning another birthday party for Jeffery."

Carly glanced at the Boston detective and wondered why he felt the need to come all the way to Windsor to plan something that could have been decided over the phone. Then again, Vivi and Ian's home was about as welcoming as a home could be; there had been plenty of times she'd wanted to curl up on their sofa and stay for a spell.

Turning her attention to the living room, she was about to suggest that they claim two seats together on the couch when she heard the back door open, heralding Ian's return with the steaks, while, at the same time, a knock sounded on the front door. From her spot beside Drew, she watched Vivi scan the room, maybe looking to see if they were missing anyone, before moving toward the front door. Ian came in through the kitchen and set the platter of steaks down as Vic stepped through the open front door.

For a moment, everyone froze. Perhaps in surprise at seeing him at all, but more likely in shock at seeing him in such a state. His eyes were red, slightly swollen, and bloodshot. His hair stuck out at odd angles, like he'd been running his fingers through it and tugging it into spikes. And under his open jacket, his shirt was only half tucked in.

"I'm so sorry," Vic said, his voice breaking as his eyes traveled around the room wildly.

"Vic?" Vivi said as Ian came to stand beside her.

Vic's eyes bounced around the room and, briefly, Carly wondered if he was on something. But then his gaze landed on Ian and a look of sadness washed over his expression that was so primal, she felt her own heart stutter.

"I'm so sorry," he repeated, holding Ian's gaze.

"For what, exactly?" Ian asked, his voice hesitant.

"I hated you. I . . ." He paused, cleared his throat and ran a palm over one of his eyes before looking back up. "I might still hate you, I don't know."

"Vic? Are you okay?" Vivi asked. She made to step forward, but Ian held her back.

"And you," Vic said, swinging his attention to Carly.

She felt Drew's presence at her back.

"I've let you down, too. I've fucked up my job and left you to clean everything up."

"Vic? What's going on?" Lucas asked. On the other side of the room, he'd barely moved from his location but he had stepped into Vic's line of sight. Vic stared at Lucas, but Carly couldn't tell if her chief actually saw him or not. Then his lips trembled and he looked away, back toward Ian.

"You were everything I was supposed to be and I hated you for it," he said.

She saw a look of confusion come across Ian's face. Vivi reached over and took her husband's hand.

"I hated you because you were always so sure, so confident about every damned thing. About your place in the world, with your military service, your job, your family, your wife. You were what I was supposed to be and, most of all, I hated you because," he stopped and rubbed both of his eyes as he gathered himself together. "Most of all, I hated you because I hated myself."

No one said a word while Vic struggled with what he wanted to say next. Only Lucas, shoving his hands into his pockets, moved.

After a long moment, Vic cleared his throat again and looked up. "I'm gay," he said, keeping his eyes on Lucas but speaking to the room. "I've known since I was a kid and I've hated myself ever since. I grew up in a family that wouldn't, that *won't*, accept it. It's a sin, it's an abomination against god, it's unnatural," he said, no doubt mimicking what he'd heard growing up.

"I grew up hiding who I was so I could stay a part of a family who wouldn't want me otherwise. The older I got, the more cowardly and spiteful I became." He cast a glance at Ian. "I couldn't stand up to my family. I couldn't tell them about that part of who I am, and I hated myself. I hated that I had to choose between my family and myself, and I let that anger and frustration turn me into a man I liked even less." His voice cracked as he spoke. "And I took it out on you," he said, meeting Ian's eye. "And because I couldn't deal with myself, I didn't want to deal with anything, so I left too much to you." He swung his eyes back to Carly. "I'm so sorry, to both of you."

Tears gathered in his eyes and he looked down, blinking them away.

"Vic?" Lucas said.

Vic looked up. Even as his lips trembled, he opened his mouth to speak. "I told my family today. They, uh," he paused and turned his eyes toward the front porch. "They reacted like I knew they would. I'm not welcome in my parents' home anymore, or those of my brothers. I shouldn't care. I'm a grown man, I shouldn't care what they think . . ."

His voice trailed off as his gaze dropped to the floor by his feet and Carly's heart broke for the chief. He had left her with more work than he should have and he had been a colossal ass to Ian, but no one should be forced to make the choices he'd made and no one should lose a family because of whom he loved. As if sensing her sorrow for her boss, Drew brushed his fingers over her arm then reached down and intertwined them with hers.

"I'm a wreck, Lucas. You know I love you, but I'm a wreck. I have no family, I've fucked up my job, and while I have a home, I'm not sure I want it anymore, because, well . . ." Because it would be too hard to live in the same area as the family who'd kicked him out was left unsaid.

"I don't know who I am or who I can be once I, well, once I sort all this out," Vic's voice shook with emotion and his eyes pleaded for some kind of acceptance. "I'm not much, Lucas, but if you want me, I'm still yours."

Carly glanced at Vivi. Finding out that Lucas, her deceased brother's partner, had found someone new and moved on wasn't something someone should learn in public. Lucas also turned his gaze to Vivi, and in that look Carly saw his regret, his pain at having hurt her. Vivi stared woodenly back at him, but beside her Ian gave a little nod. Lucas hadn't been looking for permission to go to the man he so obviously cared for, but he did seem to want their blessing. Another look of remorse flashed in his eyes when Vivi didn't respond. But he crossed the room and wrapped his arms around Vic.

Without another word, Lucas led Vic out of the house. A few moments later, the glare of headlights flashed through the living room and the sound of Vic's car faded away as the two men departed. There was no doubt that they had a lot to discuss.

"Vivienne?" Ian said softly to his wife after several moments of silence had passed, everyone waiting for her to give them some direction.

"I just," she paused and looked around but didn't quite meet anyone's eye. "I need a few minutes," she said, slipping her hand from Ian's and heading toward their bedroom.

Carly made to follow her but Drew's hand tightened on hers and held her back. "Ian, why don't I take care of slicing the steaks?" he asked.

Ian glanced around at everyone staring at him before meeting Drew's gaze. "Thank you, that would be great," he said, then followed Vivi out of the room.

"Brian, maybe you can help get everything else set out?" Drew suggested as he made his way toward the platter.

"Of course," Brian responded. "Naomi, do you have Jeffery?"

Naomi cast a concerned look in the direction of Vivi and Ian's bedroom, but she nodded and moved into the living room with the toddler to take a seat.

Following Drew into the kitchen, Carly watched him cut a few slices as she pondered what had happened.

"Did you know?" he asked.

"That Vic was gay? No," she answered with a shake of her head. "He hid it well."

"That must have been difficult for him," he said, cutting another slice. "Was he as awful as he said?"

She popped a small scrap into her mouth and nodded. "Yes. He was terrible to Ian," she said once she'd swallowed. "It was one of those things I never understood. He did dump a lot of work on me, but he was pleasant. I always knew that, if I needed him, he'd back me up. At first, he was a bit gruff with Marcus too, but since the accident, he's been nothing but understanding about the time Marcus has needed to recover. Which is why it seemed so strange how awful he was to Ian."

Drew finished slicing the first steak and moved it to the side as he started on the second. "Sometimes what motivates people, what drives them to act one way or another, is something the rest of us will never know."

"And sometimes, we find out," she finished his thought.

"Not that it excuses the behavior," he added.

"But it does explain it," she countered. She could only imagine the frustration and anger and pain Vic must have felt, struggling on his own. She agreed with Drew that Vic's situation didn't excuse his behavior, but she couldn't help feeling some empathy for his struggle.

"Do you think Vivi and Ian will join us?" he asked.

"Eventually. It must have been a shock to her, but she'll rally.

At least for tonight. I imagine it will take her a little longer to fully process what's happened."

"Why's that? I mean, I know she and Lucas are good friends—didn't she know he was gay?"

Drew already felt like such a part of the community to Carly, it hadn't dawned on her that he didn't already know Vivi and Lucas's story. As he finished with the second steak, she told him that Vivi's brother, Jeffery DeMarco, and Lucas had been partners but, because Jeffery had been in the military when the "don't ask don't tell" policy was still in place, they'd had had to keep it fairly quiet. When Jeffery was killed, Lucas had relied heavily on Vivi, since she was one of the only people with whom he could mourn his loss openly. Naomi and Brian had known, as had Lucas's parents, but he and Vivi had been the two who'd felt the loss most acutely.

"It must have been hard on Lucas, then—to fall in love with *yet another* man who felt he had to keep the relationship a secret," Drew suggested.

So caught up in how *Vic* must be feeling, Carly hadn't thought about the situation from Lucas's point of view, but what Drew had said made sense. And it would explain the several instances when she'd seen Lucas storm out of the police station. He'd told her that he and Vic had argued over some police procedure or another. But after what Lucas had gone through losing Jeffery, she could understand why he'd feel conflicted about entering into another relationship that was essentially clandestine.

"How's the steak coming?" Brian asked, halting further conversation.

"It's ready," Drew said, sliding the platter over to him.

Brian took it and placed it with the rest of the food that had been set out on the countertop. Then, slowly at first, the guests started approaching the buffet. As they settled themselves with food and drinks, conversation flowed again. No one had forgotten what had happened, but everyone seemed focused on bringing the conversation back to the gathering's original purpose—to exchange updates on Repetto. When Vivi and Ian joined them a few minutes later, no one, including Jeffery, who toddled over to his dad with Rooster on his heels, skipped a beat.

The first topic—the bullet—was covered quickly. So far, it hadn't yielded any additional leads, and Sam and Daniel were still trying to track down how the gun had moved from DC to LA, then to Washington State. They believed that, by tracking its movements, they would be able to identify who in DC had owned it at the time of the killings. Carly had been hoping for more information from them, but it was a tedious process and she was grateful they were sticking with it.

As for Jason Moran, Brian's investigation into him had given them all some breathing room. Based on the utility readings on the boat where Moran was stashed—which were indicating that Moran's computers were in passive mode rather than active—the twins had been able to confirm that Moran wasn't actively seeking out people searching for information on the killings, but rather sitting back and keeping an eye on the traps, trip wires, and other monitors he had put in place. Which meant that, as long as they didn't trigger any of his alarms, Naomi and Brian had more freedom to dig into things, like Sophia Davidson's old e-mails and Repetto's financials, which the twins agreed were now their priority.

After Carly provided both her mother's business and her personal e-mail information to Naomi, Vivi spoke up for the first time. "This is all very interesting and important, but I have to say, I think what Drew found out from talking to Ken Weston is the most interesting of all."

All eyes turned to Drew.

Carly knew he'd been to Ken Weston's office and that the man himself hadn't been there, but she was surprised to hear that Drew had caught up with Weston in the forty minutes between her last conversation with him and her arrival at Vivi and Ian's.

Drew, who'd finished his meal, placed his empty plate on the coffee table and sat forward, propping his elbows on his thighs. Looking at her, he said, "He called me just before I got here," which let her know that he hadn't withheld anything. "And let's just say I'm glad Marcus is on his way down to Florida tonight, because Ken did in fact load information onto a microchip for Sophia a few days before she was killed. He doesn't know what the information was, but he did it."

"He didn't ask any questions of Sophia?" Vivi asked.

Drew smiled. "He had a bit of a crush on her. She was nearly old enough to be his mother, but apparently, age didn't matter to him. He was young and wanted to impress her, so he was more interested in getting it done in a fast, flashy way than in asking what it was she wanted put on the chip or her reasons for doing it."

"But this wasn't in any of the reports," Daniel said, setting his plate down and leaning back in his seat as he rolled his wineglass between his fingers. "Did he not talk to the FBI after she was killed?"

"He did," Drew replied. "And though he didn't remember the name of the agent he spoke to, the man he described sounded like Repetto."

"So Repetto knew there was a chip, likely with information on it, but he didn't know where it was," Joe said.

"And because he didn't know the horse world, he probably didn't know it was common practice to chip horses," Carly added.

"And since he didn't know that, the most logical conclusion for him to have come to would have been that she gave it to you and Marcus when you left for LA," Drew finished.

"Which would explain why he seems so hell bent on the idea that we have information. And why he's coming after us after all these years." Carly sat back in her chair and took a sip of wine before she spoke again. "But it's been almost fifteen years, wouldn't he think that if we had it we would have turned it over by now?"

"My guess is he thinks you have it, but that it's incredibly easy to hide, especially given the size of the chip," Vivi said, setting her own plate down as Jeffery crawled into her lap. "He probably thinks you don't even know you have it. If Marguerite had told him where you were, or if he'd found out some other way, my guess is both you and Marcus would have experienced a series of serious break-ins by now."

"Because he would have come looking for it," Carly said quietly. She wondered what would have happened if Marguerite had given in and told Repetto where she and Marcus lived. Would he have let Marguerite live? Would the worst that would have happened been only break-ins?

"He would have killed her anyway," Drew said from beside her. She turned to find his watchful eyes on her.

"He couldn't let her live after doing what he'd done to her, so she would have died either way," he continued. "I have no doubt that she knew that, too. And I also have no doubt that she knew if he found you, he wouldn't have stopped with break-ins. When he couldn't find what he was looking for, he would have gotten desperate. Eventually, he would have come after you and Marcus. She knew that."

The truth of his words settled in her mind, but all she could bring herself to do was nod. "What about Lorraine? You have people watching over her?" she asked, worried for Marguerite's aunt.

"I do," he replied. "It's the same company Ty and Dani work for, but of course they aren't on the job, since Dani couldn't go incognito now if she tried."

She smiled and nudged him. "Be nice. The poor woman is six-and-half-months pregnant with twins."

"And she doesn't let any of us forget it," he said with his own answering smile.

"So, Marcus lands tonight?" Daniel asked.

"Yes," Joe answered. "He does. He and Trudy have an appointment with the current owners of Seraphina tomorrow morning. With any luck, he'll be back tomorrow night."

"By tomorrow night, we could have all the information we need to bring Repetto in," Drew said, rising from his seat and collecting dishes.

"Assuming the chip has the information and isn't too degraded, it shouldn't take too long to pull the data," Brian said as he rose to help.

Drew held his hand out, reaching for Carly's plate. As she handed it to him, she asked, "Does Marcus know any of this?"

"About Ken Weston and the chip? Yes," he said, looking at his watch. "I e-mailed him the details. If he didn't get it while in flight, he'll have it when he lands in five minutes. "

Carly glanced outside. With all the people in the house, it was the only quiet place to talk. Her eyes darted back to Drew, who was watching her, though still collecting dishes. "Do you mind?" she asked with a gesture of her head to the darkness outside. He'd know what she was asking.

"Of course not," he said, waving her out. "I'll get these. Go call your brother."

She smiled then leaned in and brushed a kiss across his cheek. It was the first public display of affection she'd shown him and, for a moment, Drew looked stunned. Which, combined with the excitement of what they might learn in the next twenty-four hours, made her laugh.

"It's not a secret, you know," she said as she started to move away.

"What's not?" he asked, turning to watch her go, his hands loaded with plates.

"That you kind of like me," she said, with a teasing grin.

Drew gave her a reproving look, one that looked more for show than anything else. "Yes, well, I should think it's also no longer a secret that you feel the same way about me."

She wondered how she could have ever thought him aloof and distant. When she looked at him now, she saw everything she needed to in his eyes: how much he cared—about her, about her brother, about doing the right thing. No, she'd been wrong about him. And she was very, very happy about that.

"I should think not." She gave him a coy wink, then turned to go call her brother.

CHAPTER TWENTY-ONE

DREW WATCHED CARLY WALK AWAY, a stupid grin tugging at his lips. He hadn't ever seen that playful look in her eye. He knew it was mostly because they were close to getting some answers, close to bringing some closure to what had happened to her family fifteen years earlier. All the same, he liked it. He liked seeing her genuine smile, he liked seeing that extra little sway in her hips as she walked away, and he liked that she now seemed comfortable enough with him to show casual affection in front of her friends.

Suddenly reminded of the presence of those friends, he turned back to the room. Most of them were busy clearing dishes or wrapping up leftovers, though he didn't miss the speculative look Vivi cast him. But then Ian came over and said something to her and she handed her husband the dish she'd been wrapping up, said something in return, and headed out the back door.

Vivi had participated in the conversation that evening, but he hadn't missed the distant look in her eyes. He thought about what Carly had told him about Vivi's brother and Lucas, and despite his understanding of just how much courage Vic had needed to do what he had done, and the fact that he wished nothing but the best for the two men, Drew also understood Vivi's heartache.

He walked through the kitchen, placed the plates he'd been carrying on the counter, and continued outside to find Vivi sitting by the fire pit. The cold night air wrapped around them, but she hadn't brought a jacket and sat hunched over her knees trying to stay warm. Thankfully, he'd grabbed one off a hook by the door on his way through the mud room so he draped it over her shoulders before taking a seat beside her. Looking back at the house for a moment, he saw Ian watching them through the window, but Vivi's husband didn't come out.

"Did you meet Dani Fuller during Garret and Kit's party?" he asked.

She turned and gave him a questioning look, "Yes."

"Her parents were killed when she was thirteen," he said.

"There seems to be a lot of that around," Vivi responded.

"She saw it happen," he added.

He heard Vivi suck in a quick breath.

"They were shot, execution style, in their own home," he added softly, thinking back to the couple he'd known since the day he'd been born. He leaned forward, continuing as he rested his forearms on his thighs and stared down at the slate patio stones. "Dani went into some kind of shock after that. For years," he added. "She ate and functioned, but she didn't really *function*, if you know what I mean?"

The question didn't need an answer, but Vivi nodded.

"A few years after it happened, I couldn't take it anymore. She and her sister had come to live with my parents, who were their guardians, and I watched her waste away. I was at college by then, but one day we went for a walk and I promised her that if she got healthy, I would do everything in my power to help her find the man who had killed her parents. She believed me, thank god, and that day, she told me what happened, everything she'd witnessed."

"How could you promise such a thing?"

Drew lifted a shoulder. "The bravado of a twenty-year-old? I don't know, but I knew I had to do something to get her back from wherever she'd gone. And it worked. I knew I was going into the CIA by that point, so she and I worked on getting her strong. I came home from school most weekends to check on her and eventually started to train her. She got stronger and followed me into the agency in the end.

"I brought her onto my team and we stayed together until

the day she left. I supervised her training, her missions, her career. Everything about her."

"That's quite a commitment," Vivi commented as she pulled the jacket tighter around herself.

Again, he shrugged. "By then it was second nature. I don't think either of us thought about it much." He paused and followed the line of one of the stones with his gaze before speaking again. "But then things changed. We finally got a lead on the man who'd killed her parents. Twenty years had passed and we finally had a lead."

"What did you do?"

He looked up at the question and offered Vivi a small smile. "We followed it, of course," he said, looking away. "And in doing so, Dani met Ty, her future husband."

"But did you ever catch the man?"

"We did, but while we were doing that, Dani and Ty were falling in love."

"And that was a bad thing?"

"Not for her, it wasn't. But for me, it was," he paused, thinking back on that time. "For me it was about as close to devastating as it could be. Of course, I didn't recognize it at the time. At the time, I, well, I wasn't very nice. To either of them," he added. "I said some things, mostly to Dani, that I wish I hadn't. But somehow I couldn't stop myself."

Vivi kicked at a pebble on the flagstone. "Why's that?"

Drew rubbed a hand over the back of his neck. "With the benefit of time and some very uncomfortable introspection, I came to realize that I needed Dani to rely on me as much as she had needed me to rely on. Only she was changing and I wasn't. And I wasn't ready for that, because if she didn't need me anymore, I wasn't sure what good I was to her or what kind of role I would play in her life."

"You were afraid you'd have no role in her life," Vivi clarified.

"That was part of it."

"And you're telling me this because you think I may be feeling the same way about Lucas?"

"That's part of it," he repeated. "But the other part of it was that, if I didn't have her to focus my energies on, I knew I would have to start thinking about myself—what I wanted from my life, what I wanted from my career . . . It was much easier to ask her the hard questions than to ask myself."

He paused, waiting for Vivi to respond.

After a few moments, she turned her head toward him and spoke. "You don't think I'm over the loss of my brother, do you?"

He gave a small shrug. "I don't know. Are you?"

"I don't think it's something you ever 'get over.'"

"I agree. But we do have to come to terms with it and what it means in our own lives."

"And now that Lucas has found someone else, I'll have to focus my energies on my own life. And I'm not going to be able to avoid coming to terms with the loss of my brother and my parents anymore, am I?"

"Maybe, and if that's the case, it's an uncomfortable place to be. Speaking from personal experience."

They sat in silence for a long while before she spoke again. "How hard was it?" she asked quietly.

"Hard to say," he answered honestly. "I'm still working through it. I'm happy for Dani and Ty, and my relationship with her is really good now—more equal, more the way a friendship should be. But," he paused, flexing his fingers against the cold. "But as for the rest, figuring out my career, my shit? I don't know, I'm still working on it."

"And how long has it been?"

He smiled. "Longer than I'd like."

"Crud," she muttered beside him.

Silence fell around them for a short while. Then she looked at him and said, "You're a pretty smart guy, you know," causing him to smile again. "I hate what you're saying, but I hear it. I'm not ready to embrace it yet, but I think you're probably right."

She stopped speaking but he sensed she had more to say. A few seconds passed, then she continued. "Since Jeffery and my parents died, it's been Lucas and me through a lot of it. Yes, we both have family, but no one else felt the loss the way we did. And since I could grieve in public and people would understand, I tried to be more aware around Lucas—aware of his needs and his wants—because he didn't have the freedom I did. Or, to put it more precisely, he had the freedom, but no one would truly understand the depth of his grief because no one else had known they were together. No one else had seen how committed they were to each other. No one but a few of us knew how deeply they had loved. And now he's found someone else to love . . ." Her voice trailed off.

"You're angry. You want to be happy for him, and you will say you're happy for him, but you feel abandoned and you're angry," he finished for her.

"But I'm angry because I'm scared, aren't I? I'm scared about what it means to my relationship with Lucas and I'm scared because of what it means to my relationship with myself and my own grieving process."

"I can't tell you why you're angry, but I can tell you that that is exactly why I was angry,"

She let out a deep sigh. "I hate this."

He laughed gently. "I know it's not a lot of fun. But you have good friends and, most importantly, you have a husband who I'd bet knows a thing or two about dealing with loss."

She looked up toward the house. From where they sat, they could catch a glimpse of someone moving around in the kitchen every now and then.

"I do," she agreed softly. "And you, who do you have?" she asked.

He didn't miss her use of the present tense. "I don't know."

"I think you do," she answered.

"It's not about me, right now," he countered.

"No, you're right, it's not. But when her situation changes, and you know it will, hopefully soon, what then?" she asked.

Drew's eyes strayed back to the window, and for a brief moment, he caught a glimpse of Carly as she entered the kitchen. "I don't know," he repeated.

"But you're going to figure it out."

After a long hesitation, he let out a deep breath. "Yes, I'm going to figure it out, because one thing my job has taught me is that I don't want to live with any regrets."

He felt, more than saw, Vivi smile. "Good, maybe we can help each other stay on track," she said, standing and reaching for his arm to pull him up.

"That sounds terrible," he said, not liking the idea of having to revisit this conversation.

She grinned at him. "It does, doesn't it? But that doesn't mean it's not a good idea."

He didn't have a chance to respond and, even if he had, he thought it was probably better not to anyway; he didn't want to encourage her. She pulled him back to the house and into the kitchen just as Naomi started serving dessert. Thankful for the distraction, he grabbed a slice of the warm apple pie and moved over beside Carly.

"She won't always be there to shield you from me," Vivi said, a friendly taunt as she brushed by him on her way to grab a few more forks from the drawer.

"You have no idea how many actual and metaphorical bullets I've dodged in my lifetime," he said. "You will not be a problem."

Vivi laughed. "Good then. I'm looking forward to it," she said.

Drew groaned.

• • •

After stopping by Kit's to pick up a few things and update Caleb on the investigation, Drew pulled into Carly's drive. Night had long ago fallen and the air had taken on a winter chill. He saw the light from her sitting room glowing warmly and wondered if she'd made a fire. If not, he thought that might be the first thing on his list of things to do. Well, second, after he'd given her the proper greeting he hadn't been able to give her at Vivi and Ian's.

"Come in," she called when he knocked.

Shaking his head with a smile and knowing better than to comment on her lack of security, he entered the house, locked the door behind himself, and set the alarm. After dropping his overnight bag on the floor by the stairs, he felt déjà vu when he walked into the living room and found her lying on the couch tucked under a blanket watching more videos.

His thoughts about making a fire died when he saw how cozy she already looked, so he walked over and dropped a kiss on her cheek, not wanting to interrupt her viewing.

She surprised him by hitting pause on the remote and pulling him down into a deep kiss.

An hour later, they were both ensconced on the couch, covered in the blanket with the video back on. He lay behind her on his side wearing only his boxers and she lay tucked up against him in nothing but his shirt.

He tried dutifully to stay awake as they watched round after round of horses, but the drone of the announcer's voice combined with his long day and complete lack of knowledge of the sport had lulled him into near sleep. But his eyes shot open when he felt her tense up against him.

"Carly?" he asked.

She was so intent on watching whatever round was happening on the screen, she didn't answer.

He said nothing as he watched her younger self finish the course, but when she hit the rewind button to watch again, he spoke. "Everything okay?" The video didn't show much more than the horse and rider and he had no idea what had captivated her.

"I'd forgotten about this horse," she answered as she hit play and the round started again.

His eyes went to the screen to see if he could see what was

special about the animal she watched so intently. The video seemed to have been shot somewhere warm and near the ocean. He guessed Florida, based on what he'd picked up from her about where many of the shows took place, but he couldn't be certain. What he could be certain of was that every time the horse cantered toward the ocean, its head came up. Even Drew could see the animal's hesitation.

"Why is it doing that?" he asked, propping himself up a bit to get a closer look.

"Balking at the ocean?" she asked.

He nodded, knowing she could feel, if not see, it.

She didn't answer right away. Instead, she leaned forward and reached for the case he presumed had held the video. After a moment, she fast-forwarded to another round with a different horse. The first horse had been brown with a big white mark down its face. This one was also brown, but had a black mane and tail. And a wild look in its eye that told Drew he wasn't going to enjoy watching this round.

Sure enough, the horse seemed to gallop to every fence, come to an almost complete stop, then spring over the jump. Each time the horse approached a fence, Drew's heart just about stopped.

"What are you looking at?" he asked.

"That's Charley," she said. "Believe it or not, he went on to become an extremely successful grand prix horse. He represented the German team in the Olympics twice."

His eyes strayed back to the screen—to the animal who seemed to leap more like a cat than any of the other horses he'd seen her ride. "And?" he asked.

"When we first saw him, he was horrible," she said.

To Drew, it didn't look as if the animal had improved much.

"He was on a farm in France and had more or less been abused," she continued. "He was four years old at the time and we were there looking at a two-year-old when my mom saw him. They refused to show him to her at first, knowing the reputation my mom had for raising jumpers, they said he wasn't fit for jumping.

"I don't know why my mom didn't believe them, but she pressed them until they agreed to bring him out. I remember my first thought about him was that he was incredibly unhappy. And he was mean because of it. He seemed to hate everyone and everything around him. It was more sad than anything else because horses, like people, aren't born to hate. Sure, they have personalities, and some are grumpier than others, but hate doesn't come naturally to a horse," she said, then paused as she watched the rest of the round before rewinding it back to the beginning again.

"Anyway, my mom knew that too, and figured even if the horse wasn't meant to jump, someone had taught him to hate, and she couldn't stand that. So we bought him and brought him home with us."

"What happened then? Clearly he learned to jump. Sort of," Drew managed to say as he watched the on-screen Carly pop nearly vertically over another jump.

"We put him out to pasture for about six months," she said. "We gave him treats, brushed him, loved up on him a lot, but didn't ride him. When he started to trust us, we put the saddle on him and just walked. I spent hours on the trail with him. I didn't ask him to do anything other than be who he was. Eventually, we got him back into work. We weren't sure what we were going to do with him, but after a year, he was one of the sweetest, funniest horses we'd ever had."

How a horse could be "funny" eluded Drew, but he took her word on it. "And then you got him jumping again," he said, as the round came to an end.

She sat back against him but kept her eyes on the screen. "We did, and when we did, we figured out why he had behaved the way he had when we first saw him."

"And why was that?" he asked, finding himself genuinely curious.

"You see the way he jumps," she said with a gesture to the screen. "It's different. Not at all correct, comfortable, or efficient.

But it was the way he jumped and if left alone he was remarkable at it."

"But the place you bought him from was trying to make him into something he wasn't," he said, catching on.

"Exactly. And because of that, he was lashing out and acting like a horse he really wasn't."

"But what about that brown horse?"

"The *chestnut*?" she asked, casting him a smile over her shoulder.

Apparently, they didn't have *brown* horses, but they did have chestnut ones. "Yes, the *chestnut* one." He could help the little eye roll that accompanied his correction, even though she'd already turned away from him.

She rewound the video even more, back to the horse that balked at the ocean. "That's William. He hated the Florida season and we couldn't figure out why for the longest time. Anywhere else, he was a champion hunter. A different kind of jumper than Charley—Charley was meant for the big fences and speed. William was built for the hunter ring where the fences aren't so high and horse and rider are judged on form, confirmation, those sorts of things."

Drew nodded, despite the fact that none of what she said meant anything to him. He could see the difference between the kinds of fences Carly jumped with William versus what he'd seen her jump with Charley or Athena, but he didn't know the importance of that difference. "And?" he asked.

"And after having him down in Florida for three seasons and having him perform so poorly there when he won everywhere else, my mom and I did some digging into his past. Turns out he was born in Holland and brought to England when he was a yearling. The problem was, it was by boat, during a storm. The boat foundered on the sand when coming into the Thames and got stuck. The non-live cargo was left on the boat until they could haul it out, but the horses, the only live cargo, had to be brought in by hand."

"By hand?"

"They made the horses swim."

Even he could see how that could traumatize an animal. "Why couldn't they bring food for them and keep them on board? That seems a lot easier, doesn't it?"

"They could have if the storm hadn't been so severe. They were worried the boat would capsize. They weren't worried about it sinking, the water wasn't deep enough for that. But if the boat tipped over, they knew the horses would injure themselves and they weren't sure if they would be able to get them out."

"So they swam them to shore, in a storm," he said quietly, feeling empathy for the huge beast.

"They did, and in the process traumatized at least William, maybe some of the others as well."

"So what did you do?" he asked.

"My mom had a friend in Florida who lived on the beach. We let him live there for a few months, had someone take him on walks near the water. He never grew entirely comfortable with it, but eventually he wasn't as anxious about it and that's what we wanted for him. He loved to show and we hated to see him anxious about anything. After another year or so, he was able to show the Florida circuit without any issues."

Drew liked this insight into her life with her mom and with the horses, but he didn't know why it seemed to have such an impact on her now, so he asked. "What made you react when you first saw William on the screen?"

She tilted her head in thought, then shifted onto her back so she could see him. "Do you remember what Vic said tonight?"

It would be a hard scene not to remember. "Of course."

"He said he'd had to choose between himself and his family, and that, because he wasn't who they thought he should be, he had hated himself. And then he'd turned into a man he hated even more because of how he'd treated Ian and, to a lesser extent, me."

"And?" he asked.

"And I asked Joe earlier if he thought Vince had ever had a partner when he was manipulating my uncle. He doesn't think he did, but he's also said, on numerous occasions, how Vince's behavior surprised him. That no one thought he'd be violent. His actions on the night he killed my mom were like the way Vic treated Ian, out of character for him. The way hate was out of character for Charley and William's behavior in Florida was out of character for him."

He narrowed his eyes. "Carly, your mom and uncle were threatening to expose him, that's motive enough to kill them. We don't need to dig into his past to figure out why he acted out of character, we *know* why."

"But what about before that?" she asked.

"Before what?"

"Before he killed them. Why did he get into the game in the first place? We know he had a big ego and big egos like to take risks, but the ego is also supposed to be responsible for self-preservation. Using his badge, his real name, his position of authority—those actions don't seem driven by someone who is interested in self-preservation."

"No," he agreed. "But they are the actions of a man who has delusions about his status in life, a man who thinks he is untouchable."

She studied him, then let out a long exhale and turned back onto her side, away from him. "I guess."

Drew let out his own sigh as he tugged her onto her back again, so he could look her in the eyes as they spoke. "Carly, what is this really about?"

He watched her struggle with her answer. After a few beats, she spoke, "I don't really know. All I know is that something isn't sitting right with me. We all agree he was, he *is*, motivated by power. But wanting power makes you vulnerable. And I can't help but wonder if someone else was involved—not a partner in the traditional sense—but maybe someone who used that vulnerability and manipulated him into acting in a certain way. Maybe even without knowing it. I know it sounds weird," she said, raising a hand to pre-empt any objection he might have. "Even to my ears it sounds far-fetched, but after witnessing Vic's confession today and then watching William and Charley, I guess the consequences that can come when someone takes advantage of another's vulnerability—intentionally or not—are just on my mind."

Knowing the trust she'd put in him in sharing her unformed thoughts, worries, and even her own vulnerabilities, he gave her words some consideration. And he had to admit that what she had said, as crazy as it might be, did make a little bit of sense. If Repetto had been manipulated from the beginning, intentionally or not, it would explain some of the inconsistencies they'd encountered between his profile and his actions.

"So, what are you thinking?" he asked.

Again, she let out a deep breath, then shook her head. "I don't know. I honestly don't. Maybe I don't want my mother's murder to be the result of one man's mission to gain power. Maybe I want it to be part of something bigger—part of some larger conspiracy—so that it has more meaning somehow."

"When in reality, there may be no reason, or meaning, to any of it?"

"Or none that would satisfy me, at any rate," she conceded. Turning away from him for a moment, she turned the television off then shifted to face him more fully. "Maybe my thoughts *are* just the ravings of a distraught child, but if there's a chance someone else was involved, someone intentionally using Repetto's thirst for power against him, someone who set this whole thing in motion, I don't want to let them get away with it because we're only focused on Repetto."

"A bird in the hand is not worth two in the bush?"

"Not at this point. But I guess, well, I guess I don't know. All I do know is that I want to be sure that—whether it's just Repetto, or him and someone else, or many others— everyone involved is brought to justice and we don't get too constrained when we look at the evidence."

He smiled. "You're a good policewoman, you know."

She made a face at him. "Yeah, I am good at my job."

"But this is about more than good police work."

"I know."

"Then let's go to bed and get a good night's sleep. We can harass Vivi about it all tomorrow," he said, rising from couch and pulling her with him.

"Sleep?" she asked wrapping her arms around him, stopping him with a grin.

"Or maybe something not quite that," he said.

CHAPTER TWENTY-TWO

WAITING FOR MARCUS TO CALL, Carly paced her office while Drew sat in a chair in front of her desk. She was glad she had gotten to know him better over the past several days because, had he actually been as calm as he appeared to be, she might have had to commit bodily injury. Knowing him as well as she did now, though, she could tell from the way his fingers curled over the arm of the chair and his blue eyes watched her that he was as anxious as she was.

"What do you think?" she stopped pacing to ask him. For the third time.

"I think your brother will do everything in his power to get that chip. And if he doesn't get it, we will get a warrant. We'd just rather not have to because of the process," he replied. Also for the third time.

"I'm being annoying, aren't I?" she asked, then resumed her pacing.

"No, you're not."

She glanced at him and saw a flash of frustration in his eyes—not directed at her. No, more likely he wanted to pull her down onto his lap and hold her, offer her physical comfort with his steady presence. But he wouldn't. He wasn't the type to be so public with his affection—and even if he were, he respected her work and her position too much to behave so intimately in her domain of authority.

She started to thank him for being so patient when his phone rang, startling them both.

Drew glanced at the number. "It's Brian," he said as he hit the accept button. "Carmichael," he answered. After a few seconds, his eyes flitted to hers then to her computer. Still listening to Brian, he motioned to her computer. "Do you mind if I . . ." he asked, gesturing to the machine.

She stepped back and waved him over. He moved around her desk and sat in her chair in front of the monitor. After scanning the screen for a moment, he seemed to find what he was looking for and clicked on an icon she'd seen, but hadn't ever used—the video conference call application.

"Got it," he said, then rattled out what appeared to the equivalent of a phone number for her account. Drew hung up and then, within seconds, Brian and Naomi appeared on the screen with Daniel in the background.

"You have news?" Drew asked without preamble, obviously more comfortable with video communication than she was, as she'd never used the application before.

"We do," Brian confirmed. "But you may want to take a seat." Drew immediately stood and offered Carly her chair then brought the other chair around to sit beside her.

"Okay," Drew prompted.

"Okay," Brian repeated. "Can you see this whiteboard behind me?" he asked, moving to the side. Behind Brian and Naomi, Daniel stood at a whiteboard with several photos taped to it and lines linking some of the images.

"Yes," Carly said.

"Then here is what we were able to find. Daniel, do you want to take over?" Brian directed more than asked.

Daniel pointed a group of photos. "Here are the suspects for the killing in the San Juan Islands that used the same gun as the gun that killed your mother and uncle. This man here, William Kenny," he said, his finger landing on a photo of a bald man covered in tattoos who looked to be in his late thirties, "is the cousin of this man here." Daniel's finger followed one of the drawn lines to another photo in a second grouping.

"And I assume those are the suspects in the LA shooting?" Carly asked.

"They are," Daniel confirmed. "And once we found this connection, Naomi and Brian were able to track the movements of Douglas Trainor." He continued to point to the cousin in LA. "It's a sporadic trail, but within a few years of the events in LA, he did make a trip to the Seattle area."

"And you think he transferred the gun at that point?" Carly asked.

"We think it's a distinct possibility," Naomi cut in.

"So that's how the gun got from LA to Washington, but how did it get from DC to LA? " Drew asked.

"Well, interestingly enough," Naomi started. "We did some digging and found out that Douglas Trainor's father, Isaac, who lives in DC, applied for a gun permit about six months after Sophia and Tony were killed and about six months before his son moved to LA."

"And?" Drew prompted.

"We're pretty sure he bought it from a pawn shop in his neighborhood," Brian cut in.

"A pawn shop," Carly repeated. It made sense, but the thought of the weapon that had been used to take so much from her and her brother being casually sold and moved about the country seemed unreal.

"Do we know why he bought a gun? Could it have been for his son?" Drew asked.

Naomi shook her head. "No, we don't think so. At around the same time there had been a number of break-ins in the area. Isaac Trainor, from what we can tell, is a stand-up shopkeeper of a small news and sundries shop. We think he bought it for protection."

"And his son likely took it from him when he moved to LA," Drew finished.

Naomi and Brian both nodded.

"Okay," Carly said on an exhale. "Can you get into the records of the pawn shop and see who brought it in to be pawned in the first place?"

Naomi made a face. "No. Other than the credit card system we used to trace the purchase, the shop seems to have no electronic records of anything. This is one that is going to require some boots on the ground."

She looked at Drew, who seemed to be contemplating the information. "Drew," she said, drawing his eyes to hers. "I can't leave right now." With Vic god-knew-where and Marcus in Florida, there was no way she could leave.

His face went distant, then his gaze met hers. "I'll take care of it. Naomi, do you have anything else?" he asked, cutting off any protest or question Carly might have about his plans.

"That's it from us. We're waiting to hear from Marcus, as I'm sure you are too," she answered.

"We'll let you know when we hear from him," Drew responded.

"And if you hear from him first—" Carly said.

"We'll let you know," Brian cut in.

They ended the call and she stared at the now empty screen. But Drew's movement beside her brought her back.

"Drew?"

He tapped the desk with his fingertips once, twice, then a third time.

"Drew?" she repeated.

"Right," he said pushing away. "I'll be right back. Stay here. Don't go anywhere."

And then he was gone.

She frowned at his retreating form but realized there would be little good in calling him back. Mostly likely, he'd gone off to book himself a flight to DC. She let out a deep breath and sank into her chair. If she couldn't go, at least she had Drew to go for her. It was the next best thing. Or so she kept telling herself.

An hour and a half later, when her frustration level had reached its maximum peak, Drew came waltzing back into the station with Vic, Lucas, and Ian. Carly had just handed some paperwork to

Sharon to copy when the four men walked in and paused in front of her.

Her gaze fell on Vic, Lucas, and Ian individually before landing on Drew. "The four of you make for quite an impressive sight," she said. And it was true. Vic looked much better than he had the night before. His eyes still held a bit of a haunted look, but he appeared stronger and, if possible, more grounded. Beside him, Lucas's tall frame all but dared someone to say something. And on the other side of Lucas stood Ian, looking as pragmatic and practical as always.

"What's going on?" she asked.

To her surprise, Vic was the one who stepped forward to answer. "Drew filled us in on the situation. I'm sorry about your mother, about Deputy Silva, and for, well, everything you're going through right now while also trying to hold down both your job *and* mine. Obviously, you're better at it than I am. Oh—" He turned and caught Sharon's attention with a gesture. "Sharon, you've met Lucas Rancuso before. He's my partner, personally, but today he's also here to help out."

Carly couldn't keep her eyebrows from shooting up. Even Lucas looked a bit startled. But both Ian and Drew appeared to be holding back smiles.

Sharon let her eyes travel over Lucas before they landed back on Vic. Carly could see him holding his breath—he might have made his announcement with a lot of bravado, but he was clearly anxious about his long-time receptionist's reaction.

Sharon rolled her eyes and began reshuffling the papers Carly had handed her. "It's about time you settled down, Chief."

Vic blinked.

"Of course I knew," Sharon said, answering his unasked question. "I know your family probably gave you a hard time, but, no offense, they always were an opinionated lot. And usually of the wrong opinion, if you ask me," she muttered.

After a pregnant pause, Vic spoke again. "Okay, well, um, now that we have that out of the way," he said with one of the first easy smiles Carly had seen on him in months. Turning toward her, he continued, "So, we figured out the best way to get you down to DC."

"Me? Down to DC?" she asked.

"Did Marcus call?" Drew interjected before anyone could answer her question.

Carly hesitated and glanced quickly in Sharon's direction, then with a gesture of her head toward her office, she led the four men into the room. Drew shut the door behind them.

"He did call. The owners agreed. It turns out they knew my mother and never believed any of the stories they'd read in the papers about the connections to terrorists."

"So do they have the chip?"

She shook her head. "Not yet. The vet couldn't make it out until this afternoon. But he'll be there around two and they'll do the procedure then. Marcus is booked on a flight back at five. He should be back to the lab by nine thirty."

"Good. That's good," Drew said.

"Yes, that's good," she repeated. "Now what about DC?"

"We're going to DC," Drew said. "We have just enough time to swing by your house and pack a bag. We meet the plane in about an hour over by Great Barrington."

"The airport's in Albany," she replied, already starting to gather the few things she'd brought to the office with her.

"Private plane," he said, holding her coat out for her to slide into.

"Yours?" she asked, reaching for her purse.

Ian, Lucas, and Vic hadn't moved much but all were watching the interaction between her and Drew with interest. She wondered how the three of them would fare together and what Drew had said to get Ian on board, but she figured she'd have time to ask him on the flight.

"The company's—my *family's* company's—plane," he stated, clarifying that his reference to the "company" did not mean the CIA. "I called as soon as I left the station earlier. It's based in New

York so the pilot flew it up. He should be landing any moment, then he'll need to add fuel and run a pre-flight check. Then we'll be off."

She turned toward Vic, "And you—"

"We got this," he said, holding up a hand. "I'll be fine. I should have stepped up a long time ago. And if I need any reminding of that, Lucas and Ian will be here."

She cast a skeptical look at the other two men and Ian gave her an encouraging smile.

"Carly?" Drew stood by the door with his hand on the doorknob.

She said a grateful goodbye to the three remaining men then stepped toward the door as Drew opened it.

Within minutes they were on their way to her house, where she quickly packed a bag and changed out of her uniform into jeans and a lightweight sweater. Shortly after that, they were headed to the private airport just over the Massachusetts border.

When they arrived, she was startled to see Caleb walking toward them carrying a black duffel bag.

"I left my car in the garage bay like you told me to. I'll be back next week to pick it up," he said to Drew, not breaking stride as he walked toward her. "Carly." He bent down and kissed her cheek. "Good to see you again. I'm just going to hitch a ride down to DC with you all. But don't worry, I'll sit with the captain in the cockpit and leave you two alone." And then he was walking up the stairs to the plane where he disappeared inside.

She turned her attention to Drew. "I'd almost forgotten he was here."

He grabbed her bag and motioned her toward the plane. "Don't tell him, he'll be crushed."

So many thoughts zipped through her mind as she boarded the plane that she could hardly grab onto a single coherent one. Except for the thought that they were close. After all the years and all the secrets, they were going to bring her mother's killer to justice, and maybe, just maybe, get some answers. That one thought seemed to occupy every breath she took, so it wasn't until they were airborne that she started a conversation.

"How did you find Vic?" she asked. Seated in a wide, comfortable leather chair facing the front of the plane, she looked at Drew, seated in a similar chair across a table from her.

"I figured Vivi would know where Lucas was and Lucas would know where Vic was."

"And Ian?"

"He was home when I talked to Vivi. He offered to come along in case we couldn't find Vic and needed a local law enforcement officer to take over."

"Wow, that was nice. Of them and of you."

"I could have gone down to DC by myself, but given that Marcus is likely to be bringing back the smoking gun, I thought you might want to be in DC when Franks brings Repetto in."

The idea of seeing Repetto face-to-face, of having him pay for what he did, had been something she'd wanted since they'd first put a name to the deed. But now, hearing Drew acknowledge that they really were that close—close enough to plan on arresting Repetto—made a wave of uneasy excitement ripple through her body.

"Thank you," she said, turning her head away to look out the window. Suddenly, she blurted, "Why are you doing this?" Her question was born of her own insecurities—why her? Why was he doing everything he was doing for *her*? And what did it mean for them in the long term? But when he responded, she knew he'd heard her question differently.

"Why am I doing what, specifically?" he asked. His expression shuttered and though, to an outsider, his voice would sound nothing but calm and professional, Carly knew her question had hurt him. He had not heard her insecurities, but his own. He lived in a world where everyone questioned everything, and to him, she had just cast his feelings, his intentions toward her, into doubt.

"All of it," she answered. "The task force, the plane, making arrangements for me to go to DC and the pawn shop . . ." She let her voice trail off and hoped he'd heard the real question this time. But even if he had, even if he'd recognized that her question had been more abstract than specific, she knew there were two answers he could give: why he'd done all those things or why he had done them *for her*.

He drummed his fingers on the armrest of his seat and switched his gaze out the window before he spoke. "Because we have an opportunity to get some answers and finally close this case. As for the trip to DC, we're not going there just to follow up on the pawn shop—we also need to look into the rented yacht, the hired hacker, and the people we think Repetto has already approached to take your uncle's place. We need boots on the ground."

Although it didn't come as a surprise, the fact that he'd decided to answer with logic rather than emotion disappointed her. But since she had been the one who put the distance between them to begin with, even though it had been done inadvertently, she could also be the one to bridge it. So she did.

Unbuckling her seatbelt, she stood then moved around the table to his side. His gaze followed her in question. She paused a moment, then slid onto his lap facing him, straddling his thighs. His hands came to her waist, whether consciously or not she didn't know, and his fingertips brushed the skin above the waistband of her jeans.

"You pulled away from me," she said.

His blue eyes met hers.

"I know, it was my fault. I didn't, well, I didn't ask the question the way I should have. It's just," she paused and took a deep breath. "With everything going on, it's a bit overwhelming. And, well, as much as I hate to admit it, I had a burst of insecurity. I'm not questioning your motives or your feelings for me, Drew. I didn't mean for my question to come out that way. But my life isn't clean. I *know* I'm headed for an emotional train wreck when this is all over."

Again, she paused then pulled up all the courage she could. "I'm not much of a catch. I don't know what I have to offer you.

That's what I meant—I meant to ask why you are doing this for *me*?" she said, laying her doubts on the line.

She expected him to pull her into his arms and hold her, but he didn't. Instead, he raised his hands and bracketed her face with them. Leaning his forehead against hers, he closed his eyes for a moment then answered the question she'd asked.

"I'm doing this because I'm selfish, Carly. Being with you makes me want to explore again. You make me want to *feel* and you make me want to *want*. Until I met you, thinking about my life was something I avoided at all costs. My future felt more like a black hole teeming with uncertainties and unknowns—definitely not a place I wanted to venture into and not a place I'd drag someone else. But when I'm with you, those thoughts—those questions, those unknowns—aren't so scary. I still don't know any of the answers, and I have no idea what life will bring for us, but for the first time, I can actually catch a glimpse of what it might be like to navigate all the opportunities that are part of that uncertainty. Whatever it is we do, or whatever it is we make of this thing between us, isn't going to be easy," he stopped and exhaled before continuing.

"There's too much in our pasts and so much doubt about what the future will bring for both of us for it to be anything other than a long road. But that's a road I want to take now. Because of you. And hopefully *with* you."

He held her gaze, and because she knew he had more to say, she said nothing.

"I can't pretend to know what you're feeling right now. Everything you and Marcus have been through, everything you *will* go through," he paused again. "But I do know how important all this is to you, and because it's important to you, it's important to me. That's why I'm doing this for *you*, Carly."

His eyes were earnest and sincere, and it was then that Carly felt the full impact of what this man could mean to her. She didn't believe in love at first sight. She didn't even believe in love in two weeks. But she did believe in the possibility of love. And in that moment, when their breath mingled and their eyes held, she knew that if love was possible for her, it was possible with this man.

"Thank you," she said. Sometimes those words, that phrase, felt so inadequate. How could two words possibly convey the depth and truth of what she felt? But today they did, and she sensed it in her body just as she saw it reflected in his eyes. Their presence together, in this moment, was more intimate than anything else they had ever shared.

Drew gave a small smile then dropped his hands back down to her waist as the plane hit some turbulence. Startled, she tensed, and his hands tightened, holding her steady. She glanced out the window, as if the sky would tell her whether or not it had been a one-time bump or if more were to come. When she looked back at him, his smile had grown bigger.

"You don't much like flying, do you?" he asked.

She rolled her eyes and shook her head as she slid off his lap and onto the seat beside him where she promptly buckled her seatbelt. And tightened it. "No, I don't. I flew a ton when I was kid. Back and forth to Europe all the time. Flying to horse shows, all that kind of stuff, but it's still not my favorite thing to do. And yes, before you spout statistics, I know it's safer than driving," she said, holding up a hand to stop him from teasing her.

They hit another bump and her hands dropped to the armrests. Drew reached over, picked one up, and held it in his. "I wasn't going to point that out."

"You were," she said, gripping his hand.

"I wasn't," he countered. "But I *was* going to point out that you probably feel safer driving because you're in control," he added.

"Are you insinuating that I'm a control freak?" She arched a brow at him.

"'Freak' isn't the word I'd use."

"Are you the pot or the kettle?" she asked with a laugh.

He smiled. "I'll be the pot. Kettles have more curves."

CHAPTER TWENTY-THREE

DREW WATCHED CARLY AS SHE leaned her hip against the pawn-shop's counter and tapped a piece of paper on the glass. By all outward appearances, she looked like a plain-clothes police officer doing a routine job. But the intensity in her eyes gave her away.

"It was nice of Vivi to arrange a search warrant for us," she said, keeping an eye on the back of the shop. The shopkeeper, who had been cooperative, was back there pulling his paper records for the gun.

"And for the FBI escort." He gestured toward the agent waiting for them by the door. The man had met them at the private airport and introduced himself as Agent Damian Rodriguez. Agent Rodriguez and Ian went way back to their days as Rangers. In other words, he was someone in the agency they could trust.

Carly glanced over her shoulder at the man, who winked and gave her an are-we-having-fun-yet look. She smiled, looking like she was about to say something, but abruptly cut herself off when the shopkeeper, an older man who appeared to have more skin covered in tattoos than not, came walking toward them from the shop's office.

"Here we are," he said, handing a consignment slip over them. Carly took it, read it, then handed it to Drew.

He looked over the name and address of the person who had consigned the gun, as well as the information pertaining to the gun itself, to confirm that it was the one they were looking for. Stapled to the slip was a receipt for the amount paid by Isaac Trainor, further confirmation that it was the right gun.

"Do you know if this man ever brought anything else in?" Drew asked, pointing to the name of the man who'd brought the gun into the pawn shop.

"My filing system isn't the greatest, I go by year and then name. I didn't see anything else from him in the year you were looking at, but I didn't go through any other year."

"But if he was in a lot, you'd remember him?" Carly pressed.

The man nodded. "I have a few regulars and I can say he isn't one of them."

Drew slid the consignment slip and receipt into a clear evidence bag. "Thank you for your help."

"Anytime. I like to keep things above board here," the shopkeeper replied. "Knowing I cooperate with law enforcement keeps some of the characters I'd rather not do business with away."

With that, they turned toward the door. Agent Rodriguez opened it for them and the three of them proceeded out to the sidewalk.

"Get what you need?" the agent asked.

"We have a name and an address—whether he's still at that address, we'll have to see. Do you have someone who can run a search for us, Agent Rodriguez?" Drew asked, holding out the evidence bag.

"Call me Damian, and yes, I do," he said, reaching for the information.

As he made the call, they made their way to the government issued SUV he'd picked them up in. Five minutes later, they had an address for one Louis Charles, aged fifty-four, and some additional personal information on the man who had once had possession of the gun used to kill Sophia Davidson and Tony Lamot. He had no criminal record, paid his taxes, and, for the past two years, had lived in an apartment above a small breakfast and lunch place he owned in one of the gentrifying neighborhoods in DC.

"You okay?" From his position in the front seat, Drew turned back to look at Carly, sitting in the back. While he knew DC well, he was glad to have Damian navigating the streets so that he could focus on her. She seemed to be growing more and more quiet with each passing block.

After giving Damian a quick glance, she looked back at Drew. "Just thinking," she said.

"About?"

"How would Louis Charles come across a gun that was used to kill my mother and uncle? From what Damian said, he seems to be a stand-up guy who's built a better life for himself in the past fifteen years. I mean, the address the pawnshop guy gave us isn't in the best part of town *now*. Back then, I can't imagine it was a place anyone like Vince Repetto would have set foot in, willingly or not, without a lot of backup. So where did their paths cross? Or did Repetto have a partner familiar with that part of town? Or did he just hire out the killings?"

Drew studied her face as she turned to look out the window. "You still think someone else might have been involved," he said.

"I don't know. I guess I'm getting ahead of myself. Yes, I think there might have been someone else involved in the whole scheme. But I suppose it's just as likely that he hired out the killings and whomever he hired had a connection with Charles—which would explain how the gun ended up with him in that part of town."

"If there's a link between Charles and Repetto—a link that would explain how the gun came into Charles' possession—Naomi and Brian will be able to find it. Do you want to call and give them the update? Ask them to follow up?"

At his mention of the twins' names, Damian chuckled.

Drew turned toward him, then, deciding not to ask, turned back to Carly, who already had her phone out.

Dialing, she said, "I'll ask them to dig into it. I also want to see if anyone has heard from Marcus yet."

Drew sat back in his seat. Half-listening to her side of the conversation, he watched the streets go by. Men and women in suits flooded the sidewalks, walking purposefully. He felt a kind of kinship with the nameless masses. Usually, he was one of them, going about his business as if it were the most important thing in the world. Granted, his "business" often truly was crucial, to the nation at least. But as he watched a man talking on his phone walk directly into a woman staring at a device in her hand—neither bothering to acknowledge the other—he wondered just how much bravado there was in thinking he was anything more than a cog—a replaceable cog—in the machine.

"Drew?" Carly's voice came from behind him.

He turned to face her.

"You okay?" she asked, parroting his question from a few moments earlier.

"Fine, what's the story?" He glanced quickly at her phone then back at her.

She hesitated then answered. "Naomi and Brian will look into Louis Charles and let us know if they find anything interesting. Marcus got the chip and is on his way to the airport now. We should know tonight if it has any information on it."

They would know that night if they had what they needed to bring Repetto in. Or if, after so many years, the chip had become too degraded and unreadable.

"We're here," Damian said, pulling into a parking spot along-side a renovated building. All three of them craned their heads to get a look at the brick townhouse. From the information Damian had provided, they knew that each of the two upper floors con-tained a two-bedroom apartment. Both had bay windows looking out onto the street, and with new glass, clean trim work, and restored brick, the building looked well tended and welcoming.

The ground floor café, according to the writing on its large front windows, served southern-style breakfast and lunch. Booths and a counter could be seen through the windows, as well as an open kitchen. It looked a bit retro with black and white tiled floors and red vinyl seating, but also clean and well kept.

"Ready?" Drew asked.

Both Carly and Damian nodded and the three of them climbed from the SUV. A door on the left side of the building led to the apartments and Damian took the lead, stepping up to the entrance and ringing the bell.

"Yes?" came a male voice over the intercom.

"Agent Damian Rodriguez, sir, with the FBI. Would you have a few minutes to talk?"

There was a pause and Drew saw a curtain flutter in a window upstairs. "Who's with you?" the voice, presumably that of Louis Charles, asked.

"I have Deputy Chief of Police of Windsor, New York, Carly Drummond, and a consultant, Drew Carmichael, with me, sir," Damian responded.

"Show your ID," the voice said.

Damian pulled out his badge, looked around, then held it up to the small camera Carly pointed out over the door. A few seconds later, the door buzzed to let them in.

A short black man with graying hair was waiting for them on the first landing. "Come on in," he said, waving his arm toward the open door of his apartment. "Sorry to be so brusque. This is a good neighborhood and all, much better than where I used to live, but you can't be too careful."

"No, sir, you can't," Damian agreed as they followed the man into his living room.

"Are you Louis Charles?" Damian asked.

The man, who couldn't have been more than five-foot-three, nodded. "I am."

Damian turned to Drew and Carly to see who wanted to lead. Drew cast a look at Carly.

"Mr. Charles," she started.

"Call me Louis," he interrupted.

"Louis, about fourteen years ago, you took a handgun to a pawn shop near the neighborhood where you used to live. Do you remember that?"

He frowned and Drew's heart sank. He didn't want this man to play dumb with them, or worse, truly not remember. But then the older gentleman surprised them all.

"Of course I remember," he said, making a face. "It was the strangest damn thing," he added.

"Strange?" Carly asked. "How so?"

"Now look, I know what you probably think. A black man living in that neighborhood, of course he'd have a gun." Louis slid his hands into his pockets and rocked back on his heels. "But the thing is, I don't like guns. Never bought one, never wanted to shoot one. I had a boy, my son, in the house with me, I always thought I'd rather us take the chance if we got robbed than have a gun in the house neither of us knew how to use. You know what I mean?" he said, looking up at them.

"Owning a gun is a big responsibility," Damian said.

Again, Louis nodded. "It is. If you're gonna own it, you should know how to shoot it, and back in those days, I didn't have the time, money, or inclination to learn to shoot properly."

"So how did you come across it?" Carly asked.

Louis shook his head. "I don't rightly know. Now, I know that sounds strange, and like I said, the whole thing *was* strange. But the truth is, one day I just found it."

"Found it?" Drew repeated.

Again, Louis shook his head. "I know, sounds crazy, but that's the truth. There was a clog in the toilet one day so I took the top off to look in the tank and there it was."

Everyone was silent. Of all the things Louis Charles could have told them, this hadn't entered any of their minds.

"Had you been in the house long?" Damian asked after a moment. "Could it have been left there by the previous tenant?"

Louis shook his head one more time. "We'd been in that apartment more than eight years and believe me, with a growing boy and the bad plumbing, we'd had to take that toilet apart more than once."

The story was just strange enough that Drew found himself believing Louis—that and the fact that the event still seemed to befuddle the man was probably what convinced him.

"Do you have any idea how it could have gotten there?" Damian asked.

Louis shrugged. "Not really, no."

"Had you had any visitors in the weeks before finding it?" Damian asked.

Carly's phone buzzed and Drew cast her a glance before returning his attention to Louis.

"Excuse me," she said, stepping a few feet away.

Louis shook his head at Damian's question. "Not so much as I can remember, but you have to know, I was working like a dog back in those days. Eighteen-hour days weren't unusual."

"And your son was home alone a lot," Drew said.

"He's a good boy, always was. He's a lawyer now. Here in town. He got a scholarship to a special high school, then to college. Worked his way through law school. Signed on with one of those fancy law firms. The first thing the boy did was put a down payment on this place and move us out of our old neighborhood. Always did say I should be cooking for a living," the father said with obvious pride in his son. "We renovated the café together, then the apartments. He still lives upstairs. Not spending his money on silly things—he still takes the metro to work."

"Is this your son?" Carly asked, picking up a framed picture and rejoining the conversation.

Louis smiled. "Yes, that's my boy. High school graduation. He was valedictorian."

"You must be proud," she said.

"Yes, I am."

"How did he end up applying for the scholarship to the high school? Did his school counselor tell him about it?"

Louis let out a cynical laugh. "They didn't have any counselors at that school in our old neighborhood. Couldn't get any to stay more than a month or two. I was working so much that Cole spent some time at a local youth center. It was there he learned about the scholarship. Got a lot of help there too. I wasn't so well educated, didn't even graduate high school, but that doesn't mean

I don't know the value of education. Wanted something better for him, wanted him to have more opportunities than I did and I knew education was the way. I encouraged him to go to the youth center and they were good to him. Tutored him, mentored him, all those things."

"Sounds like a great program," she said. "Is it still around?"

"It is. Much bigger now than it was back then, but it's still around. Cole helps out there regularly too."

"What's the name of the place?" Carly asked.

Louis eyed her, sensing, as Drew did, that the question had more meaning than she was letting on. "Youth Roots," he answered. "Is there a problem with them? And what do they have to do with the gun?" he asked, his eyes narrowing on her in curiosity.

"Maybe nothing," Carly said. "But do you remember this day?" she asked, holding out her phone to him.

Louis hesitated, then took it. After a moment, he smiled. "Of course I remember. The local newspaper was doing one of those ridiculous feel-good stories—you know the type: the local-poor-boy-does-good kind of thing? Anyway, they came to the apartment to take pictures of Cole with the board of directors of Youth Roots," he said, handing the phone back to Carly.

Silently, she handed it to Drew.

He looked down at the image she'd brought up. A young boy, presumably Cole, surrounded by six adults—two women and four men—everyone smiling. Tapping the screen he enlarged the image to read the caption. Cole Charles stood surrounded by the board of directors of Youth Roots, including Olivia Laturna Repetto.

"Was anyone else here that day?" Drew asked. "Anyone other than the board members and the photographer?"

Louis looked away in thought, no doubt trying to recall that day many years ago. "There was another woman, the wife of one of the board members," he said. "And the husband of one of them too."

"Do you know which woman brought her husband along?" Carly asked.

Drew could hear the excitement in her voice and Damian, no doubt sensing it too, seemed to come to high alert.

"Yes, that one," he said, taking the phone back and pointing to Olivia Laturna Repetto. "They were off to celebrate an anniversary right after the photos were taken. Going to the Caribbean or something like that."

"Is this the man who was here?" Drew asked, handing Louis yet another image, on his phone this time.

"Yes, that's him. Looks a little older in that picture, but that's him. Do you think he brought the gun into my home? Why would he do something like that?" he asked.

Carly looked to Drew to take the lead, no doubt because he had more experience evading questions than she did. It was a somewhat dubious compliment.

"At this point, we're not sure, Louis. We're trying to find the origin of the gun and whether Mr. Repetto had anything to do with it or not. You've given us an idea of where to go next, so thank you."

The man rocked back on his heels again and seemed to be debating whether to ask any more questions. In the end, he said nothing.

"Thank you for your time, Mr. Charles," Carly said.

"Louis," he corrected.

She smiled. "Thank you for your time, Louis. We truly appreciate it."

He lifted a shoulder. "Anytime. Anything I can do to help."

Drew and Damian also thanked him and the three of them took their leave.

Once they were all buckled into the SUV and he was steering it into traffic, Damian asked, "Want to tell me what that was about?"

Drew glanced back at Carly, planning to take her lead on just how much she wanted to share.

She was looking out the window, but he didn't miss the smile that was spreading across her face. "We're closing in, Damian. We're going to be able to bring my mother's killer to justice."

• • •

Carly had drifted off to sleep hours earlier, but Drew sat, quiet and alone, at his computer in his DC apartment. Occasionally, his eyes would stray to the river that swept past his building. In the cool October darkness, the lights that lined the river walk reflected crisp colors on the still water and leafless tree branches swayed in a gentle breeze. But despite the beauty of the hour, his eyes stayed mostly fixed on his computer screen.

Marcus had returned from Florida with a treasure trove of information embedded in the tiny chip Seraphina had been carrying around for close to fifteen years. Naomi and Brian had done a preliminary scan of the data and it was clear from the material they were gathering that Joe hadn't been exaggerating when he'd described Sophia Davidson as organized. She'd created spreadsheets documenting each of Repetto's visits—noting the day and, in some cases, length of each visit. She must have made her brother sit down and go through it all with her as well, because beside each entry she'd included a summary of the conversation between Repetto and Tony. The summaries included notes as to whether the information that had changed hands was information Tony had passed on to Repetto or if it had been information Repetto had asked Tony to pass on to others. And in the latter case, she'd noted to whom Tony had passed the information.

And, of the four times Repetto had asked Tony to pass on a "rumor," Sophia had noted that, not long after he'd done so, at least two of those people had lost a significant amount of money. Of course, neither investor had ever come forward with a formal complaint about the rumor, as they would have incriminated themselves for insider trading, but, having been friends with those investors, Sophia had known of the losses, if not the exact extent of them.

Naomi and Brian were looking into these particular "rumors" and the fallout from them, as well as the flow of information that went the other way, from Tony to Repetto, and, no doubt, linking it to stock trades Repetto made soon thereafter. Not having insight into what Repetto would have invested or gained, Sophia had not been able to provide a direct link between what her brother had told the agent and what Repetto had used. But the information she had provided allowed Brian and Naomi, who had full access to Repetto's accounts at this point, to make those connections.

The twins were sending Drew bits and pieces of data in real time and he was culling through it to make his own set of files. He planned to take a risk the next day that no one knew about and no one would approve of. But he hadn't worked at the CIA for nearly two decades without picking up a few tidbits about human nature and the impact of good intelligence—good intelligence could often be, and often was, more persuasive than any other form of communication.

Adding the most recent piece of data Naomi had sent to the open file on his computer, he heard Carly shifting in his bed. They'd come back to his apartment after visiting Louis Charles, sent some e-mails to update everyone on what they'd learned, and then gone to dinner. A couple of glasses of wine with the heavy Italian meal had been enough to soothe her adrenaline, and at around ten o'clock she'd started to drift off. Once she'd been sleeping soundly for a bit, he'd slid from the sheets and made his way to his computer. Where he'd sat for the last four hours.

Again, he heard her shift. After taking a look at the latest file Naomi had sent, Drew saved everything to a thumb drive then shut down his computer. For a number of reasons, he didn't want Carly to wake up and find him missing from the bed. Not only did he not want her asking too many questions about what he'd been doing, but he didn't want her waking up alone either. So, after placing the drive next to his wallet on the dresser, he slid back into bed beside her.

Watching her profile in the ambient light of the city, he hoped she was emotionally ready for the day to come. Vivi and Damian had obtained an arrest warrant for Vince Repetto just moments earlier, something he'd tell Carly when she awoke in the morning. Between finally being able to question Repetto and the evidence everyone else was tying up, including documenting the movement of the gun, taking statements from other people Repetto had used in his schemes, and tracking Repetto's finances, he expected to have the situation all cleaned up, all neat and tidy, within the next thirty-six hours—a blink of an eye compared to the near fifteen years both Marcus and Carly had been waiting.

"Drew?" her voice, heavy with sleep echoed in his room.

Rather than answer and wake her more, he gently pulled her against him. She rolled over, slid an arm across his chest, and nestled her head against his shoulder. A few minutes later, he felt her breath even out as it whispered across his skin. He just hoped that the following night she'd feel as at peace.

CHAPTER TWENTY-FOUR

CARLY WATCHED AS DREW SLID a thumb drive across a table toward a man who looked to be about her age. He also looked vaguely familiar, but she couldn't place him.

"My contact information is on this drive, once you've had a look," was all Drew said.

She could tell from the flash of guilt that came into Drew's expression when he saw her standing there that he hadn't wanted her to witness the exchange. She glanced down at the man at the table, who'd turned his attention back to his book, then she looked back at Drew.

"Everything okay?" he asked, obviously wondering why she'd returned from the restroom so quickly.

She thought about pressing him, asking what he'd given to the man, but she didn't want to put him in an awkward position. He'd been spending most of his time with her, on her case, but he still worked for the agency and she thought it was entirely possible that what she'd just seen was agency business.

"Everything is fine," she said. "I need a key to get into the restroom."

Saying nothing about what she'd just seen, he motioned her toward the counter of the busy coffee shop where he'd suggested they stop on their way to meet Vivi, Wyatt, and Joe.

The three agents were flying in that morning to meet Damian and the small FBI team Damian had put together to execute the arrest warrant on Vince Repetto—something she could hardly believe was really happening. She hadn't wanted to delay, hadn't wanted to stop, but Drew had convinced her by reminding her that getting to the airport early to meet Vivi and the others wouldn't actually make them arrive any earlier. So they'd stopped.

When she came back from the restroom a few minutes later, he gestured to the line and said, "Latte?"

"Yes, please."

"And maybe a croissant?"

She pursed her lips, but nodded. He had been trying to feed her since they'd risen from bed ninety minutes earlier. But after he'd told her about the warrant, eating breakfast had fallen off her list of priorities for the morning. She didn't think she'd be able to stomach even the simple pastry, but saying "yes" was easier than saying "no."

Fifteen minutes later, they were again headed to the airport. Ten minutes after that, her three friends were stepping through the airport doors, each giving her a hug before climbing into the SUV. Vivi was the last in and she lingered for a moment, her eyes searching Carly's. She was grateful for Vivi's concern, but she wanted nothing more than to get on with the day.

As if sensing her desire, Vivi gave her a small smile and asked, "Are we ready to get this show on the road?"

Carly's stomach fluttered and she gave Vivi a nervous smile in return.

"Then let's get to it," Vivi said.

When they were all seated in the large SUV, Damian placed a call to the team he'd had put in place as soon as the warrant had come through, confirming that Repetto was still at home. Carly had thought it would have been fitting to arrest him in his place of work—a job he'd abused so horribly—but in the end, she'd been convinced that quickly and quietly was the best option.

The morning traffic made the relatively short distance to Repetto's home feel interminable—she felt like she could have walked there faster. Of course, walking herself there faster wouldn't have done any good. Neither she nor Drew had any jurisdiction over the arrest. She wouldn't be able to do anything but watch unless, or until, the FBI gave her permission to do otherwise.

Beside her, Vivi reached over and gave her hand a squeeze as they made their way north. Idly, Carly wondered about Repetto's wife and how her husband's arrest would affect her—his arrest for not just a slew of financial crimes, but murder as well.

Deep in the files Naomi and Brian had found on the chip from Seraphina, Sophia had included information about a security company that backed up all the CCTV cameras they'd had on the barn—a company Repetto had known nothing about.

Repetto had, of course, viewed the footage from the night of the murder provided by the primary security company, a company that only stored data for seven days. He'd reported that the house hadn't been visible, only the barn, and as a result, the FBI hadn't taken any footage into custody. He'd been wrong though. About two things.

Most of the footage *had* been of the barn, but there had been a single camera angled in such a way as to see the parking area near the house. The second mistake Repetto had made was in assuming Sophia Davidson had not arranged for a separate company to take and store all the CCTV footage beyond the seven days provided by the primary provider.

No doubt, Sophia had originally intended to use the video to back-up her assertions regarding the dates Repetto had visited. But inadvertently, she'd also provided them with what they needed to prove Repetto had visited Sophia and Tony on the night they'd been killed, *and* within the window the coroner had ruled as their times of death.

Both the evidence of his arrival at the Lamot/Davidson house and the way they'd been able to track the gun, though that was admittedly circumstantial, had been enough to persuade a judge to include murder charges in the arrest warrant.

"You okay?" Vivi asked as the SUV came to a stop in front of an elegant home in Chevy Chase, a wealthy suburb of DC.

Carly felt her heart constrict as she glanced over at her friend.

She had never seen Vivi wearing either an FBI jacket or a bulletproof vest, and the sight made her smile a bit. No one was anticipating any problems, but it was good to be prepared. Ian would have approved.

"Yes, or rather, I will be once he's in custody," Carly answered with a glance toward Joe.

They'd jointly decided that Joe would be the one to make the arrest. Vivi, Damian, Wyatt, and the two agents who'd been watching Repetto, would be backup.

Vivi studied her for a moment. "Then I guess we better get to it. Damian?"

"My two guys are waiting for our signal," he answered.

"Then let's give it," Vivi commanded.

In unison, Joe, Wyatt, Vivi, Damian, and the other two agents exited their cars and made their way to the front door. The two agents she didn't know circled around the back, but the rest, led by Joe, knocked on the dark wood door.

Carly saw a woman appear and, even from where she sat, she recognized Vince Repetto's wife, already dressed and made up for the day. She didn't work, so Carly wondered where she might be going, but the thought slid from her mind as the woman, clearly confused, opened the door and let the four agents in.

"How are you, really?" Drew asked from the front seat with his head turned back to look at her.

She tore her attention from the front door to meet his steady gaze. "I'm glad we were able to include the murder charges."

Emotion flashed in his eyes and she knew he didn't like the fact she'd even had to say those words.

"Me too," he said quietly.

A beat passed then she let out a long exhale, preparing herself for his response to what she was about to say. "Drew, we got lucky with the video evidence that had Repetto's car on it. Maybe we should see if luck is still on our side."

"Meaning?"

"Meaning, maybe we should keep looking to see if there was

someone else involved," she said, then held her breath, waiting for his answer. The look on his face shifted and she hated what she saw there. Pity, definitely, but maybe a little frustration too. She looked away, forcing herself to breathe. "Look, we know he involved someone else when he confronted Marguerite, why not when he killed my mother? You know as well as I do that having *someone* else involved is the only way to make sense of some of his actions."

"Carly," he said after a beat, his voice soft in the car.

She kept her eyes trained on the front door of the house.

After a few moments, he let out a long breath. "Look, if there was someone else involved, everyone will do their best to find that person. Joe and Vivi and the rest of the team will interrogate Repetto today and then take what he says and run it through their systems. If there is anything there, you know they, or Brian and Naomi, will find it."

When he said nothing more, she turned back toward him, his blue eyes still steady on hers.

"I don't know what they will find," he spoke again. "I honestly don't. But if you're asking if I *think* there was someone else involved in what he did to your mother? Then, yes, I agree with you, there probably was. But was it criminal? I don't know. And Carly, it's possible we will never know."

She studied the painful honesty in his eyes. He didn't like telling her that she may never get all the answers she wanted. And she liked hearing it even less, even though she needed to. Because she knew, but hadn't admitted to herself, that unless Repetto told them himself, or they found some evidence of a partner, they—she—might never know the entire truth. And, somehow, she'd have to learn to live with that.

She sighed and rubbed her temples. He reached out and took one of her hands in his. She started to thank him for everything he'd done, but then Joe came walking out of the house guiding a hand-cuffed Repetto ahead of him and her breath caught in her throat. She watched Vivi, Wyatt, and Damian follow Joe out onto the porch as the other two agents came around from the back of the house.

Vince Repetto looked remarkably similar to the man she'd known as Vince Archstone nearly fifteen years earlier—time had been kind to him. He was still trim and cut a figure in his suit. And, even with his hands cuffed, he looked like a man who knew power.

Joe led Repetto toward the other FBI car and opened the rear door. Repetto paused before sliding in and his eyes went to the front door of his home. Carly's gaze tracked his and there she saw his wife accompanied by her father, Senator Laturna, who must have joined the couple for breakfast.

Olivia Laturna Repetto stood there in her designer dress with one arm wrapped around her petite waist, her other hand covering her mouth. On both her wrists, gold and diamond bangles glistened in the morning sun, their glamour at odds with the look of confusion and shock she wore on her face as she watched her husband being led away.

Beside his daughter, Buzz Laturna stood firm, his body straight and strong, with one arm draped over her shoulder and his unblinking gaze set on the unfolding situation.

Carly wondered what the woman's father might be thinking—was he proud of his son-in-law, believing this to be a mistake, or had he thought his daughter had married beneath her and the situation was finally proving him right? Senator Laturna gave no indication of his feelings and as soon as the car door closed on Repetto, he ushered his daughter back inside the house, no doubt to call a high-priced attorney.

Vivi, Wyatt, and Damian stood by as Joe and the two nameless agents pulled their car, with Repetto in the backseat, onto the street, then made their way back to the SUV. Vivi gave Carly's hand another squeeze when she and Wyatt climbed into the backseat.

They spoke little on the ride to the FBI office and Carly appreciated the few moments of quiet they gave her—moments to prepare for what would come next, for what she would or wouldn't hear during the interrogation they'd agreed to let her listen in on.

Before she realized where they were, Damian pulled into the garage under the J. Edgar Hoover building. They hadn't wanted to alert Repetto to her involvement, so rather than risk a chance hallway meeting, she'd agreed to wait in the car until he was situated in an interview room. What felt like an eon, but was probably no more than ten minutes, passed before Damian received the call clearing them to go up.

On their way up to the main floor to pick up their visitor badges, Carly's mind buzzed a mile a minute. As the elevator rose, so did the tension in her body. Her shoulders twitched, as if unable to contain the energy vibrating inside her and she felt as if she might explode. Subtly, Drew's hand wrapped around hers, grounding her body, if not her mind, and she stilled.

"Carly?" Vivi said.

Carly turned to look at her friend.

"I have a surprise for you," Vivi said, her eyes flitting to Drew. She held her phone in her hand and Carly realized she hadn't even noticed that Vivi had taken a call.

She frowned. This didn't exactly seem like the best day for surprises. "Yeah?" she asked as the doors opened onto the lobby.

And there stood Marcus.

She stared in disbelief, then walked into her brother's hug. She hadn't realized how much she had wanted him there, how much she had wanted them to do this *together*, until he was there, holding her in his arms.

"How did you get here? Isn't there only one morning flight down from Albany?" she asked, referring to the flight Vivi and the others had caught.

Marcus gestured in Drew's direction. "He had his plane bring me down. He thought we should be together."

That, more than anything, nearly caused her to lose it. Blinking away the gathering tears, she gave her brother one more squeeze then turned to face Drew. "Thank you," she said.

He said nothing, just gave her a small smile as his eyes bounced to Marcus.

Marcus owed him a thank-you too, but given that her brother was still less than thrilled about him being a part of her life, that might be asking too much at the moment.

She glanced back at her brother and hesitated when she noticed the assessing expression on his face as he watched Drew. Why it should catch her attention, she didn't quite know—after all, Marcus hadn't been a fan of Drew's from day one—but it had. She tried to push it aside as they walked toward the reception desk for their visitor passes, but when they paused and Marcus put a proprietary arm around her shoulders and leaned in to ask her how the arrest went, it clicked like a guillotine falling into place.

"Carly?" Marcus asked, sensing something and drawing back.

She glanced around—everyone was looking at her, expectantly. "Can you," she started, then paused and took a deep breath. If she didn't want to freak anyone out, especially Drew, who was watching her with hawk-like intensity, she needed to calm the rush of adrenaline that had burst through her system.

She swallowed. "Damian, can you get my visitor badge for me while I make a phone call?"

The agent tilted his head. "Of course."

"Carly?" Drew said.

"I, just give me a minute, I need to make one quick call," she said, then stepped away before anyone could ask any questions.

After dialing the familiar number, she held a quick conversation with Naomi. She could feel Drew and Marcus's eyes on her back, and even the occasional questioning glance from Vivi, Wyatt, and Damian, but she didn't turn their way. What she wanted Naomi to look into was such a long shot that she didn't want anyone else to know about it yet. But she had to try. Drew had prepared her for the possibility that she might have to live without knowing all the answers, but if she didn't try this one thing, she knew she'd regret it forever.

"Everything okay?" Drew asked when she rejoined the group.

She didn't know if it was or wasn't, but she nodded.

"Do you have my pass? Are we ready to go up?" she asked Damian.

In response, he handed her the badge, which she clipped to her shirt just as the man she'd seen Drew talk to at the coffee shop walked in.

His step faltered when he saw all of them gathered around the reception desk, but then his gaze focused on Drew and he continued toward them. As he approached, Carly could see that he held a small thumb drive in his hand—similar to the one Drew had given him a short time earlier, but of a different color and shape.

"This is for you," the man said, holding the drive out to Drew.

"Everyone, this is Jason Moran," Drew said as he took the device and handed it over to Damian.

Jason's eyes darted between all of them, but when he spoke, he spoke only to Drew. "I've left contact information on that drive, along with details of everything Vince Repetto asked me to do. There are also scanned images of the contract he gave me and the warrant he showed me. I have the originals—I thought it best if I kept them for the time being. When you get to the point that you need me, you'll be able to find me." With that, he turned and walked out.

"Drew?" Vivi was the first to speak as a surprised silence had followed Moran's departure.

Everyone turned to Drew to hear his response.

He shrugged. "Naomi and Brian said he skirted the edge of legalities but didn't cross it. I figured if he knew what Repetto was doing with the information he was providing, he wouldn't want to be involved."

"So what was on that thumb drive you gave him this morning in the coffee shop?" Carly asked.

"Data Naomi and Brian had pulled from the chip, along with the reports we'd pulled together on the death of your mother and uncle, as well as Marguerite," he answered. "Pretty much everything that would prove to Moran the kind of illegal activity he was supporting or facilitating."

"And what do you think is on that?" Wyatt asked, pointing at the drive Damian held.

"Other than the specifics of what he just said, my guess is details he gathered on Marguerite that will help prove he was tracking her, along with how he erased her from the system, and probably also the reasons he was given as to why he was being asked to do it," Drew said.

Everyone looked at the device. Then Damian grinned and shrugged. "I'll guess we'll find out won't we? Let's drop this with an analyst I trust, then head up to the interrogation room."

Several minutes later—after the flash drive had been left in the hands of an Agent Lamb—Carly, Marcus, Drew, and Wyatt watched Vince Repetto drink a cup of coffee from their vantage point in the observation room. Damian had relieved the previous agent and now stood guard in the interrogation room while Vivi and Joe remained in the hallway going over some last minute details before starting the interrogation. As they waited for Vivi and Joe to begin, Carly took the opportunity to study Vince more closely.

He wore a dark blue suit with a light gray button-down shirt and a steel gray tie with thin dark-red stripes. His mahogany hair had turned a bit gray at his temples, but with his Mediterranean skin and dark eyes, the effect was more striking than aging. He sat with one ankle resting on his knee, his deep brown eyes traveling around the room with a lazy kind of curiosity. Leaning back in his chair, coffee in hand, he looked like he was the one waiting to do the interrogating, rather than the other way around, such was his calm, confident exterior.

And that confidence didn't falter even a tiny bit when Vivi and Joe walked into the room. Which meant that he was either a better actor than they had anticipated or was delusional about his situation. Even Carly found Vivi, her own *friend*, a bit intimidating. She didn't look stern or attempt to appear bigger than she was—either in size or ego—but Vivi's confidence, confidence that communicated itself in every move she made, seemed to fill the room.

As for Joe, well, he was an imposing guy with nearly fifteen years of anger for motivation. To Carly, Repetto's bored gaze seemed childish when compared to Joe's eyes, which seemed to say he'd been to hell, stayed for a drink or two, and was considering going back and taking Repetto with him.

She couldn't help the tiny little smile that crept onto her face at Joe's appearance. And judging by the way Repetto's fingers stopped twirling his coffee cup, she wasn't the only one to sense Joe's intensity.

"Franks." Repetto acknowledged his former partner with a nod.

Joe said nothing in response as he shut the door.

"Vincent Repetto?" Vivi asked, establishing his identity for the record.

Damian, no longer needed in the interrogation room, joined Carly, Drew, Marcus, and Wyatt at the observation window.

"Yes," Repetto answered. His body language didn't change, but his voice held a hint of something, perhaps concern or maybe curiosity.

For the next two minutes, Vivi and Joe went through standard procedures, notifying him that the interview would be recorded, verifying with him that he'd been read his Miranda rights, and introducing themselves—or re-introducing themselves in Joe's case—as well as reviewing the charges being brought against him.

"Do you understand the charges, Mr. Repetto?" Vivi asked.

For a moment, he watched her. Then he dropped his foot to the ground, leaned forward and smiled as he put his paper coffee cup on the table. "I do, but consider this my official request for a lawyer. In fact, I believe he's already on his way," he said, knowing they couldn't question him further once he'd made the request.

Joe let out a low chuckle as he leaned against the wall in the corner of the room and crossed his ankles. "You'll be waiting a while, Mr. Repetto."

Repetto's bravado didn't falter a bit. "I doubt it," he shot back.

His persona, when seen in contrast to the quiet certainty of Joe and Vivi, became almost a caricature of itself.

"Well, actually, he's right," Vivi said, sliding a sheet of paper across the table. "We forgot to mention, you're being charged under the USA PATRIOT Act."

Beside her, Carly heard Marcus mutter, "What the fuck?"

Drew chuckled in response.

She straightened and strained to hear what Vivi would say next. The PATRIOT Act was meant for terrorists. *She* might think what he'd done constituted an act of terror, but even she had to admit that it would be a hard argument to make in front of a judge. So what was Vivi doing?

"The PATRIOT Act?" Repetto repeated. His voice still held disbelief, but in it, Carly heard the first strains of real concern.

"Yes, according to your after-incident report, Anthony Lamot was involved in funding terrorist activity, is that correct?" she asked, knowing full well Repetto would have to answer in the affirmative, since he'd created that part of the record.

Slowly, he nodded then answered, "Yes."

"Well, since we have proof that you engaged in financial dealings with him, that means that, potentially, you have also conducted financial activity with terrorists which, as you know, comes under to auspices of the PATRIOT Act. And, as a natural-born citizen of Canada, not the United States, the judges are currently debating whether or not to officially classify you as an enemy combatant," Vivi said. Not a single ounce of emotion came through in her voice and Carly suspected it was that, more than anything, that got to Repetto. Emotions were not running high. Mistakes had not been made. No, this allegation came from someone who knew what she was doing and didn't care one iota about him or his record with the bureau.

"But she knows—" Marcus started, but Drew cut him off.

"Vivi knows a great deal, Marcus, including how to run an interrogation," he said.

And then what Vivi and Joe were doing clicked, making

Carly smile. They all knew full well that Tony and Sophia weren't involved in terrorist activity, but the official record said differently. Knowing the kind of legal power Repetto had access to, Vivi and Joe had opted to use Repetto's own words against him in an effort to cut him off. By arresting him under the PATRIOT Act and invoking enemy combatant status, they had ensured that it would be a good long while before any legal counsel would be allowed to walk through the door. In the meantime, while the powers that be debated whether to transfer him to a federal civilian court or a military one, Vivi and Joe would have unfettered access to Repetto. Once they got what they needed, they could disprove the terrorist links at a later time and clear Tony and Sophia's names.

Still smiling at the brilliance of the plan, Carly continued to listen until her phone, vibrating in her pocket, pulled her attention away. Glancing at the number, she moved away from the one-way glass toward the back of the room—away from Marcus and Drew's curious looks.

Without greeting, Naomi said, "You were right."

"Can you send me what you have?" Carly asked.

"Yes, we only have the tip of the iceberg but we'll put together some reports and e-mail them to you. Can you get them on your phone?"

"Yes," she answered. Then she spied a printer in the observation room and thought she might be able to go one better, but she'd have to look into it first.

"Give us twenty minutes and we'll have gold for you."

"I owe you, big time," Carly answered.

"Just get him and we'll call it even."

Carly smiled as she hung up. Briefly, she let the feeling of pending triumph wash over her.

"Carly?" Marcus drew her attention back to the window onto the interrogation.

"Yeah?" She stepped in between Marcus and Drew. With Wyatt and Damian on the other side of Marcus, and Vivi and Joe inside the interrogation room, she had to admit to feeling a bit invincible. They were going to get Repetto. One way or another, they were going to get him.

"I'm not answering that," Repetto said to some question Joe had asked.

After a few more minutes, it became clear those words were going to be Repetto's refrain. "I'm not answering that." It was either that or complete silence.

"Well, this is going to be fun," Marcus said. His impatience rolling off him in waves. Irritating, negative waves that interfered with the excitement she felt creeping into her body.

"Damian, is that printer wireless?" she asked, nodding her head toward the printer, but not taking her eyes from the trio on the other side of the window.

"It is," he confirmed. "Why?"

She pulled her phone out and started looking for the wireless devices available in her area. After a few seconds, it showed up on her list. "I may need to print something in a bit," she said, connecting the device to her phone so that as soon as she received the e-mail from Naomi she could print it.

Once the connection was confirmed, she turned her attention back to the interrogation. Sort of. Repetto's consistent response came on the heels of every question, so Carly let her mind turn toward coming up with a plan to talk to him herself. She'd need to convince Vivi and Joe to allow it, and in order to do that she needed to be clear not only about *what* she intended to say, but, more importantly, *how* she intended to say it. Just delivering the information Naomi had gathered would rock Repetto, but if she delivered it right, she could destroy him.

Finally, after what seemed like ages, her phone vibrated with a new e-mail message. "Found even more. We're still looking and verifying, but this should give you a good start." Attached to the message was a text document. Quickly, Carly opened it, scanned it, then sent it to print.

The machine whirred to life, startling the men in the room, who turned.

"Sorry, I need to print something," she said, taking the three steps to the machine and grabbing the papers as they came through the feed.

"What's going on?" Drew asked, pulling his attention from the interrogation altogether and turning to face her.

"Just an idea I had," she said, scanning the pages. There were only three, but three would be enough. For now.

"Care to share?" he asked.

At his tone, she looked up to find him watching her, arms crossed, feet apart.

Telling Drew and Marcus was the first of her hurdles—she knew they'd insist that Vivi handle delivering the new information. And while she had every faith in Vivi and Joe, Carly wanted to be the one to put the nail in Repetto's coffin. Not because she was feeling vindictive, but because, for what felt like the first time since Marguerite had been found, this was something she knew she could do to help the case. True, she had never interrogated someone like Repetto. But that didn't mean she'd never been in this type of situation.

"Carly what the hell is going on?" Marcus demanded, joining the conversation.

"Marcus," Drew warned, no doubt disapproving of her brother's tone.

Marcus shot him a quick glare, but otherwise kept his focus on her.

"I want to talk to him," she said. In for a penny, in for a pound.

Everyone seemed to respond at once.

"Not a chance," Marcus said.

"No way," Wyatt and Damian echoed.

Drew asked, "Why?"

Drew's response seemed the only reasonable one, so she focused on him. "Because I know why it started," she said.

Drew eyed her with quiet contemplation, but Marcus wasn't so sanguine.

"Like hell! There are a hundred and one reasons why you will not be walking into that room," her brother barked, not even bothering to ask her what she knew. "You're not qualified, you're too involved, and he still has no idea you and I are a part of this, to name a few."

"I have to agree," Wyatt weighed in. "It's not a good idea."

"What's in those documents, Carly?" Drew asked, indicating the sheets she now held protectively against her chest. She didn't think either Drew or Wyatt would try to snatch them from her, but Marcus, well, she wouldn't have been surprised if he tried.

She took a deep breath and met Drew's eyes. "I was right," she said. And that was all she said. It took longer for it to sink into Drew's brain than she thought it should, but when it did, only the tiny little tightening of his lips gave him away.

"Let Vivi handle it," he said.

"I want to do it," she responded.

"Someone tell me what the hell is going on," Marcus demanded.

Neither she nor Drew paid him any notice.

"Why? Why you?"

She had expected the question but not the slightly panicked look in Drew's eyes.

"Because I want to," she replied.

"Or because you discovered it, you want to be the one to deliver the news?" he clarified. "That's nothing but ego talking, Carly."

"Maybe," she answered. "But that still doesn't change the fact that this is something I'm good at."

"He's not one of your horses. You aren't going to dig into his psyche and expose the truth of his actions."

"It's not the truth I'm going to expose, but his weakness. He'll expose the truth after that."

"It doesn't work that way," Drew said, the insistence in his voice now bordering on anxiety.

"What doesn't work what way?" Vivi asked. Everyone in the room spun to find her standing in the open doorway. They'd been so caught up in their discussion, no one had noticed that Vivi and Joe had taken a break from the interrogation room.

"Vivi, may I speak to you in the hall?" Carly asked, before anyone could interject.

"Damn it, Carly," Drew said as he ran a hand through his hair, mussing it so spikes stuck up at odd angles.

"Whatever the hell you think you're going to do, it's a bad idea. You have no idea what you're doing," Marcus added.

She debated whom to respond to first, but the frustration and fear—fear for her—in Drew's eyes won out. She walked up to him and took his hand in hers. "I know you don't think this is a good idea, but I'm asking you to trust me."

"It's not about trust, Carly," he said, gripping her fingers. "You know I trust you."

"I know you don't want me to confront the man who killed my mother. I know you're worried about me and what it might do to me if I don't get the answers I want. I *know* you don't want me to do this because you care about me. But I'm telling you now, if I don't get the answers I want, I'll somehow learn to live with it. I may need your help, but I promise you, I will learn to live with it. But if I don't even try?" she paused and shook her head. "If I don't even try, I'm not sure *that* is something I could learn to live with. So please, Drew, tell me I can do this, and also that, if I come out of there with nothing more than what we have now, you'll be here to help me figure out how to accept that."

He hated it. She could see it in his eyes. He hated what she had asked of him, but she knew as well as he that he wouldn't deny her. After a long moment, he raised her hand, still wrapped in his, and rested the back of it against his cheek. "I know you can do this, Carly," he said, brushing a kiss across the back of her hand. "And, whatever happens, I will be here when you walk out of that room."

She wanted to wrap her arms around him and hold on tight, if just for a moment. But she didn't. Instead she brought his hand to her lips and, mimicking his actions, placed a kiss there. He gave her hand one last squeeze, then let her go.

"And you Marcus," she said, turning to her brother. "I know this past year has been hard on you. I know this isn't the life you thought you'd have. But contrary to what you may think, and you don't seem to be thinking highly of anyone or anything these days, I *do* know what I'm doing. For the first time in a long time, I feel like I know *exactly* what I'm doing.

"I'll let your lack of faith go this time, because I know it isn't really *you* saying what you've said to me. But make no mistake, my forgiveness won't extend forever. I love you. You're the only family I have left. But you need to figure your shit out and start being the decent human being I know you can be."

She didn't stop to see his reaction, but she did catch a glimpse of Wyatt's wide-eyed expression as she turned toward Vivi. "Can we step out into the hall now? I have a favor to ask you."

Vivi's eyes bounced from Carly to Drew to Marcus, then back to Carly, and she arched an eyebrow. "Of course," she said, standing back and motioning Carly through.

Taking a deep breath, Carly walked out.

CHAPTER TWENTY-FIVE

DREW WATCHED CARLY WALK INTO the interrogation room. She paused after shutting the door and met Repetto's gaze.

"Do you remember me?" she asked.

For the first time since they'd started the interrogation, Repetto's face lost some color. Whether he remembered her from before or he was only now putting two and two together, he knew who she was.

"I'm Deputy Chief of Police Carly Drummond," she said as she walked toward the table. "Or you may remember me as Carolyn Davidson," she added, taking a seat across from him.

Repetto didn't deny knowing her, but other than his initial reaction to her, he didn't confirm it either.

Carly sat across the table from Repetto and took a moment to simply watch him. She'd folded the pages she'd printed in half and occasionally tapped them on the tabletop as they sat in silence.

"She doesn't know what the hell she's doing," Marcus muttered from his spot beside Drew. "Vivi, how could you have let her go in there?"

"Give her time, Marcus," Vivi responded.

The seasoned agent's calm tone caught Drew's attention and he turned to look at her. Standing with her arms crossed, she watched the interrogation room with her head tilted a bit to the side and her brow furrowed ever so slightly, which made her look more curious than concerned. Her body language gave him a bit more confidence in whatever plan she and Carly had put in place.

He switched his gaze back to Carly, who had leaned forward slightly.

"I have to say," she started. "I was a bit surprised to read your profile once we'd identified who you were and what role you'd played in what happened—from the financial crimes to the murders of my mother and uncle, and finally, of Marguerite."

She paused and tapped the papers again. "Marguerite surprised me. I mean, I can see why you would have gone after my mom and uncle, since they were a direct threat to something you were actively involved in—it was a reaction to the situation. But Marguerite? That was planned. Well planned too, for the most part. Not well enough, of course, but most murders aren't, are they?"

Drew thought the question was rhetorical, but she paused.

Repetto eyed her but said nothing.

"Oh, that's right," she said. "You only worked white-collar crime. You didn't handle a lot of murder cases. You wanted to, though, didn't you? You requested a transfer to the anti-terrorism group a few years ago, and a few years before that, you wanted to transfer to the serious crimes division. Of course, Deputy Director Perelli denied both, just as he'd denied all the other transfer requests you put in for," she said, adding the last bit of information as almost an after-thought.

Carly took a deep breath and exhaled. "Anyway, like I said, given what we know about what you did, your dossier came as quite a surprise. Husband of Olivia Laturna, member of two country clubs, white-collar crime specialist . . . doesn't really read like the profile of a murderer, does it? And it's not as though you needed the money, right? Because, let's not forget, you're also the son-in-law of Senator Buzz Laturna. What is he, a two-term senator now?"

"Three," Repetto corrected automatically.

Carly bobbed her head. "I guess that's right. Time flies, but I do remember him, your father-in-law, coming to the house once to see if he could get my uncle to bankroll one of his campaigns, must have been the first one, since my uncle was long dead for his second and third runs." She paused again and Drew saw the back of her head shift slightly. If he could see her face, he'd bet she was looking off into the middle distance.

"My uncle turned him down, of course. Anthony Lamot was old-school Southern Democrat. Don't get too many of those these days, do we? Obviously, their politics didn't align."

"Is there a reason you're here?" Repetto asked condescendingly, finally showing some sort of emotion.

"See? Now *he's* questioning *her*," Marcus muttered.

"Shut up, Marcus," Vivi shot back, not taking her eyes from the room on the other side of the glass. Beside her, Joe shifted on his feet. Tempted to turn and see how Marcus had taken her rebuke, Drew resisted, knowing if he did so it would only piss Marcus off more.

"I guess I find it interesting that pretty much your entire life is bankrolled by your father-in-law. Your expensive wife, your house . . . I'm pretty sure there is no way you could afford your luxury cars or country club memberships without his help. I wonder if he pays your credit card bills too. Is that a custom suit? Definitely something Olivia would approve of," she added.

Drew watched as Repetto's jaw tightened. For the first time, it occurred to him that he should be worried not just about Carly's emotional safety but her physical safety as well.

"Vivi?"

"If he moves, Damian is right outside the door," she answered, obviously thinking the same thing.

"Of course, nothing is too good for his only daughter, is it?" Carly continued. "He appeared quite protective of her this morning, maybe even a little proprietary, and it wouldn't do to have her living in whatever kind of apartment or house in the suburbs you could afford on your government salary. I mean, don't get me wrong, I know how much you make, and it's decent, but I think we both know it's nothing compared to what Senator Laturna has, is it? Certainly not enough to keep his daughter living in the style to which she's accustomed."

"Of course it's not," Repetto managed to say. He still wasn't saying much, but she had persuaded him to say more than "I'm not saying anything."

"And they never let you forget it, do they?"

Repetto's eyes came up sharply at the comment disguised as a question.

She shrugged, feigning a nonchalance Drew knew she didn't feel. "I don't know much about your wife, other than her spending habits, but Buzz Laturna is an arrogant son of a bitch who's hard to even watch on TV. I can't imagine what it's like having him as a father-in-law, but I have to believe he makes your life a life a living hell. Maybe not overtly, but in that subtle, insidious way he seems to have," she added then paused to observe Repetto, who now seemed to study her with something close to curiosity. He wasn't ready to talk yet, but he definitely wanted to know what she'd say next.

"I imagine he'd be the kind of guy who measures worth in dollars and I'd bet his daughter is the same. But I'd wager that, while Olivia might actually get a thrill out of telling her country club friends about her FBI-agent husband, Buzz probably doesn't have much respect for you or what you do, does he?" Carly asked.

She let the question hang and, after a moment, Repetto gave a small nod.

Letting out another long exhale, she shook her head, as if commiserating with him, but not going quite that far. "Yeah, I kind of thought that would be the case. He's not one who cares for the common man, is he? I mean we're all so, well, common."

At this, she paused, unfolded the papers, and took a look. Repetto leaned forward a bit, but unless he stood, and he was smart enough not to, he wouldn't be able see the content of the pages.

Carly took another minute to look then refolded the papers.

Repetto frowned.

"So this is how it is, Vince," she said, using his first name for the first, and probably only, time. "We have enough to convict you. We have the paper trail of all your financial transactions and my mom left a pretty robust set of files that documented conversations you had with my uncle. It's been pretty easy to tie those conversations to some of your more profitable financial investments."

"Then why are you spending your time talking to me?"

Carly cocked her head and took a moment before answering. "Well, you see, some friends and I have been having a disagreement about *why* you did what you did, not necessarily *what* you did."

"Assuming I did anything, you think I'm going to tell you? And since the crimes you just listed are financial crimes, assuming I did anything, I think the reason *why* would be obvious. Money." It was the most they'd heard him say since he'd walked into the room.

"But that's the thing, you *have* money. Well, granted, it's not yours *per se*, but it is at your disposal. So while money *is* the obvious answer. I don't think it's the correct one." Again, she tapped the papers on the tabletop and studied the man across from her. "It's really all about power, isn't it?"

The question hung between them and though Carly continued her line of reasoning, she took her time before picking it back up.

"Living with a man who constantly makes you feel like you could never live up to his standards has got to be, what's the word?" she paused. "Aggravating? Frustrating? Probably something even stronger than those two emotions would be my guess. But beating your father-in-law at his own game—making money—now *that* shows some balls," she said. "It *had* to feel good to be trading in information and money he could only hope to have access to."

For a long, charged moment, Repetto stared at her. Drew knew, and he had no doubt Carly did too, that this was the turning point in her line of questioning. Repetto would either take the bait she had laid out, or he wouldn't. And if he didn't, they'd get nothing more out of him.

"Why the hell does she care *why* he did it, we just want confirmation that he did. Hell, I don't even care if he confesses, we have enough to build a solid case against him without him saying a word," Marcus said.

Drew could feel Marcus's frustration, and between that and

the tension in the observation room, it felt like they were standing inside a pressure cooker. But even so, even knowing that as a more seasoned agent he should be defusing that tension, he couldn't help his response.

"Lay off, Marcus, and trust your sister. Finding out *why* he did it is a means to an end, not the end itself," he snapped.

"Then what the hell *is* the end?" Marcus demanded.

Drew felt no need to respond. Repetto had started to speak.

"I'm not admitting to any of the charges," he said. "With regard to my wife, she enjoys what her father has provided for her but she doesn't judge people the same way he does. Surprisingly."

"And Buzz?"

Repetto let out a cynical laugh. "You're right that Buzz Laturna is a judgmental son of a bitch and his scales always tip in the balance of money. For those beneath him, which in his mind is nearly everyone, beating him at his own game, one-upping him when it comes to investments and making money would definitely be a way to have the last laugh," Repetto said.

"I thought so," she said, then seemed to mull something over before speaking again. "I would think, even if you couldn't say anything to him about what you'd done, assuming you did anything, which we're not," she added as he opened his mouth to object, "it would be satisfying. Just knowing you beat him, just having that little secret to hold onto. The last laugh, as you said."

Repetto hesitated, then sat back in his chair. "Yes, I imagine it would be satisfying."

At that point, with that statement, Drew knew Carly had him. He didn't know exactly what she had, but she had him where she wanted him.

"Yeah, it's interesting you say that, Vince, because I have something I'd like to show you." She unfolded the papers.

"What's on that paper?" Drew asked Vivi.

At the same time, Marcus asked, "What is she showing him?"

Vivi smiled but kept her eyes locked on Carly. "Investment information."

Drew chanced a look at Marcus who met his questioning gaze with one of his own. They didn't have the answers, but at least Marcus's hostility seemed to have abated.

"What's this?" Repetto asked, taking the pages from her.

"These are some of your father-in-law's investments over the time you were using my uncle to manipulate the market," she said.

Repetto's eyes came up. He glanced at her over the top of the pages before dropping his eyes back down to the data she'd provided him with.

A few minutes passed in complete silence—the kind of silence that would have ratcheted up tension under normal circumstances, however, in this case, Drew felt a sense of calm come over the observation room. He knew where this was going and Carly had gotten them there. They still had a long way to go, but the confidence he felt in knowing they'd get there was only overshadowed by the tremendous sense of pride he felt on her behalf. She'd been right all along and she hadn't bowed to what he or Joe or Marcus had tried to tell her. And because she hadn't bowed, she was going to get not only Repetto's confession, but was quite possibly going to be the architect behind one of the biggest political scandals to hit Washington in decades.

"This column, this one on the right," Repetto said, pointing to one of the pages he'd spread out on the table. "These are my investments, aren't they?"

"They are, yes."

"And this column on the left, these are Buzz's?" His voice, heavy with incredulity had pitched up.

Carly nodded.

Repetto's eyes went back to the pages. And as he read, his face became redder and redder.

"Are you telling me—"

"That your father-in-law was manipulating you all along?" she asked. "If that's what you think I'm telling you, then, yes, you're right. He was."

She paused long enough to lean forward and point to something. "Have you noticed that for each transaction you made, there's a timeline from when you talked to my uncle, to when you made your initial transaction, either a buying or selling of stock, to when your father-in-law did the same, to when you both made money?

"You see, if you look at this transaction here—according to my mother, this is when my uncle told you his friend's company hadn't been awarded the big government contract they'd been promised. You sold your stock before word got out and then, look here," she said, pointing to something else, "a few days after you sold your stock, your father-in-law sold his. I'm guessing you shared a broker?"

Repetto nodded, but it looked more like an automatic reaction than one done with any thought.

"So, you know, your secret wasn't a secret—and worse yet, he even outdid you trying to outdo him," Carly said, pointing to something else on the page. "Look here, at this transaction. Here is where your father-in-law sold this chunk of stock. A few days later you sold your shares as well. And then, a few days after *that*, again, according to my mother, you asked my uncle to circulate a rumor about that company going bankrupt. The stock plummeted and while you rebought your original quantity of shares—leaving you with a nice chunk of change *and* your investment intact—your father-in-law rebought—at pennies on the dollar—six times what he'd sold it for before the crash. When the price recalibrated after the rumor was put to bed, he sold the excess off, leaving him, like you, with the same quantity of stock, but a hell of a lot more cash."

She stopped talking, letting what she'd said sink in.

"I'm thinking he probably suggested starting that rumor would be a good way to make a quick buck," she started up again. "But of course, it wasn't worded like that when he suggested it to you, was it? He was probably sipping some scotch, throwing around 'gossip' as if he respected you, and maybe tossed this one out, like 'I heard this company might go bankrupt. Now, mind you, I don't believe it, but if I did and I sold my stock now and rebought when the price dropped, I could make a killing.' And you took it and ran with it.

"He knew all along how to play you. He knew if he treated you as worthless, you'd do whatever it took to prove him wrong, because you're better than he is—smarter, savvier, more charming. And he manipulated you the entire time. The entire time, when you thought you were pulling something over on him, he was feeding you lies and pulling your strings and making you dance to his tune. And on those same illegal transactions that made you two million, he made twenty-six million."

Drew watched Repetto as Carly sank the sword in deep, exposing his ultimate weakness, his ego. Now it was time to see how violently that wounded ego would lash out.

"So now, the thing is, Vince, we have you for a whole slew of crimes," she said. "But we also have information here that will allow us to at least arrest Senator Laturna for insider trading. I'd like to get him convicted too. Now, there's no question it's too late to save yourself, and I'm not offering any deals, but after everything he's done to you—the manipulation, the lies, the years of making you feel like less of a person, all while he was profiting off of you—well, since you are going down, how do you feel about finally taking Senator Buzz Laturna down a few notches and bringing him with you?"

EPILOGUE

CARLY ROLLED OVER IN HER bed and watched the snow falling outside her bedroom window. It had been four months since that day in the interrogation room and on lazy days like these, she couldn't help but reflect on all the changes that had happened since.

Downstairs she could hear Drew futzing with the coffee pot. That was definitely one change. Still working in DC, he flew up every weekend to see her, or sometimes they met in New York City. They'd even been to Maine twice to visit Dani, Ty, and all three kids. Really, it didn't matter where they were, they just tried to spend as much time together as they could.

And time was easier to come by now. Vic had hired not only Josie Webb but also an older, more experienced officer named Travis Brantley. He'd also re-instated Marcus as Deputy Chief of Police when Carly had resigned two months earlier. She hadn't quit completely, but she'd become a part-time officer.

Vic was still struggling with his family, but he was also cautiously stepping into this new phase of his life. Each day he seemed happier with himself and the people around him, and he was definitely more engaged than she'd ever seen him as the chief.

Of course, he was now considering a move to the Boston area to be closer to Lucas and had started to look for his own replacement. Carly didn't know what would come of that or what kind of candidates he would find, but he was being diligent about screening them. He'd also left one full-time position open so the incoming chief could hire one of his or her own, so to speak, as a way of creating some instant investment in the team. It was all very well thought out.

As for Marcus, he was sticking around in his reinstated role, but she often wondered how long that would last. Since they'd been officially released from the witness security program, they'd each been given access to the family funds and businesses that had been held in trust for them all this time. She had no interest in the business side, but Marcus had loved it, and she wondered if he was contemplating leaving law enforcement to take up the reins of the family ventures. He'd had meetings with the board of directors for the holding company that controlled all those ventures, including Bill Wycoff, the man who had worked with Deputy Director Perelli to arrange for the storage locker, and had visited several executives, but other than that, he'd been closed lipped about his plans.

Carly flopped onto her back and her eyes caught on a new pair of boots, still sitting in the box they'd been shipped in. She smiled. Now that she was only working part time, she'd taken Trudy up on her offer to spend some time at the barn. Actually, she'd been spending more than "some time" there. More weeks than not, she was there all four days she had off. She was picking her riding skills back up again, getting in shape, and remembering how to read and respond to different horses. Trudy had a handful of horses from the jumper circuit that Carly was helping her rehab for friends and clients—some had been through traumatic experiences and some were coming back from injuries. Each time Carly worked with one and felt a little bit of improvement—in its mind or its body—a surge of pleasure washed through her. She didn't think she'd ever get over the high that came with knowing she was reaching—truly communicating with—an animal.

But she wasn't just riding and working with the horses. She was also getting up to speed on the changes in the industry, and in the fifteen years she'd been out, there had been many—the show rules, the gear, the types of feed available, and even the medicines. For each hour she spent with a horse, she spent at least the same amount of time learning about the care and management of the barn and its inhabitants.

And she'd never been happier.

"Carly," Drew called from downstairs. "Come here for minute."

Smiling to herself at how comfortable she and Drew had become in each other's lives, she tossed the covers off, grabbed her cashmere robe—the warmest she had—and slid on a pair of slippers. Outside, a winter storm had blanketed the valley and though her house was warm, staying cozy was still a mental necessity.

"What's up?" she asked as she hit the bottom of the stairs.

"In here," he called from the living room. She turned to find him sitting on the couch with his feet up on the coffee table, mug in hand, watching TV. Only he'd paused it.

"What are we watching?" she asked, sitting down beside him.

"This," he said, restarting a morning news segment.

A newscaster in a navy blue jacket with her dark hair clipped back was introducing a new story. "And in breaking news this morning, the jury for the trial of Senator Buzz Laturna has returned a guilty verdict and for the first time in decades will be sending a sitting senator to prison."

The image on the screen cut from the newscaster to the sketches of the courtroom, media cameras having been barred from the trial. "As I'm sure you remember, Senator Laturna was being tried on several counts of securities fraud and insider trading linked to his former son-in-law's activities. His former son-in-law, Vince Repetto, a federal agent at the time of *his* arrest, was also convicted of securities fraud and insider trading, as well as three counts of murder for the deaths of Anthony Lamot, Sophia Lamot Davidson, and US Marshal Marguerite Silva. One of Senator Laturna's former security officers was also convicted in connection with the death of Deputy Silva. Repetto's testimony of his father-in-law's involvement in his schemes was a key component of the prosecutor's case."

Drew turned the TV off, cutting off the rest of the broadcast. They knew enough already.

Feeling him watching her, Carly turned to face him.

He smiled. "You done good with that one," he said with a gesture of his head to the television.

She shrugged, but smiled back.

He tugged her over until she was tucked up against him. He'd had some papers in his lap, but moved them to the arm of the couch as he took her hand in his.

"You really did," he said, his voice turning serious. "You knew from nearly the beginning, from when Joe started talking about Repetto, that something was missing from the picture."

"I was kind of lucky," she said, tracing his fingers with her own.

"Maybe. But you were right to keep pressing, to keep asking the questions. And even though we both know that, morally, Laturna was also at least partly responsible for the murders, I'm glad we could at least get him on something. That we could at least hold him responsible for some part of what happened with Repetto."

She exhaled and rubbed his palm with her thumb. "Yeah, me too. And even though he wasn't necessarily an accessory to all of Repetto's crimes, not in the legal sense anyway, I'm glad we were able to play a part in showing him for who he really is."

And for a long moment, they sat, comfortable on the couch, wrapped in each other's arms, watching the fire. She was about to get up and grab a cup of coffee when Drew's arm tightened around her.

She looked up in question.

He picked up the papers from the arm of the couch and scanned them.

"What are those?" she asked.

"Do you know the old VanDurst farm?"

She frowned in thought. "That big place just beyond Trudy's?"

"That's the one."

"I do. It's that place with the old stone house, isn't it? I've always loved that house. It has a kind of, well, I don't know, charm, certainly, but a little something more. A little something kind of enchanting about it," she added, thinking of the building.

One of the older houses in the area, it was quite large for being made of stone—not large by modern standards of mini mansions, but large by the standards of historical homes. Built of gray stone, it had three floors in all, although the top floor looked to be quite small and may have, at some point, been the servants' quarters. It also had rows of windows, climbing roses in the summer, and a large porch that had recently been added off one side.

"It sits on about four hundred acres," Drew said.

"If I recall my history right, it was one of the largest family farms in the area when it was first settled. I'm sure it's changed hands several times since then, but it's always been known as one of the bigger estates."

"This is the contract to buy it." Drew handed her the papers he'd been holding.

Stunned, she sat up. "Excuse me?"

He cleared his throat and sat up too. "Yes, well, I thought maybe we could, you know, buy it. We could spend this summer renovating the house and then the winter making plans for a barn and pastures for some horses, for you, and also a small training facility, for me, that we could start building next summer."

She stared at him for a long, long moment. She understood the words coming from his mouth, but somehow they weren't sinking in. Not until she noticed that the pulse on his throat had become visible and was beating rapidly.

Drew Carmichael was nervous.

"You mean, move in together?"

He hesitated, then replied. "To start."

"And build me a barn so I can get back into the business?"

"I know you've liked working with Trudy. The farms abut each other, so you could still share trails and maybe share some training, horses, that kind of thing."

"But you said a training facility for you," she said, not knowing what he meant by that.

He cleared his throat again. "Well, by next summer I'll have been with the agency for twenty years and, well, I'm planning to retire."

"Retire," she repeated.

"Sort of. I want to get more into the family business, I shouldn't leave that to Sam and Jason anymore. Especially now that my dad wants to spend more time traveling with my mom and retire himself. But, well, I've also been talking with Rina, my boss, about doing some consulting work for the agency."

"Consulting?" she was starting to feel like a parrot but she truly didn't know what "consulting" with the CIA looked like. Was it like what Caleb Forrester, Kit's brother did? If so, she wasn't sure she was going to like that.

"Yes, consulting. You know I like working with agents and I like training. I've posed the idea to Rina that I set up a small training facility up here where agents, one or two at a time, could come up and stay for a few weeks before heading off on assignments. While they're here, I'll work with them to make sure they're prepared for what they're going into, both physically and mentally."

Okay, that made sense and she could see him enjoying the work. "What kind of training facility are we talking about?"

"I've walked the land and there are a few hills on it, which is great. On the back side of one, deep into the woods, is a little clearing that could be accessed from a road on the other side of the property."

"Away from the main house is what you're saying?" she clarified.

"Exactly. I'd build a small facility there that would include accommodations for up to four people, a study room, a workout room, maybe a shooting range, things like that," he clarified.

She wasn't sure how she felt about living near a bunch of spies, but Drew wouldn't do anything to purposefully put her, or anyone, in danger. "And you'd work with them here, in Windsor, for a few weeks before they went off to wherever they were assigned?"

"That's what Rina and I are talking about now. Of course, it would depend on whether or not you agreed." He paused then took her hand in his. "I know this is a big decision, for both of us. But I also think it's the right decision. I want to be with you. You want to be here. Windsor has grown on me too, and this," he said, gesturing to the papers she still held in her other hand, "Well, this lets me have the best of all worlds, I think. You, work, flexibility. And I hope you agree it's the right thing for you too."

"This is big."

He nodded, looking nervous again.

"This is long term, isn't it?" she asked.

He let out a short laugh. "I certainly hope so."

"Marriage?" she asked.

He smiled. "Maybe. I figure I'll wait for the idea to feel comfortable to you and then you can ask me."

She laughed at the reminder of his previous attempt to wait until she felt comfortable with him to make the first move. At which he'd failed. And she hadn't minded. She didn't think she would mind if he failed to wait her out again.

"Well?" he asked.

She looked into his eyes and felt no doubt about her answer. She smiled and he pulled her onto his lap.

"You could be waiting a long time," she teased as her arms went around his neck and she brushed her lips over his.

"Maybe," he said, kissing her back. "But I doubt it. I don't think I have to tell you I'm not a patient man."

"No, you're not," she said, leaning her head to the side so he could make his way down her neck with his lips.

"*And* I am very persuasive," he said, sliding a hand under her robe.

She laughed softly. "Yes, you are," she agreed, knowing full well that he wouldn't wait long. And she was just fine with that.

ACKNOWLEDGEMENTS

As ALWAYS, MY FAMILY AND friends are my rock (or should I say *rocks*?). Without them, life would be a lot less interesting—not to mention immeasurably harder—and *way* less fun. And, once again, without my editor, Julie Molinari, well, I'm not sure where I'd be—we went through the trenches with this one and I couldn't ask for a better ally.

Keep reading for a preview of Tamsen Schultz's upcoming book,

A DARKNESS BLACK
WINDSOR SERIES BOOK 6

Darkness. Covert operative Caleb Forrester has always preferred darkness over light, keeping his grief and shame in shadow. But just as he starts to question this existence and let go of the years of blame he's carried, his best friend's widow calls upon him to help her stop a murder. It's a request he can't refuse, even though he knows that traveling to the remote New Hampshire mansion to reunite with Cate will put him face-to-face with memories he's spent more than five years trying to forget.

Life. After suffering two searing losses less than a year apart, widow Catherine Thomson has worked hard to let go of her guilt, move forward, and rebuild her life. But when a murderer threatens the wealthy family she works for, it's Cate's history that may save them. To help her investigate, she calls on Caleb—a man she trusts though may no longer know—and when it becomes apparent that it's not just the family who is in danger, Cate realizes that revisiting the past she's so painstakingly put behind her may be the only way she can help Caleb find his own redemption.

Betrayal. It's everywhere. The Whatley family has generations of secrets and resentments that Caleb and Cate must wade through if they have any hope of preventing the murder. But it's Caleb's own disloyalty that shocks him to his core when he finds he's falling for Cate. Caleb knows that stopping the killer isn't going to be easy, but finding the strength—and forgiveness—to forge a future with Cate could be the hardest thing he'll ever do.

CHAPTER ONE

CALEB FORRESTER SCANNED HIS SURROUNDINGS. There were too many kids. They were everywhere. His chest tightened as a baby crawled between its father's feet. He opened his mouth, about to call out a warning, then stopped himself. He shouldn't—doing so would bring attention to him—but if the man wasn't careful, god only knew what could happen to the infant. Fortunately, the man reached down, scooped the baby up, and walked off.

Caleb let out a small sigh of relief then tried to loosen the constricting collar around his neck. The material of the black outfit he wore seemed to trap his body heat and reflect it back onto him in waves. His feet, confined in unfamiliar shoes, ached. He couldn't remember the last time he'd felt so uncomfortable—a sobering thought, especially considering he was there willingly.

"You're gonna dance with me, right, Uncle Caleb?" Emma Hathaway said, interrupting his thoughts from her perch on his lap.

He glanced down at the curly haired four year old dressed in a puffy dress and shiny shoes and found her big brown eyes watching him. He wasn't her uncle, not by blood, and Caleb rather suspected that Emma's mom, his friend Jesse Baker Hathaway, had given him the moniker just to make him sweat.

"Of course I am, sweet pea," he replied.

Tucked into a corner farthest away from all the action, he eyed the dance floor. He should be in South America or somewhere in North Africa or the Middle East. How he had come to be wearing a custom tuxedo at a decadent reception in the quaint little village of Windsor on a chilly fall evening waiting to dance with tiny little person, was lost on him.

Only it wasn't. Not really. Caleb watched a couple move into his line of sight—his younger sister Kit in the arms of Garret Cantona. Caleb had been to Windsor more times in the past year and a half than he had in the several years preceding put together. And it was all because of Kit. The strained and tumultuous relationship they'd had for years was a relationship he was now trying his best to rebuild.

As the music played, Kit slid her palms from Garret's chest to behind his neck then tilted her head up. Garret smiled and obligingly leaned down and brushed a kiss across her lips. Caleb looked away. He may be much closer to his sister now than he had been since they were kids but that didn't mean he had to sit there and watch his best friend kiss her. He had to draw the line somewhere, he thought as he turned his gaze back to the little girl who sat upon his knee.

"When, Uncle Caleb?" Emma pressed as she played with one of his jacket buttons.

"When this song ends, peanut." It was a slow one; a song that had many couples swaying—Kit and Garret, and Emma's parents, among them.

But not the bride and groom. Caleb swung his eyes over to where Drew and Carly Carmichael stood. Carly looked stunning in her gown, and Drew, with his fingers laced through hers, did not look the least bit interested in letting go of her. Smart man.

When he had first met Drew, Caleb hadn't taken kindly to the fact that the CIA agent had involved Kit in the trafficking of intelligence. Then, when Caleb's and Kit's two worlds had collided in a spectacular mess eighteen months ago, Drew had been caught in the middle. But despite that less than auspicious beginning, somehow, all these months later, Caleb now found himself with Drew as a friend. And during his frequent visits to Kit, Caleb had become, if not friends, then at least friendly, with most of Kit's social circle, including Carly. All of which explained his attendance at Windsor's wedding of the year.

Again, he tugged at his collar—god, he hated tuxedos. He thought about untying the bow tie altogether but as he glanced around at the well-dressed guests and his gaze landed again on a smiling Carly and Drew, the phrase "suck it up buttercup" came to mind. There were more important things to think about—like the happiness of his friends—than his minor discomfort.

Caleb let out a small sigh of resignation but then a baby howled and his heart leapt into his throat. His eyes jumped in the general direction of the sound and he started scanning the crowd to locate the specific source.

"That's just Charley," Emma said.

"Charley? Matty and Dash's baby, right?" Using a four-year-old for intel was a new low for him.

Emma nodded. "And he has a sister, too. Daphne."

"What about those two?" he asked with a nod to two little boys chasing a balloon.

"That's TJ and his cousin, Andrew. They're Carly's new family."

Caleb wasn't exactly sure what "new family" meant, but when he saw the boys run smack into the arms of two women, it made sense. Dani Fuller and Sam Carmichael pulled the boys onto their laps, laughing as they both proceeded to tickle their sons. TJ and Andrew seemed pleased with the tickle attack for approximately two seconds; then they both clambered off their respective mother's laps and dashed off. Caleb had met Dani at around the same time he'd met Drew. He knew she'd been an agent at the CIA too, but had left the agency several years earlier. Sam, her twin sister, was married to Drew's brother Jason. Carly's new family.

Caleb turned his eyes away from all the family. His stomach churned and he felt his pulse kick up. There were too many people, too much family, too much *love*.

And just having that thought made him feel like an asshole.

He didn't have anything against love, but having been more or less a loner for the past decade and a half, being relaxed in social situations, being comfortable with the casual intimacy of family and love, wasn't one of his strongest skills. But he did like seeing his sister happy, and as she came back into view—still in Garret's arms—it was quite clear that she was.

He smiled at the sight as he felt Emma tug at his bow tie.

"Is it crooked?" he asked, looking down at her.

"No," she said, bending it back and peering at the knot. "I just want to see how it's tied. My daddy wore the other kind of tie and my bows don't look like this."

Caleb smiled again. Emma liked to figure things out. She was a little like her brother James, a math and science savant who was currently out on the dance floor with his girlfriend.

"What's James's girlfriend's name?" he asked.

"Chelsea. She's nice, but I don't see her as much anymore since she went to college." Emma stumbled a bit over the word "college."

"That happens."

"Did you go to college?"

No, he thought. He'd had an education of a completely different kind. He'd spent his time and money teaching himself how to navigate the dirtiest, scummiest, least ethical people and places on the planet in an effort to destroy an empire his own father had built. It had been a far cry from the hallowed ivory towers his ancestors had graced.

"Let's go dance," he said as the song changed to something more upbeat, but not so upbeat that he wouldn't know what to do with his feet.

Dropping her question with a squeal, Emma slid from his lap and caught his hand in hers.

Her fingers and palm felt so tiny in his and, in a rush, memories of a different time, of a different child, sucked the breath from his lungs. He nearly yanked his hand back and made for the exit, but Emma turned and smiled at him.

He forced himself to breathe. He didn't have the right to pull away from her. He didn't have the right to hurt her feelings by breaking his promise to her. He knew that. He believed it. Still, his heart raced and his mind began to spiral down into a deep, dark place.

A place where children died. A place too black with sorrow to even allow the light of mourning in. A place where parents buried their babies and silently went crazy from the pain.

"Uncle Caleb?"

He looked down. They'd come to a stop on the dance floor. He couldn't dance. He couldn't do it. He had no right to celebrate.

"Caleb?"

At the sound of Garret's voice, Caleb's eyes came up. As his former partner in the world of black ops and covert assignments, Garret Cantona was about the only person who could understand the crippling impact of a memory.

"Are you okay?" Kit asked from within Garret's embrace.

Well, maybe Garret wasn't the only one. Looking into his sister's eyes, Caleb took a deep breath, inhaling her strength. She'd been through hell and still managed to love. Still managed to laugh. Still managed to dance.

He nodded. "It was just a moment, I'll be fine." Both Garret and Kit eyed him, but when Emma tugged on his hand, he turned his attention to the sprite. Moment by moment, he willed his feet to move. Thirty seconds later, he was dancing with Emma, truly dancing—spinning her around and making a promise to himself to always be her favorite uncle.

Not wanting to break his promise, he let her convince him to escort her around the floor for another two songs. And when a slower song came on, he swung her up into his arms and swayed to the music, to her unending delight.

David and Jesse smiled as he slid by them with their daughter in his arms. As he twirled her around, he caught sight of Vivi DeMarco and her husband Ian, dancing together with their son Jeffery. His eyes took in the swell of her belly, and even though his breath hitched slightly at the thought of another baby being brought into this world, he made a mental note to ask Kit when her friend was due with her second child.

Garret tapped Caleb on the shoulder. "May I cut in?"

"I don't know, peanut, what do you think?" Caleb asked, drawing his head back to look at Emma.

She looked at Garret, then at Caleb, then back again at Garret. "Is Kit going to dance with Uncle Caleb if I dance with you? I don't want him to feel left out."

"Yes, Kit is going to dance with her brother," Kit said, stepping around Garret as Caleb handed Emma over to him. The little girl grinned, obviously pleased to have two dance partners vying for her attention.

"He's not going to be nearly as fun as me, Emma, so you know where to find me when you get bored," Caleb said as he took his sister's hand in his.

"Ha!" Garret said as he gripped Emma and orchestrated a dramatic three-spin move away from them.

"I didn't see him twirl you like that," Caleb teased as his sister's hand came up to rest on his shoulder and they began moving to the music.

"Because he knows I'd probably get sick on him if he did."

Caleb's eyes shot to his sister's. She wasn't one to get motion sickness and so the most obvious reason for her to be feeling nauseated was . . .

"You should see your face," she said with a laugh. "But no, I'm not pregnant if that's what you were wondering. Just getting over a little touch of the flu."

Garret and Kit had been together for over a year and a half and had never mentioned marriage or kids, at least not to him. Knowing how happy they were, he hadn't given it much thought, but seeing so many kids there that night, along with so many other happy couples, he wondered.

"Do you want kids?" he asked, not sure he really wanted to know the answer. She was still his little sister and he just hadn't ever thought of her as having kids of her own.

Kit shrugged. "Probably not, but we'll see. We have so many

friends with kids that we certainly aren't lacking for babies to spoil or kids to act as surrogate aunt and uncle to."

Caleb wasn't quite sure what to say. Kids, and whether people had them, wanted them or didn't, was one of those topics he preferred to avoid discussing. Because whatever he said always felt like the wrong thing.

"What about you?" she asked.

A sharp pain lanced through him.

"I'm not even in a relationship," he managed to say.

She tilted her head and studied him. "I didn't mean *now*, it was a general question."

He shook his head. The thought wasn't one he could let himself contemplate. Not here. Not now. Not with so many families surrounding him and memories knocking at the door waiting to be let in.

Eyes the same golden color of his looked back at him. Caleb was about to make a stupid comment to deflect the tension coiling in his body when Kit abruptly stepped away. "I'm feeling a bit tired. Do you mind if I sit the rest of this one out?"

He wasn't sure if she was truly tired or had sensed his growing discomfort, but he nodded and led her to a seat. "Can I get you anything to drink? Some water or tea?" he asked.

She shook her head. "Why don't you go outside and have a look at the moon. It's full tonight and should be rising on the horizon about now."

He hesitated.

She smiled and squeezed his hand. "Go, Caleb. Go get some fresh air and let me know if I'm going to have to finagle Garret's jacket from him when we leave. It was starting to get chilly when we arrived for the reception. You can let me know if the temperature has dropped much more."

He knew she was bullshitting him then. She'd never have to finagle anything from Garret, ever. Despite the continued weirdness of having his sister and his former partner living together, he was grateful that Kit was with a good man.

He nodded and made his way toward the exit. The wedding reception was being held in a refurbished barn on the grounds of an upscale bed and breakfast. It was a huge building with exposed beams, rough-hewn wood, and long distances between exits. When he found one, Caleb stepped out into the cold night air and onto a large flagstone patio. He imagined that for warmer weather events, the big rolling doors to his right could be opened to allow guests to flow freely between the inside and outside settings.

As it was, on that cool evening, he was the only one out there. He looked up at the sky and saw the first evening stars twinkling dimly in the dusk. The moon hung over a darkened hillside, bright and unapologetic. Not quite full, but close.

Behind him, he heard the strains of music coming from the barn, along with the constant murmur of conversation punctuated by the laughter of one or another of the many guests. He hadn't been to too many weddings in his life, but even he knew that this one was something special. It wasn't flashy but had all the casual comforts money could buy, and he knew Carly and Drew had been more interested in creating an atmosphere that let them celebrate *with* their friends and family rather than one that placed them at the center of all the attention and festivities.

Not five minutes of quiet had passed when Caleb heard a door open and close behind him and he didn't need to look to know who had followed him out.

"Everything okay?" Jesse asked as she slid an arm through his.

"Yes, everything is fine."

"Liar," she countered, but didn't press further.

Jesse was like that. Of all of Kit's friends, she was the only one who had never been intimidated by him and she'd been the first of them to claim him as a friend. She was also the one he now counted on to look past his lies, forcing him to ask questions and confront his own doubts. He didn't always like it—hell, he rarely liked it—but she was also the only one who ever seemed to have any answers for him. She wrapped them up in questions and gave them to him, like little gifts, for him to unwrap when he was ready.

But tonight, he wasn't ready. And she seemed to sense that.

"I never thought I'd see the day when you wore a tux," she said, leaning into him a bit.

"I never thought I'd see the day when you came up to my chin. What are you wearing, six-inch heels?"

She bumped him with her hip. "Be nice," she said with laughter in her voice. "And it's not my heels, it's my hair. My hairdresser went a little overboard today."

He chuckled. Jesse Baker Hathaway claimed to be five-foot-two, but he'd swear she was five-foot-one if she was an inch.

"Emma seems to be doing well," he said.

"Mmm hmm," she nodded. "She is. It's been a little rough this fall though, since James hasn't been around as much. He's been so busy with school and then, when he does have free time, he tends to go visit Chelsea at college. Emma misses him a lot, and it's been much quieter at home, but she's getting used to being more or less the only child."

"I'm sure that will be very tough for her. Being the only child."

Again, she bumped him with her hip. "Stop," she said, laughing quietly in the night. "She's not totally spoiled."

"Not totally, no," he answered. "At least not until I come to town."

"Or send ridiculous gifts. Really, the four-foot stuffed pumpkin was a bit much."

"Just getting you back for having her call me Uncle Caleb."

"You love it."

He kind of did, so he said nothing. The silence of the night seeped into his bones, as did the cold. He turned to look at Jesse to make sure she had a coat on.

"You should have something warmer," he said, eyeing the wrap she wore around her shoulders.

She shook her head. "I'm fine," she paused. "How are you, really, Caleb?"

"I'm fine," he mimicked her.

She sighed and he knew she was about to say more, but in that moment his phone buzzed in his pocket with a text message.

She rolled her eyes and shook her head, as he reached for the device.

"Gee sorry, I have to get this." He held his phone out, waving it in front of her with an unrepentant grin. But then he saw a name flash on the screen and his grin died.

"Caleb?"

He hit the ignore button and slid his phone back into his pocket.

"Who was that?"

"No one." He was aware of the slight tremble of his hand in his pocket as he answered Jesse.

"I saw the name," Jesse said. "Who is Catherine?"

He was about to say "no one" again when his phone vibrated. He heard it. Jesse heard it.

"Aren't you going to answer it?"

"Drop it."

"Oh, hell no," she answered with a knowing laugh. "Wrong answer, Caleb. In more ways than one, that was the wrong answer, and you know it."

He did know it. Jesse had raised two boys, dealt with the loss of a less than stellar husband, and was no shrinking violet. He hadn't thought about his command before he'd issued it. Had he done that, he would have realized that, of all the things he could have said to Jesse, telling her to drop it was the exact wrong one.

He exhaled. "It's nothing, Jesse. Please."

The "please" gave her pause and for about three seconds he held out hope that she would let it go.

"Caleb, I don't know who Catherine is, but I can feel the tension in your body now." She gave his arm, the one she still had hers looped through, a gentle nudge to prove her point. "Only someone who means something to you would cause that kind of reaction."

And that was where she left it. With a little something for him to think about. A question posed as a comment. Because she was right, there were very few people who would cause him to react the way he had. So, what did Catherine mean to him?

"She's Tommy's widow," he said softly.

Her quick inhale gave him some satisfaction. Tommy was someone he didn't talk about. Caleb would like to say he didn't ever talk about him, but that clearly wasn't the case. There was one person who knew. Unfortunately, she was standing right beside him.

"Maybe it's time," she said.

He turned his head and looked down at her green eyes.

She didn't blink or back down. "I'll leave you to it," she said as if it were a forgone conclusion he would do the right thing.

Behind him, he heard the sounds of the reception grow louder and then quieter again as Jesse opened and closed the door to the barn. His phone buzzed again. His fingers curled around the device in his pocket. It was warm from being close to his body, the edges sleek and sharp.

It vibrated in his hand.

He made his way to a bench at the edge of the patio and pulled it from his pocket as he sat with his back to the reception.

"Caleb?" the message read.

The second message said, "Is this the right number?"

He stared at the phone for a long moment, his fingers feeling clumsy and uncoordinated.

"Hi Cate," he typed back. "Yes, it's the right number."

"Thank god," came the immediate reply. Then, after a moment, "Are you anywhere near the eastern seaboard? The north part?"

His eyes lifted. The bucolic Hudson Valley spread out before him. It was too dark to see the colors of the leaves but he knew, in the light of day, fall was still making its statement there in the Northeast.

"Yes," he typed back. Then he waited. And waited.

"Cate?"

"Never mind," she replied. "Sorry to have bothered you. I'm glad you're stateside."

Never mind?

"Cate."

He could all but hear her sigh.

"Honestly, Caleb, I'm sorry. It's nothing, just me being paranoid. Give me a call sometime and we'll catch up."

Dismissed. Only it didn't work that way.

"What's going on?" he wrote. "Where are you?"

Nothing came back.

"I swear to god, Cate, I can track your phone if I need to."

"Nice to know you haven't changed. I'm in New Hampshire. Working a job."

"And?"

She paused again before answering. "It's weird. Something strange is going on but it could just be the people I'm working for."

"Strange enough that you texted me after five years?"

"I'm not the only one with a phone." No hesitation there. He let out a deep breath.

"Where are you?"

"New Hampshire," she wrote again.

"Where in New Hampshire? Specifically," he added.

"I'm managing a family reunion at The Washington House. It's a private home not far from the resort."

Caleb ran a hand over the back of his neck and turned his attention to the stars. He wasn't one to really believe in heaven and all that, but he wondered what Tommy would be thinking right now—that Caleb should go to her, or stay the hell away?

Behind him, he heard the shriek of one of the many kids attending the reception. A shriek of laughter and love.

He rubbed his chest then returned his clumsy fingers to the screen of his phone, typing, "I'll be there in six hours." Then he shut the device off and slid it back into his pocket, not wanting her to give him any excuses to back out.

● ● ●

Catherine Thomson stared at her phone for a good long while. She'd texted Caleb back, telling him not to come, but had received nothing in response. She shouldn't have contacted him in the first place.

Standing in the kitchen of the carriage house that had been converted into a large three-bedroom guesthouse, she listened to her daughter in the bathtub upstairs. Elise was singing a song with her nanny, Jana.

Cate stepped outside onto the small front porch and shut the door quietly behind her. The chill of the night seeped through her light weight sweater and jeans, but she paid it no mind. Reluctantly, her gaze went to the small building about five-hundred feet to her left. Looking at it wouldn't conjure Caleb, but she could feel his presence already occupying the empty space.

For a fleeting moment, she regretted not having housed any of the five staff members in the renovated ice house, but it hadn't made sense to put one or two in the one-bedroom guest quarters while leaving the rest in the main house. So all five were housed on the third floor of The Washington House, like servants of days gone by. And the former ice house was vacant.

It wouldn't be for long.

The thought of Caleb Forrester being so close caused her stomach to tighten and she had to will herself to breathe slowly. It had been five years since she'd seen him. Five years since . . .

Abruptly, Cate switched her focus across the driveway to the back of the main house. Warm light glowed from the windows of the grand dame of a building. Some locals called it a castle, some an eyesore, but there was no denying that The Washington House wasn't content to be obscure.

Originally built in the late 1800s as the hunting lodge of a prominent Boston family—though calling it a "lodge" was akin to calling the houses of Newport "cottages"—the four-story white stone home boasted sixteen bedrooms, twenty bathrooms, three billiard rooms, two parlors, two bars, servants' quarters, and much more. It was the perfect location for the Whatley family reunion, an event Cate had been organizing every year for nearly a decade.

Only this year it was different.

Her eyes traveled over the windows at the back of the main house. There were sixteen people inside, twenty-one if she included her staff, some of whom were serving dinner just then.

She glanced at her watch. Caleb would be there in less than five and a half hours.

It was a good thing.

It was a good thing, she told herself. Because she was fairly certain someone inside that house was going to be murdered.